Second Edition © Tempest & Brolly™ 2016

ISBN-10: 0-578-19612-3
ISBN-13: 978-0-578-19612-1

Winding Up Strangers in Bars

Barf Loko

ONE

Seattle, Sun Oct 12th, 2014

We used to take pains to make them look like suicides, but not anymore. That just works itself out now. In a few hours housekeeping will find this one. The next day the newspapers will report it was a suicide and the housekeeper who knows better will have had a brief and cruel peek behind the veil; a glimpse into the world behind the world.

I wonder, what else will it cause her to question? What other suspicions about the world will this prompt? Will she begin rethinking what she's been told about 9/11? The Kennedy assassination? The moon landing? Will she wonder if anything she's ever been told is true? Or is it all lies? Is the earth even round? How deep does the rabbit hole go, Alice?

A cherished part of unwinding after an assignment: Imagining life for the person who discovers the murdered, once they've seen the next day's paper declaring it a suicide. So here I sit with that reward now, that and my Jameson. The bar is quiet; the TV is muted with the captions on. Dr. Tobias Anglethorpe is on the screen speaking to the press, about his Supreme Court case no doubt. He's taken his fight for assisted suicide to the highest judicial power in the land. There's not a thing wrong with him, no terminal illness, no diminished mental capacity; he's of perfectly sound mind as has been confirmed by a battery of shrinks. He just wants the legal right to end it all because he's sick of being around us, the teeming moronic rabble that is humanity. I can't blame him, just seems like a lot of trouble to go through when he could just drive out to the desert, quietly take some pills and vanish into his final reward without so much as leaving a note. But that wouldn't be nearly as much fun as dragging the entire country into court, would it? Or he could just piss off my people. Everyone who fucks with us seems to wind up dead from suicide. But I don't think he really wants to die. He's just winding us all up.

I like to sit alone with my thoughts like this at the end of a prosecution, but not too alone. Of course I could just sit by myself back at the safe house and drink undisturbed but I prefer the potential of unwanted company while I unpack my thoughts. I'm not a people person, I'm an anti-people person and being an anti-people person presumes the presence of people to rid yourself of. Solitude doesn't accommodate that. In my experience, I've found that the quickest way to meet unwanted people is to sit alone in a hotel bar and hope no one sits next to you. So that's what I do.

This hotel bar is otherwise empty, save for the blowhard in Goretex who sidled up to my left 20 minutes ago. His Crown and rocks is sweating so his bar napkin sticks to the bottom of his glass every time he lifts it. I finish my Jameson neat and signal for another while he prattles on about some behavior experiment he read of online. Something about Rhesus monkeys who were punished with a jet of cold water every time one of them tried to fetch a banana from the top of a ladder.

"After a while they don't even look at the ladder, let alone think of climbing it." the know-it-all in Goretex is saying.

"So they don't even spray the monkey who goes after the banana," I follow, "they just spray the other monkeys?"

"Right, and after a while the other monkeys will freak out and attack the one who goes after the banana. They do it every time." He says between anxious sips of his Crown and rocks. "It got so they didn't even have to spray them anymore. The monkeys would just start thumping anyone who so much as looked at that ladder."

He waits for a response; I wait for my drink and stare down at my mobile.

"Every so often they'd switch out the monkeys, one by one, 'til there wasn't a single monkey left who'd been sprayed." He continues, "Anytime one of the new ones went for the banana, the other monkeys, they'd beat him senseless. They hadn't even been sprayed themselves, they just knew that's how things were done around there."

I relish watching him bristle at my non-response as the bartender brings me another Jameson neat. I think I like Jameson because it tastes like Band-Aids. Something about that seems very appropriate for liquor. Liquor should taste more like the hospital than the candy store.

Goretex is next to me shaking his head now in some approximation of pity as he says, "Sort of tells you something about the human condition."

I let his pronouncement hang in the air for a moment. I sip, he tenses.

"Really? What does it say?"

"Well, I guess it's sort of sad." Goretex bandies, a little less confident,

"Half the time I don't even think we know why we do the things we do or think the way we do."

This is why I love it when the Prelacy sends me to prosecute a writ in Seattle. This city is a gallery of wind-up toys. You just pick one out, open him up and marvel at the simple gears and clockwork. It's like that anywhere, really, but these people are certain they're nothing if not smart, anything but incorrect or unjust. That's what makes it so fun winding them up. Winding up strangers in bars, that's what I do instead of church or yoga.

"That's' what you take from it?" I ask, "Some cynical critique of humanity?"

"Well, yeah. What's your take?"

"I don't take anything from it. It's just culture. You're describing culture, that's all."

"Culture? How's that culture? You're saying culture makes us dumber? That sounds a little bit racist to me."

Why is anything beyond the threshold of inconvenience or insult ascribed to racism with these blockheads? A genuine problem for some people is reduced to a convenient clearinghouse for every pang of paranoia with these morons. 1690s Salem had its witchcraft, modern day Seattle has its racism. Here on earth nothing changes but the names of the gods and the villains. Today, we kneel at the altar of Hawking and gird ourselves against the devil of some ubiquitous, omnipotent white oppressor. Yesterday it was Jesus we prayed to and witches we feared, then it was America and liberty we adulated while we trembled before the specter of authoritarianism. It's all bullshit.

"So not getting sprayed with cold water, that sounds dumb to you?"

"No, that's not it at all. I mean, how much of what we think and do is just mindless obedience?"

"I think you miss the point. The point isn't that humanity is some monolith of mindless obedience, the point is that most of the traditions you don't understand inform a culture that keeps you and every monkey around you from getting sprayed with cold water."

The blowhard in Goretex wrinkles his face, visibly offended and says, "Why do you keep bringing up culture? What's any of this got to do with culture?"

I finish my drink and before dismissing myself, turn to the man and say, "Believe it or not, culture isn't only about spicy food and funny hats. It's about making life predictable. It's mostly just about not getting sprayed with cold water."

I leave enough cash to cover my tab and the bartender's tip then head out the door for a different bar to wind up and turn loose on the world.

TWO

Los Angeles, Thurs Sept 25th, 2014

About three weeks ago, I was back in Los Angeles looking to celebrate some good news by going out and winding up strangers in bars. I can't say precisely when I began this practice but I do know it was after I'd moved back home to Los Angeles from Seattle a few years ago.

About a year after Afghanistan I wanted to start over somewhere new, somewhere I could re-invent myself and explore being another person entirely. So, I moved to Seattle, having never been there and not knowing a single soul. I just loaded up a U-Haul one day, drove up the 5 for 24 hours and settled in, living out of motels at first, eventually finding roommates, making friends and planting roots. I lasted almost three years before it all came crashing down and I found myself running back home to L.A. in defeat. What felt like an entire city ablaze with disgust for me shrank in the rear view of another U-Haul as I drove south; ashes to ashes, dust to dust, U-Haul to U-Haul; me in a nut shell.

On this particular night though, I was looking to let go a little but more importantly I wanted to celebrate. My celebration would of course be a one man affair. That's pretty standard for me, I'm mostly a loner and that's the way I like it, more accurately the way I think it has to be. What I was celebrating was the news I'd received earlier that day from Sébastien, my sponsor within the Prelacy. On this day he told me that upon satisfactory prosecution of my next writ I would be advanced in rank and lodge to Sword Hand in the Tentacles of Abraxas, the second highest lodge within the Prelacy. This was a big deal for me so I wanted to cut loose some.

My plan was to find a dive or two I'd yet visited, tie one on good and wind up a stranger or two I'd yet aggravated. My short list of unexplored new dives was a bar called the Sans Souci in Eagle Rock and another called McHenry's in Burbank. I ended up at the Sans Souci in the early evening keen to stretch my legs and see what was what.

The décor at this old hole in the wall would've been referred to as swanky back when it was new; lots of Naugahyde and Mahogany with brass fixtures. The bartender was over 60 and he told me straight away that he wasn't sure he wanted to serve me because of my long hair. I liked that. This was a place with a lot of character. It seemed a shame to try and wind anyone up there but I'd already found my seat at the bar and had every intention of at least enjoying a few drinks before heading down the road.

After my first Jameson the number of patrons in the Sans Souci had doubled to four. Down the bar from me now sat a pair of old timers who'd just walked in, pensioners by the looks of them and they were on a first name basis with the bartender. Randy as it turns out. On the other side of the bar opposite the old couple sat a gruff looking blue-hair who busied herself playing video bingo or some such bar game.

While Randy cleaned glasses and kept an eye on things I occupied myself with cable news on the old color TV above the bar, there Dr. Anglethorpe was rattling off names into a bouquet of TV news microphones.

"...Dennis Rodman, Rod Blagojevich, Elizabeth Hasselbeck, Macklemore..."

`Every time the press surrounded him he would simply ignore their questions and move right into some curt preface like, "We'll keep fighting the good fight until justice prevails and I am legally permitted to leave this rotten *bleep* *bleep* planet to stupid sons of *bleep* like..." followed by his endless list of names which rolled out of his mouth with the most transparent contempt. It was the finest piece of performance art I would likely ever see, except he was totally unambiguous and seemingly sincere.

The story goes that in Oregon last year Dr. Tobias Anglethorpe obtained three different sworn and notarized statements from three separate psychiatrists, all of them very reputable and all of them declaring him completely of sound mind and in perfectly good mental health. He then obtained copies of his medical records and two separate opinions from two separate medical doctors declaring him in optimum physical condition. Dr. Anglethorpe, certified to practice assisted suicide in the State of Oregon then proceeded to conduct his own euthanizing by lethal injection on the steps of the Capitol Building in downtown Salem.

The good Doctor was interrupted, promptly arrested and brought up on charges of unlawful attempted suicide among other things. Since then he had escalated his case to the highest court in the land. What has followed is perhaps the most absurd circus in the history of the American justice system. If for nothing other than the fact that every time the press questioned him about the case, he would explain that he was simply seeking to legally end his life so he didn't have to go on living in the same world as those he would name from his list. Since the first day this trial hit the news cycle, Dr. Anglethorpe has used every moment on air to publicly shame a seemingly endless roll call of celebrities, politicians, athletes and notables, the very people he cannot bear to live in the same world as. It has been hilarious and it is the news cycle gift that keeps on giving.

"...Ram Dass, Jared from Subway, Alex Trebek, Alex Rodriguez..."

Dr. Anglethorpe continued rattling off names from his list when an obese, butch looking woman in a Los Angeles Kings jersey filled the seat to my right, looked up at the screen and shook her head in casual disgust.

"Oh, god. I can't stand this idiot." She mumbled. "Randy, put on the Kings game, would ya, hon?"

I was a fast fan of Dr. Anglethorpe and his absurd fight for freedom so I thought it pretty apparent that this woman would be my first dance partner for the night. I was going to enjoy winding her up. How can you hate Dr. Anglethorpe? He's the only good thing about this world right now.

Randy reached behind the register for the TV remote and switched the channel to the Kings preseason game against the visiting Ducks.

"You a Kings fan?" the woman turned to me and asked.

"Went to my first game on my 7th birthday."

"Nice."

"Got their asses kicked by the Blackhawks."

"Oh. Was that back when they wore the Purple and Yellow outfits? I like those."

"Forum Blue and Gold" I corrected her.

"For 'em what and huh?" she wrinkled, turning to face me.

"Forum Blue and Gold. When Jack Kent Cooke chose the colors for the Kings and the Lakers, the colors were to be officially referred to as Forum Blue and Gold."

"That's stupid. It's purple and yellow. That's not even blue, it's purple."

"It's Forum Blue and-"

Before I could even get the last word out of my smartass mouth, my new favorite Kings fan had belted me so hard in the teeth that I fell back on my barstool and onto the floor. Laying there on my back looking up at the ceiling of the Sans Souci, my bitten tongue swelling, I thought to myself, "That didn't take long. I should have plenty of time to check out that place in Burbank."

THREE

Seattle, WA – Sun Oct 12th, 2014

For as long as I care to remember, I've been wrong about everything. Primarily, I've been wrong about what I want far too often to ever be certain of what I want. Being aware of that fact hasn't spared me suffering from desire though. I can still want with the best of them, I'm just usually disappointed with whatever it is I thought I wanted once I've got it. The dog that actually catches the car.

I'm also usually wrong about anything I think I know for sure. Being aware of that fact hasn't spared me suffering from curiosity. I can wonder with the best of them, I'm just usually way off when I decide I've figured something out. These days I'm down to just a few certainties; primarily, I am certain that there is far too much certainty in this world. I'm also certain that most people are morons, that I'm no better than most people and that there is one vital indulgence which keeps me sane: getting drunk in bars and disabusing strangers of their certainties. That shameful little ritual I refer to as "winding up strangers in bars"; my frequent meditation which renders me mostly harmless to myself and chases off any misfortunate soul who might've thought to call me friend, if only for a few rounds.

If I indulge this compulsion every few days I'm satisfied and I can remain safely solitary. More honestly, if I'm disgusted with myself enough, I'm at no risk of building a network of enablers. A circle of friends is vital to people who aren't crazy. For me, they become nothing more than possessions to wind up, so I wind up strangers instead and stay as far from friendships as I possibly can. Someday maybe that can change, but for now this is what's working.

On my way up 6ᵗʰ Avenue in Downtown Seattle I see a tow truck broken down in the middle of the street. That's ironic enough but even better; this tow truck is pulling a tow truck. The driver has left the cab and is hopelessly trying to push his truck out of traffic. Everyone is losing their minds and honking at him on the already congested one way. The drizzle isn't making his day any easier and I feel like he could use a hand.

"Hey!"

He looks around for whoever's yelling at him and it takes him a moment to pin me. When he finally sees me I sense his relief immediately.

"Hey, you want me to call a tow truck?" I yell.

"Fuck you, asshole."

That was fun. I think I even just giggled a little bit.

I shrug and watch the guy struggle with his tow trucks a little longer before I get bored and take the circus down the road a ways. Content that my Prelacy obligations have been fulfilled and feeling a little gust of satisfaction from winding up the guy in Goretex earlier and now this tow truck driver, I'm keen to spend the entire rest of the evening winding up other strangers in other places. I continue north on 6ᵗʰ toward Denny telling myself I'm wandering without destination. I know I'll just wind up at the W, though. I usually do when I'm here in Seattle. Even within the solitude of my own head I'm too dodgy to admit that I'm certain of where I'm going. Still, I know that I'm heading toward the W if nothing better catches my attention along the way. I'm staying open to getting swept up in something spontaneous and unexpected but the bar at the W is a good enough default for when that doesn't happen. It probably won't be as empty as I'd prefer but I'll figure out how to make it all work. It only takes one stranger and a few Jamesons neat to re-center myself and the W can accommodate those conditions just fine.

I drift on toward anywhere but the W on my way to the W when I feel my mobile buzzing. I stop and read a message from the Prelacy's Scrivener. He issues the writs so he'll be inquiring about the status of my prosecution earlier this evening.

J.S. – Art thou the Folded Hands?

Me – Nay, 'tis I, the Red Hand.

J.S. – Whither go ye, Red Hand?

Me – Where so ever faith shall guide.

J.S. – Hast thou faith given ye a sign?

Me - Indeed.

J.S. – Very well, what is the sign?

Me – It is the Scale.

J.S. – Very well, hast thy writ been prosecuted?

Me – In deed it has and none hath seen.

J.S. – Very well, take ye your leave, Honored Hand.

And that's the end of that. I'm off the clock officially and left to my own devices. That exchange is identical to nearly every other one from that number. I have never even met the lodge Scrivener. For all I know he's a chat bot or some kind of AI.

I generally avoid agonizing over the odd fact that I've only met a few other members of our order. Most were superiors in the order, and met under circumstances of Prelacy ceremony.

The Prelacy is a secret society with a rich history but along the way I've learned some truths our order might prefer I hadn't. Through my own recreational investigation, I've come to suspect that our order is only about 30 years old, though our elders will swear to it being over a thousand and they draw its fabled lineage all the way back to the Merovingian dynasty of continental Europe. That's hokum. We're none of that, though I would imagine most of the devout among our order have eaten that bullshit story right up. Our society is indeed secret though. Our level of secrecy makes UFOs jealous. Makes the Illuminati look like LinkedIn.

We are in fact so obscured from sight that not only the public at large but our rivals, our raison d'etre, they don't even fully know we exist. Our own membership is in fact barely aware of one other. If I've ever encountered another member of the Prelacy outside of ceremony, I wouldn't know it. Reason being is we're expected to kill any member we've met outside of ceremony. This fatal concern is why we diligently guard the secret of our association, each and every one of us. Suffice it to say, we're not exactly in it for the fellowship. No spaghetti dinners and pancake breakfasts in this order. No fund raisers for children's diseases, no bingo night, just pure skullduggery.

Like any secret society, we have our symbols; foremost among them is an icon that consists of a simple bee within a hexagonal border but there are others. We also wear our hair below the collar to honor the warriors and tribal Kings of pre-Roman Europe. Meroveus, Clovis, Vercingetorix, Arminius and on and on.

Though we have our signifiers, they are vague and few and it is unwise to keep or collect articles that refer to our symbols, as you might imagine. The only items I possess with our bee icon are the gold mini-bars the order pays me in for the completion of the tasks they assign; the prosecutions of their writs, as it were.

By now I am on high alert anytime I lay eyes on a grown man with longhair, let alone wearing a bee symbol. I get suspicious whenever I see any bee symbol or icon anywhere. It's like driving a Volkswagen Beetle. You don't even see them on the road until you own one, then suddenly they're all over the place. I never realized how ubiquitous the symbol of the bee was until I'd joined the Prelacy, now I notice them everywhere and it freaks me out. If I meet someone with a tie-pin of a little bee I get suspicious. I see a sports team with a bee for a logo and I'm set to wondering. At this point I view the entire state of Utah with suspicion and the whole bee thing has really ruined the Wu-Tang Clan for me. If I had to wager which of them is in the Prelacy, my money's on Killah Priest.

As a corollary of this strictly enforced secrecy we don't wear any regalia or accoutrements to denote membership save for the long hair. No cool sashes, no fez, no medallions, no rings. The only regular symbolic indications of my affiliation I come across are those gold bars that are a pain in the ass and expensive to liquidate. If you're not selling them back to the Prelacy for currency, good luck. Selling the Prelacy's gold bars outside of the Prelacy requires melting them down and recasting them without the bee symbol on them, then you still have to find a buyer who isn't buying them at a rip-off exchange rate. I just sell them back to the order whenever I need cash. I pity the soul desperate enough to trade those bars publicly with the bee icon still on them. It happens from time to time I've been told but it doesn't end well for the person found doing it. It's exactly this degree of concealment that has supported our successful obscurity for so long. By now everyone has heard of Skull and Bones but I highly doubt Skull and Bones have heard of the Prelacy.

Though our secrecy is so severe that we're mostly obscured even from other members, we do have our opportunities for fraternization and ceremony. If summoned by a lodge elder, fraternizing is not only permitted but encouraged. Perhaps the greatest opportunities to learn about this order I belong to have come from those sparse moments of permitted socialization. A great deal can be gathered about our secret society from other members at the rare ceremonial feast. It is there, in strict numbers and under watchful eye that Prelates are permitted to rub elbows with one another. I've met just a few other members under the ceremonial eye of our elders but those Prelacy shindigs were really informative in the way of Prelacy lore, not to mention a pretty good time. It's exhilarating to think that had those members and I by chance learned of our shared association outside of ceremony we would be locked in mortal contest. Because we had met under ceremony, we were now relieved of such duty altogether. Were we ever to run into one another outside of ceremony now, we didn't have to worry about the whole thing where one of us had to kill the other. We were however forbidden to acknowledge one another. We are strictly instructed to avoid even casual mingling outside of ceremony under any circumstances. Though members may on occasion encounter and recognize each other, they are to proceed strictly as strangers.

When you encounter a ceremonially known member of our order outside of ceremony, the rule of thumb is always leave the room of encounter in opposite directions and endeavor to keep at least one room between the two of you. This degree of compartmentalization is so operationally secure that it gives the war vet in me a camouflage boner and the neurotic obsessive in me Sudoku boner. The Prelacy is in fact so compartmentalized that I don't even know the names of most other lodges within the order, I know of mine, The

Path of the Sword and just a few others. There is the Path of the Cloak, which I know of because it was offered as my only other optional path of advancement through the Prelacy hierarchy. Once I'd leveled past the initiatory rank of Blind Apprentice I was offered advancement through the Path of the Sword and the Path of the Cloak, I chose the Path of the Sword. The Path of the Sword is the Prelacy's muscle, to put it bluntly. We whack people. The Path of the Cloak is our intelligence arm. They spy on people. The other lodges I know of are the Path of the Disciple and the Prelacy Guard. I had learned of those two through fraternization under ceremony. Disciples are a lodge of scholars within the order and the Prelacy Guard are our internal police force. I hear they're dicks. Nobody likes cops.

Even our order's name is a big secret. We're never to speak the proper name outside of ceremony, not even to ourselves. It is never to be written down and never to be said aloud. Our ceremonial name is French; it is le Familier Prélature de Arbitres Infernales. On the rare occasion I even hear it referred to outside of ceremony, it's simply called the Prelacy. The Familiar Prelacy of Infernal Arbitrators if you're nasty. The Prelacy is nothing if not a secret society that makes all the rest look like the Red Hat Society; of that much I'm certain.

Certainty, that old hang-up of mine. It seems to me when certainty is what we long for most, it is a certainty that our longing will be rewarded with endless conundrums. I'm not even certain of death and taxes. The Prelacy has rewarded me with a small fortune in gold no one's been able to tax yet and I suppose that whole death thing is something you sort of have to see for yourself. I've seen other's die, to be sure but how dead are they? How do you know something's dead when you can't even describe the experience of being dead? I can't be certain.

There are just so few things I will permit myself to feel certain of; the sun rising in the east and setting in the west, I'm an asshole when I'm drunk and dangerous when I'm not. I'm certain that most people are morons, I'm certain that I'm as much of a moron as any stranger I've ever wound up in a bar and I suppose add to this small list of certainties that the Prelacy will most certainly issue a writ with my name on it should they ever find out what kind of moronic fuck up I really am. Finally, it is with absolute certainty that I consider joining the Army to be among my biggest mistakes. I think that about covers it. Those are the things I'm certain of; everything else is still a jump ball.

FOUR

Seattle, WA – Sun Oct 12th, 2014

As certainty would have it, I wind up at the W's ground floor after pretending it might happen otherwise for a few blocks. I enter, leaving a hankering for anywhere but here and pasty Seattle atmosphere on the other side of its glass. The ambiance inside is as bright, warm and phony as the building's red carpets and crystal fixtures. Just up the escalator is a sort of open walled bar area situated in the middle of a moderately trafficked lobby. I don't know much about architecture so I guess I would call this a lobby bar. By any name, there's no sense of privacy or anonymity here. No shadowy corners to vanish into, no flat screens to fix the eyes on. The bar is well lit and the bartenders, chipper females uniformed in white button downs, red six button vests and black slacks. This bar conflicts with my every sensibility, yet I wind up here every time I'm in Seattle. With a self like mine, who needs enemies?

I seat myself in a conspicuous place at the center of the bar and wait to be accosted by some business casual Happy Monday with the fleeting, affected gregariousness that a third Appletini has installed. I make eye contact with a tired-of-smiling twenty-something bartender whose name badge reads Jilly. That name; now there's a sunny facade on a Seattle storm cloud. I lean in and tell her I'd like a Jameson neat, double. My tone, just above whisper-volume elicits a look of belabored patience, the fifty in my right hand tempting something closer to enthusiasm. Somewhere along the line I learned that talking low forces people to listen. I also learned that bartenders dislike a customer who doesn't speak up when they order as much as they dislike one who holds their fare so visibly. I'm off to a bad start as I so enjoy, though I never, ever wind up bartenders. Always treat the bartender nice. The bartender is your friend even though they hate you, and make no mistake, they fucking hate you.

Jilly pours the easiest order she'll get all night as I watch her deciding whether I'm worth the trouble, even on a slow night. She "there ya goes" my whiskey, neat and I "keep the change" her for her trouble. She goes from less-than-annoyed to bubbly like I give a fuck.

I don't really care if she's nice to me or if she snaps to when she sees my glass is dry. Her job is dealing with the worst assholes the city can muster and I don't need her to make me feel like Penny Royalty. If she gets too busy or just can't be bothered it's no worry, that's why I carry a flask.

I tip well and I make nice but I don't believe much in the urbane deceit of politeness. I over tip because I used to live with a bartender and I've long ago memorized every litany and lament these pre-offended sob-minstrels can sing. I know them all by heart and I can sympathize with every single one of them because dealing with the public is a hellish way of making a living. With one pissy look across a bar those irritating bleats about complex drink orders and bad tips come flooding back to me the same way the whir of a chopper makes flashes of the 'Nam come bolting back to throb the shrapnel in a war vet's ass.

Did I just compare living with a whiny bartender to surviving 'Nam? Yes, I did. I wouldn't dare compare it to Afghanistan because I know from Afghanistan; it's nowhere near as bad as living with a whiny bartender. Like most personal antagonisms of the conscience, this one can be quieted with money and a polite decorum. It's worth it because I'm not going to start isolation drinking any time soon. I like to drink alone in a crowd, not alone in a room. I have to be out here among the miserable, going through the motions with the rest of the genteel haters. The storm clouds with sunny facades. I'm bitter, not better.

I take a sip when through the corner of my eye it seems that the seat next to me has filled; a male presence, commanding posture, not a slob. Before I can get too puffed up about this potential new cat toy in my perimeter, I deflate with the realization that it's just Al. I like Al, though it's not apparent by the way we get on. Regardless, it's not a good thing running into him here right now. I grit my teeth and wait for him to speak.

"You gonna sit there lookin' down at your Mick piss water all night or are you gonna say hi?"

It's never good running into Al in a public place, mostly because no one else can see him.

FIVE

Los Angeles, CA – Thurs Jun 6th, 1991

It was the same summer Sailor got sent back to Sinaloa and my mom dragged me back to Illinois again. I was eleven years old and after coming and going over and over since first grade I was only just beginning to fit in with the other kids. No small accomplishment for the only gavacho on the block.

"Chale! Those are my quarters, fool!" Sailor said laughing, his skinny digit pointing out the slimmest distance between the wall and the coin he'd just tossed.

Rigoberto Abeja wasn't just our friend, he was an irreplaceable fixture in our collective identity, but then again we all were. There was Rigo, Marcos and Salvador. Sailor, Chico and Joker respectively and then there was me, Huero. Huero's pretty much the standard nickname the white guy gets in any neighborhood like ours.

Sailor was Sailor because, for some reason the way he walked meant he was Sailor. His family called him that and it had been his name since he was a toddler. We only ever heard the name Rigo spoken in class.

Marcos Ybarra was Chico, a name he got from the older homies because he was so slight. It would come to be an ironic nickname once he hit his growth spurt but the name would stick, none the less.

Salvador was Joker because that was his dad's name. Sal's dad was a veterano from our neighborhood who was doing life in the pen. Sometimes nicknames got passed down for no better reason. His dad's sense of humor didn't get passed down, that much we know. At least that's what we figured. Maybe his dad didn't have one either. None of us really knew his dad; we just

17

assumed he must have been funny if everyone called him Joker.

"Hells nah, mira fool. You're short, that's all me!" Chico protested, pointing at the quarter he'd thrown before Sailor's.

That's what we did before and after school in those days. We pitched pennies, or more accurately quarters; a game of stakes that involved tossing coins at a wall, the purse going to whoever got closest to the wall with their toss.

We all gathered around the four coins to scrutinize the distance between them and the wall of the corner store we stood outside of every day. Mine and Joker's coins had hit the wall, disqualifying us but Chico and Sailor's were neck-and-neck; we couldn't tell who'd won the round.

"That one's yours, yeah Chico?" I asked pointing to the one that had just been tossed. The fun of this game wasn't so much tossing of the coins as it was arguing over the results.

"Nah, I'm the one on the left." Chico said.

"You're short, fool." Joker said.

"Bullshit, look!" Chico urged, bending down over the coins and beckoning closer inspection.

"You're gonna believe you own eyes?" I said.

"Huero, don't be that guy." Chico cautioned. My tendency toward being a difficult little smart ass goes pretty far back.

As we argued over who was closest, Mando showed up prompting us to acknowledg that minor mood breaker to one another with the same knowing look that said "Fuck, here comes Mando."

We liked Mando but he was kind of a dick to us. Four years older than me, the youngest of us-but for some reason all too keen to hang out with us youngsters though he was never invited.

"What's the word, Peewees?" Mando said as he walked up and joined our circle.

We gave him the mandatory reception of glad hands, back pats and nods and a round of what's-up-Mandos.

Mando was Mando. That was his actual name and that's what everyone called him. Mando Pentecost. He was a member of the neighborhood gang but he didn't dress like a cholo and he never had a nickname. His casual rejection of conforming to those things was off putting. It suggested he didn't have to observe tradition if he didn't want to, which came across as powerful, even intimidating. No tattoos, no khakis, no Chuck Taylors or house shoes, no bald head. Mando wore basketball shorts, Adidas slides and his hair was a messy black porcupine. He had a reputation for fighting well above his years and even the older homies gave him respect. Mando liked us and we liked him back but that doesn't mean he was one of us.

"Hey, let me use this to get a forty, the old Chinese lady will sell to me if she's working." Mando said, stealing the purse from our game of pitching pennies. We didn't protest. It was a quarter lost to each of us which amounted to a dollar in total. Mando probably knew none of us drank beer, so he'd just hustled himself a good one.

"Mando, get some gum too, eh." Sailor said.

Sailor was the boldest of us. He wasn't going to let Mando tax us without taking something back for it. He was smart like that and it was little details like this that kept people from running over us roughshod every single day.

"Will do." Mando said as he disappeared around the corner and into the store.

Mando returned with a 22 of King Korba and no gum. Nice try, Sailor. At least you gave it a shot.

"What happened to the chicle?" Sailor said.

"Oh, shit, I forgot, eh." Mando said.

We all just looked at each other and smirked. No surprises there. That's sort of how it worked around our neighborhood; you always knew what someone was going to do but if you didn't make your stand anyway, then it just got easier and easier for them to walk all over you.

Mando twisted the bag around his bottle of King Kobra then cracked it, took a big drink and offered to pass it around; no takers. After he took another swig he studied us for a moment before speaking.

"So when are you little putos going to get put on the varrio?" he asked. "Is it on or what?"

We'd been dodging this pressure for a while now. Somewhere after we stopped playing GI Joe by the railroad tracks and started hanging out in front of the corner market the neighborhood homies started in on us about getting jumped in. Sailor and Chico hated the idea, Joker didn't like it but said he knew it had to happen and my dumb ass thought it was exciting that they wanted us.

By this time, the cholo era in Los Angeles was winding down as most kids were finding more interesting lifestyle pursuits that didn't require hospitals, jails and funerals. Things like Rock-a-billy, Punk Rock and Mod culture, skateboarding, scooters, hip hop, Harley Davidsons, raves. For some reason we didn't find our way to the cool table quick enough to discover those diversions. We were pretty much nerds and complete nobodies at our school as much as around our own neighborhood. We never featured ourselves being a part of anything trendy or fun.

"Nah, fool. Why do you guys even care what we do?" Sailor laughed.

His confidence gave us all a feeling of security.

"You're from the turf, Sailor, we just want to make sure you guys are alright." Mando said. "We don't want anything to happen to you little vatos."

Sailor just sucked his teeth and pantomimed kicking dirt in dissension. The rest of us milled about nervously.

"So what're we doing? Pitching pennies or what?" Mando asked, digging in his pockets to pull out what was most likely one of the quarters he took from us earlier. "You game?"

I didn't have any more quarters so I faded back with Sailor while Chico and Joker buoyantly rose to the challenge. As the sun went down Chico, Joker and Mando pitched round after round, Mando winning most of the arguments over who was closest. When Mando was done with his bottle of King Kobra he headed toward the store with his winnings to get another one.

"Hey, for real though. You vatos have to figure it out because it's coming up a lot. Homies want to know if you're down or what." Mando said as he counted his change and parted for the entrance of the corner store. Once he'd started for the door, he halted as something caught his eye.

"Hey, you see that burgundy '72 down the street?" He asked us, pointing down the block with his chin. We all looked and acknowledged.

"Yeah, I see it." Sailor said.

"El Sereno boys, trucha."

El Sereno was a neighborhood down the hill and to the south of us. Our neighborhoods had been at war with each other for decades. Sailor, Chico, Joker and I had even been having problems with a group of El Serenos we'd run into at the malls and swap meets lately. While I think my friends were snapping alert, I was just scared. Those dudes from El Sereno who'd been fucking with us were older and pretty intimidating. I wanted to feel brave and badass but in the back of my mind I was hoping it wasn't trouble lurking in that maroon Caprice.

Mando popped his chin up and chest out toward the old Chevy as he watched it creep around the corner and once they were out of view he continued on, yard-strutting toward the front of the market to get another beer.

While Mando was gone Sailor broke our tension by asking us for our thoughts about getting initiated into the neighborhood.

"Fuck that shit." Chico said. "Cholos are corny. I just want to ride skates and kick it with you vatos."

"Yeah, I do too." Joker said, "But we don't get to pick that life. This is Boyle Heights, fool, not the Valley. We have to be smart."

"All that shit about protecting us?" Chico said. "And right before he points out that lowrider? Mando's just trying to scare us." Chico laughed. "Fuck that, I ain't joining shit."

"We can put it off but the truth is we're going to have to do it sooner or later." Joker said. "We all know it, we're just hoping something happens so we won't have to."

"What do you think, Huero?" Sailor asked me.

"I don't see why we don't do it." I replied.

"Fucking Huero. C'mon, man." Chico said. "Fuck these guys. We're nerds, why do they care what we do?"

Things got quiet for a while and then Mando returned, fresh squeezed 22 of King Kobra in hand.

"You youngsters see that Caprice come back around?" Mando asked as we all answered our nos and uh-uhs.

"You guys don't know that car?"

We shrugged and shook heads waiting to hear more.

"That's Chango from El Sereno's ride. The older homies smoked his primo last week so don't slip."

"Yeah, we know who he is. Him and his homies have been fucking with us whenever we see them around." Joker told Mando.

"You're sure that's his ride?" Sailor asked.

"Yeah, I know his car." Mando said. "You can tell it's his because of the bondo on the right rear quarter panel. It's him for sure. That's Betsy. That car's been in Northeast for 15 years. She used to be one of the older homie's from here."

That's the thing about big cities. They're really just a bunch of small towns, except there's no distance between them. That car was over 15 years old and it had probably never been 50 miles from its first owner.

"Hey, you guys should bounce." Sailor said to me and Chico. "It's getting late and if that fool Chango is creeping around looking for static I don't want you guys out here."

We just laughed.

"Yeah, right. We're not going anywhere." Chico said. I just stood beside him in support.

Sailor looked at Mando who shrugged and said, "It's cool with me if you guys kick it. Just keep trucha. That fool is crazy. It ain't on me if it pops off."

The five of us went back to watching or competing in another penny pitching contest, which was inevitably won by Mando's arguing. After Mando had contested his way to enough for another 22 he spied the burgundy Caprice slowly rounding the corner down the street yet again.

"Hey, it's already dark out and I just saw those fools make another pass; you little homies should probably bounce." Mando said, chambering a round in his automag and placing it back in the holster clipped to the inside of his waistband. "I'm gonna call Kiki and Corndog, I'll be right back."

Sailor, ever the grown up brains of our group ordered me and Chico to go home which we refused to do.

"Serio, if you don't leave, I'm gonna make you go." Joker said, backing Sailors command that we retreat to safety.

"Chale, we're not leaving you." Chico said. I just stood with my chest out in support again, offering no word on things.

"If they want to stay, let them stay." Mando advocated. "I'm strapped, we're all good."

Joker just shrugged and Sailor shook his head, evidently uncomfortable with the prospect.

"Alright but if anything happens, you guys don't try to be all tough or anything, you head straight for the railroad tracks and run home, entiendes?" Sailor said sternly, making sure to look each of us right in the eyes for acknowledgement of what he'd just told us.

Leaned against the wall were me and Chico's skateboards and as Mando returned from the payphone on the other side of the corner store he picked mine up and and gave it a once over. "You guys anygood?" He asked awkwardly pushing mongo in his slip-ons with no socks. Chico and I just laughed at the clumsy skateboarding demo, much to Mando's amusement. "Am I getting off or what? Is this how you do it?" Mando clowned. We laughed. We liked it when Mando acted goofy like this because we knew he was patronizing us and that was as close as we'd get to respect from him.

"Mando, What'd Kiki and Corndog say?" Sailor asked casually keeping an eye down the block for that '72.

"No se. I just paged them the code for out-of-towners. We'll see if they come through."

In those days, no one really carried cel phones but pagers were pretty common and there were a series of codes someone could message with, letting the person they'd paged know what they were trying to get in touch about.

Kiki and Corndog were older homies, a pair of cousins who-as far as I could tell-drove around all day in Corndog's primer grey '65 Impala with a Mossberg pump under the bench seat. Every time I saw them they were drinking cheap wine, high on brick weed and just driving around. They were a pair of characters and they never seemed to take anything serious but I don't think they had to. They had that Mossberg and that '65. For them, that was all they needed; everything beyond that was gravy.

Sailor and Joker went back to pitching quarters at the corner store wall while me and Chico watched Mando clown around on my skateboard. Before long the sun had completely set and it was time to go. For me and Chico anyway. Sailor and Joker gave us a shake, said their goodnights and told us they were going to hang out with Mando until Kiki and Corndog showed up. Before we could change our minds Sailor told us to get going. I started to worry that Mando was going to make me ask for my skateboard back but he wound it out 'til the last moment and then handed it to me.

"Don't forget your deck, Huero." He said handing it over and giving me a playful shove as Chico and I walked off toward the railroad tracks. To see it all, you'd think I was raised around bullies but things like that little shove were just a casual display of fondness and good faith in our world.

Chico and I made the trek home along the railroad tracks safely and uneventfully, parting ways at our usual spot.

"Alrato,Huero."

"Alright, Cheeks," I said, Cheeks being short for Chico, "mañana."

The next morning was the last day of school before summer break. Sailor didn't show up at the railroad tracks where we normally met to walk to school. When Joker finally arrived he told me and Chico that Sailor's folks were sending him back to Mexico because of what had happened. When we asked what he was talking about, Joker ruefully explained that Mando had been shot to death standing in front of the corner store where we were last night. Chango and his boys from El Sereno, no doubt. Sailor's parents had found out about it when the police drove him home.

Sailor had explained to Joker this morning that last night's events sparked a discussion between his parents about getting him out of harm's way and teaching him a lesson. They were worried that because he was born in the States he was getting too spoiled, didn't respect how hard they had worked to give him a life here. They worried that he seemed keen to just throw it all away hanging out with the local riff raff so they decided a couple months in the old country might give his perspective a little tune up. If only Sailor's folks knew how much he disliked that local riff raff, wanted us to have nothing to do with them. No sense worrying about that now, though. Sailor was going back to Sinaloa and there was nothing we could do about it. Summer, something we normally looked forward to now held a dread prospect without Sailor and even Mando.

A month later, my mother had run into financial problems and was full speed ahead into her routine solution; loading up the U-Haul and dragging us back to stay with her family outside Chicago, something she'd been doing over and over for the previous 7 years. I never told her about Mando and she remained oblivious.

SIX

The Prelacy's lore is extensive and richly rendered throughout a library of guarded occult texts and mysterious artifacts, though as I've hinted, it's all bullshit. It's all an elaborate evangelical contrivance. Propaganda aimed at the development of zealous devouts within the lodges.

The dissemination of these inspirational fictions begins in the initiation phase and continues as the member levels through the order's enlightened degrees. All prospective members of our lodges receive the title of Blind Apprentice once they are ceremonially returned to the sea in the Prelacy's initiation ritual. Whenever a Blind Apprentice is initiated into the order he is permitted intercourse with the primary article of Prelacy lore, The Codex Merovingi. A seemingly ancient and ornately illuminated book that contains the gospel stories of the Prelacy's origins during the Merovingian Dynasty. As with all of the artifacts of our order, the sponsor or advocate will only permit his ward to view it in his presence.

I read the book in fascination and committed most of it to memory over the course of a weekend in Santa Barbara a year or so ago. Alas, because I came to the works of Edward Bernays and Nicolo Machiavelli before I came to the Codex Merovingi, I saw it for what it really is: nothing more than an attempt by my newfound friends to buy up real estate inside my head. I've embraced the fiction and regurgitated its finer points whenever it could advantage me but I've always known better than to hold it as any vessel of cosmic truth or spiritual insight. It's just cultist clap-trap.

Power resides where people believe it resides, it depends entirely on the appointment of its constituents. Kings have long manufactured their claims to thrones with fables of divine lineage which appeal to their devotees. The

Merovingi made the claim of being sired by a beast-god called a Quinotaur which emerged from the sea, Ragnar Lodbrok boasted of being the progeny of Thor, even the burgeoning Caliphates of modern Arabia wage war over which lineage they trace back to their prophet. All monarchs can fortify their potency with fables of divine ancestry. I quite like our order's little tale of sacred providence, phony as it is.

The first book of the Codex Merovingi is the Gospel of Childeric I, King of the Salian Francs. It tells the story of the birth of his father Merovech, son of that sea monster with the head of a bull, the torso of a man and the tail of a fish; the Quinotaur. The Merovingian Kings are closely associated with the sea in all of their lore. In fact they are fabled to have come from the sea and ultimately been driven back there after generations of being the Kings of Frankia.

The Merovingi were colloquially known as the Long Haired Kings. This is the reason men of our order must wear their hair past the collar as I do, though I've worn mine long for years anyway. I'm alerted by men with long hair as much as I am people wearing the image of a bee. The Merovingians wore their hair long both in defiance to Roman custom and as a tribute to the long haired tribal chieftains who ruled continental Europe before Rome.

Among the more odd trappings of our house, all members must be born under the zodiac sign of Pisces, that is they must have been born between February 19th and March 20th. That is downright crazy to me but no more crazy than anything else we do, I suppose.

I don't mind the Prelacy's preposterous lore. It's like the pageantry and role play found in any other fraternity or religion, I just can't buy in to it as a devout. For me, we're no more than a secret guild of assassins who target rich bankers. Ask one of our more devout members and they might tell you we're fulfilling prophecy. I don't go in for all of that. I'm just a weird loner who likes to drink whiskey, loves to wind up strangers in bars and harbors no sympathy for the wealthy elites our order is wiping out like so many bountied wolves.

SEVEN

Seattle, WA – Sun Oct 12ᵗʰ, 2014

"Still sore over Hamburg?" Al asks.

He likes to draw me out in public because he knows I don't want to be that crazy guy talking to himself at the bar. That's one of the rubs about being crazy, you don't want anyone to think you're crazy.

"Go away, Al." I say under my breath, face and lips pulled taut as I stare ahead.

"Kid, you can't keep blaming me for the Austrian. It wasn't my fault and it wasn't yours either. You gotta let it go and get on with it."

The Austrian was a young millionaire, an extraneous casualty of a writ I had to prosecute in Hamburg last spring. He was what most people would call a douchebag but I took a shine to the guy. I also had a mostly unblemished record with the Prelacy before that writ and it might have stayed that way if not for Al. His interloping in Hamburg had delayed my promotion to the rank of Sword Hand and thereby, my initiation into the Tentacles of Abraxas, an advanced lodge within the Prelacy. I was in deed still a little pissed at Al, to be sure.

I take another pull from my glass and resist verbalizing any response.

"Suit yourself kid, but there was nothing either of us could have done to save him."

He's not trying to make me feel better; he's trying to pass the buck. He's the reason things went sideways in Hamburg and he knows it. It's taking all of the composure I can muster to keep from swinging at him right now.

But wouldn't that be cute? The stand-offish weirdo sitting alone at the bar is swinging at the air now. Yeah, that's a good look. I grit my teeth and hope he leaves soon, or at least stops talking.

"You'd think a guy who spends his free time winding up drunks for fun would be able to see it when someone's doing the same thing to him."

No sooner am I about to launch my drink at the annoying specter of former Raiders owner Al Davis than he's vanished into the ether. In his place is a repulsively gorgeous woman who is just now pulling out the barstool he'd been sitting in a second ago.

Of all the empty seats in the house why pick this one? I count myself lucky I didn't just coldcock some beautiful woman with a rocks glass. Al's going to get me in trouble someday. It's as if he's set on it.

Al gone, replaced by this abomination of fortunate genetics, I reflexively set to composing myself and focus on doing the only thing a guy like me can do in the proximity of such stunning beauty. I make a spectacle of my forced disinterest. Of course she doesn't notice and there's no way I'm going to say anything to her. I might have to walk to the Ace Hotel down in Bell Town if she doesn't go away. There's no winding up beautiful women, it's either impossible or so easy it's unsatisfying. I still have my ritual re-centering to attend to. If she stays long I'll have to move on. Then again, maybe I don't feel like winding anyone up tonight. Maybe I just want to sit here for a while and pretend I don't notice her.

While she stands there being flawless to a fault, I go on pretending I don't know she's there and catch up with Dr. Anglethorpe's latest antics on my mobile's newsfeed.

"Paula Deen, Chief Keef, Toby Kieth, Banksy, Simon Cowell"

EIGHT

A lot of what I know of Prelacy lore has been learned from lodge elders and their access to our historical artifacts. Through brief conversation I've been able to gather little bits of information about the politics of our order but not very much. Tidbits, mostly about my own relative significance within the order, little beyond anything personal. They really don't let on much. Beyond those limited perspectives I've pieced together some things on my own. Things they would probably prefer I left uninvestigated.

As far as my own station within the Prelacy I'm told that I am the only American in the lodge. As I was once told by my sponsor Monsieur Sébastien, "In the U.S. there is no shortage of capable candidates who are perfect for apprenticing but most of them are incontrovertibly loyal to precluding endeavors. Running banks, corporations or blindly faithful to military and intelligence services." I take that to mean all the good psychos are already brainwashed.

Much like the Prelacy's lore, their story of how they found me was nothing short of bullshit. To hear Sébastien tell it I was tested at age three and selected to begin conditioning immediately. They say the conditioning occurred throughout the normal routines of my formative years, completely unbeknownst to me or anyone close to me. That when the time was right I was located and tapped for apprenticing and every day of my life has been in preparation for that moment. I was basically selected and groomed to be a Blind Apprentice in the Prelacy from childhood. My rank now is Red Hand and if things go well, soon enough I'll be a Sword Hand and level past the Path of the Sword and on to the Tentacles of Abraxas. Had things gone better in Hamburg I would have already done this. I know very little about the Tentacles of Abraxas beyond that it is the second highest lodge within our order.

I don't believe the nonsense about being selected as a child. Like I said, they want to buy up as much real estate in my head as they can. That's a normal imperative for any cult . I do wonder how they came to tap me, though. I tend to think one of them held a position in the Army and decided I suitably filled the profile they were looking for but I can't imagine why. I was only in the Army briefly and I never saw the sort of action that would impress them. That could've been enough to bring me to their attention, though. I also had a brief run as a fraud investigator in the banking industry where I uncovered some pretty startling things, so it's been in my head that maybe they found me that way. Whatever the case, I don't buy in to the hokum about divine destiny or any of that. Whenever their stories go off the deep end I tend to just nod my head and quietly dissent.

Now, through personal inquiries via the miracle of the internet, a Los Angeles public library card and corroborations made from my own independent study of the Prelacy's records and codices, I've outlined a different understanding of Prelacy history than what they purport.

By my best estimation the Prelacy started around 30 years ago. No millennia old royal legacy in Europe. The order is more likely just a bunch of aging 1960s radicals who've rebranded themselves with 21st Century fascinations resembling the Illuminati and Freemasonry.

The true beginnings of the Prelacy can be traced to a series of bloodless banking coups in the early 1990s. Through the successful extortion of executives inside Banco Internazionale dei Commercianti e Industriali, or BICI, one of the wealthiest international banks in Italy, the Prelacy began a campaign of undermining and disruption within global banking that had turned the world on its ear no less than what might have happened had those same bankers been left to their own devices.

In the summer of 1992, with a very sly bit of intelligence gathering and corporate espionage the Prelacy was able to collapse BICI into insolvency, never to be seen again. With this success they sought to scale their operation and replicate that action across the banking world. It only took a few years to notice an unfortunate trend. In the resulting power vacuum of their big takedowns, a different bank would always step in to fill the toppled institution's vacancy. BICI was replaced by Banco d'Italia Popular which quickly became twice as powerful as BICI was. Bank von Bayern was toppled only to be replaced by a now more powerful Kaufmannsbank und Vertrauen. Algonquin Trade & Trust collapsed only to make way for a bigger, more belligerent Manahattan BB&T. The list goes on and on. After similar operations throughout Germany, Italy, Greece, and England it became apparent that destroying the banks simply consolidated their power and made the world even worse for the common man. Still, hardly a soul noticed what was going on. Most of the citizens of Europe and America went about their routine of spending money they didn't have on things they didn't need to impress people they didn't like. Business as usual.

In the wake of these pyrrhic victories, the Prelacy seems to have suspended operations by the mid-90s but apparently they did not disband. From the mid-90s and up until a few years after 9/11 there just isn't an awful lot of information about their activities. I've sifted through suppressed topics and conspiracy theories all over the internet as much as in mainstream periodicals and for all I can see the order went dark for a decade. The Prelacy elders themselves are very hush on our order's activities during this period as well. Anything the Prelacy was up to between 1996 and 2007 is pretty well stifled and squelched. The most glaring questions being what if any part did they play in 9/11 and the American recession. The most I can gather is that through this period the Prelacy was focused on incubating their own cells within banking. A silent campaign of establishing moles with very little substantive action taking place, save for some insider trading and put optioning to syphon off operational capital. This era of quiet is, by my estimation, where the Prelacy went from ambitious radicalism to shadowy cabal of wealthy zealots. In short, they went dark to make a lot of money to finance their next phase of action, which is occurring now.

I was tapped for Apprenticeship in 2012 which Is around the time the Prelacy resumed actions against their targets. Around 2011 people began to take notice of a spate of Banker suicides. One by one, a wave of bankers who'd taken the proverbial plunge from their towering corner offices grew and grew, while making hardly a ripple in mainstream news media. Independent online news sources however picked up on it right away. Bankers falling like flies in London, New York, Geneva, Lichtenstein, Frankfurt, Vienna. At first, hardly a soul even noticed but when a few dead bankers became a dozen and counting, suddenly some of the more alert people peeled their eyes from the antics of the CIA's radical Islam puppets and social media' scourge of Social Justice clicktivism to wonder, "Won't someone with nice hair on CNN or SkyNews tell me if these dying bankers are something I should feel afraid over?" And that's about as far as the average person's interest was stoked. Most people I suppose just dismissed it all as money doing what money does and bankers doing what bankers do. If these weren't legitimate suicides, then they were just bankers being killed by the usual dark forces and that was hardly any man-bites-dog concern. Nothing so important as whatever Kanye was getting up to or whoever Justin Bieber was pissing off. Or on.

The truth of course was actually far more inspiring than a bunch of suicidal bankers. In fact, these weren't suicides at all. These were murders and there were particular details that made it apparent that they weren't the result of corporate espionage or a dark culture of blood and money within banking. These were the result of a Robin Hood . A Killin Hood, if I'm being clever. That is exactly why the truth of what was occurring had to be suppressed. If the common man knew there was a secret cabal of unknown psychopaths going around murdering the most corrupt bankers in the world it might inspire uprisings. Killin Hood and his Murdery Men might severely destabilize anything resembling business as usual throughout the European and American markets and that just would not do. That might even inspire hope and that simply would not do. That would be evidence of real justice and in this day and age, real justice had to be suppressed. The only thing that seemed to keep people inline was constant injustice. Doctors to make you sick, bankers to rip you off, judges to lock away the victims and set free the criminals. Those were the true pillars of a functioning society and anything reasonable had to be hidden if not destroyed. Anything so life affirming and justified as a fraternity of shadowy assassins going around and killing the kings of hell had to be obscured, distorted. Plain and simple.

So the Prelacy began, not 1500 years ago with the birth of a God-King and an eternal destiny but maybe just 20 years ago with a few collapsed banks and a pragmatic goal. It started as an ambitious terror operation to restore a sense of civility and fear among the oligarchs of the Western world. At least that's my suspicion. It's a lot more believable for me than some 1500 year old magical cabal.

Unsurprisingly, the Prelacy's continual assassination of the banks' leadership has had little if any effect as best I can tell. It was certainly less problematic than assassinating entire banks, as per the Prelacy's old methods but it's all been just as pointless. For every banker the Prelacy has taken down there have been dozens more eagerly awaiting promotion to take the place of their institution's fallen King.

In less than one year of undertaking the current mode of operation the cabal had realized the futility of its endeavors but they would not let it go now. The Prelacy settled for what it relented was its true mission: to become a simple institution of tradition; to wage an endless war and make it a simple fact of life for the banking elite: when you are promoted to the top role in one of the top banks, it is a morbid truth that you were less than 90 days from the grave. No goals, no ultimatums, no demands, just tradition; just the simple cultural transmission of a corollary dread. The underlying idea being, I suppose, that after a while maybe these monkeys would all stop looking at the ladder. Stop getting sprayed with cold water, as it were, to put it in Rhesus terms. Thank you Goretex blowhard in that Seattle hotel bar.

In just these last few years that is exactly their fact of life, the bankers; the tradition they all began to live with. The fact that they were wedded to a dark, hateful specter with no hope of reconciliation or mercy, a force of nature. Without exception every single executive promoted or hired to fill the top role at these banks had fallen to the sword and not one arrest had ever been made, nor would it be.

This is where, I believe, the occult accoutrement of the Prelacy justifies itself. I think it's bloody clever to make this cabal seem ancient and unstoppable, a centuries old spiritual imperative that could not be bargained with. It's apparently worked in turning it's assassins into zealots and it's apparently helped in the spread of terrifying rumors and ghost stories among the banking elite. Diabolical smart, if you ask me. It makes me wonder about my dear Sébastien. What was his pedigree? Was he a Frankfurt School academic? A disgruntled FARC or IRA king? Some sort of rogue CIA reactionary turned Robin Hood? Who were the power elite in my Prelacy and what was their real game? Whatever the case, they hadn't put the banks on the run in any meaningful way but they had given them a new, dark reality to live with.

Conventional wisdom would have it that there would be little problem for these banks to ferret out a few psychopaths who were vexing them. After all, these banks could readily wield the political process of any nation they operated in. None the less, exerting that control down the chain was easier said than done. They'd hired millions of dollars' worth of elite investigators, fixers, intel experts and henchmen to zero effect. They were being bested by an ideological adversary and no amount of money or political influence could remedy that. By year two of the Prelacy's campaign of assassinations they had made it impossible for the big banks to hire outside their companies whenever they needed to fill their top executive positions. Less than three years into the campaign the bankers had come together and asked for an identity, a list of demands.

"Who are you and what do you want from us?" the last words of an executive who was delivering the bankers' message, a written plea for negotiations handed to a Prelacy assassin as he was prosecuting his writ.

The response?

"We are to you as the Tentacles of Abraxas. Do not presume to bargain for we cannot be satisfied." Written in the blood of that same murdered executive next to his corpse.

I estimate it's been little more than 30 years since the founding of The Familiar Prelacy of Infernal Arbitrators. There have been countless banking institutions toppled, undermined, hi-jacked and plundered, hundreds of executives murdered in that time and the public hasn't seen a single honest word about it in the press ever. Since the 38th corpse was found the bankers have colluded among themselves to make each murder appear a suicide, an accident or death by natural causes. Ideally, they are able to suppress any headlines what so ever. It's been the only way they could trick prospects into filling their executive positions. It's the only way to continue business as usual without startling the markets. Such irony. All the Prelacy need do now is prosecute our writs and the bankers themselves take the pains of covering up the crime. It's poetic. At this point there's no chance of a Prelacy assassin even getting found out unless they are caught in the commission of the act. We kill them, they cover it up. Piece of cake. Easy as pie. I scream, you scream. Dessert has one more s than desert because you'd never want seconds of a desert. A mnemonic device from third grade English. Did I mention I'm crazy? So is English. So is 3rd grade. So is the desert.

Crazy brings me back to the Prelacy and the banks. The entire dance between the bankers and the Prelacy seems just pointless and insane to me. While a great deal of the world still pins it's currencies to the dollar, the dollar hasn't been on the gold standard for decades. The dollar seems more and more every day like some kind of virtual currency that isn't backed by anything more than human collateral and that human collateral amounts to little more than an unskilled labor surplus. Still, the Prelacy wages their futile war as a matter of tradition and I am complicit. Who knows, maybe a currency piggybacked on the value of a labor surplus is worth waging war over. What do I know?

I don't know shit but after just a few decades, this war seems to me like little more than a matter of tradition. A cultural dance both sides know the steps to and will not disengage from. There's nothing to suggest that the Prelacy has gained or affected any actual influence over the banking industry as a result of all this. The world is still careening toward hell in the same old tedious hand basket. From my side of the green visor, the Prelacy is effectively nothing more than a coven of blood thirsty psychos who have found a group to prey on, a group whom the world won't miss or lament.

We are an odd and noble tradition as old as banking itself if you ask our elders but I don't buy it. I just like being a part of the machine that forces the suits to settle their debts in blood. That's my kind of crazy.

NINE

Seattle, WA – Sun Oct 12th, 2014

If I'm honest with myself I really loved it here in Seattle when I relocated after Afghanistan; that is until I didn't love it anymore. Seattle was an adjustment at first but I eventually found my groove, once I got past the Seattle Chill; an infamous perception that Seattlites are cold and indifferent to newcomers. After a while, that fabled chill thaws and you make friends but for me it seemed like most of the friendships I'd made were convenient and insincere.

I don't hold it against people if they don't like me. I'm obviously not that easy to be around, but that's not my point. My point is everyone here likes you but none of them like you. I don't trust people who think they're friends with everyone they know. It's perfectly normal to dislike others but being tolerated is just insulting. The deal is, that's one of the big things people in Seattle seem to pride themselves on, their tolerance. Anywhere else in the world a person doesn't like you, they tell you go fuck off somewhere else. In Seattle they just sort of put up with you and call you their friend. In Seattle, people you see regularly are called friends, regardless of how you feel about them. People you've barely known for a year will refer to you as "their boy from way back". I didn't get it at first but once I'd assimilated myself, this practice became the foundation of a very destructive pathology. Once I'd embraced their custom of pretending to be friends with people you can't stand, I became a danger to myself and everyone around me.

How does this imperative of getting along at all costs emerge in a culture? What safety mechanism does it presume to provide? It seems extraneous. Is there some fear being blunted? Is there a terror in the collective conscious that everyone might suddenly be at each other's throats if they aren't all pretending to play nice? It made me wonder if the urbane veneers I came across weren't each masking a snarl of red fangs. Reminded me in a way of the Southern states and their mandatory politeness with its roiling contempt just beneath the surface, but these Seattlites were passive psychopaths who mostly had no fight in them, unlike the diabetic lard-assed, personal mobility riding hordes beneath the Mason Dixon. Those people have 30 seconds of wind and 24 hours of fight, every single day.

As time went on it became apparent to me that my go as a Seattle transplant didn't take and I just went back home to Los Angeles rejected, killed by kindness and relieved to be back among the violent ignorance and shallow materialism where I guess I belong.

Maybe Californians are the only thing they can't tolerate in Seattle. If so, who could blame them? We have a well-earned reputation for importing a culture that people would prefer stay quarantined in the Golden State. Lately we'd become more like the Golden Horde; an endless golden wave of invasive dudebros and whoogirls taking jobs, raising rent and challenging patience everywhere we landed; a perpetual din of loud cellphone conversations and near-perfect food orders being returned.

Right now there is a perpetual din in this bar that I happen to have nothing to do with, Californian or no. I'm sitting quietly but underlying my still reflection is a constant hum, not much louder than the ringing in my ears. That ringing in my ears is from tinnitus and it's probably the one thing I actually brought home from Afghanistan. I like to collect little trinkets from the places I've been in the world but one place I let that slide was Afghanistan. Still, it sent me home with something, whether I wanted it or not; a ringing in my ears from military ordinance.

The constant hum I'm hearing here in the bar is a combination of bustle and chatter from foot traffic and the ambient electronic music being pumped in overhead. It's just loud enough to let you know you're out in the world but it's not intrusive. Currently that calming white noise is colluding with the whiskey and the woman sitting next to me. The three of them have thrown in together in a conspiracy to soothe away my itching to cross swords, to wind up strangers in bars. I'm starting to feel downright pacified and if I don't find some distraction soon I might as well head back to the Prelacy safe house and call it a night.

Relaxing into the rest of the night would be fine but that's not what will happen if I go back to the safe house. I'll just be trapped in my own head if I go back there. I need to be out here swimming in the tides of casual melee looking for distraction. Maybe it's time to walk to the Ace or take a cab to one of the many quiet dives in Phinney Ridge. I'm about as turned up and full of shit as I can get right now, but there is neither the potential for friend or foe where I am sitting. No conversation to be had but the one with myself; nothing cooking with a beautiful woman sitting next to me.

Beautiful people are always going to be people who can't be wound up. Those are the people who are completely used to getting everything they want right when they want it. Those are the people who can spot a fraud like me after one nominal exchange of barbs or pleasantries. They don't engage if there's nothing in it for them and they can tell right away that with me, there's nothing in it for them. People who aren't beautiful can't imagine anyone's just plain diabolical. People who aren't beautiful don't even see me coming. They can seldom dismiss me any more than they can avoid rubber-necking a car crash in traffic.

I can turn a room full of 120 IQ uggos on its ear in three Jameson's but put me in front of one halfwit with great tits or sixpack abs and I'll be exposed for the giant nutcase I am. That's just simple chemistry. Things being what they are, I still can't resist the temptation to imperil myself and that's why I haven't pulled the rip cord on this place already. I should have left for another bar a full minute ago. If I weren't on my sixth Jameson neat I'd have shook the spot within one drink of this disgustingly beautiful woman's arrival. Yet here I am, like she can't see me working and like Al might not show up to my right at any minute to ruin everything. I'm always looking for somewhere to wreck my ship but I'm just too far out to ever hit a reef.

I might be lying to myself that there's any reason to stay but you've got to lie to yourself from time to time or you never take any risks. Might never learn to ride a bike, let alone leave the house. I've always figured it's a given, we lie to ourselves. My whole thing has been to make sure that the truth is a pleasant surprise, not an earth shattering revelation. Like how right now I'm telling myself there's no chance in hell she'll talk to me. That's one of the rules. No breaking the ice. If they don't speak first, can't wind them up. And there's no chance she's going to speak first.

I should really get going. What am I even doing still sitting here? What is it I even want to happen? This is running in place, I need to find something else to do.

As I finish my Jameson and shift in my seat to leave the beautiful, black haired woman next to me turns and says, "Do you have..."

I didn't hear the rest but I'll sure pretend I did just to keep things rolling.

TEN

My advocate-that is, my direct superior in the Prelacy-is a man whose official title is le Grand Maître Honoré Sébastien de Saint Étienne, Courtier du Roi en Attente de la Prélature Familier de Abitres Infernales. A Knight-Errant in House Merovingi, he is known to me personally as simply Sébastien. A man 25 years my senior, Sébastien tells me he began his apprenticeship in our order when he was just a few years younger than I am now. I've expressed my doubts about the Prelacy's existence prior to the Reagan administration but he has been a tremendously stabilizing influence on my life so I do not quibble with him over these things. My respect for him is total and I shudder to imagine what my life might be like had I never met him.

The story of how I came to know Sébastien is a little embarrassing for me. I met him when I was a few years out of the Army and home from my little jaunt in Seattle. At this time in my life I was directionless and doing a little truth seeking. A little searching for myself, cliché as it sounds. It's important for me to admit that at the time I may've been vulnerable, impressionable and weak minded. Though I would always prefer to present myself as determined and self-assured, I seldom am. In those days, I must have thought it was worth my time seeking truths but of course that has simply not been my fortune, then or now.

I was in my late 20s and utterly lost, looking for purpose, looking for answers, a mentor, anything to guide me. I'd been on this self-seeking bullshit since well before Afghanistan and by now my search had led me to a number of unfulfilling things: Zen Buddhism, pathological altruism, psychedelic drugs, ultra nationalism, classical liberalism, hard drugs, yoga, soft drugs, sobriety, chaos magick, radical critique, nihilism, hedonism, asceticism. I had tried just about every mundane system and spiritual philosophy that wasn't in the Abrahamic pantheon. Or Scientology. In spite of my distaste for the Abrahamic faiths, I found something about Gnosticism that resonated with me at this time. As I was quick to do then, I sought to learn more about it. This is what led me to cross paths with Sébastien.

After looking into services on the internet, I went to a Gnostic church in West Los Angeles where I attended a very non-denominational, very generic Sunday service with a lot of very normal, unremarkable looking people in the pews. At the end of a very common-sense sermon and some awfully vanilla music I left the pews feeling underwhelmed by it all. Straight away I was back to wondering where I might go digging next for wisdom when as if out of nowhere, Sébastien, eccentric and infallible looking in his white on white suit and jacket to match his back-swept shoulder length white hair and Van Dyke beard. All accessorized in gold accents. Cuff links, buttons, pocket watch, medallion and cane pommel. A vision of the modern wizard, to be sure and I was immediately taken in.

"At last, at last he arrives." His first words to me, such persuasive presentation. How does one react to that from a stranger, one who dressed as if Merlin were a Gilded Age mystic version of Colonel Sanders?

I don't recall any of the silly things I might've said to him that day really, but I remember most everything he said to me. He had me rolling those words around in my head for weeks afterward.

"Godefroi de les Anges, sainte de le tronne, returned from the tides. At last, at last he arrives."

I was dumbstruck. I had no idea what this snazzy dressed old guy was trying to say to me but three semesters of high school French at least indicated he had called me by a name that was not my own and then called me "the saint of the throne". The name, Godefroi sounded like he was saying Goodfwah. The entire presentation was strange though dramatic and flattering, to be sure. Eccentric people are a dime a dozen in Los Angeles yet he still stood out to me as distinct from any weirdo that tinsel town and its adjacents could muster. He just crackled with adventure and import.

When I asked him who he was he replied, "l'eminence gris en blanc. The power behind the throne, my dear Godefroi."

Again with that name, Godefroi. All very powerful sounding words but I had no idea what he was talking about. I only knew that I wanted to know more; that I wished he weren't a challenging and mysterious person but a book that I could simply take away and read undisturbed and know every secret contained within. He had told me he was "The Grey Eminence in white" and I still don't fully understand what that means to this day.

Before parting ways that day I remember asking him his name and with what seemed like a very self-satisfied flourish he introduced himself as "le Grand Maître Honoré Sébastien de Saint Étienne, Courtier du Roi en Attente de la Prélature Familier de Abitres Infernales, at your service." I would learn soon enough he had given me his title and rank in the Prelacy. Something he would never tell the uninitiated under consequence of death.

I remember naively asking him then if he'd been a Gnostic for very long, to which he replied that he wasn't at all. Further perplexed, I asked him if he'd be back for next week's service and he said that he would and that he would see me again then. And that was that. Though I didn't know it then, I had just met the man who would offer me apprenticeship in the Prelacy.

Though I had no idea that day, I would soon be starting a new life entirely unlike any reality I'd ever imagined let alone thought possible. These days I'm probably not as impressed with his eccentricities, I may not buy all that Sébastien tells me of the Prelacy or my place within it but for every ecclesiastical myth he can't help extolling, for every overly animated flourish or dramatic presentation he is prone to, there are a dozen thoughtful insights into managing my own unmanageable mind, for living in this world I never fully felt a part of. For that, it is with burning revere and noble-worthy respect that I regard this man, my mentor, Monsieur Sébastien de Saint Étienne, Chevalier Errant of House Merovingi.

ELEVEN

Seattle, WA – Sun Oct 12ᵗʰ, 2014

I'm standing here bewildered, offering my flask to the knock-out in casual black separates. Straight, shoulder length black hair, short bangs, natural looking no-make-up style make-up. Square, Scandinavian jaw and soft almond shaped Finnish eyes, slightly lighter than olive skin. Scandinavian? A local then, I'm guessing. A bit too subtle in the way her look is put together to be local, though. Seattleites are too afraid someone might not be able to tell they're unique and important, so they don't put much faith in subtleties. To be honest, she's far too attractive to be a local. Seattle can't help being a little dumpy. There's no point looking good if the rain's just going to ruin it. It's all fleece and Goretex when it's not leather and denim.

She's old enough to have spent a few years failing at something in New York, I guess. Maybe she's the local who's returned home in defeat, but that doesn't add up either. I don't detect in her someone who settles for the emulation of success let alone settles for failure. No, she can't be local. I'm alert now for a Scandinavian or Baltic accent. That might make more sense.

With a confident stare, she takes my flask, unscrews the top and drinks. I wait for her to return it, which she doesn't.

"Thanks, but I didn't ask if you had a flask, I asked if you had a loaded pistol I could borrow."

Humor, but that's the sort of on-the-nose coincidence that redlines my paranoia. Of course I have a loaded pistol and of course she's not serious. This is the part where I'm supposed to ask her if she's had a rough day but I'm not quick enough for banter. I'm still a bit stunned.

"Oh, wow. Look at your face." She says. "You actually do have a loaded pistol. Yikes."

I'm always being betrayed by my stupid face. I think I've made it pretty clear that I feel transparent around these types. It doesn't help that her distracting good looks are making my cognitive process a half-cycle slower.

She gets inside my three feet of personal space and suddenly my fight-or-flight response is engaged. Apparently I'm not running.

"Let's see if I can guess what kind of gun you have." She says in an indistinct American accent, leaning in.

I offer no response but take back my flask since it's in reach now and shoot her a look of suspicion.

She backs away again to size me up.

"Mid to late thirties, well groomed for a hair farmer. You do the bare minimum to stay in shape but you're not a fat mess. You wear trainers and that black military style jacket so when you're in Europe you don't stick out like a Yank." She's showing off. "Whiskey neat." She says nodding toward my short glass. "Jameson" she continues nodding at the flask I'm now holding again. She grabs my glass, finishes it and says, "I'd say you're muscle, maybe a PMC or, oooh, I know! Maybe you're an assassin! Yeah, that's it."

Awkward.

She goes on, "You wouldn't be carrying a High Point. No low cost hoodrat pistols for you. Hmmmm, HK USP is too tacticool for you, but then a Beretta is too cliché. You're too vain for that."

Ouch, harsh. I know I said that I was transparent to people who were used to getting their way but this isn't what I meant by that at all. Not at all. That's not what's at play here. I'm not being sized up, I'm being flat out profiled. Opened wide, contents forensically parsed. It's absolutely stimulating. I still can't make her accent. It's as neutral as her wardrobe. This is getting good.

I unscrew the cap on my flask and grinning with interest, I take a pull. "Go on." I say.

She takes a breath and with a look that indicates she's already bored with me says, "You're too particular for something so standard and one-size-fits all as a Glock 9 and you like to have the elite shit no one else does, I'm going to say you're an AF-1guy. A Strike One racing pistol most likely. Not one of the flashy anodized rigs, though. Something with matte finish grip and brushed finish on the slide for you. You don't do flashy."

Now I'm actually a little uncomfortable. That's completely out of left field and it's nail-on-the-head right. My guess is she didn't pull that out of the ether. That has the ring of beforehand knowledge and this is all unfolding quite fast.

"AF-1? Why an AF-1?" I ask?

"I don't know, they're hot shit, cool kid tech, and you're an early adopter" she says pointing at my blackphone, the encrypted mobile device of choice among Prelates and intel spooks.

She's right. I do have an enthusiastic interest in my tools which makes me prone to exploring innovation and novelty. I squirm inside with a little shame. Maybe she did just pull that out of the ether.

"And where'd you learn so much about guns?" I ask.

She reacts with a coy grin. Suddenly I pity the trail of arrogant men she's left dismantled in her wake.

"and Americans trying not to look American?" I add. "And thumbnail profiling?"

"I don't know, you tell me, smart guy. How does a girl like me, who could just get by on good looks wind up developing these skills?" she asks. "You tell me where I would learn these things."

This is getting fun and I'm beginning to hope it doesn't trend in that direction much further. I'm hesitant to engage. Nothing like this has ever happened. My life in the Prelacy has been completely anonymous and none of my jobs have brought me into contact with state operatives of any stripe. As profiling goes, I'm in over my head. I've been trying to make her without any confidence in accuracy. I've picked up some profiling skills instinctively as a paranoid psychopath in a clandestine cabal, I've studied the skill of profiling recreationally as well but tradecraft hasn't really been a big part of my Prelacy training. I'm not sure I can keep up.

I shrug and say, "What? You're asking me where you learned to pick a man apart? I don't know. public school?"

She laughs, well more of a snort.

"Don't deflect. You're enjoying this." she says. "Tell me."

Where is that little stormcloud, Jilly? I really need more whiskey right now.

"Well you're certainly attractive enough to be Mossad, but then again your facial phenotype and affected neutral American English have me leaning toward Russian SVR."

"That's lazy. You're not even trying." She says.

Where is this all going? If the banks have finally figured out enough to strike at the Prelacy through some powerful state's intel service, why me, why here and why not use private contractors? Is she Academi? I hate those assholes. Them and Google are the dodgiest of all the freelance muscle and intel firms. Besides, she's way above their cap. Who the fuck is this woman? For the first time in years I feel something like panic. Is that fear?

The bartender thankfully spares me for a moment, interrupting our little game.

"Sir, can I get you another Jameson."

I nod and return my attention to the woman in black standing next to me.

"What about you? Are you good?" Jilly asks her.

"I'll have what he's having" she responds, barely breaking her focus.

"Two Jameson neats. OK." she says as she removes my glass.

"So what is it then? Who are you with? The Vatican? FIFA? I don't know, tough guy. I admit it; I'm out of my element here." I say.

Jilly returns with our drinks and the mystery woman is smirking at my jaunt. She leaves me guessing for another beat or two and just as I'm about to jump out of my skin from anxiety she lets me off the hook. Or reels me in, to use a more accurate visual.

"I'm a Cloak in the Prelacy," she leans in and whispers. "I need you to come with me and no one in the order can know about any of this."

TWELVE

I came to Seattle gassed on Tom Robbins' romanticized caricature of the city, I came enamored with its legendary musical history and I came in search of my tribe, an imagined culture of continental refugees, down to earth individualists who were as sick of prejudice and gangsterism and materialism as I was. I also came with the misguided notion that I really liked the rain.

I've said I'm no good with certainty, though so let this be an illustration of that. I was certain these were things I might find in Seattle and I was certain that once I'd found them, these were things I wanted. Eventually, I learned that the Seattle of my benign prejudice was not the Seattle I would experience and those certainties were utterly jejune.

Seattle is a beautiful city and it may have been everything I thought it would be, once upon a time. When I had finally gotten there in 2007 it was little more than a New York City themed amusement park where the children of middle class Midwesterners went to drink off their 20s and 30s emulating an experience they didn't have the courage to actualize in New York. By the time I left Seattle my only sympathy was for the locals who just wanted their old city back as much as I wanted to live in the one that had vanished before I ever got there. So I left by the same bridges I would have raised, had I my druthers. The irony of that conceit is not lost on me. Still, I wish those born there lots of luck getting rid of the rest of us who came in search of a similar fable.

I had a girlfriend when I was there, Andrea Naslund, a Minneapolis native who loved underground hip hop and indie rap and wanted to be a Social Worker once she'd finished her Master's program at the U Dub. We moved in together too fast but we lasted a couple of years regardless.

Most of the time I lived there I worked as a fraud investigator in the loss prevention department of The Cascadian Bank & Trust's corporate headquarters. 10 hours a day, five days a week I would sit in the Cascadian Tower downtown. Just me and about 15 of the creepiest authoritarians the Federal Trade Commission, Secret Service and FBI ever shit-canned and sent off to seek work in the private sector. I would clock in every weekday and sit with them drinking coffee, tracking the activities of Armenian, Russian and homegrown Aryan criminal enterprises that were ripping off the bank tens of thousands of dollars at a go.

One night when I'd stayed late and was bored, sticking my nose where it didn't belong, I uncovered the laundering of $100 million dollars by a Russian oligarch way back in the 90s. After the collapse of the Soviet Union, there was an exodus of former state functionaries who had been hiding money in accounts all over the world before the fall. "The Russian Paper Chase" as it's known. Many of those who were able to launder their skimmed stashes arrived in the United States wealthy and welcome.

As it turns out, The Cascadian B&T had laundered $100 million for a somewhat well-known former party member named Aleksander Chikurov, shortly before he made his way to his new home just across the lake in Bellevue. Lucky for me, I turned up this information snooping around and found myself fired within the week. I was taken by plain clothes security to a dim office on an unlisted floor where I was given a creepy starchamber-like exit interview, given some not-so-veiled threats, advised I'd be blackballed from any employment in banking anywhere again, ever and swiftly escorted from the premises. It scared the shit out of me but that isn't the worst of it. They stiffed me on a $10k bonus I'd earned that quarter and my girlfriend left me a day later.

Everything kind of went to shit all at once but that was just a coincidence. The reason Andrea left me had nothing to do with me getting fired and everything to do with some things that were going on around our circle of friends, some things that were going around about me. In the span of 48 hours I was jobless, homeless and friendless in a city where they can tolerate anyone but a jobless, homeless, friendless Californian. When it rains it pours, even in Seattle.

The thing with me losing my job is whatever, but the thing that cost me the woman I thought I loved and the friends I thought I had, that's more indicative of a damaged pathology I've been trying to get a handle on for most of my adult life. Jobs are easier replaced than friendships and love. I don't feel any kind of way about getting fired from The Cascadian but what I did to lose Andrea and my friends just shames me.

In those days before I'd determined myself to go through life a loner, before I'd discovered that winding up strangers in bars protected me from accumulating a circle of enablers and protected hapless strangers from my pathology, I was a different kind of asshole; the kind that let people trust me so

I could use them. That doesn't quite say it though, that almost sounds too vague and sympathetic. I didn't just use them, I put them up to shit they would never do and I would usually do it for my own benefit if not for my own simple amusement. And I did it for no other reason than I didn't' give a shit about them. I would let people get close to me, not because I liked them, but because of their social proximity to me through mutual friends. The same sin I condemn in Seattlites if I'm being brutally honest. If I had a sincere friendship with one of their friends, but I couldn't stand them, I would pull them close anyway just so I could mentally abuse them. Manipulate them, gaslight them, goad them into doing ruinous things they would never do on their own.

It all unraveled when it came out that I'd cost a man named Charles his multi-million dollar IPO and worse, ruined his engagement and caused him to get a DUI that sent him to prison. Though this was only one of many snafus that would reveal themselves in my wake upon leaving Seattle, this was the one that actually cost me something. And that's the only thing a psychopath like me can really get his head around, the stuff that has blowback. I couldn't be bothered to remember the stuff I did that didn't directly affect me but I'm sure it's all just as bad.

Charles was engaged to Andrea's best friend Margaret. Andrea and Margaret had grown up down the street from each other in Minneapolis. They'd been best friends since third grade and they moved out to Seattle within a year of each other, Margaret for the NYC amusement park experience and a year later Andrea to pursue her secondary degree in Clinical Social Work or something like that.

I had no business with Andrea and to this day I wonder how I even wound up with her. At this point I chalk it up to alcohol and low self-esteem. Hers, not mine. If she knew her own worth she wouldn't have wasted her time with me. Wherever she is now I hope she knows how to spot a bad apple, but I doubt it. I'm not the only person fighting with their pathologies. Wonderful people always seem to find a way to wind up with bad apples.

Charles was a frat boy dickhead. That's no justification for winding him up so hard but it explains why a person might not like him, if I'm permitted to generalize. Where I'm from, the correct thing to do when someone like this is constantly in your sphere of influence is tell them to fuck off somewhere else. By Seattle rules your duty is to never fatigue, always stay vigilant and avoid fucking with them, pretend to like them until something happens to actually endear you to them or until you finally give up and just decide you'll like them because fuck it, they're always going to be around anyway. On a long enough timeline, maybe that would have happened for me but as it were, I gritted my teeth every time I saw Charles and I saw him involuntarily about three times a week for the entire time Andrea and I were together. Suddenly I begin to understand Seattle. Maybe Seattle's view of friendship isn't regional, it's temporal. Maybe at a certain age, your friends aren't just the people you'd take a bullet for. Maybe they're just people you see all the time. Maybe there's hope for me yet. Charles not so much. He's fucked and that's all my fault.

Charles had invented some algorithm that he said would turn the capacitive touch screen on a smartphone into a functional scale for weighing out small quantities of elicit contraband. I don't know enough about this stuff to assail or confirm its accuracy but I had my doubts. Never the less, the market doesn't always demand verity as much as novelty so his Skaylr app was doing just fine in spite of being denied placement in key distribution markets. It was even the subject of a massively read takedown piece online that declared it a "fraudulent piece of shit" but that just proved to be a demonstration of the "all press is good press" philosophy because that silly little app had racked up a verified 8 million downloads from the Skaylr website on its own. Truth be told, kids who didn't have any use for it just wanted it on their mobile because it was a cool little conversation piece. It didn't matter if that "fraudulent piece of shit" could or couldn't accurately weigh out a gram of weed or a teener of coke, the investors came a-calling.

On the night of this big party to celebrate Charles' selling his soul to some snowboard moguls who'd invested and wanted to fold Skaylr into their new app market's IPO, I displayed a stones to birds ratio of at least three to one and I was hardly even paying attention when I did it. In just a few short hours and probably less than 6 Jamesons neat I had unconsciously wound Charles up for the worst night of his life and he's still in the joint paying the price for ever believing I was his friend.

The first shitty thing I did was loudtalk an app that could determine blood alcohol levels in earshot of Charles' investors and anyone else at the party I thought was influential. No one wants to get a DUI and one by one I had everyone in their launch party talking about an app that could determine your blood alcohol content through solving a series of funny little puzzles. The app was called 2drunk and if you failed its tests it both called you a cab so you avoided a DUI and locked your dialer so you couldn't drunk-dial your ex. It was some little known app I'd discovered that wasn't even on the big app markets and in a couple of hours it was on every phone in that launch party.

The second shitty thing I did was get high with Charles investors and undermine him. I had them looking to dump Charles and pick up the guys behind 2Drunk after a few rails in the bathroom at their launch party. After that I went out and goaded Charles into a fight with his fiancé Margaret so he had an excuse to leave because I needed a ride home. Let that sink in. I needed a ride home so I made a happy couple fight. Once they were pissed at each other, Charles was free to give me a ride home. And I needed a ride home.

Charles dropped me off at home and went down for a DUI on his way back to the launch party. The next day his investors dropped him and Margaret dumped him before he could post bail, mostly still sore about their fight the night before and emboldened by his sudden social meltdown of lost investors and a 5th DUI.

Once the dust had settled I had sleepwalked through decimating

Charles' business, broken up his engagement to my girl's best friend Margaret and gotten him busted for his 5th DUI which put him on his way to the joint. That's one hell of a wind up, and all done to someone I let think I considered a friend. I never once considered him a friend, the dude made my skin crawl but that's no excuse for how horribly I single handedly fucked his whole life. I could've just told him to fuck off somewhere else. Instead, I played out my own pernicious version of that Seattle institution, pretending to be a friend.

When people started to talk a little in the aftermath, my name kept coming up and it eventually became a consensus that I was the catalyst for all of it. The only thing no one could settle on was whether or not it was intentional. That much precise destruction had to be purposed, right? It had to be intentional, yeah?

Shit, you got me. I wasn't watching, I was busy destroying. Did I ever sit and plot it out on a dry erase board? No. Was it entirely my fault? Yeah. Needless to say, after I got the axe from the Cascadian and Andrea gave me the boot, I hopped on the 5 and headed home to Los Angeles.

In the lonely times that followed, I came to develop the little ritual that has kept things like this from ever happening again; winding up strangers in bars. Pitiful as it is, it works and I'm not in residential care drooling all over my hospital gown from elephantine doses of psych meds. I walk that dog every few days and it may shit in a yard or two, but it sure doesn't rip out any throats. It is what it is.

THIRTEEN

Seattle, WA – Sun Oct 12th, 2014

"I heard you was talkin' trash, like it wouldn't get back to me."

Oh for fuck's sake. Now? Right now? God damn it. Al, why right now?

"Oh, I do love these little moments when I get to talk and you just have to sit there and try to hold it together. Good times, kid."

Normally, I'm used to Al pulling this shit. He doesn't do it very often but I know he's not above it. He thinks he's being funny. He'll pick a bad time every now and then just for his own amusement. I'll typically have to deal with him popping up with some silly one-liner or making monkey shines in the background of whatever situation I'm in the middle of.

Trying to talk my way out of a traffic ticket? Al might pop up behind the cop doing the old "invisible blowjob" pantomime. Concentrating on a passage from one of the sacred codices that Sébastien is reading? There's Al in the corner of my eye whistling Yakety Sax and doing the Charleston.

"C'mon, kid this is fun! It's like that photo bombing thing you kids do, except it's real life. Reality bombing! I'm reality bombing you, kid! That's fun, right?"

I want so badly for him to go away. I wish so badly that he was a physical entity so I could wring his neck.

"Don't go cold on me, Killer" the woman in black says to me. "I'm serious. You have to come with me, I'll explain on the way."

"Don't do it, kid. It's a trick. She's gonna get you swept up in all kinds of shenanigans." Al teases with a cat-that-ate-the-canary smile.

I finish my drink and rise from my bar stool trying not to seem disengaged but she's too quick for me to play it off. She's most likely thinking that my mind is racing over her announcement that she's from the Prelacy, and it will be once I can focus on it but right now goddamned Al Davis is over her shoulder wiggling his tongue at her ear and making "Oh" faces. Fucking frat boy, I swear I can't stand him.

As we head for the door and I try to refocus, the woman in black is saying something but I can't hear her.

"That's it, kid. You're a goner. Fish food! I tried to warn you!" Al pesters from behind us.

Lucky for me he's not following us.

We exit the W and a cold rush of air sobers me just enough to acquiesce.

"OK, wait, we've got to slow this down just a bit. Who are you again?"

"I told you as we were walking through the lobby." She says, "Where did you go?"

"I'm sorry, I just sort of lost-"

"I am l'Honore Manteau Madame Aureline de le Pyrénées, Poignard de la Couronne en le Prélature Familier de Arbitres Infernales," she says with a pause then adds "but you can just call me Arlene for now."

Her rank and title. Both unheard of to me before. If my French is right, her title is Honored Cloak and her rank is Crown's Dagger. I have no idea what that means. The Prelacy is so vast and mysterious that I honestly don't even know how much I don't know about it. She said she was a cloak so I know she's part of the intelligence division within the order. This is the most shit-your-pants fun I've had in the Prelacy since my first big job in London. Much like that time, I hope I get to live through it.

"Yeah, about that," I say as Arlene walks to the curb to flag a cab. "I'm a little confused as to why you're not trying to kill me if you're one of us."

"I'll get to that soon enough, Godefroi," she says to me as a cab pulls to the curb and she opens the door. "And don't you go getting ideas about that yourself. If anything happens to me there are others who will see to it you don't see sunrise and worse."

"The thought hadn't even crossed my mind."

"Shut up and get in."

Arlene instructs the cab driver to take us to West Seattle via 3rd through Pioneer Square. I sit quietly watching the street drool by through wet glass sorting out my suddenly busy head. I really should be putting a bullet in this woman's temple and the cabbie's next. I am in deep shit with the Prelacy if this ever comes to light with the elders. Then again there's a lot the Prelacy doesn't know about me. A lot I'm sure they would kill me over if they knew, so I'll just have to manage.

"Godefroi, I'm going to tell you now a little about what is happening." She says in a hushed tone. "Give me your Monolith." My blackphone.

"Why?"

"Fine, we'll use mine."

Arlene pulls out her blackphone and begins typing a message onto the screen then hands the mobile to me.

The screen reads:

"You are in grave danger and the future of mankind depends on your survival."

I snort an involuntary laugh that startles Arlene and our driver both. For someone who seems to have a file on me she sure doesn't know me at all. I have absolutely no interest in the future of mankind. I just like being a party to the terror of rich banker assholes. I have no cause, I'm not a crusader. I'm a psycho who is fortunate enough to have found a comfortable niche.

I can feel Arlene's glare burning a hole through me as I turn to meet her knit-brow intensity. I'm actually unable to respond. There are a thousand things I want to say bottlenecked somewhere between my brain and my mouth. What am I supposed to tell her? That this is the funniest thing I've ever read? That I fucking hate mankind? Should I ask her if she has any last words? I'm intrigued, a bit more than intrigued maybe.

I look down at her mobile device and snort again. She's losing patience. As I look at the people walking down 3rd in their normal, naïve routines, some happy to be out for a night on the town, others sick of being trapped outdoors, I wonder if Arlene is just now thinking about whatever her plan B is.

I glance over at her and the look on her face has gone from intense to something indistinct. Resignation? Fear? Is this what emotionless looks like? Surely this pokerface wouldn't kill me if I'm the last hope of mankind. Would she?

I laugh again. I can't help it, it's the stupidest thing I've ever heard. The last hope for mankind. How fucking stupid does she think I am? In a matter of minutes I've gone from perhaps the greatest moment of intrigue I've ever experienced to losing a little respect for the Prelacy.

"Look, I love you guys. I love the mystery, the dramatic flair but c'mon. We all know this shit is just some clearinghouse for psychos like me who-"

"Shut up and type it on the mobile then hand it back to me." She interrupts. "But first I want you to take a deep breath and think very deliberately about what you are going to say to me. This may seem like a joke to you but it's not a joke to me."

She breaks her stare to point her eyes down at her lap and I follow them. Sitting there in her lap is an unsigned writ with Sébastien's title and rank indicated for prosecution. The only person on this cursed planet whom I care a lick for, my mentor and my advocate within our order. Apparently there is a plan B, one that I am not keen to abide. Suddenly none of this is funny. Absurd, yes but not funny.

I look back down at her mobile and delete what she's typed. In its place I punch in my own message and hand it back.

"My apologies, Madame Manteau, I am at your service." It reads.

She looks up to find my eyes waiting for acknowledgement and I smirk a little, in spite of her grim revelation. She breaks into a slight self-satisfied half smile and shakes her head at my insubordination as our cab continues down 3rd.

FOURTEEN

From the Codex Merovingi

Excerpt from

l'Évangile de Chilpéric II

Translated from the **Le Volume du Maire du Palais**
from memory by Foster Revell,

formally *l'Honoré Godefroi de Les Anges de le Prélature Familier des Arbitres Infernales*

Chapter XIV, vs. 23-34

23. From the sea, and to the sea and from the sea once again. Long-Haired Kings like the tide itself. 24. God-Kings of Frankia, who took a rib from the corpse of Rome and made it into the back bone of Europe. Once and future Kings. 25. Hail Merovech, Hail Europa. Death to Rome.

26. As did Clovis and all ours after, I wear the cross, yet hold none higher than Meroveus the father. 27. Though I fight and die for Frankia my loyalty is to House Merovingi first, the true God-Kings of Europe. 28. Ever in shadow shall I work toward returning our lineage to its rightful place atop Europa and beyond, in kingdoms seen and unseen, in lands known and yet discovered.

29. Though we soon shall be driven back into the waters from whence we came, back to la Meuse and up into the Frisian Sea, our agents and arbiters shall remain. 30. A prelacy of hellbound adjudicators familiar only to us shall carry on our work under cover of shadow. 31. That we may one day return to

sit the throne as destiny has ordained.

32. By cunning of dagger, under shadow of cloak, we shall direct the powers of Rome, as well as the Levantine money changers and the crowns of all Europe. 33. And when the time has come and each of the Chatrangé pieces are in their appropriate places, from the Sea once more shall come the next son of Merovech to rule over all. 34. Verily, verily. Hail Merovech, Hail Frankia, Death to Rome. Forever and Ever.

FIFTEEN

Hastière, Belgium – Wed Feb 29th, 2012

"Honoré Druide, does this one come to be returned to the sea?

"Oui, Maître." Sébastien said to the man on the shore addressing him.

"and Honoré Druide, does this one come to be restored in the eyes of Meroveus?"

"Oui, Maître."

The brisk river smell on this Belgian shore triggered an anxious feeling that shimmered in my stomach and quivered out through the nerve endings in my limbs. Initiation rites could do that I supposed. Everything felt so appropriate though. Even the blindfold, silken and cool on my face felt welcome and customary.

"Honoré Druide, by what name shall the candidate be known within the Prelature?"

"Maître, he will be called Monsieur Godefroi de les Anges"

The numbing cold of the River Meuse at my knees and thighs kept me sharp, still I was unprepared for any of this night so far. Just moments ago I was sitting on a bench near the shore reading alone while I waited for Sébastien to meet me for a birthday celebration, my 32nd. The next thing I knew Sébastien was instructing me to follow him through the cold, blindfold and all. I knew what was happening, that I was being initiated into the Prelacy, but I still had no idea what that meant or entailed.

"Monsieur Godefroi de les Anges, were you born under the signe des Poisons?" asked the man in the blue cloak.

"Oui, Maître." I responded as Sébastien had coached me to do beforehand.

"Very well, Monsieur Godefroi. On what date?"

"Leap year, 1980, Maître."

A response that caused a stir which was hastily quelled by the man on the shore, whom I'd seen earlier in his blue cloak.

"Shhh! Reverence, children! Reverence!" he continued, "Very well, Monsieur Godefroi, Meroveus accounts your merit and welcomes you. Are you prepared to return?"

"Oui, Maître."

"Very well then. Honoré Druide, please return the candidate's blood to the Sea."

Sébastien then grabbed my hand tightly and cut across my palm with a ceremonial dagger he'd been keeping in his belt. I felt blood run down my hand into the cold la Meuse and its frigid lapping stung the wound.

"Godefroi de les Anges, please remove your blindfold and read the passage from the Codex Merovingi." the man on the shore commanded.

I removed the soft black scarf covering my eyes and there was Sébastien holding the Codex open and pointing to the passage I was to read.

And so I read. It was a verse from the Gospel of Childeric III, Chapter XXIX, vs. 17, the scripture known as the Oath of the Infernal Arbitrator.

"De la mer , et à la mer et de la mer une fois de plus . Je vous salue, Mérovée . Par la ruse de poignard , sous l'ombre de manteau , nous dirigerons les puissances de ce monde , visibles et invisibles . En vérité , en vérité . Je vous salue, Mérovée toujours et à jamais ."

As I finished reading there was a hush. In the stillness all I could think of was the tide licking at my cold legs and my stinging hand. The clashing sensations distracted me from the moment. After a pause I heard the man on the shore, the man in a blue cloak, spoke again.

"Sons and Daughters of Meroveus I present to you - l'Honore Greffier Monsieur Godefroi de les Anges, Aveugle Apprenti de la Prélature Familier des Arbitres Infernales."

A small but thunderous applause came from the people I had hardly noticed were standing in a semi-circle on the shore before us. Men and women in black cloaks like the one I wore. I stood dumbfounded as Sébastien, standing there in his white cloak grabbed my still bleeding hand and wrapped it with the scarf removed from my eyes a moment ago.

"Come, Monsieur Godefroi. We go now to celebrate your return." Sébastien said as he clapped me on the shoulder. Still slow to get my bearings in the dizzying dream that was the moment, I waded to shore a few paces behind the old white wizard.

We followed our party up into the local forest and greens on foot, finally arriving after 15 minute's trek at a rustic château hidden among the trees. The rest of the night was a grand and aristocratic dinner where wine was served in ancient crystal on ancient wooden tables atop ancient woolen carpets. It was positively hypnogogic. By the end of the night I had met and spent time getting to know each of the eleven other elders who presided over my initiation. Maître Xavier de St. Exupery, a man just a few years older than me but as formidable and wise it seemed as any of the elders, l'Honore Maître Monsieur Herman de Boheme, a hardy man whose oaken stature and echoing laugh coaxed forth images of barbarian heroes, and even Our Grand Maître Chilperic XI de Antwerp, the blue cloaked man who'd conducted my inititation rite, highest ranking member of the Prelacy himself, le Roi en Attente. I felt as though I had finally found a path in life, a track to follow, a place to belong. A people. Formidable enough that they could not only guide me, but whom my pathologies could not ruin. I felt safe.

As the welcome dinner wound down and members trickled out, I dismissed myself to the solitude of a balcony overlooking the forrest and stream where I might reflect. I was soon joined by Sébastien who didn't break the silence, only hunched against the rail and quietly surveyed the bucolic panorama below.

"I feel like I've made the best decision of my entire life." I finally said trying not to disturb the calm.

"But you didn't decide a thing, mon ami." Sébastien responded. "We chose you, rather you returned to us as we knew you would."

"Fair enough," I laughed, already making a habit of dismissing Sébastien's Prelacy jargon, "it just feels good to belong. "

"Belong is precisely the word to use, Young Godefroi. There could be no more apt a word, as you belong here. House Merovingi are your people."

It felt good to hear. It felt foreign. Was this relief? Belonging was a new concept for this loner, as it had been every time I'd ever belonged. I paused to palate the impression. After a moment I broke the calm once more.

"I worry about the religious aspects of the Prelacy, Sébastien. I have a distaste for these things. I understand all fraternities have their rituals and bunk, and that's fine, but if there is a spiritual component of the Prelacy I'm afraid I can never be devout."

"My dear Godefroi, we are not a church fellowship.", Sébastien laughed as he reassured, "We are the martial order of a hidden empire, displaced and throneless."

"Whatever, just don't ever try to turn me on to Jesus." I laughed but Sébastien did not join, he became quite sober in fact.

"No, mon ami. We revile the Roman lie." Sébastien said, "Nothing more than a deceitful propaganda to weaken our house's resolve."

"How's that?"

Sébastien let the question hang in the air for a moment and took a breath before responding.

"If you were Caesar and you had your eyes on Europa, the homeland of warrior kings like Clovis I of the Merovingi or Armaenius, Prince of the Cheruschi, who would you prefer they worship? Would you have them and their armies fighting for the blood offerings demanded by warrior gods like Wotan or would you have them laying down their weapons and passively turn as commanded by this Roman god of yielding and guilt who admonished them 'render unto Caesar what is his?"

"Sort of puts a sinister spin on the Christian commandment to turn the other cheek. Never thought of it like that."

"Sinister, indeed."

As the silence returned we continued looking down at the starlit tree line, a cool wind drafting up the hillside beneath us.

SIXTEEN

Seattle, WA – Sun Oct 12ᵗʰ, 2014

Arlene pecks rigorously at the keypad of her mobile for a few blocks before handing it back to me. I take the little device and stare down at the wall of text she's composed to digest it all as we crawl through Pioneer Square traffic in our cab.

The message on screen reads:

"I belong to a subversive faction within the Prelacy called The Restored Covenant of Arius. Though our own accord predates the Prelacy itself our renewed compact is hardly more than a few centuries old. What you need to know right away is that you are being lead down the garden path by the Prelacy's elders. Much of what you've been told by Sébastien has been true, but a great deal has been kept from you. To the elders, you are the fulfillment of prophecy. This might sound exciting but I can't imagine you'd like what that actually entails. The short version is Sébastien has been grooming you for a mission of sacrifice from which you won't return. It is vital to the fulfillment of their plan and if you complete his mission successfully it will have global implications which would change the world as we know it, for the worse. Much, much worse. It is the task of the Restored Covenant of Arius to intercept you, to keep you from this mission, keep you alive and offer you an alternative that can thwart the catastrophe you were meant to initiate. We are depending on the unlikely kindness and trust of you, a man whom we are certain has none. This is why we have elected to leverage your cooperation with this writ which you most certainly don't want to see prosecuted. When we have crossed the bridge into West Seattle the driver will take us to a rendezvous in a safe location, where you will meet two other members of our Covenant. We will brief you in greater detail at that time. As I warned earlier, there are pieces which will be set into play should anything happen to me before we get to the rendezvous point. Please hear us out before you make the most important decision you'll have made since joining the Prelacy."

I let her words sink in for a moment in silence. I'm surprised to find myself moderating a legitimate, fearful impulse to kill her and the driver and vanish into the dishrag mist of Pioneer Square night. Is this fear? Both a fight and a flight response? Before long my fearful urge gives way to seductive curiosity, the desire to know more. I will wind this out a little and see what's revealed. This impulse to engage seems to be my curse. There is a sound logic to it, none the less. If I were I to snuff her now and report to Sébastien, I would not only be setting her side into play, shy of some valuable intel, I would be eliminating an access point forever. I might never learn whatever knowledge of the Prelacy her cabal held for me. I don't like being manipulated or challenged like this and I resent her forking gambit but I'll suppress all that and continue on with her to the rendezvous. I want to find out what they know.

I feel Arlene's quizzing gaze in my periphery. I draw a deep breath and offer a reassuring nod. Looking out my window I watch Downtown Seattle disappear into a grey veil as we cross the West Seattle Bridge.

"Driver, our destination in West Seattle is the Maharajah. Do you know where that is?" Arlene asks.

"Yes, I do. It is on California." Our driver says half-shouting over the jihadi Nasheeds he's listening to on his stereo. Islamic war songs set to electro-pop sounding backdrops I recognize from Afghanistan all those years ago have made their way here more recently and they've sure gotten a radio friendly sounds since I last heard them. While we're sitting here quietly quibbling over an accord to thwart the end of the world, our cab driver is fantasizing about nudging it forward. I hate this fucking planet. I really do and I don't want to save it. I convince myself that the only thing keeping me from putting a bullet into both of these people's heads is my curiosity about what this Covenant of Arius knows that I don't. That and the fact that we're doing 60 over the Puget Sound on the West Seattle Bridge.

"We have to use some measure of precaution moving forward. It was a little risky for me to approach you in public." Arlene says. "I was running out of time and I needed to act."

I nod.

"We will be safe at the rendezvous but I'm not fully confident the Prelacy is still unaware of the Covenant by now." She continues, "It's just a normal precaution to secure trusted locations which are out of the way if we need to meet other members of the Covenant."

"Ya think?" I chide, considering the elders would expect us to assassinate each other, not meet up for drinks. Pretty hard to explain four of us in a room together chit-chatting. If I'm dead in a week without any warning it wouldn't surprise me. It's hard to be sure just how omnipotent the Prelacy is.

The elders present it as infallible but that's sort of a corollary of wielding power, appearing all-knowing and all-capable.

"Don't worry. The Prelacy's formidable but we simply don't have the man power to watch each other constantly. Long before any of us were born the elders made sure that our internal police apparatus would remain minimal." Arlene explained.

"For fear we might become a paranoid hydra of self-surveillance like the Soviets had. Like the CIA and the Vatican have." I said

"Right, they didn't want that to happen to us so the Covenant has used that to our advantage a bit."

I nod and digest that nugget of intel with quiet satisfaction.

We sit in silence for a few more minutes while saccharine-tinged pop tunes about beheading infidels and apostates fill the cab. A few turns past crossing the Puget Sound we pull up in front of a lonely looking dive of an Indian Restaurant. The street itself is dimly lit and feels like a ghost town. The lack of foot traffic in the neighborhood is reassuring. I want an anonymous exodus when I get done killing these creepy zealots. But not before I've heard what they think they know. Am I really going to round out my night by killing this Arlene and her two cohorts? That's a lot of wet work all at once. That'd be a new wrinkle.

SEVENTEEN

Los Angeles, CA – Mon Nov 9th, 1992

Constantly starting my life over somewhere new has been a learned strategy, not something I developed on my own. I'd become so adept at rebooting my entire persona and entire life by the time I was 12 that I'd end up manufacturing my own tabula rasa over and over throughout the rest of my life; in the Army and Afghanistan, after that in Seattle and eventually in the Prelacy.

The longest running iteration of me began when I was 12 and it endured through my mid 20s when I would try to put it all behind me by joining the Army. Moving back to Boyle Heights just in time for my teen years would prove to be a dangerous proposition. Spending the entire duration of my teens there would prove to be a molder of character qualities kind men have little use for but survivors depend on. My mother moved us back and forth oblivious to it all but for some reason, we actually stayed for good when we returned to Boyle Heights a few months before my 13th birthday.

I arrived in class a familiar stranger returning to mostly faces I recognized but not the ones I was looking for. I was worried Sailor never came back from Sinaloa and worse, I was scared that something may've happened to Chico and Joker since I'd last seen them over a year ago. The school day wound on and I went through the motions of acquainting myself with new teachers and explaining myself to old bullies over and over until I finally saw Chico. My excitement and relief at this sight for sore eyes can't be overstated. He was standing at the bike racks after classes and I barely recognized him. Six feet tall now and at least 250 pounds, he'd grown a foot in the year since I'd last seen him. Chico was more like an Oso now but that's not all that had changed.

"Chico! What the fuck, homes?"

"Orale, Huero! You're back?"

"Yeah, we'll see how long this time." I said giving my good friend a handshake, which he quickly pulled into a powerful hug.

"Te sales, fool. If your mom goes back to Chicago again, you come stay with my family. We missed you, bro. No more of this back and forth shit."

I couldn't tell if he was joking or being patronizing, facetious but it felt good to hear someone say those words. Feeling like you actually belong somewhere isn't a familiar feeling for kids who move around a lot, so I soaked it up. There's no way Chico could know how that hit me and in that moment I think I decided I was done leaving Boyle Heights whether my mom was or not. This time it was for good.

"Where's Joker?" I asked.

"Him and Sailor go to Garfield now but we always meet up at Joker's pad after school."

"Sailor's back?" I asked, trying to contain my excitement. I didn't want to seem too much like an excited puppy but that's exactly how I felt being back among these friends.

"Yeah, he was only gone for the summer. He came back and he's been doing firme ever since, getting good grades y todo. His parents said they would shoot him back to Sinaloa y ya estuvo if he got into any more trouble."

"The thing with Mando? How did he get in trouble for that?"

"He didn't. His parents just freaked out because he was there when Mando got smoked."

"Fuckin' Mando, man."

"Yeah, sucks,eh. Rest in peace."

We let the conversation go cold for a moment after the mention of Mando but the mood couldn't stay dark for long, given the reunion that was in the making.

"C'mon fool, we'll take the railroad tracks to Jokers. Him and Sailor are probably there by now."

"What's there to do at Joker's"

"His jefita lets us kick it in the garage. After Mando, all our parents started tripping about us hanging out in front of the tienda so we just kick it in Joker's garage now, iron clothes, bump oldies or whatever. It's firme, you'll see."

"Like a legit clubhouse or what?"

"I mean, we can't party or take gynas back there but we sneak a few brews every now and then. It's tight; better than pitching pennies in front of the tienda."

"You still skate?"

"Chale."

That was a no. Things had definitely changed in the short time I was away.

In about 15 minutes we were walking up to an open garage off the street and toward the back of the property Joker's mom rented. Inside I could see Sailor creasing a pair of tan khakis while Joker fiddled with a boombox on the workbench behind him

"Hey, look who I found." Chico said as we approached.

Joker and Sailor stopped what they were doing to come over and greet their long lost pal. Hugs and handshakes, pats on the back were quickly abandoned for the more casual ribbing and teasing seen among good friends in our world.

"Damn, Huero, are you trying to grow your hair long enough to cover up your ears or what?" Joker quipped about my hair that was much longer than the buzz cuts they'd all started wearing since I'd last seen them.

"Leave him alone, fool. If your ears looked like an Impala driving down the street with both doors open you'd try to do something about it , too." Sailor feigned defense.

"At least I don't look like a cold bare ass. You look like moldy peaches, all three of you vatos." I teased, referring to their stubbly bald heads.

We laughed as Chico and I sat on the old couch in the garage while Joker and Huero returned to their tasks. I resisted mentioning it but couldn't help noticing Sailor and Joker had changed as much as Chico. Though Chico had only grown bigger and Joker had some kind of whispy little mustache coming in, there was a marked change in dress for the three. All of them now wore the standard cholo uniform of Ben Davis work pants, Royal Comfort t-shirts, slingshot undershirts, low top Chuck Taylors and shaved heads. It was pretty apparent to me that they had finally caved and gotten put on the hood. I felt a little out of place next to them in my nearly collar length hair, casual beach wear and skater shoes but they didn't make any mention of it beyond some good humored joking around. They just embraced me as one of them, like always and I was too relieved to be back for giving it any more thought.

"Hey Huero, since you're back I've got an idea." Sailor said. "We should ditch school tomorrow and take the bus up to the Galleria. Try to spit game at Valley Girls or whatever."

"Nah, fool. You can't ditch, Sailor." Joker protested. "You'll get in trouble with your jefe."

"It's cool, I'm doing good. He won't trip if he finds out."

"I don't know, eh." Joker said.

"C'mon Joker it'll be fun. We haven't done that in a long time." Chico pled.

"We can play hide and seek in the mall like we used to." I shouted. My newly solemn and grown up friends laughed at this and I immediately felt embarrassed.

"What?" Sailor said "You guys think we aren't going to play hide and seek? That's the real reason I want to go."

Hide and seek in the Galleria was sort of a neighborhood tradition that went back with the youngsters. We'd all been playing hide and seek in the enormous mall for years now and as part of my homecoming it seemed like a celebratory revisiting of tradition I would relish, though we may be getting a bit old for it. Well, maybe they were. I couldn't wait.

We hung out in Joker's garage as we listened to oldies and the guys ironed their next day's clothing until the sun went down. Afterward, Chico and I said our goodbyes to Sailor and Joker, then made our way home by the railroad tracks as we always had.

"Alright, mas alrato, Huero." Chico said making his way toward the front door of his house.

"See you tomorrow, Chico." I said and made my way home to yet another rundown apartment my mom had rented for us.

Around 10 am the next day, the four of us were stepping off the RTD bus in front of the massive Glendale Galleria shopping mall with the intent of fucking around and doing anything but think about school. We spent the first hour there just walking the length and breadth of the place oohing and aahing over gaming consoles we couldn't afford, interesting styles of tennis shoes we couldn't possibly get away with wearing and of course blondes from north of the Ventura Freeway we could never muster the courage to talk to. After a meandering lap around the building's ground floor and catwalks, we shared a lemonade from the food court and decided what to do next.

"You already know what's next, fool. Not it." Joker said.

"Not it!" Chico and Sailor chimed in after that which left me the odd man out. It would be my job to find these guys which, in a place this big might take the rest of the day.

"Alright, but no fair moving around. You guys have to stay in your spots."

"Pshh, already making excuses. Este vato." Sailor ribbed.

"Don't trip, fool. We won't cheat." Chico said.

"Now go to the bathroom and count to 100." Joker said as the three got up from the food court table and headed off in opposite directions.

I walked to the bathroom trying to imagine where Sailor and Joker always hid. They had a spot somewhere that was impossible to find so I knew my best bet was to focus my energy on finding Chico. As big as he was now it would be a good strategy, besides the fact that Joker and Sailor obviously had found the perfect hiding place years ago. I couldn't remember the last time anyone had even found them hiding, though I doubted they cheated.

After counting to 100 I started my trek through the enormous shopping center in search of Chico. I had a hunch he would either be sitting in front of the array of TVs situated in the Penney's home electronics section or maybe looking at Lowrider and Thrasher magazines in B. Dalton. I figured on giving the stores a quick once over on the way to those locations and then rethinking my strategy after that if my hunt hadn't yielded any results. I think my excitement about playing hide and seek there presupposed I would be doing the hiding.

After 10 minutes of trying to be nonchalant about scanning the inside of every store on the way to B. Dalton I found something but it wasn't Sailor, Joker or Chico. It was something I didn't want or expect to find. Looking across the rows of record racks in Music Plus I spied Mando's killer, Chango with two of his friends. He had to be 19 or 20 years old by now and he looked terrifying, more so than I remembered. His friends even worse. It wasn't the face tattoos , long before they had become so common, let alone the black ink sleeves they all had in varying degrees of completion. It wasn't their free-weights physiques they'd been building in garages, backyards and jailhouses. It was a an intangible communicated by their demeanor. They exuded ruthless, fearless cruelty. They wore it like a crackling aura that warned people to steer clear. I went stiff as a chill jolted through me and eyes forward, walked as swift and inconspicuous as I could manage. Would they recognize me from the times they'd harassed me, Joker, Chico and Sailor? Might they be looking for Sailor and Joker who had seen them kill our friend Mando one summer night over a year ago? I didn't want definitive answers to those questions. I only wanted to be far from their line of sight.

Once I'd gotten outside their field of vision I double-timed it toward B. Dalton in hopes of locating Chico. I began wishing for a miracle, that I might first find Sailor and Joker to warn them. I didn't think it paranoid that I wanted us all to get out of there as fast as possible.

I came across Chico just two doors past the record store where I'd seen Chango and his friends. He was inside of Radioshack playing some kind of handheld electronic game when I ran up on him, nerves frayed and fear redlining.

"Aww, damn. I knew I should've read magazines in the back of B. Dalton. I made it too easy but I wanted to play this game, though."

"Chico, we've gotta find Sailor and Joker and shake the spot!"

"Why, what'd you do?" Chico asked, laughing at my panic.

"Nothing, fool, it's not funny; we've gotta bounce."

"Why?" Chico pressed as I was pushing him out of the store.

"Chango. I saw Chango and his homies."

"Put that on something."

"On anything, I put that on my mom."

"C'mon. I don't know where they hide but I think it's somewhere on the second story by Macy's."

I didn't ask how he knew, I just followed. As we were rounding the corner out of Radioshack I locked eyes with Chango coming out of Music Plus. I could tell by the look on his face he recognized me and Chico. He may not have known from where or how but it was apparent by the look of contempt on his face that it didn't matter, he just knew the he knew us and that he didn't like us.

"He seen us, fool. Fuck we've gotta bounce, eh." I mumbled nervously to Chico.

Chico turned around and right then we heard a "Hey!" I turned to see Chango and his two cronies quickening their pace to catch up with us. Without breaking into a run, we sped up a little and at the next doorway Chico casually turned right into me, pushing me into the store. We were in Macy's and as soon as we'd rounded the corner out of sight Chico broke and I followed. We got as far as the back of the Men's section before Chico told me to duck. I spotted Chango and his homies rounding the corner into Macy's as I ducked low enough to be obscured by the rounders of menswear.

Chico and I were skulking further toward the back when we heard a voice coming from behind us. It was Rocklynn Coleman, the youngest brother in one of the last black families who lived in our neighborhood. He was dressed in office casual and wearing a Macy's name tag.

"Psst. Chico, what y'all hidin' from, homes?" Rocklynn whispered, slyly looking in the opposite direction of us.

"Rocklynn, you work here?"

"Yeah, what's up, y'all hidin' from them eses walking up this way?"

"Yeah, you can see them?" Chico asked.

"Yeah, they almost here, sneak over and meet me by that elevator by layaway. I know where you guys can hide out 'til they bounce."

"Fuck yeah, Rocklynn." Chico said.

We duckwalked, below sightlines to a pair of elevators just outside of the Men's department where Rocklynn was inside the elevator holding the door open for us. Just as we rounded into the blind of the elevator I saw Chango and his friends had spotted us and were closing ground. The elevator doors closed on Chango just out of view shouting, "Yeah, you better run, putos. You think we won't find you?"

"Holy shit, that was close." I gasped, nervous and scared. "Did he see you, Rocklynn?"

"Nah, fool. The doors closed before they even got close."

"Firme." Chico said, catching his breath.

"What y'all do to them fools?" Rocklynn asked.

"Nothing, they're just some dicks from El Sereno. They're always picking on us." Chico said.

"Yeah, they're dickheads. They're always in here doin' dumb. Fuck those guys."

"We're still in chinga though. They're just going to check the 2nd and 3rd floors for us."

"Check this out." Rocklynn said as he pushed the G button and the 3 button simultaneously. In no time were were transported to a basement level of Macy's not indicated on the elevator controls. I felt like I'd just seen behind the veil of reality. How many other buildings had secret floors. How many other hidden worlds were out there right under my nose?

"Man, thanks Rocklynn." I said.

"Thanks, Rocklynn." Chico said "I know the homies give you and your family a lot of shit but you're alright with us, homes."

"Don't trip." Rocklynn said, exchanging fist pounds with us both. "Just hang out down here for a while and when they're gone I'll come down and walk you out though the service entrance."

The doors closed behind us and we walked to the back of the basement level warehouse.

"Ah, hell no. How the fuck did you guys find us?"

"Aw, bullshit, you fools are cheating! Is this where you hide every time?"

Joker and Sailor just doubled over laughing, Chico and I falling in with them after a beat. Sneaky bastards had a good thing going while it lasted. This was their big secret hiding spot we'd always suspected they had.

"Did Rocklynn show you?" I aksed.

"Mayate Rocklynn?" Joker asked puzzled. "How would he know?"

"He works here. He just showed us how to get down here because we were running from Chango." Chico said.

"Chango's here?" Sailor asked, sobering quickly.

"Him and two of his homies were chasing us when we seen Rocklynn working." Chico said "He helped us get away down here."

"Fucking Rocklynn. That's firme." Joker said.

"Simon, eh." Sailor said "Rocklynn's firme gente. We owe him."

"Big time. We gotta look out for him with the older homies, que no?" Joker said.

About 20 minutes later, Rocklynn came down and fetched us, took us to another secret floor between 2 and three where he showed us to a maintenance corridor which led to a service entrance and exit. The four of us nervously scanned the parking lot as we walked to the bus stop and caught our ride back to Boyle Heights. On the ride home, Sailor, Joker and Chico explained to me that it wasn't safe for me to be around them if I wasn't going to go through with initiation into the neighborhood. They impressed upon me the importance of meeting with the older homies to discuss my initiation and I agreed. Things had picked up exactly where they'd left off, as if I'd never even gone. Just a few nights prior my mother and I had left Chicago in another U-Haul. As it turns out, one thing that shouldn't have made the trip with us was my sense of childhood. Living in Boyle Heights again, I'd have no more use for it.

EIGHTEEN

Manattan Beach, CA – Tues May 15th, 2012

"You just got me fired, motherfucker!"

"What'd you expect?" I laughed.

"You think this is a joke? I'm gonna fucking kill you!" Mike screeched.

Moments before this, Mike and I were sitting at the bar having a civil conversation about the ethics of online surveillance. I didn't know Mike, had only just met him but now he was going to kill me, or so he was saying. Mike was of the opinion that if the government wanted to spy on its citizens, that was just fine. Being that I encrypted all of my limited online interactions I didn't really care one way or the other but Mike was pretty passionate about the topic. I was on my third whiskey and having fun winding him up so I figured I'd recreationally defend the position that any sort of online surveillance was morally repugnant, government or otherwise. This really upset Mike. He didn't like that at all.

"Unless you're some Bond villain, I highly doubt the government cares about what's in your emails." He ridiculed. "Bottom line is if you've got nothing to hide, you've got nothing to worry about, Bro."

Mike was spending the day drinking Long Island Ice Teas by himself and hitting on Mandy, our bartender at this brightly lit Manhattan Beach pub. Playing hooky from the dealership, as he'd told me earlier. Mike sold new Cadillacs. Bravo. The sun was out and he said he'd been a good boy for long enough, that he deserved to take a day for himself. For sure, Bro. Who wouldn't understand that?

I excused myself to use the restroom.

"You want another whiskey, Bro?" Mike asked.

I accepted his offer because I decided it would make what I was about to do sting that much worse.

"Mandy! Another Long Island for me and a Jameson straight for my Bro over here," I heard Mike tell our bartender as I walked away, "hey Mandy, do a shot with me!"

I'd observed Mike's full government name on his credit card sitting at the bar earlier. Michael A Bertrand. As I walked slowly to the restroom I located Mike Bertrand's facebook account and as expected his security habits were complete shit. Everything about him was on full display for anyone to see and of course anyone could post to his wall. He even had his employer linked in his profile. Cadillac of Orange in Tustin. Nothing to hide, nothing to worry about, right Mike?

I turned around and snapped a pic of Mike doing Patron shots with Mandy. I took that photo and a few others I had snuck earlier (Mike slamming a yard of ale, Mike flexing his biceps with Long Islands in each hand, Mike grabbing Mandy's ass, Mike doing key bumps by the jukebox) and posted them to his wall from a sock puppet account I had on Facebook for fucking with people. After that I tagged his employer in the photos along with a few other people who seemed important to him, "Mike is in a relationship with" and other's he'd been frequently tagged with. After that I went to the bathroom. Fun times.

When I got back Mike was screeching and I laughed and laughed. Christ, I'm an asshole when I've been drinking.

"Bro, I just got fired from the dealership! Why would you do that?"

"Why are you acting like a donkey? You've got nothing to hide, right?" I replied, laughing.

"What?! Are you serious? Are you fucking serious?"

"What? You've been a good boy, man. You deserved a day off. Fuck that job if they can't see that." I said.

That was it for Mike. He lost it after that. Mike's barstool knocked over, he jumped out of it so quick. As he was coming at me I saw Sébastien walking in the front door. I'd forgotten he was meeting me here. He was the entire reason I was here in the first place.

Sébastien was meeting me here today because he'd told me he wanted to learn more about what I did for recreation. He didn't quite understand when I told him that the entirety of my hobby, my religion and pastime was winding up strangers in bars. Well, he was just in time to see what that was all about.

Mike launched himself at me in what I took to be some sort of mixed martial arts maneuver, crouched, forearms by his face looking for purchase on my neck or shoulders. I calmly moved out of the way as Mike ran head first into one of the pillars holding up the roof, and just like that, Mike was on the ground snoring.

Mandy, our bartender was backed against the shelves behind the bar with a look on her face like she had just smelled a diaper.

"What was that all about?" she asked.

I shrugged and told her he was mad about something I said on Facebook.

"Oh my god, what a loser! People who get mad about facebook are so dumb." she said as she resumed the pressing business of looking busy. I got the impression that what had just happened was was regular fare in this place. Nothing to see here, just some musclehead knocked out in the middle of an empty bar. Tuesday by any other name.

"I know, right? Facebook?"

I returned to my seat and welcomed Sébastien who had spotted my whiskey neat and pulled up a barstool next to it.

"Hey, Sébastien," I said extending my hand which he shook firmly, "sorry you had to see that."

"Is this what you mean by winding up strangers in bars, Monsieur Godefroi?" he asked.

"Pretty much."

"Forgive me, I am not sure I understand." He said, his aristocratic French accent making me feel stupid and American. It never had that effect on me but I had just showed him something that triggered what I surmised was the fabled stereotype threat. Times like these I longed for a more idling mind.

"Nutshell? I'm annoying. That's my thing. I like to find quiet bars I've never been in and pick someone to irritate until they want to kill me."

Sébastien paused to attract Mandy's attention and ordered a House Red. He looked down for a moment to gather his thoughts before he spoke.

"Godefroi, this is the strangest hobby I have ever heard of." He said. "In fact, I don't think this is a hobby at all, I think this is a pathology."

"Well, I also like to read the classics and collect Nazi and cold war and samurai artifacts but I didn't think showing you that would be very interactive or nearly as interesting."

Sébastien just shook his head. Was that pity?

"What did you say to this man to make him attack you?"

"I told him spying on people is wrong."

Mandy arrived with Sébastien's wine, immediately warm to his charm. Sébastien was nothing if not charismatic.

"Do you know why you do this?" he asked.

"That's a long story but I do. The short version is it's fun for me. I look forward to doing it and if I don't do it every few days things start getting weird."

He drew a breath and sipped his wine as I squirmed a little, waiting to hear his thoughts.

"I think we should find another bar so that I may observe you doing this with a more adroit focus."

I wasn't expecting him to say that. I didn't think Sébastien was prone to delivering lectures on conduct or anything like that but I wasn't expecting him to take this sort of encouraging curiosity in what was, for me, a somewhat embarrassing and personal fixation. I liked that I never felt judged by Sébastien. He always made me feel safe, accepted.

"Yeah, probably ought to shake the spot before ol' Mike here wakes up." I said nodding at the 250 pound dudebro snoring on the floor.

Sébastien laughed and paid Mandy for Mike's drinks as well as ours, and judging by the smile on her face tipped her generously, as was his fashion.

"Very well then, Monsieur Godefroi. Off we go."

NINETEEN

Seattle, WA – Sun Oct 12th, 2014

I'm finding the balmy air along with the smell of curry and sandalwood inside the Maharajah are a welcome contrast to the twelve feet of Seattle climate between the cab and the front door. The way that Arlene has seemed to indicate a familiarity with this place doesn't wash with the way she's giving me leash to decide our seating. The place is mostly empty save for a quiet party in a booth by the door and a few men scattered at the bar. Hendrix's "The Wind Cries Mary" is playing on the jukebox. So much for bucking cliché, Seattle. This city never shuts up about Hendrix. At least in Minneapolis you can go weeks between Prince songs. Put Sublime on a Jukebox in Long Beach and the whole bar groans. No such dignity in Seattle, just boundless, proud over celebration. Hendrix, Nirvana, Pearl Jam everywhere while they conveniently pretend Kenny G never happened.

I suspect Arlene would prefer we secret ourselves away in a dark corner far from view so I lead us up to the most visible place at the bar next to a pair of obvious locals in smart-guy glasses and sensible fleece. Big, burly guys outfitted like academics. Looking like a lit professor is de rigueur in these parts, even if you hammer nails for a living.

The bartender is attentive and likable. A welcome start. He nods and I order a pair of Jamesons neat. Arlene is texting someone on her mobile, our rendezvous contacts I suppose.

"Our friends are still a good 20 minutes out." She says, never looking up. "Relax and enjoy yourself but don't cause any problems."

"I don't foresee any problems in this place." I say surveying the bar with my built-to-offend smirk. The bartender brings our drinks and I tell him

Arlene's paying, which she does. I've decided the drinks are on her for as long as this all takes to play out.

I've never felt very handy with guile so I seldom bother. I'm usually hard enough to peg just being myself but I'm easy to see through when I'm lying. In any case, I figure it's apparent to Arlene that I'm feeling a bit had, a bit resentful being that she made such a plaything of me initiating all of this. It was probably her smartest move in attempting to engage me. It worked, anyway, all Mata Hari sexy. What an easy mark I made and now here we are. She broke the ice, isn't dead and I've come along to hear her out. Mission accomplished, so far. I'm feeling pretty adversarial about it all, so I really want to take it out on these people sitting next to us at the bar. Arlene can see that.

"You know what I'm talking about, Godefroi." Arlene cautions. "I did my homework on you before we met, don't fuck this up."

"You've got nothing to worry about."

"I doubt that. Your outlandish little sport of vexing strangers at every tavern you come across is quite storied."

"Everyone has their quirks." I shrug.

"It's beyond me how anyone might find it fun getting beaten up and thrown out of bars for fun." Arlene says.

"I don't always get beat up and thrown out." I say, pausing to take a swallow of Jameson. "Sometimes the other guy gets thrown out."

"Whatever the case, don't start up here. We've important business at hand." In her affected neutral accent I've already taken a shine to. How I loathe the attractive.

Yes. Saving the world, of course" I mock. "I'll be on my best behavior."

She knows I'm lying. Like I said, I'm no good with guile and people like her see right through me.

"You hear that, man?" the 6'5", 300 pound would-be intellectual in fleece to my right asks rhetorically. "Fucking best guitarist ever lived, man. A true son of Seattle."

"Godefroi, don't." Arlene pleads.

One of my odd little rules is I never break the ice. I mind my own business but once someone's initiated conversation they're fair game. Sorry, Arlene. What can I say? I'm a magnet for this shit. I smile and shrug at her as I turn to face my challenger.

"Hendrix?" I laugh. "The guy cribbed his famous style entirely from Leslie West while he was living in New York."

"God damn it, can you not?" Arlene seethes under her breath. "This guy is a dim wit and he's going to flip out if you fuck with him."

"He's not a dim wit, Arlene. This man is clearly a genius by simple virtue of residing in the smartest city in America."

"What'd you say about Jimi?" the mountain of UW swag demands in disbelief.

"I said that your true son of Seattle left this dead-end backwater as soon as he was 18 and never looked back."

"Great, here we go." Arlene said. "I guess I finally get to see this legendary fatuity played out in the flesh."

"Buddy, you've got 10 seconds to take that all back before I rag-doll your ass out the front door." My prospective dance partner advises.

"That means I've got 10 more seconds to educate you about Johnny Alan Hendrix." I reply. "The most Seattle thing your boy Jimi ever did was play the guitar with his teeth, which is something he stole entirely from an uncelebrated local named Butch Snipes."

"5 seconds, smart ass."

"He thought so much of Seattle that he held auditions for the Experience in London." I add.

"That's it, you've got to go, dickhead!"

Just as this giant is about to rebut my thesis with the genius and curt rejoinder that is physical violence, Arlene steps in, along with the big man's sidekick and the bartender.

"I want to apologize for my friend, please let me buy you guys a couple of drinks and we'll move our little party over to the corner." Arlene offers.

"No, I think you guys should leave." Grunts the sport fleeced hulk from the other side of his phony tech-bee glasses.

"Why? You and I don't see eye to eye on the true nature of God so the lady and I have to leave?" I agitate.

"You, shut up." Arlene commands.

I might be crazy but I'm not stupid. Jimi Hendrix was amazing and I love his music as much as the next guy. I also know that every single thing everyone has ever been taught about anything is a big fat lie and most people are just regurgitating uninvestigated bullshit they've credulously accepted as gospel. Take Jimi Hendrix. People will generally go casual jihad on you for suggesting that Jimi is anything less than a god just as quick as a Sunni in the Arab world might dust off the gallows over your disparaging the Prophet. Even the most banal iconoclasm can get you killed or beaten, just about anywhere you go. Some places, you don't bad mouth the Queen. In the States you don't do things like suggest Tupac was an overrated ripoff of a Texas rapper named Scarface.

That's one of the pillars of my unusual hobby. It's petty and self-indulgent but I just love extolling the indefensible truth and then weathering the violent reactions it elicits. I keep hoping that someday I'll wax contrarian in the presence of strangers and their reaction will be puzzled reflection, not bared teeth and flying fur. I won't hold my breath.

"Bartender, can you please get these gentlemen a double of whatever they're having, on me?" Arlene says amidst the simmering fracas.

"No problem," the bartender says, "you guys mind maybe taking it to that corner booth over there while I smooth things out with our genteel locals?"

"C'mon, smart ass. Let's sequester ourselves before you ruin everything." Arlene says, hooking me off of my stool by the elbow. I follow Arlene to a secluded corner booth out of the bar area's sight lines where we settle in and wait for her comrades.

"So that's what it looks like? Monsieur Godefroi de les Ange's fabled pastime of winding up strangers in bars." Arlene said, hardly shifting her attention from of her mobile's screen.

"Well, to be honest that was more like a scrimmage than a full scale wind-up." I say.

"I'm just trying to understand better, is there a time factor involved?" she asked.

"Like how?"

"I don't know, is it more enjoyable for you to slowly build things to a crescendo or do you feel more successful if you can just turn the whole place upside down with a few words?"

"It varies, I guess." I shrug, "I've always thought it could be fun to work a longer angle if I had a friend who was in on it, but so far this has only been a one-man show."

"So this is like a con-game?"

"Well, not really. Con games yield a material reward. I think this has always been more about exposing people to their own hypocrisy and blind stupidity."

"From where I'm sitting it just looks like ruining a stranger's buzz for no good reason."

"More like ruining a parrot's buzz for no good reason. People are just parrots. They have no idea what they're saying, they just love the way words sound coming out of their mouths." I might be drunk.

"Perhaps your nom de Prelature should have been Monsieur Quixote de La Mancha."

"I think you understand perfectly."

"I worry that the fate of the world is in the hands of such an irrational and petty idealist."

"I thought you were going to say lunatic."

"You're not crazy, Godefroi. I imagine Sébastien has convinced you that you're crazy but you're not."

I'm not crazy? She's never seen me argue with Al. I suppress a shudder at the thought of him appearing again.

"You're wasting your time, I can't be buttered up." I say. "I am most assuredly insane and idealism is just a foible I like to play with. I don't believe in anything." Yup, I'm drunk.

I've really reached that point where I'm drunk, I know I'm drunk and I don't give a shit who knows it. I begin to wonder how hard it would be to wind up Arlene. She seems completely unflappable but right now I think I could. Somehow I avail myself of the unlikely common sense to put that off for another day.

"So, Sébastien doesn't fret over your resistance to his sacrosanct Prelacy lore."

"I'm not sure I want to sit here and listen to you disparage the person who's done the most for me in this lifetime. Sébastien has been a mentor and confidant, always understanding, never judgmental."

"Understood, Godefroi, I'll tread lightly with regard to Sébastien?" she says "So I take it you're not a devout Prelate."

"No, I don't believe in Prelacy lore. I don't believe in the bitter, vain desert god of the Abrahamics, I don't believe in the neutralizing idiotic passivity of Eastern philosophies, I don't believe in Nationalism, I don't believe in Globalism, I don't believe in individualism, I don't believe in collectivism, and I don't believe in the boogeyman." I fume. "It's all a load of shit."

"Nothing is real. Everything is permitted."

"Bartol." I light up, "Now he was on to something. Every one of these institutions people put their faith in are run by corrupt men who believe in nothing more than power, if not then they're run by insane zealots who believe in outrageous prophecies and ludicrous gods." I rant, "We keep waiting for the right philosophy to come along and save us when it's not philosophy that's our problem, it's us." I'm three sheets full sail now and there's no stopping myself when I get like this, "As the venerable American philosopher George Carlin once said, 'the public sucks, fuck hope.'"

"So what? You're a nihilist?"

"When I'm not busy being a hedonist or a stoic or a cynic." I blather, "I'm whatever I need to be at the time. To survive, that's what I am, same as everyone else."

"When in Rome..." she acknowledges.

"Do as the Vandals" I finish and take another drink.

"You're a contrarian, that's what you are."

"I don't know what I am and it's probably none of my business." I slur. "So why don't you tell me what you are now?"

"Which me?" she asks. "l'Honore Manteau Madame Aureline de les Pyrénées is a Prelate and an aspirant to a title in House Merovingi."

"So you worship the son of a half-bull, half-fish beast named Meroveus and you really believe that bullshit about the Kings of Europe returning from the sea to rule the world?"

"Outwardly, yes, In the presence of Prelacy elders, that is how I present myself."

"But you don't really believe that stuff?"

"Of course not."

"So what's your thing?"

"Members of the Restored Covenant of Arius are monotheists. We believe there is a god, but we reject all churches and hideout within the Prelacy as well as many other institutions. We do not believe in demi-gods. No praying to saints. No worshipping Jesus, nor Mary, nor Muhammed. We don't believe in old testament legalism and we don't believe in the need for an organized church of any kind. We believe there is god and there is the person and the relationship between the two is a private matter."

"So, you're kind of like Deists or Gnostics."

"I don't object to your characterizing us as Deists but Gnostics, I'm not so fond of that likening. Many among our number have in fact identified as Deists. Many of your land's founding fathers were in fact Deists as well as members of the Covenant hidden within the body of Freemasonry."

"Right." I mock, "Here we go."

"Take it as you will but many of your founders, Adams, Franklin, Hamilton, Washington, Jefferson, these were Protestants in culture but Deists in belief and practice and they were members of our Covenant."

"Whatever." I wave off. Tinfoiler hokum. "So why a cabal within a cabal? It's so much cloak and dagger."

"Because until the establishment of your homeland, any influential men who espoused a churchless monotheism seemed to always meet with merciless opposition, often death."

"Such as?"

"Well, the Pharaoh Akhenaten and Jesus Christ to name a couple notables."

"So, you believe Jesus was a real person?"

"I do."

"But not a god?"

"Nor the son of god, just a man; an inconvenient and controversial Deist whom Rome needed to silence, as he was stirring up rebellion among Caesar's Hebrew subjects."

"So why does your sect hideout inside the Prelacy?"

"Because we've been there from the start but it's not the only place where we're found now. You can find us hiding among the bodies of Masonry, the Vatican, in fact all of the Abrahamic faiths and even various Pagan systems. We're hidden among the corporate elite, the bankers and the heads of state throughout the world."

"But I don't understand how you account for your Covenant's origins within the Prelacy"

"When our dear long-haired King Clovis I of Frankia converted to Christianity in the fifth century he did so as a political subterfuge. He outwardly represented himself as a worshipper of the god of Rome and he tithed to Rome while secretly he founded the Prelacy."

"To preserve the Cult of Meroveus and the traditions of House Merovingi."

"Correct. All of this, you already know from your level studies but there was another burgeoning philosophy among the Franks at this time. One that wasn't comprised of fictions meant to manufacture consent to Roman or Merovingian power."

"Which was?"

"Why, Monotheism of course. Haven't you been paying attention?" she jabbed. "The ante-Nicene heretic Arius was finding a great deal of support among the Frankish tribes for his ideas of God and how God and man related. He proposed a God who didn't require the intercession of emperors and popes. Who didn't require kneeling before statues or letting Rome walk all over you. Didn't require tithing to Caesar."

"That couldn't have gone over too well."

"And he proposed a God who wasn't the son of a ridiculous half-fish, half-bull who raped a queen and spawned a royal lineage."

"The nerve!"

"Do you believe in God, Monsieur Godefroi?"

"Doesn't matter. If he's real and I don't believe, it makes no difference."

"Logic. Not much wiggle room for a god to thrive under logic but I understand why people feel safer within it."

"It works for me today. Might not tomorrow." I slur with a shrug.

"So, in short, The Covenant of Arius actually existed long before the Prelacy and many of the first Grand Maîtres in the Prelacy were already members of the Covenant in secret, of course." She said.

"This rabbit hole goes pretty deep." I say, mustering as much patience as I can. "To be honest, I like a good story so I'm paying attention, for now but it all just sounds like more propaganda."

"Propaganda does not have to be untrue. The best propaganda is in fact truth."

"Bernays."

"Correct. The reason the Covenant needed to form as a secret sect was because people were being persecuted as heretics for daring to presume a relationship with god that circumvented Christ or Rome. The covenant was less a church than a secret fellowship."

"And so when Clovis formed the Prelacy he had no idea that some of his appointees were furtively members of this secret fellowship?"

"You get it. And the Covenant remained quietly active under the wing of the Prelacy for centuries. Over time our members have gained influence not only in the Prelacy but as I've said, in institutions like the Vatican as well."

"So it's true that there are Prelates in the Vatican right now?"

"Absolutely. Within the Church there are Prelates loyal to House Merovingi as well as Prelates who are members of the Covenant."

"This is a lot to digest."

"Godefroi, there are Catholic Saints who were Prelates. Amandus of Flanders, Audoin of Rouen, Eligius, and many, many others. Clovis intended for the Prelacy to covertly infiltrate every seat of power in every principality and that is exactly what they have done."

"And so among all of the Prelates who were able to embed themselves in these powerful courts, a handful of them must have been loyal to the Covenant of Arius?"

"You're a quick study, Godefroi. The Covenant is everywhere House Merovingi is and we have spared humanity horror after horror by undermining the Prelacy as well as their rival cabals over the last 1500 years."

"My problem with all of this is that believing any of it requires me believing in Prelacy lore, which I don't."

"You don't have to believe any of it. All you have to believe is that the Prelacy elders believe all of it and they think they are fulfilling prophecy."

"I can accept that, for now anyway." I comport.

"That is an important step toward a vital accord but we will have to continue this discussion later as it appears our friends have arrived" Arlene says checking her Monolith.

TWENTY

Boyle Heights, CA – Sun Aug 11ᵗʰ, 2013

"Fuck you, Al! I'm not listening to you!"

"What'd you say?" Guitar Tommy asked a little confused.

Guitar Tommy was a bartender at the Copper Bucket, the local dive I was actually a regular at. I did have my staple haunts despite my penchant for being a jackass tourist on other people's home turf. I always did my best to behave at the Copper Bucket. The one thing no wants where they're a regular is to get 86ed. That is, to get thrown out for good. The quickest way to get 86ed is to get shitty drunk and make a mess, piss off the bar staff or any of the other regulars. I always minded my Ps and Qs at the Copper Bucket. No winding up strangers on the home turf. Ever.

"I wasn't talking to you, Tommy, I was talking to him", I said gesturing at the empty barstool next to mine.

"Yeah, there's nobody there, Foster."

Foster. My birth name. The name I'm known by outside the Prelacy. Foster Revell. Seems almost irrelevant at this point. I almost never hear that name anymore.

"Nah, s'okay, he's there you jus can't see him."

The first time I saw Al was on this day. It was over a year ago but it feels like it's been going on forever. Well, frankly it felt like it had been going on forever by the end of that first day.

"Foster, if you're so trashed you're seeing people who aren't there, I have to cut you off."

As it turns out, I was sloppy drunk on the home turf on this day, a prime candidate for being 86ed. Anyone who drinks everyday has a certain line they're aware they shouldn't cross, a time to stop drinking and go home, at the very least. I had crossed that line hours ago, before I'd even left the house.

"Nah, s'okay, Tommy. 'Nother whiskey neak." I managed to sort of enunciate. "It's this guy, Al. He showed up at my house this morning before I started drinkin' so it's not the whiskey."

"How's that?" Guitar Tommy asked, as puzzled as he was interested. I think that must've been the moment I broke crazy and revealed that the quiet guy who hadn't caused any problems at the Bucket was actually anything but normal.

Earlier that day I was going through my morning wake up routine. Shit, shower, shave and all that. I walked into my living room still in my robe when I was startled by a figure out of the corner of my eye. A man poised next to the curio which held some of the collectibles I'd acquired throughout my travels with the Prelacy.

"Is this thing real?" the man asked, pointing to an authentic WWII Walther P-38 I had on display.

I nearly jumped out of my skin. Right there in my living room was this roguish looking stranger attired in quirky mid-century playboy chic. A self-assured looking early middle-aged guy, his tailored grey suit and black turtleneck reminded me of the Man from U.N.C.L.E. He looked familiar but I couldn't place him. Honestly, I think the only reason I wasn't attacking him like a wild chimp was because he didn't seem the least bit threatening. He was relaxed and matter of fact in his manner, this throwback in my living room. Just casually standing there like I had walked into his office by appointment.

"How did you get in here? Who are you?"

He just ignored my questions, shrugged off the pistol and moved down the cabinet where he began handling a Kriegsmarine Dagger. He shot me a judgmental look and shook his head.

"Nazi bullshit." He sneered.

"Put that down. It's valuable."

"Why do you gotta make everything such a bore?" he said.

"What?"

"This is fun, what we're doing here right now. Why do you wanna spoil it." The sharp dressed stranger scolded, "Don't spoil it."

He was now fiddling with a set of Schutzmannschaft branded Matryoshka dolls I'd acquired on a writ in Donbas.

"Russian nesting dolls! Little ones hidden inside the big ones, like your creepy little secret club."

"They're Ukrainian. Put those down."

"It's like I'm pointing at the moon and all you see is the dirt under my fingernail." He said. "I thought you were smarter than that."

"Look, I don't know who you are but you better start explaining why you're standing here in my living room." I said stifling a nervous laugh.

"I'm Al, kid. The name's Al and I'm in your living room because, I don't know, you seem like you need a friend. And you've got all this weird stuff here. I wanted to check it out."

I recall feeling like I needed to get mad. Like I should be flipping out on this guy but I couldn't muster it. Should I be scared? I remember wondering this but I just didn't feel threatened by him. I had my eye on him none the less.

"What's all this bullshit?" I asked gesturing toward his pretentious outfit.

"What's what bullshit?"

"This fuckin' hipster gangster get up you're trying to pull off here. You look like you're gonna smack around one of Don Draper's girls or something."

"Say what?"

"You look like if 1960s Hugh Hefner ran a casino."

"Hef?! You know Hef? Hef's my rock. He'd like that." Al said, "Good eye, kid."

"Oh, you know Hugh Hefner?" I played along.

"Know him? Hell yeah I know him. I better know him. We ran some operations for the CIA together back in the '60s."

The guy in my living room, Al, was dressed like he was from the 1960s to be sure, but there was no way he was old enough to have even been alive in the 1960s, let alone worked for the CIA back then. My weird-o-meter was redlining. Every time this guy said something it seemed to reveal nothing but more mystery.

"What did you say your name was again?"

"I'm Al, kid."

"Al what?"

"Davis. Al Davis. You know, football?"

Of course it was Al Davis. Who else? The ghost of the former Raiders owner was just standing there in my living room poring over my collection of WWII paraphernalia and giving me grief for it.

"What's with all this stupid nazi shit, kid? I fuckin' hate the Nazis." Al sneered, looking at me like I was crazy. Creepo-crazy, not seeing-ghosts-crazy. We were off to a good start.

"I like historical artifacts. It's not all nazi stuff, man. There's other stuff, too."

Al just side-eyed me in contempt and kept on poking through my curio.

I'd forgotten I was standing there in my robe and started to feel a little awkward. As I was trying to think of something to say to Al my mobile rang. I picked it up off of the coffee table and looked up to let Al know I had to take a call, but he'd already vanished. I looked down to see who was calling and saw that it was the Copper Bucket. I let it go to voicemail. They were just calling to let me know I left my bank card there last night. Not a big deal, I already planned on heading down there later anyway.

I spent the next couple hours reading about paranoid schizophrenia and hallucinations on the internet. I also started drinking to counter the onset of anxiety this all triggered.

Usually when something shocking happens, I suppose the urge is to tell someone. You had to go to the Emergency Room because your pet Spider Monkey bit your nose off? Might not be time for a selfie but you're gonna at least want a strong friend you can relate that to. You stumbled on a suitcase full of hundreds by the railroad tracks? Definitely not a good idea to run and post a status update but you've got to tell somebody. The ghost of Al Davis was in your living room wrinkling his nose at your Totenkopf pin? Yeah, maybe keep that one to yourself.

The whole thing had me feeling pretty alone and scared of myself, more so than usual. Still, I suppressed the urge to reach out to Sébastien, my mentor and only confidant. Instead, I was keen to bury the entire event far from view of anyone. I'd have to carry this load on my own like so many others. No one but I could be allowed to know how far my sanity was deteriorating.

So I started drinking. Before I'd even put on pants I had finished the bottom half of a handle of Jameson and I still had to go down to the Copper Bucket to pick up my card from the night before. I knew better than to tell myself I'd only stay for a couple drinks and hoof it back home. I'd never succeeded at just popping in there for a couple of drinks, or anywhere else for that matter. My resolve was to simply do no harm.

To the Copper Bucket people I was a quiet loner. A random, in the contemporary parlance. A regular, but a random none the less. Always the outsider, even in places that know me by my given name. The Bucket was a local dive where the regulars were your usual assortment of L.A. hard-cases and lowlives. Bikers, cholos, rock band assholes. I was the quiet square who came in a couple times a week, kept to himself and tipped well. I wouldn't say I was well liked but to say I was merely tolerated wouldn't quite say it either. I was exactly who I needed to be at the Copper Bucket. Mostly anonymous, but worthy of being treated like an actual person. Given the time put in to cultivating that comfortable framework and the close proximity to my home, the Copper Bucket was more than just a place to go out drinking. It was in certain terms a sanctuary. A place of calm and retreat for me, with Slayer on the jukebox.

I tried to shake off the cobwebs with half a joint of Hindu Kush. For sure it repaired my uneasiness but it didn't do a thing for my vigor. As a result I dragged ass around my apartment for another half-hour laboring over which black t-shirt to wear with which black Levis. You think that sounds stupid, you should see me on laundry day trying to perfectly match all of my identical black socks. Identical to you, maybe. I slid into my black denim jacket and patted myself down for essentials: wallet, keys, lighter, mobile. Fuck, where was my mobile?

As I walked to look for it on the charger in the kitchen, there stood Al. Early 2000s Al with the band-aids on his head and the black satin Raiders bomber. No. Just no, I was not going to be alright with this. Was I going to have to go outside myself for help with this? No way I trusted the institutions of medicine and psychiatry. If I told Sébastien he'd know what to do but I couldn't fathom bringing this to him. Ha ha, nope.

"Who died, kid?"

"What?"

"What's with all the black? Did someone die?"

"Great. That's just great. The undead owner of the Raiders is standing here in all black lecturing me about wearing too much black". How much crazier could this day get?

"Touché." Al agreed, giving his own presentation a once over.

The initial fit of running into him again settled in to a sort of resignation.

"Are you going to tell me what this is about?" I think that was a plea. "This is really making me feel crazy and I don't like it."

"Stop ruining everything, kid. This is fun, you and me. Just roll with it."

So I broke a perfectly good toaster throwing it at him. I launched it right at his his crypt-keeper looking face and naturally it just broke on the wall behind him. When I calmed down and surveyed the result of my assault, Al had vanished and my toaster lay on the counter and kitchen floor in pieces.

I drew a deep, calming breath and told myself a lot of things. This wasn't really a ghost or a hallucination, it was just my imagination (strong coping, that one), that this was nothing to worry about, it was a harmless delusion that could in fact be fun (relax, you've got the good kind of crazy!), that maybe he really was a ghost and this had something to do with Prelacy lore (you're not crazy at all, you're just a divine champion on a mystical quest and people who think that are never crazy!) I needed to sit down. All of this not being crazy was making me crazy.

I returned to my seat on the couch and nervously massaged its soft black leather cushions hoping to settle my mind. I thought about phoning a regular I knew from the Bucket for some Xanax. I figured that would put an end to this whole day if it didn't snuff out Al altogether. My problem with that was I had a strong fear of treating my craziness with anything that wasn't alcohol or weed. Xanax was a stop-gap measure that could quickly balloon into perpetually fighting off a consuming psychosis for the rest of my crazy life. I decided I would need to manage this using the devils I knew.

"C'mon, kid. Let's go have some fun. It's a beautiful day outside."

"I've gotta go up to the Copper Bucket to get my bank card. You can't come with me, Al." I pleaded. He was sitting down the couch from me now. I couldn't stand to look at him.

"Why do you have to do that?" he asked.

"Do what?"

"Cut off your possibilities."

"Possibilities? What possibilities?" I asked, "The possibility of freaking everyone out at the Copper Bucket because they see me talking to my imaginary friend, Al Davis?"

"You're doing it right now."

"Doing what, Al?"

"Trying to control everything." Al said. "Is that the only possibility you can imagine if I go with you up to the Copper Pot?"

"Bucket. It's Copper Bucket, Al."

"Bucket, Pot. 2 field goals, a touchdown. What's the difference?"

"Well for starters, you get to try for a conversion after a touchdown and it only requires one trip down the field, Al."

"Just win, baby."

I remember giving up at that point and laughing at how absurd it all was. I thought, fuck it, maybe Al was right. Maybe I did need a friend, even if it was an imaginary friend. Or the ghost of the Raiders owner. Maybe I did need to lose control a little even if it meant not doing what I wanted all the time. At least he was funny. At least he was every bit as crazy as I was.

I collected myself, stood up and once again determined myself to leave the house. Pat down; phone, wallet, keys, lighter. All there, set. I swung wide the door and squinted at the assaulting daylight. An unremarkable groove for most, for me a deliberate labor, the surly bear trudging beyond the mouth of his warm hibernacle.

"Sunshine feels good, don't it?"

"Don't push it, Al."

Though I had reached a certain peaceable rapport with my new shadow, I was eager to establish some ground rules, assuming that was even a possibility. As we made our way down the catwalk toward the staircase I looked around to be sure no one could see me talking to my imaginary friend, Al Davis.

"Look, man. If this is going to be a thing, I need you to spare me some of the obvious bullshit this could cause."

"C'mon, kid. Let it go."

"Al, I'm fuckin' serious. I can't be talking to a person no one else can see. You have to at least give me that."

"You worry too much."

I was about to lose my shit all over again as one of my neighbors was walking up the stairs with her laundry. I bit my tongue and smiled as she passed.

"Who was that?" Al asked.

I didn't know her name and I had no intention of responding if I did. I felt like he knew I couldn't name my neighbors and he was pointing it out. This set me off a little more. It also worried me. It was already too easy to just ignore him. I didn't like how being crazy was so natural, so familiar to me. I wasn't going to like having a friend I couldn't punch in the face or just avoid whenever they pissed me off. Worse, a friend I couldn't wind up for shit. As I considered how right he was about me being a control freak we cleared the stairs and exited the building.

"Al, you've got to cut me some slack, man." I pleaded as we rounded the exit and headed up the sidewalk. "There's nothing wrong with me wanting to avoid being that guy, man."

"You're too negative, kid. You gotta let go a little."

I guess this was what I could expect. I'd spent so much time winding up strangers and now here I had Al. The great equalizer, my imaginary friend who seemed perfectly capable of winding me up like a yoyo. It didn't seem fair, but oh, was it ever. Fair like the rest of the world never is.

I kept to myself for the rest of the walk to the Copper Bucket, ignoring Al completely as he verbally patted himself on the back for hiring the first black head coach. Art Shell? Really? His record was shit! I bit my tongue. About a block shy of the place I noticed that he was no longer shadowing me. The immense relief I felt was immediately accompanied by a certain dread of his returning. I shook it off and reconnected with my relief as I heeled toward the bar.

"Hey, there he is." Guitar Tommy said pouring my Jameson neat as I walked in.

"Thanks, Tommy." I said corralling my drink as a convict might his meal at the mess table.

I could tell by the way Tommy was regarding me that he knew I was already pretty shitfaced. It irritated me. I was never sober long enough to understand why people who weren't drunk themselves might be so pensive around drunks. I just took it personally.

"Doyers in an hour."

Christ, I really did get an early start. It wasn't even 2 o'clock and I'd been getting after it since noon.

"Who're they playing?"

"Rays are in town and Kershaw's on the mound. Should be a good one."

I nodded and peeked around at the bar to see who else was there. Chivo was at the pool table as he usually was, shooting a game with some semi-regular I didn't know. Skinny white guy with a beard down to his chest.

Chivo was a shot caller for the Avenues, a high powered Mexican gang based in Boyle Heights just up the hill. He was a square looking guy in his early 30s. You'd never know he was the bar's resident coke dealer to look at him. He just looked like your regular hardhat and lunchpail kind of guy. Red Wings, denim pants, free t-shirt. Chivo is Spanish for goat. I figured he got the name from his mannerisms. He just seemed like he was born grumpy. That sounds like a criticism but there's something charming about the fussy, impossible to impress animal called the goat. In spite of that Chivo made people at the Copper Bucket feel safe when he was around. He wasn't imposing or blustery, he was imminently likeable but, like a goat, chasing his approval would be a fool's errand. I don't think anyone knew Chivo's real name. He was usually here in the night time so it was a bit of a surprise seeing him here in the afternoon. He's the guy I was thinking about calling for Xanax earlier. Chivo noticed me surveying the bar and gave me a nod which I returned. I liked Chivo, same as everyone at the Copper Bucket.

Serena was bar backing and cocktailing I guess but it didn't seem like there was much need for her today. The place was mostly empty. Serena was an attractive half-mexican woman, metalhead. She was there most nights I was, drinking with friends if she wasn't working. Her faded chola tattoos peeked out from under her Burzum shirt which forced me to keep looking around, lest I linger too long and catch a cold look from her or worse, a smile. To say Serena was easy on the eyes understated the fact that she was intriguing and begged to be parsed. The study of humans was an empty reward, though. I preferred their mystery to their banal truth so I never lingered long on the ones I liked. Affinity is just another pathology I'd become adept at moderating.

Down the bar was Tucan. Tucan was a Mexicano from Guadalajara who by all accounts collected disability for a living. A 40 something construction worker by trade who hadn't worked a day in at least a few years. His interest in the English language didn't go much further than it's utility in obtaining pain pills from gavachos. He'd hurt his back and gotten disability in addition to a few million bucks in settlements not once but three times. He was here by himself every day from opening 'til last call. Tucan's real name was Joe but no one called him that. I'd had some pretty good drunken converstaions with Tucan about the Dodgers and how much the cops suck. Beyond that I only knew he had a daughter going to Cal State Northridge whom he was very proud of. Tucan usually had his eyes fixed on the TV which was always tuned to ESPN if it was on at all. Volume down.

Guitar Tommy was a rail-thin white kid who played guitar, obviously. He was in his mid 20s and pulled shifts at the Copper Bucket to make rent while he gambled his future on becoming a professional musician. I have a learned disinterest in most music and I've disliked the few musicians I've met but Guitar Tommy was a sweetheart. You'd have to have your hate cranked to 11 on Spinal Tap's amps to find anything wrong with Guitar Tommy. Okay, he did have stupid tattoos. A bunch of hipster bullshit. Nautical stars and swallows and script letters. Alright, he also dressed like a douche but Tommy was just a babe in the woods. I shudder to think what would happen to anyone who ever did anything to hurt Tommy in view of Chivo, Tucan or Serena. You can add me to that list but I'm not the badass on that roll call. I might be a member of a murderous international cabal but I never said I was Roadhouse Swayze.

"You doing alright today, Foster? You seem stressed." Guitar Tommy probed.

Temptation. Stupid as it sounds I actually had to fight the urge to spill my guts to kind hearted, easy to please Guitar Tommy. I was drunk and my judgment was impaired enough to actually consider unburdening myself.

"Fuckin' Raiders." I said shaking my head. Best I could do.

Tommy just shook his head in pity.

"You rang?" Al's voice from behind me.

Fuck my life.

TWENTY-ONE

Sun Tzu said that if you wait by the river long enough, the bodies of your enemies will eventually float by. Logic follows that if you want in on the action you'd better arm yourself and head up stream or, I don't know, maybe you should just stop hanging out with all those assholes down at the river.

Life's busy enough without getting a ledger going. Once you start keeping track of losses you never get back to even. At some point you have to stop trying to force your rivals to square their debts and just go downriver and wait for their corpses to float by.

That's' what's worked for me, anyway. At some point I just stopped worrying about getting even with people and started distributing damage randomly wherever I lit, the leaves of my ledger spiraling out from me like the big bang as I spun and erupted, redistributing debt to whoever got close. Didn't settle my ledger but it sure kept me too busy administering damage control to ever mind the tally.

Before I started winding up strangers in bars I was just a run-of-the-mill psychopath. Mostly I'd spend my time trying to fit into new places or wearing out my welcome in old ones. In those days I still thought I could be normal if I worked at it but I'd usually last about two and a half years somewhere new before I started running low on friends and high on peril. These days I know better than to think I'll ever be normal. I stay careful not to let anyone close, for my own well-being as much as theirs. The scariest thing in this world for me has always been me.

I've noticed that everyone loses their temper from time to time. Maybe when they have a lot going on in their life; so much shit just coming at them from every direction that they finally fatigue. It's understandable when someone can no longer moderate that swelling impulse to lash out. Maybe they'd done alright up until that moment, quietly weathering a shit storm without so much as a complaint or even a whiny facebook status.

For some reason though, along comes that one co-worker or acquaintance who's committed the least of trespasses but it just happened to be the single load which couldn't be bore. Under the weight of everything else being shouldered, even the sane person finally breaks. The guy who, one nog over the line at the office Holiday party lays into the pushy, overly perfumed Jesus Freak no one can stand but pretends to like out of pity and respect for esprit de corps; she wouldn't shut up about the War on Christmas and it was time someone straightened her out so off came the gloves. Or the Orange County soccer mom who goes off on the sidelines at her son's AYSO game, right there in front of God and everybody, the Mexican coach is a racist because he doesn't sub in her tow-head shitstain even though he just runs around aimlessly out there and boots the ball into the sideline bleachers anytime it comes near him. Or the bartender who finally takes out his long-simmering rages on the unlucky frat-bro who just ordered five Lemon Drops, two Buttery Nipples and a round of Jager Bombs, then tipped a buck. At some point on any time line even the most even-keeled normie will go raped ape on someone over something so beneath their outrage, they'll wish they could take it back.

How often is this tenable, though? Once a year? Twice ever? Every other weekend? Three times since high school? How often can a person get away with losing control like that before finding themselves at a much different station in life? Divorced, unemployed, at the mercy of the court. Can you lose your temper every month? Every decade? I wonder because I don't know from normal. This never happens for me. I don't lose my temper. I do things differently. I'm just using temper tantrums as a model to illustrate what it's like to really scare yourself. An angry outburst tends to frighten a person who usually manages their outrage without falter. I use this understanding of anger management to draw an analog to my own personal psychosis.

Most of us will at some point catch ourselves looking around a roomful of startled faces frozen, waiting to see where our anger is going to take things. That's perhaps something everyone's at some point experienced, to their own mortification. Waking up in abject terror at the things you're capable of, not so much.

What sort of behaviors will have a man packing his bags and quietly vanishing into the night as an aftermath is arranging itself to collapse around those left in his wake? What sort of thing drives a man to take wing and reinvent himself in a new place every so often, wondering if this time, will he make it 2 years? Five years? A decade? How long before he pulls the whole thing down around him and moves on again?

Any loose nut can get themselves canned from the AT&T call center for telling a customer she's a sassy cunt but that guy isn't capable of the destruction that's shakes me from a merciful dream and delivers me to a waking nightmare. It is however a starting point for understanding me.

Safe to say that at some point, probably in childhood, most of us figure out that losing our temper doesn't solve anything, in fact only exacerbates a bad situation. We learn to catch ourselves escalating things in our heads and to switch tactics. This is where me and normal people part.

Confrontation triggers the fight or flight axiom, as we know. Sometimes we rush in, fists flailing at a perceived threat but most of the time we just opt to wait by the river to see if someone we hate floats by. And then there's me. I tend to take an option which is seldom seen. I become threatened by the most banal things that are no actual threat at all and my threat response is not fight or flight. What happens to me is I become engrossed, curious, engaging.

I wind up in arms-length of someone I've snap judged as loathsome and rather than fight or flee, I want to own them. I want to lure them with rapport and wind them up to do stupid, ruinous things. Sometimes it yields a black eye or a view of someone's back walking away, mostly it yields a human being to manipulate. This is why I spend my days alone now but not long ago this pathology was a source of devastating trouble for me and anyone in my sphere of influence.

Instead of making an ass of myself getting belligerent over a spilled beer or a swiped parking spot, I would become disgusted by a style of beard, an affected stride or a shade of lipstick, then smile and engage as if I hadn't just decided I hate this person. I'd befriend, become a little too charming and dole out awful advice. I'd find myself instinctively manipulating and I could hardly even control it. On my worst days I didn't even catch myself doing it. The way most people have to watch out for their temper, I would have to watch out for my glad hand.

I've since figured out that winding up strangers in bars is my best strategy for managing my pathology. Before I ever arrived at that method I found myself having to constantly take inventory, develop other metrics and strategies for moderating my manipulative impulse. I'd have to consciously look at things like, "OK, I know I'm going to get people doing all sorts of crazy shit, all the time and most of the time I'm not even going to realize I'm doing it. So, how often can I allow myself to do it? How much of it can I get away with? How often am I going to be totally conscious of fucking with people and still unable to resist the impulse? If I'm in relaxed company maybe it's twice a week for five or six hours at a go. I might catch myself doing it ten times that week. If I can resist influencing people eight times I'm only dicking around in other people's heads twice a week. Let's just call it 100 times a year. If I can do this 99 times in 100 without getting caught, I'm in damage control once per year. If I can moderate the damage 50% of the time I can make it in this new town for two years, maybe five if I stretch it and exceed projections."

I would much rather be a normal person, babysitting a little temper but my reality is moderating full-blown psychopathy. The same way someone else hits a rough patch, their car just broke down, wife makes them sleep on the couch or whatever, they count to ten, go for a walk, take some deep breaths, punch a pillow, go to the shooting range, whatever it takes. I can't do any of that. What I do is wind up strangers in bars. It's the only thing that works for me and if I don't walk that dog every few days now it will shit all over the house so bad that I'll have to burn it to the ground and start over someplace new. I can't do that anymore, not since the Prelacy.

Winding up strangers in bars isn't so weird. Other people let off steam in similar fashion. On any given Sunday there's a guy in some sports bar watching a 42" flatscreen in horror as the $50 he put on the Raiders to cover slowly vanishes. Everyone in the bar will look at him stunned when he loses his temper and calls the guy he owes $50 a "passionate faggot", then breaks his own phone against the wall. That's' pretty bad, sure. Giving in to your temper can cause real problems but this only happens for him once or twice a year, so he's got that going for him. It's not that abnormal, maybe just offensive and definitely indignant. His friends will tease him about it for a couple weeks and in a month no one will even remember it happened at all. "He's a character" his friends will say. "Classic Steve-o" they'll joke if it's ever even brought up again.

Then there's me. No hilarious violent outbursts from me. That same Sunday for me plays out much different. I'll be sitting at the bar alone in a new town, enjoying a Jameson neat and my own company. I'll be minding my own business, trying to appear normal by staring at sports on the television, half hoping nobody bothers me. Inevitably some interloper sidles up to my left. This by itself is enough to trigger my territorial circuit and have me thinking about calling the guy a donkey and smashing him in the face with my rocks glass. If I were the temperamental type, this innocuous compromise of my personal perimeter would have already spurred me toward telling the guy he smells like a swim through pigshit and dresses like he hasn't left the house yet.

He hasn't even opened his mouth, let alone acknowledged my presence but I can see it coming and for me, that's enough to make me think about binding him with the zip-ties in my glove box and lighting up that pack of Newports on the bar in front of him, just to put them out all over his fat greasy face. But I'm not the demonstrative, temperamental type. I don't fight and I don't flee. I like to talk to them.

So in the old days, I would strike first and compliment him on his disgusting lard-ass sweatpants. I'd look at his piece of shit phone and tell him, "I used to have one of those back in college. Man, I love retro.", then cause him to feel even more insecure about his shitty old pre-paid by making a show of looking down at my shiny new mobile while I surreptitiously google the image on his t-shirt. I'd sit and study the band name on his tee and after five minutes of digesting the vast mythology of The Insane Clown Posse I would set to engaging this rube about the thing closest to a religion for him. Before long I'd be amazing myself at how I could take what little bit I've learned of

Shaggy 2 Dope and Violent J in five minutes and relate it all to the most dazzling, abstract insights my new friend's tiny brain can follow. After three beers the guy not only thinks I'm the foremost authority on the Insane Clown Posse, the one thing that matters most to him in life, but he's starting to see me as some sort of enlightened guru who speaks to him in the esoteric language of his beloved Juggalo tribe. He's bewitched. After a few more beers he'd pretty much take to heart anything I might suggest, which is why he's broken his stupid old phone against the wall and called the guy down the bar a passionate faggot. I goaded him in to putting his last $50 on the Raiders to cover and made him hate his phone. Making friends already, things are off to a good start in my new town.

But for how long? How long until that moment where I'm just doing this on a bigger scale, pathologically manipulating an entire network of these townies, watching them put me on their shoulders only to abuse them? How long until a roomful of them has that "a-ha" moment where they catch me doing it. Before an entire neighborhood of pre-diabetic juggalos or curly mustachioed ass-wipes and early adopters, or an enclave of "photographers" and "DJs" and "musicians" I've hypnotized awakens from the illusion I've crafted around them. How long before the pitchforks and torches are at my apartment door screaming for the monster? How long until the mask of sanity fails to convince, how long until the snake oil patrons want their money back? How long until I have to pack up in the middle of the night and move the circus to a new patch of dead grass?

If only it were ever something so little as a broken phone or fifty bucks when the house of cards comes down around me. By the time I'm found out it's usually been a few years of influencing anything from a small, insular group of lost souls to an entire network of financial assassins and hitmen who will eventually come looking for blood. That's what shakes me from sleep in the middle of the night and has me terrified of what I'm capable of doing. And unlike a problem temper, I can't control it. I can't count to ten and watch it dissipate. I can only dog sit it, take it for short walks every now and then.

If it weren't for winding up strangers in bars I'd still be surrounding myself with fast friends to victimize for personal amusement and for very little material gain. I'd still be moving on to new places every so often to start over fresh. Thanks to my shameful little barroom ritual I'm mostly alone in this world now. I'm seldom in the company of others save for a couple of acquaintances and the odd stranger I find myself harassing in a pub somewhere every few days, all just to exhaust any dangerous social urges.

When I'm not helping the Prelacy tear the world apart in exchange for a small fortune in gold bars you can find me on a bar stool somewhere, recreationally making strangers hate me and then leaving them to stew, careful to never make friends, careful never visit the same bar twice. Those are my rules. Well, OK, I usually try to keep one bar where I'm considered a local. In this one place I'm careful to remain mostly anonymous and mind my manners. I strictly forbid myself from winding up a single soul in my regular bar. No winding up strangers on the home turf. That's the rule.

Other than that, they're all fair game. That's what's kept me sane, stable and problem free for the last few years. No long term connections that inevitably become a network of enablers waiting for me to make them complicit in their own ruin. It's just me and a new bar every few days where I get drunk and irritate the shit out of a few strangers. Crazy as it sounds, that's what's working.

I should thank the Prelacy every day for counting me among their number. If for nothing more than the fact that they are a group I shouldn't dare fuck over as they' could squash me like a bug. And I am thankful for that but frankly, they're as full of shit as I am and they're going to kill me when they find out the truth about me; that my stupid penchant for mischief actually has fucked them over like it has everyone else who's stayed in my corner for very long. Groucho Marx once said, "I wouldn't join any club that would have me as a member." Groucho was perhaps too kind hearted and far smarter than I'll ever be. In spite of his declaration against being a joiner, I wonder if he wasn't in the Prelacy. I should look into that.

TWENTY-TWO

Downtown Los Angeles, CA – Mon Aug 12ᵗʰ, 2013

Sébastien was bailing me out of L.A. County's Men's Central jail after I'd gotten 86ed from the Copper Bucket the previous night. I'd started having words with Guitar Tommy about cutting me off. He saw me arguing with Al at the bar on the first day he began appearing to me so Tommy wouldn't serve me anymore. My arguing with my invisible friend and then Guitar Tommy escalated into a pretty big tussle with Tucan and Chivo and pretty much everyone else at the Bucket. I wound up fighting with Chivo and his long-bearded white friend Leon out in the parking lot which went well I suppose, considering I lived to tell about it. The cops came just as I was picking myself up off the ground. When all was said and done I wound up getting booked on a disturbing the peace and a drunk in public while the rest of the bar went back to enjoying the night minus one crazy weirdo.

Sébastien and I went to sit in the sun at MacArthur Park and talk a little bit about what happened. We met there frequently but this time he was seeing me in perhaps a different light. I was filled with shame and regret over wearing out my welcome at one of the only places that would have me to begin with. I couldn't bring myself to reveal the detail about arguing with my imaginary friend Al Davis at the bar. I just wasn't ready to reveal that to anyone. If it weren't for Sébastien's calming influence I think I'd have just packed my bags and moved somewhere else that very day, like I've always done when the going gets rough.

"Where would you go, mon ami?" Sébastien asked

"I don't know. Back up to Seattle maybe?"

"Seattle? You've lived there, yes?"

"For a few of years after Afghanistan."

"You like it there?"

"No. I mean, yeah but, I don't know. It's like anywhere else." I tried explaining. "It's nice but it's got its drawbacks. Usually, anywhere I go, those drawbacks are me."

My words hung in the air for a moment before Sébastien turned the conversation.

"This is something you do, is it?" Sébastien asked. "You like the fresh start?"

"I always mess things up right when they're going well. I think I do it when I get bored. Things become too routine so I stir shit up."

Another little silence. This might make me feel nervous or judged if I didn't feel so at ease around Sébastien. Honesty isn't exactly an efforted trait for someone who tends to lay everything plain but it doesn't mean it comes painlessy. Honesty gets me in trouble. A lot. Still, it was always easy being honest with Sébastien.

"Is this perhaps how you found yourself in Afghanistan?"

"Yeah, maybe."

"Tell me about this time in your life, Monsieur Godefroi."

"I'm gonna go to the churro cart and get us some churros. You want a churro?"

"Godefroi, leave that for now. Tell me about Afghanistan."

"Not much to tell. I went there for a year and made a mess of that, too. Had to leave before I even saw much action, really."

"What happened?"

"I don't know," I shrugged, "Same old story, I'm an asshole. COs didn't like me, enlisted men didn't like me, PMCs didn't like me."

"But what got you sent home?"

This takes some sorting out in my head. I'm sure there's a simple way to tell it but it's all still somewhat confusing to me. I breathe and then take a swing at making sense of it for the old wizard as much as for myself.

"The short version is I stumbled onto a heroin deal between a couple hajis and some PMCs embedded with us. Prior to that, those same PMCs had threatened me with blue on blue next fire fight we saw.

"Blue on blue?"

"Yeah, like, they were going to kill me in combat and report it as a friendly fire incident, like an accident."

"This was a common thing?"

"I don't know. It sure seemed routine to them but I know fuck all about what goes on. I was in way over my head in Afghanistan. None of what went on over there made sense to me."

"So what happened?"

"All I know is that my superiors somehow got wind of it and they sent me home. I don't blame them. We were at war and those guys shouldn't have to deal with the kind of internal conflicts I was causing just by being there. I had no business joining the Army. I was way out of my depth."

"You did not like the structure? The violence? The being far from home? What was it?"

"I thought I would like all of those things but I never really figured out how to fit in. I couldn't make it work."

"And yet here you are thriving within the Prelacy where you have the most strict and consequential of rules to follow, where you are required to prosecute our writs regularly and you are traveling all of the time."

Sébastien pointing out this irony gave me chills. I fretted that my pause was suspicious but I bore down and managed to pull off a casual response.

"Go figure."

"You're an odd bird, Monsieur Godefroi."

"Yeah, I think I give everyone that impression."

We sat quietly, watching the ducks on the pond for a beat before Sébastien broke the silence again.

"Tell me, what became of these PMCs you saw buying the heroin?"

"Far as I know, nothing. CO got me sent home on a General Discharge and everything there returned to business as usual I figure."

"And you never saw combat?"

"I was in firefights on patrol a couple of times."

"But you had never sent someone to their final reward before choosing le Chemin de l'Epee?" The Path of the Sword, my lodge within the Prelacy.

"Not a soul."

I labored at casual cool through another of Sébastien's uncomfortable pauses.

"How are you finding your chosen path, now? Have you acclimated?"

"Had a little bit of a bumpy start I guess but I think I've found my groove."

"You are indeed an odd bird, Monsieur Godefroi. Rare and charming in your own way but odd." Sébastien chuckled.

TWENTY-THREE

Los Angeles, CA – Tue Jan 22nd, 2013

About six months after my initiation rite in Belgium I was promoted to the rank of Black Hand or Main Noire, my first rank within the Prelacy. At this time I was asked to choose my lodge, my novice path of advancement in the order. Within the Prelacy there are different regimental disciplines, each with differing duties and courses of study that a member must advance through. There are the Path of the Sword, the Path of the Cloak, the Path of the Disciple and the Prelacy Guard to name just the ones I'm aware of. I was offered a choice between the Path of the Cloak and the Path of the Sword.

"It is quite a simple decision, Monsieur Godefroi." I recall Sébastien's gentle assurance.

"My choices are basically being a spy or being a soldier? I don't like it." I griped. "What if I want to be a wizard?"

"You should know we have no such thing as wizards within the Prelacy, dear Godefroi. You must choose to be a Cloak or a Sword. That is your choice."

"Well, why can't I be a Scholar? Don't you have Scholars?"

"In deed we do, alas you are not a Scholar, Monsieur. The path of the Disciple is reserved for those who are devout in their reverence for Prelacy lore. You have been given the choice of these paths. Either you are to be a Cloak or you are to be a Sword."

"I don't know. I can't decide."

"Confusion is merely the inversion of curiosity, Monsieur Godefroi.

Why not simply ask yourself which path you find more intriguing, which path begs your interest?"

"You think I should be a Cloak?"

"I offer no opinion."

"What do Swords do again?"

"They are the martial path within our order. They carry out our military actions."

"And the Cloaks?"

"They engage in espionage. They are our intelligence apparatus."

"Well, I guess I like fighting more than I like sneaking around so I'll follow the path of the Sword."

"Very well, Monsieur Godefroi." Sébastien sighed. Was he surprised? Disappointed? I couldn't tell.

I chose le Chemin de l'Épée, the Path of the Sword, little knowing what it actually entailed. I only knew it meant I had selected what Sébastien called the martial path within the Prelacy. I had no idea that I would soon be an assassin for the order. I think if I had known, I might have chosen the Path of the Cloak, so I'm glad I didn't know. I've come to really enjoy being an assassin, though I'm shit at it.

With my advancement came a new rank and title. I was no longer l'Honore Greffier Monsieur Godefroi de les Anges, Aveugle Apprenti. No longer a Blind Apprentice, I had become l'Honore Arbitre Monsieur Godefroi de les Anges, Main Noire, I was now a Black Hand. All very sinister, mysterious and intoxicating.

There was of course another little ceremony but nothing so elaborate as my initiation. No trip to Belgium, let alone a big dinner in a castle. Just a small ceremony one night on the beach up in Santa Barbara with Sébastien and the ranking master in le Chemin de l'Épée. A man I recognized from my initiation. It was the burly and heroic looking l'Honore Maître Arbitre Monsieur Herman de Boheme, Gardien de l'Épée. After the ceremony I was given my own Monolith, the Prelacy's blackphone they used for encrypted mobile communications. I was also given some instructions and a strange book titled Le Livre des Fontaines. The book itself appeared as a very old hardbound French book of fables but I would soon learn that its contents were stories encoded with a vital directory of Prelacy locations. Safe houses, dead drops and meeting places mostly. It was the only piece of Prelacy literature I was ever permitted to keep and each Prelate owned one.

It would be another six months before I received my first real assignment. One late January night while walking home from the Copper Bucket there came a text message on my mobile. It was from the Judicious Scrivener, the never seen man in my lodge whom I was instructed to carry out any order from. Failure to do so, I was assured came with a penalty I did not want to know.

Until this day, my orders from the Scrivener were simple things. Retrieve this gun from this location and dispose of it. Go to this other location and torch this vehicle, leave no trace. Pick up Sébastien's take out order from Zankou Chicken, get extra Hummus. This day, however the stakes were raised forever, prompted by a routine exchange of text messages on my Monolith.

J.S. – Art thou the Folded Hands?

Me – Nay, 'tis I, the Black Hand.

J.S. – Whither go ye, Black Hand?

Me – Where so ever faith shall guide.

J.S. – Hast thou faith given you a sign?

Me - Indeed.

J.S. – Very well, what is the sign?

Me – It is the Cup.

J.S. – Very well, fill thy cup at the Fountain of Stars.

All of my communications with the Scrivener began with this exchange while I bore the rank of Black Hand. The first part of this odd coding was so the Scrivener could be sure he was in fact contacting the correct party. Had the challenge of "Art thou the Folded Hands" been responded to with anything other than "Nay 'tis I the Black Hand" (or Red Hand, or Sword Hand for the higher ranks) the Scrivener would know he could say no more and take whatever counter measures were necessary to safely address the miscommunication.

The second challenge, "Whither go ye, Black Hand" was to acknowledge that our handshake had been initiated and to next determine if the Hand was occupied or available for communication. A response of "Where so ever faith shall guide" indicated that situations were normal and that the Hand was available. A response of "into Caesar's shackles" indicated distress while a response of "to pray in the Citadel" indicated that the respondent was at leisure and would be delayed.

When asked "Hast thou faith given you a sign" the Scrivener was checking the respondents current activities against previous communications. A response of "It is the sign of the Cup" indicated that the respondent was awaiting new orders while the sign of the scale indicated previous orders had been completed.

The Scrivener's message to "fill thy cup at the Fountain of Stars" was an instruction to find new orders at one of the Prelacy's many Fountains. Fountains were safe houses and dead drops located throughout the world. We had thousands of them as I understood. Up until this exchange I seldom had to look them up in Le Livre des Fontaines, the coded directory of our fountains that Monsieur Herman de Boheme had given me at my promotion ceremony.

Until this moment I had only ever retrieved orders from one of three Fountains out of the dozens located in the Los Angeles area. The Fountain of Patience was a dead drop hidden inside the Grove shopping center off of 3rd in La Brea. The Fountain of Equis was a dead drop located inside of the mens restroom at a bar called the Coach and Horses in Hollywood. One less place I could go wind up strangers. The Fountain of Renewal was a safe house and dead drop located on the top floor of The Citron, an apartment building near Pershing Square. Here was where I would invariably find my reward for successfully completing each assignment. Always in the Prelacy's gold kilo bars.

It really was like a fun game at first. I'd get my cryptic instructions from the Scrivener on my Monolith and proceed to one of these locations. There I would find a coded note instructing me to carry out something as mundane as taking one of the Prelacy's vehicles to transport a passenger from LAX to Downtown or something as nerve wracking and perilous as sneaking into a crime scene to retrieve and destroy evidence. Afterward I would always receive a text message from the Scrivener advising me that I would find my reward at the Fountain of Renewal and every time, waiting there would be these gold kilo bars with the Prelacy's hexagonal Bee seal on them. It was exhilarating. When I found out how much one of these kilo bars was worth I could've shit my pants. Something about that kind of money elicits minor pangs of terror, the worry of unfulfilled obligation. It all seemed like overpayment for what I might have willingly done just for thrills. I worried, what were they really buying from me with all of this gold?

I'd found orders in just these three locations up until this moment but the Fountain of Stars was someplace new. I remember my excitement that I'd finally have to consult Le Livre des Fontaines again to determine its location. I hadn't done that since my first orders from the Scrivener six months previous.

It was required that I learn the Prelacy's cryptography techniques in order to advance in rank and I did so enthusiastically. When I located the reference to the Fountain of Stars in Le Livre des Fontaines I decrypted its location and reacted with what I think is best described as a yelp.

"Hell yeah! We're going to London!"

The Fountain of Stars it turns out was a safe house located in London's Aldgate area. I'd never been to England and I was excited by the prospect of official travel under the orders of my lodge. I felt I had truly arrived as a Prelate, but also as a person. I had finally done something with my life.

TWENTY-FOUR

Seattle, WA – Sun Oct 12ᵗʰ, 2014

Standing at our table are an attractive, tall bald man of Turkish or perhaps Balkan descent and the man I recognize as my superior in le Chemin de l'Epee, Monsieur Herman de Boheme. Aghast panic gives way to a hunger for knowing more. There is probably a simple German word for this.

"Monsieur Godefroi, thank you for your patient assent to this perplexing engagement." The bald one says tersely as he seats himself.

I can hardly acknowledge the man as I'm fixated on the presence of Monsieur Herman. I already just want to beat the new guy up on spec. There is no one in the Prelacy without shoulder length hair so a xenophobic paranoia has taken over. I'm navigating my own drunken impulses split seconds before I can re-channel them into any form of diplomacy. Monsieur Herman de Boheme seats himself second in conspicuous deference to his cohort and I'm anxious to hear what's about to be said. I'm convincing myself I've mustered at least a painstaking look of informality if not an actual air of indifference. I doubt it though.

"Monsieur Godefroi, I want to first explain why I did not reach out to you myself." Herman de Boheme says to me in the neutral accent he typically affects when speaking English. All European Prelates speak in that intel spook's learned neutral American. It usually comes across as a chill but flip Vincent Price.

I offer no response.

"Please understand that a buffer was necessary at first." Herman explains. "If I had brought this to you and you'd elected to use the sword and not the ear, this entire operation would have been exposed. Centuries of work laid to waste. It was a much safer route, deferring to the charms of our Madame Aureline. She is nearly infallible in that regard."

Centuries of work. It never stops with these guys. Honestly, I'd never pegged Herman for a cuckoo in our brief encounters. I freakin' like Herman. A lot.

"I volunteered for this, Godefroi." Arlene injects. "I'm taking it as a positive that you seem oblivious to how dangerous that was for me."

I can't help feeling a little gassed. I try not to let it distract me. I need to stay frosty for this bald motherfucker, is what I'm thinking. I'm sitting here with two Long-Haired Kings who seem to be subordinate to this shaved-pate pussy and that's just too unsettling right now. Then again, I'm pretty fucking wasted.

"Well, are you gonna say anything, baldy locks?"

Bald guy extends his hand across the table and says, "Monsieur Godefroi, my name is-"

"Put your dick beater away. Shaking hands is for men who are standing."

The bald man isn't offended in the least.

"Well you did not stand when I arrived."

"Then you get it."

"Alright, girls, you're both pretty." Arlene says.

A run-of-the-mill stare down ensues and I stand up and head to the bar.

"What're you having, Arlene"

"I'm fine."

"Herman?" I ask.

"Soda water and rocks, please."

I ignore the bald one and order, surreptitiously chambering a round in my AF-1 and re-holstering it by the time our bartender returns with a soda water and rocks and my double Jameson. I crab-hand the drinks and head back to our table.

"Listen, the pace here needs to exceed my ability to sustain giving a fuck." I say as I slide Herman his water. "Whoever's going to do all the talking, now's as good a time as any."

Arlene looks to the bald guy who nods his green light and she takes the wheel. Good move.

"Godefroi, here's the deal, in a nutshell."

I peer over my short glass right into her eyes like she's the only one there.

"As I've indicated, upon successful prosecution of your next writ you will be nominated for a very big promotion, but I don't think you understand how big." She continues.

"It's a done deal. I'll be elevated to Sword Hand and the Prelacy's second degree tree. The Tentacles of Abraxas."

"That's where you're mistaken. The Prelacy is not the Boy Scouts or the Freemasons." Arlene clarifies. "The Tentacles of Abraxas aren't just a degreed lodge. They are the Knights of House Merovingi."

"Not more lore, please stop talking like this."

"It's the truth. Upon elevation to the Tentacles you will be a titled member of House Merovingi and all Prelacy and House secrets will be made available to you. You will enjoy unfettered movement among the novice lodges along with regular access to all Prelacy and House membership."

"And I suppose that would be pretty valuable to you guys."

"No. We have that already. One of Canan's assets is a Tentacle. Monsieur Giles de Albion, a Knight in House Merovingi who emerged from le Chemin de l'Exquisite Paragon, the Path of the Artisan."

"The what?" I ask. "Who's Canan?"

Arlene nods toward the bald guy sitting across the table from us.

"Monsieur Godefroi." The bald guy says.

"You're Canan?"

"Yes."

"And you're in the Prelacy?" I scoff incredulously, "Not with that Roman hair cut you aren't."

"No, Monsieur Godefroi, I am not in your Prelacy but I have an intel asset who is an Knight Artisan in the Tentacles of Abraxas, the Royal Court of House Merovingi."

"This is where you need to pay attention." Arlene says. "We've had an overview of House Merovingi's hierarchy for almost a century now. We have long ago duplicated most of their secret texts, we have even infiltrated them as high as the Tentacles of Abraxas. None of those things are needed from you."

"I don't follow."

"Monsieur Godefroi, perhaps I should explain." Monsieur Herman de Boheme finally chimes in.

"By all means, bossman. Please do." I patronize. "I'm all ears."

"In order to be considered for advancement into the Tentacles of

Abraxas, I had to nominate you for ascension." He explains. "This happens perhaps four, maybe five times in the life of a Path Master, such as myself."

"So, most Prelates don't advance beyond the rank of Red Hand?"

"Most do not advance beyond Black Hand, Monsieur."

This stuns me to hear. Why had I advanced of all people?

"I don't get it."

"The Prelacy uses and throws away thousands of lives but we mustn't get side tracked by that right now. That is another sorrow to be lamented another time. What I mean to relate to you right now is of paramount importance. Not just to you but to everyone on earth."

I pause to process their barrage of revelations as they impatiently watch. I dismiss the laughable, emotional notion of "everyone on earth" and try to wrap my head around just the part in which most Prelates never make it past the rank of Black Hand. I reflect on the shit show that was my first big assignment in London and cram to understand how I even made it this far.

"So why me?" I ask, trying to seem nonplussed. "You remember the Fountain of Stars when I was a Black Hand, Herman. Why me?"

"How much of the Codex Merovingi are you familiar with?" Herman asks.

"I don't know, man. A lot actually." I say.

"But I thought you weren't a devout."

"I'm not, I'm just terminally curious." I say. "If you let me read a book and tell me it's one of only eight copies on earth, I'm going to devour it, commit most of it to memory, if I can."

"So you've actually memorized passages from the Codex Merovingi?"

"Probably not a lot but yeah, and thanks to three semesters of high school French I've even translated and recorded some of it in my own library."

"Fascinating. Some say this is even in the prophecies." Canan interjects.

"What, a guy with three semesters of high school French will translate House Merovingi's most sacred text? Yeah, that's totally in there, I'm sure."

My quip is met with belabored patience and a quiet beat.

"This is absurd to you, I get it but it is no less important to those familiar with Prelacy lore."

"Yeah, well that's what I've been doing. Look at it however you want but whenever I get to spend any time with the Codex I memorize parts, then come home and record them in my own writing." I explain. "I've been doing it since my intitiation."

"Are you very familiar with l'Evangile de Saint Éloi?" Herman asks.

"The Prophecies? No, not so much." I say. "I'm mostly just curious about l'Histoire. Why?"

"I think you should study them for yourself but for now I will explain in brief."

I take a drink and wait for Herman to get to his point. I'm more engrossed than impatient by now and a mite too committed. Far too fascinated to table-flip our emergent chess game, anyway. I'm still miles from trusting anyone sitting here, though.

"Godefroi, Sébastien and others in the Prelacy see you as a fulfillment of prophecy." Arlene adds after a moment.

"If you have read it already, revisit l'Evangile de Saint Éloi. You're a Leap Year birth, from a zero year, as is Sébastien. The prophecy says that two children of Leap Year birth from zero years will replay the pageant of Clovis and Sigibert."

"Pageant of Clovis and Sigibert?"

"Yes. Clovis hired assassins to kill Sigibert and then killed the assassins and claimed Sigibert's throne." Herman explained. "This is retold in l'Evangile de Saint Dagobert, you should read that as well."

"Wait, tell me if I'm picking this up right." I say. "So you guys think that if I'm promoted to Tentacle, Sébastien will approach me about killing Grand Maître Chilperic XI de Antwerp and once that's done he'll kill me and ascend to replace him?

"As the new King-in-Waiting, yes. the highest seat in House Merovingi. That is precisely what will happen." Herman assures. "As told in the prophecy of Saint Éloi, except that the prophecy of Saint Éloi doesn't specify which of the two births of zero ending Leap Years survives and acends."

I take a moment to process what I'm being told and the gravity of it all comes crashing in.

"You guys think you have a shot at having a member of your Covenant as the head of House Merovingi!"

"But for the tiny detail about inducting you into the Covenant, you understand perfectly, Monsieur Godefroi." Canan adds.

I give Canan the stink-eye and continiue.

"So you want me to kill Grand Maître Chilperic, then kill Sébastien and blame Chilperic's assassination on him?" I demand, laughing.

"Yes. This is what we see, after which you will demand fealty from the Palace Keys and the Tentacles of Abraxas."

"Palace Keys?" I ask.

"Yes, Le Clés du Palais. They are the lodge above the Tentacles of Abraxas in House Merovingi. It's not important right now. You will eliminate Sébastien and usurp Chilperic and after that the Palace Keys and the Tentacles of Abraxas will swear fealty to you. You would be the King-in-Waiting and the Covenant would benefit from your accord with us."

"And as King-in-Waiting, why would I forge a pact with your Covenant of Arius?" I ask.

"Is our saving your life worth nothing to you?" Canan volleys.

"To saner men, I'd suppose it might be."

"So you would prefer to roll the dice with your own life rather than proceed with the certain and advantageous outcome we propose?" Canan asks,

My hand reflexively moves toward my AF-1 at the not-so-subtle threat.

"You put it like that and I'm inclined to take my chances." I say beginning to stand as Arlene reaches her hand across me in a calming gesture. I remain seated and listen to her.

"We're not your enemy, the Prelacy is, Sébastien is. We're no threat to you, Godefroi."

"Monsieur, we simply have mutual interests. We can help you survive the events to come and in turn you can help us to protect mankind from what the Prelacy will do should Sébastien ascend to King-in-Waiting."

"And upon your elevation to the Tentacles of Abraxas you will be in a position to do exactly this, Godefroi." Arlene adds.

"Once you're Knighted, it will only be a matter of time before Sébastien propositions you." Herman says. "Once that has happened, the Pageant of Clovis will have begun and it can end in only one of two ways."

I take a slow sip off of my whiskey neat and consider all I've heard. Just a few hours ago I was simply going through the motions. Winding up some know-it-all in a Hotel bar while I imagined myself someday making Sébastien proud of his charge. Satisfied in his patronage, his sponsorship of this otherwise wayward cyclone of calamity. Now I'm listening to this would-be seductress, along with a man I thought I admired and some bald headed douche try to convince me that I should kill not just my mentor but that I should also kill the head of our order. I'll admit, I'm now suspicious of Sébastien and just as angry at them for that as I am at Sébastien for misleading me, assuming any of it is true.

"OK, here's the good news for you three." I begin. "I'm intrigued enough to wind this out so I'm not going to kill you all right now."

I don't get hung up on their stupid smirks and secreted glances. I don't care if they think they're humoring me.

"Now here's the bad news. You've got until the Judicious Scrivener contacts me about my next writ." I continue. "If I'm not convinced there's a good reason to join your covenant by then I'll kill Chilperic and Sébastien myself and wage war against you from the comfort of my new throne."

""I suppose this is more than we'd honestly hoped for, Monsieur Godefroi." Canan says. "Monsieur Herman and I will remain in contact through Madame Aurilene."

"I'd imagine you will because Arlene's staying with me until this is all sorted."

"Relax, Muscles. That was part of our plan." Arlene chides.

"I wouldn't be so excited about that." I burp. "Because if I don't like where this is going I'll have killed you long before I get to Sébastien and Chilperic."

"You and I both know, you're not killing me or anyone else." Arlene says. "Just play along and let's try to make the best of these next few days, Whiskey Warrior."

TWENTY-FIVE

From the Codex Merovingi

Excerpt from

l'Évangile de St. Éloi

(aka the Prophecies)

Translated from the **Le Volume du Maire du Palais**
from memory by Foster Revell,

formally *l'Honoré Godefroi de Les Anges de le Prélature Familier des Arbitres Infernales*

Ch: XII vs. 18-25

18. And lo, there comes a pair of fish, each born to this earth on the leap day of a zero year. 19. One from the Undiscovered Land, the other from the familiar. 20. One shall ascend the throne of House Merovingi's King-in-Waiting. 21. One shall die delivering the throne in their re-enactment of the Pageant of Clovis. 22. This, the last of our Kings-in-Waiting shall be he who returns the Merovingi from the sea and to the throne. 23. To rule over the whole of the known world and the unknown world alike. 24. And every knee shall bend and every head shall bow to the Merovingian King returned from the Sea. 25. From the sea, and to the sea and from the sea again, death to Rome, long live House Merovingi."

Excerpt from

l'Évangile de St. Dagobert (aka the Pageant of Clovis)

Ch: IX vs. 43-66

43. And with the defeat of the Visigoth Kings of Toulouse, of Aquitaine and Gaul and also Iberia, so came to pass the days of a divided Frankia. 44. The son of Chilperic I, who was the grandson of Merovech the Quinotaur's progeny did seed a dynasty. 45. This King who walked with an upright heart before him, and did what was pleasing in his god's eyes did in fact unite the kingdoms of Frankia through no higher acts than murder and guile. 46. The first kingdom he annexed was none other than that which belonged to his partner in war, trusting King Sigibert of Ripuria. 47. To Sigibert's son, Clovis I did say, "Your sire grows weak and you should be King. Usurp his throne and I shall support your claim, young Chloderic." 48. And so Chloderic, who had never considered the throne for himself, now imagined for himself no other destiny. 49. And so Chloderic who now featured himself in a crown, did set forth the pieces to lay his own father low. 50. And so Chloderic did send his agents to take King Sigibert the Lame as he lay in his sleep. 51. The mortal deed done he sent word to inform Clovis. 52. "Send your envoys to claim your share of the spoils." 53. And so Clovis did send his agents to Chloderic the Parricide. 54. And so came the agents of Clovis to survey and inspect the treasures and inspect them all they did. 55. "It was in this coffer my father used to keep all his gold coins" said Chloderic to the agents of Clovis. 56. "Plunge your hands to the bottom," they answered, "to see how much is there." 57. And so Chloderic obliged them and in that opportune moment Chloderic was struck dead by the agents of Clovis. 58. And so an unworthy son shares the fate of his father. 59. The deed done, King Clovis came to Cologne. 60. "The son of your King, my brother did plot against his father. 61. Chloderic set assassins upon your King and did have him murdered. 62. In turn Chloderic was killed by someone or other. 63. And so I say unto you, people of Cologne and Ripuria, put yourselves now under my protection." 64. When the people of Cologne heard what he had said, they clashed their shields and shouted "Long Live House Merovingi!" and raised Clovis on their shoulders. 65. And so began the uniting of Frankia under House Merovingi. 66. Hail Frankia, hail Europa, long live House Merovingi.

TWENTY-SIX

London, Thurs Jan 24th, 2013

From what I'd recently begun to understand there is a great and secret war which rages behind the veil of what is seen and behind that another one. Lift that veil, another and beneath that another and another and on and on and on. To paraphrase the famous insight, it's not turtles all the way down, it's war. It's war all the way down. This realm is like a giant Matryoshka doll made of secret wars. Not a war between good and evil. That simple axiom is nothing more than the fiber from which the top-most veil is woven. This world would be a lot less complicated if there were simply a single war between a pair of simplistic ideals. By a certain age it becomes apparent to anyone, that even on the surface of things, the warriors of this world all fight with their lives as stakes for their particular virtue, their sense of good. We're just babes when it occurs to us that there is no evil, just a million shades of good. It's just good all the way down.

There has come to be a popular notion that behind what is seen, there is a single, omnipotent, omniscient group of elites, a secret roundtable where the powers behind all of the world's thrones gather to orchestrate all of the world's wars, pestilence, famines, death, mold its morals and ethics. A so-called Illuminati, this secret circle of occulted potentates who control our media, our banks, our educational institutions, our statesmen and our churches, all to keep us pacified, subservient, enslaved. How jejune. If only.

These days people seem to religiously dismiss every world event, every sickness or conflict, every plane crash or market crash, every political intrigue or banker suicide as the work of this Illuminati. The same way the ancient Greeks would blame their Gods for everything, from an outbreak of war to a nominal inconvenience, all the doings of the Gods. The world now attributes this level of power and influence to their loathed Illuminati. Scapegoat for whatever worries you. Raining on the day you'd planned to golf? Curse you, Illuminati! War in Donbas? Damn you, Illuminati!

That lazy, superficial paranoia isn't unfounded as it turns out. The world is ostensibly being directed by secret actors behind the scenes everywhere. That part no one is mistaken about. The part where the public gets it wrong is assuming a single, powerful group at the top is behind everything. There's not. The world is indeed fucked and the reason behind it is not a single secret cabal, but a thousand of them, all clumsily overlapping, rampant with turncoats and moles and saboteurs constantly undermining one another. Things are so out of control that an Illuminati would actually be an enormous improvement. But that's just not in the cards.

What we get instead is that Matryoshka Doll made of secret war inside of secret war inside of secret war. Secret wars where every army is soldiered by double and triple agents who hide conflicting loyalties, constantly subverting one another. It confuses and confounds everything so that even the most common sense public policy can never make its way into accord let alone law. Compound that with the perpetual mobilization of 7 billion useful idiot footsoldiers who click their mouses and raise their protest signs in city centers worldwide, then disappear once the bombs start dropping, only to be replaced by idiots like me who thought the GI Bill sounded like a good head start on life.

In this dynamic the most trivial outbreak becomes a pandemic and every little struggle seems like the end of the world. The average person seems to be living in a reality where they feel their every conflict and every decision has a butterfly effect that might cost them the war in a never-ending apocalypse. No one feels agency, no one feels safe and no one feels happy.

By the time I'd met Sébastien the world had gotten so disorienting that I actually began to envy the terrorists and guerillas I'd see on television in their despotic hellholes. "They seem like they know what they want. Like they think they know what's best and what works. I really wish I did." Until the Prelacy my only outlet for feeling justified was being the adversary of whatever some blowhard in a bar was saying.

By the time I'd gotten to the Fountain of Stars in London I was finally starting to feel like I had some sort of place in it all. Some sort of bearing. Like I'd found my war and my side to fight for. I was ready, or so I thought.

The Fountain of Stars was a modest 6th floor flat in London's Aldgate area. When I arrived that evening the concierge at the desk recognized me, seemed to expect me even. He presented me with a set of keys and a blank envelope and even addressed me as if I'd lived there for years. Mister les Anges this and Master Godefroi that. The whole thing felt so James Bond I could hardly keep my cool.

Upon entering the small flat there I seated myself in its tiny kitchen area and opened the envelope the concierge had handed me. A message coded in the Prelacy's standard cryptography from the Judicious Scrivener:

M. Godefroi,

The Fountain of Stars is behind the Mountains if you face West upon entering the chamber.

Destroy after reading.

Cordially,

Your Judicious Scrivener

Pretty straight forward clues for skullduggery. I left the envelope and message on the dinette and walked back to the apartment door where on the wall to its left hung a painting of the Pyrenees. Behind the painting I found a wall safe and tried the smallest key on the key ring the concierge had provided. One turn and the safe beeped then slowly opened to reveal a small leather valise. Inside of the bag were a black balaclava, 2 pairs of surgical gloves, a pair of black knit gloves, a loaded 9mm Parabellum, a map, an ornately lettered piece of paper and a photo of a man which had a coded message printed on the back:

Shenfield Station, Essex.

Charcoal Blue 2011 Subaru Hatchback

Lot 5, Space E

25 JAN 2013 FRI 5:45am

Destroy photo and writ after reading.

Beneath the photo was the first Prelacy writ I'd ever laid eyes on. A stunning and official looking document, like something a court magistrate in the 1700s might issue. The coded wording on the writ was brief and to the point, clearly outlining the operation.

I was to drive the silver BMW in the underground garage's space 46 to the location referenced on the back of the photo at the exact time stated, assassinate the man pictured who was the same party named on the writ, then calmly drive off, return directly to the Fountain of Stars and park the car in the same space 46 where I'd found it beneath the building. I was then to await contact from the Scrivener at the safe house for further instruction.

My heart leapt into my throat. I'd never killed a man. I was confident I could and figured it was part of the commitment but still I felt I was in over my head. I needed a drink. It was Thursday evening, just 8 hours from the time indicated in the message. I needed to be careful not to panic and drink myself into making a mess of things.

I could do this. I'd fantasized this was where things were likely headed but now that it was happening I felt something. Was that fear? Doubt, I think. I worried I had chosen a path in life that I wasn't suited for. Again. I'd never killed anyone, not even in Afghanistan. My mind was racing. Wasn't 32 a little old to start being an assassin? Shouldn't the Prelacy have gone with a more qualified candidate for this sort of job? I was definitely going to need a drink.

I shuffled toward the narrow kitchen area gazing dumbfounded at the documents from the bag. I set them on the dinette and began to scour the cabinets for liquor. The cabinets were generously stocked with dinnerware, food and I did not have to look long before locating a bottle of Gilbeys, a bottle of Johnny Walker Red and a bottle of Stoli, all of which were unopened. I located a glass in a different cabinet, opened the Johnny Walker and poured myself a double. After speeding through this drink and another I felt myself begin to calm. Once I'd begun to feel a little better adjusted I decided I would wash the long flight off in the shower and walk around the neighborhood in search of a pub to sort out my head and pass the time. Maybe even wind up some of the locals. That notion was quickly banished by fear of my unfamiliar surroundings and a startling commitment to the task ahead. Common sense suggested simply going to bed. Tired as I was from travel I dared not fool myself I could sleep. My brilliant plan was to drink as moderately as I could manage without getting into trouble then heading for my target in the wee hours to wait.

I showered up and poured another drink then labored over matching one of the five identical black shirts I'd packed with one of the five pairs of identical black Levis I'd packed. I'd perhaps over packed. No surprise, that. After five minutes of this needless toil I moved on to selecting the appropriate black socks and boxers and had another whiskey. By the time my shoulder length hair had nearly dried I had found a suitably matching outfit of black denim and cotton/poly blends, identical to the one I'd shed before showering. Identical to you maybe. I was also starting to feel a little warm and chipper from the whiskey. Chatty even. I mumbled an approval of my reflection in the bathroom mirror and began to pat myself down for essentials. Wallet, phone, lighter, keys. All set for leaving.

At 11:11 pm I exited the Prelacy safe house, door locked behind me and figured on killing the next few hours in whatever nearby pub jumped out at me. I exited the lift and gave a nod at the concierge as I walked by.

"Good evening, Mister de les Anges." He bid in his perfect, enviable English accent.

"Alright, you too." I drawled back, hating my own.

"Off for a pint then, innit?"

"What's that?"

"Out for a drink?"

"Oh, yes." I stammered. "Out for drinks."

"Fit birds and that at the one around the corner on Houndsditch then."

"I'm sorry wha-"

"There's a good pub, a good bar just around the corner," he repeated sympathizing with my horrible American comprehension of English English,"on Houndsditch."

"Around the corner?" I asked as he pointed. "Houndsditch?"

"Right. One called the Pig and Anvil."

"Pig and Anvil?"

"Right, if you see Charlie's you went too far. Don't go to Charlie's, mate."

"Don't go to Charlie's."

"Nah, don't go to Charlie's," the concierge advised, "Butters. You don't want it with those geezers in there, mate. Lad spot."

"Lad spot, right." I said. "Go to the Pig and Anvil."

"Right, mate. Those lads at Charlie's are bad men. Keen to hook a yank like you in the gabber for eyein' 'em cross."

"Pig and Anvil it is then." I said. "I'll see you in a few hours then, thanks."

The concierge waved me on and I made my way towards Charlie's.

While I was walking toward Houndsditch I thought how the concierge might be fun to drink with when he's not all Mister this and Master that. He seemed to have eased out of the formal steward routine he'd put on when I checked in. A fact I'm well aware of: I'm really up tight and tend to put people off before I've had a few drinks. Then again I sure do make a sport of putting them off after I've had a few. I have a pretty wide friction point and a narrow point of engage, I decided and left it at that.

Through the icebox raw of London in January, busy lights puddled off of frigid slick asphalt. The rest of my walk was one long cursed thought of how I'd packed nothing warmer than a denim jacket. I pulled my collar up around my neck and shivered and shrugged the rest of three blocks between the Fountain of Stars and Charlie's, conscientious of looking like a wet stray.

The inside of Charlie's was warm and bustling and immediately I wished I'd taken the concierge's advice about going to the Pig and Anvil. A crowd of young toughs were competing with the volume of an unseen jukebox which played some variety of dreadful sounding cockney rap wah-wah music. I found a place to sit at a counter along the glass near the entrance and decided I would order from the cocktail girl. When none arrived after ten minutes I broke down and went to fetch it myself from the bar.

I waited for the bartender longer than I thought was fair but less than I did for a cocktailer so I bit my tongue. After a time I had eye contact and gave a nod. Behind the bar, a spindly little chav in Burberry chic with a cross tattoo under the corner of his right eye slithered over and said something unintelligible. I was suddenly nervous about my order. I really shouldn't have come here.

"Double, Jameson neat."

He wrinkled and squinted, pointing an ear at me.

"Jameson, neat. Double" I said a little louder.

"Seen, seen you don't have to shout, mate."

Well, that went better than expected. Ordered my first London drink and haven't been kicked out yet. I went about pretending to look at my mobile while the bartender poured. Head pointed down I appraised the crowd through my peripheral vision. It occurred to me that if I were going to be prowling around Europe for the Prelacy I would need to work at blending in better. I looked like a yankee turd in the Queen's punchbowl. All Chuck Taylors and black denim and drawling accent. The rest of the place was all trainers and track jackets and buzzcuts.

"It's 8 quid, lad." The bartender said setting down my whiskey.

I handed him a £10 note, nodded and walked off immediately fretting because I'd customarily tipped him without a thought. I just wasn't traveled enough to know whether or not it was an insult or something. I walked back to the seat I'd found and set to drinking alone, watching London walk by on the other side of the window.

I have a habit of speeding through drinks when I'm nervous and I'm almost always nervous so it could be said that I simply have a habit of speeding through drinks. I tried to moderate the impulse and nursed my whiskey the best I could, occasionally turning to look about the bar. As is the case with alcohol and public settings, the throng of strangers began to look less and less intimidating as I drank. No chance of me initiating conversation with anyone, however. That's never me. I amused myself by taking inventory of the bovver boys at the bar laughing with their "cheeky cunt" this and their "safe, mate" that.

The most boisterous among them was a thin man, perhaps a good five years older than the rest, maybe more. He had a characteristic snapping of his fingers in a shaking motion to emphasize his boasts and insights, a pantomime that resembled the way an American packs his smokes before opening them. From what I could make out he was animating a retelling of his run in with the law earlier. He wore a black military jacket with a stylized design. Something expensive and fashionable, nothing from serving the Crown. Close cropped hair combed forward toward his scarred mug which was at least one tooth shy of a full set. Distressed designer denim lead down to one inch cuffs above a pair of blue and grey Nike Air-max 95s.

The one he was telling his story to couldn't have been much more than 20 years old. His cool, half-interest in the older scarface's boasts belied the confidence he held in his place among these older men. Muscled, anglo-indian in complexion and Bic-bald. The young tough intermittently drank from his pint between approving laughs and go-on-thens. He observed the same uniform of his crew, and I made note of a style I was keen to adopt in the interest of blending in better on future assignments. I imagined myself in the band-collared military style jacket, designer denim and trainers he wore. I decided I could pull that off a lot more comfortably than a bunch of tweeds and button downs. He'd made note of me sitting alone and occasionally peering over, which meant I'd have to stop snooping if I meant not to offend. Normally, I meant to offend but the fish-out-of-water feel of being an American abroad can tame even the most feral of line-stepping barflies.

This crew whose actual count I hadn't taken seemed to array outward from the one I presumed to be their leader, if they in fact had one. A late 20s to early 30s aged black man, light skinned, fade haircut in a West Ham football jersey who sat quietly in their midst sipping his pint and looking at his mobile. Every so often one of them would pander for his attention which he would oblige, acknowledge with a laugh or a nod and return to his texting or reading.

I returned my attention to the window and my drink in good caution. I also thought to pass some time poking around on my own mobile. Not one for engaging social media much beyond causing trouble, I still had accounts on the common platforms for entertaining myself. Facebook, Instagram, Twitter and all that. The output of celebrities, news sources and every other variety of attention-whore boosting their signals online would be a levelheaded alternative to pissing off strangers in bars tonight. Cute kitten videos and pictures of people's lunches: the pinnacles of Western achievement, the prime motivators of our culture.

"Oi bruv, haven't seen you about, what say you come over and have a round with the geezers then, yeah?"

I turned to find the scarfaced oldest of the regulars standing closer than I liked. If I decline I figured on offending him which wouldn't bode well. I looked back toward the bar to find it unusually quiet and all eyes on our exchange. Awkward.

"Sure, why not?" I said as unflappable as I could.

"Wicked, blud, c'mon then. Long tings you over here twiggin' us like a mug, innit?

I had no fucking idea what he was saying. I just followed him back to the bar and steeled myself. I was alone and far from home and they were a half-dozen if not the entire bar.

"What's your name then, guv?" he asked.

"Foster, what's yours?"

"Name's Lionel but the lads call me Pilly."

"Pilly?"

"Yeah, y'now like pillock. A pest."

"Cool, what's up, Pilly?" I greeted.

Pilly and I joined his crew around the bar where he went about making introductions.

"Oi, you tossers, listen up! This here's Foster, he's gonna have a round with the fam.", Pilly announced. "Foster, that's Monk" he said pointing at the tawny young one he was talking with earlier, and proceeded down the row, " that's Pete, Griggy, Fiver, Dunk, Aaron and that screenager down the end ignorin' us all is Grime." The last one he introduced being the one I supposed for their main man.

Each of them gave a nod as they were called off while the one called Grime just raised a hand and kept looking at his phone. I gave an awkward half wave and stood there like an idiot through an uncomfortable silence.

"Well, c'mon then lad, go and fetch us around, innit?" Pilly said breaking the tension.

I was being wound up myself for once it appeared. Every dog has his day, I guess. I might be in a pickle if I hadn't brought plenty of the Queen's cash with me. Good thing for me I made the currency exchange before leaving the airport.

I made my way to the bar and had no problem getting the attention of our bartender this time.

"Can I get a round for the crew over here?" I asked, motioning toward them.

"Sure thing, guv." The bartender said, "And you're Jameson neat, doubles, right?"

I nodded. He served me as I stood there, then proceeded down the bar serving the gang before returning to collect.

"It's £36"

I gave him two £20 notes and he brought my change.

"Is it rude to tip?" I asked, remembering my shameful walk from the bar last time.

The bartender squinted and shrugged.

"It's not really the thing to do here, mate. If you want to buy me a round as well, I suppose I wouldn't argue with that."

I offered him a round and he collected another £8 from me for his double Jameson.

I rejoined the crew of young toughs to nods and broken-fenced grins all around.

"Here he is!", Pilly exclaimed lifting his pint. "Top-flite, lad. Cheers."

"Cheers." I said lifting my glass.

I stood among them a bit nervous, trying to think of something to say. Truth, I'm not good in crowds. Social settings in general have never been my native environs. Add to that I couldn't figure out if these toughs were being naturally hospitable or setting me up to be kicked around like a soccer ball. Or football, as it were.

"So where you from, Foster?" the young one, Monk asked. "L.A.? did I guess right?"

"Nailed it."

"I could tell. You yanks stumble in here from time to time."

"How could you tell me from a New Yorker or a Texan though?"

"I don't know about Texans but New Yorkers we get alot. They all look like tossers and think they're the only good Yanks, as if there were are any."

I wasn't touching that one. I just laughed.

"And Californians?" I asked.

"You lot always sport those brass fucking kicks," He laughed nodding down at my shoes. "Those old-timey fuckin' kicks, ridiculous but you all have them."

Chuck Taylors. He was right.

"Yeah, I guess we do."

"You also can't shut up about California and that." He said. "You're not going to start in are you?"

"I really don't feel like getting my ass kicked tonight." I assured him.

"Top banter." Monk laughed raising his glass. "Cheers, mate."

I raised my drink in relief. I was doing good. So far I hadn't mouthed off and no one seemed to be in a rush to punch me in the face.

"What brings you to London?" Pilly now turned to ask.

Shit. I hadn't thought about that. I didn't have an answer and I don't think Pilly and his friends were the sort to let bullshit slide. I had to think of something. Matter of fact, I was going to have to get good at fielding questions like this if I were going to be worth a damn at being a globetrotting assassin. That whole thing suddenly seemed a world away now though. Assassin? Really? How was I going to be this cloak and dagger badass if I couldn't even blend in wherever the assignment took me? More and more this day I felt I was in over my head while everything up until this assignment had felt so easy and natural.

"Work." I said.

"What work?" Pilly wouldn't leave it.

"I'm an assassin." The alcohol said. In my state I figured the truth was so unbelievable I might as well roll with it.

"Havin' a giggle, then?", Pilly pried. "C'mon, mate don't wind us up. What do you do?"

"I'm just here-", I answered. I couldn't imagine there being a right answer. Any American with enough money to be here for business or leisure was probably the enemy of whatever outlook these guys held. "to kill some banker." What the fuck was I thinking?

"Alright, I'll leave it alone then if you don't want to talk about it."

That went better than expected. Except for the part where the news tomorrow evening is all about some banker murdered at the Essex train station. If I could trust one thing it's that these guys weren't in a hurry to go talking to cops. I'd just vanish into legend and these guys would spend the rest of their lives talking about the night they drank with a mysterious yank assassin named Foster. Assuming they would even remember my name. Sloppy tradecraft, but I wasn't going to fret over it. I'd have to get better at these things in the future though. I promised myself I'd never go out on another assignment without a good cover story if I made it through this one. Meanwhile, I'm in the most under surveillance city on earth telling the truth like a lie. I couldn't resist the fruitless scan of the pub for cameras I was making which brought a brief sense of relief.

As I was finishing up my drink and returning focus to the current threat, I wanted to think of a polite excuse to get out of there. I don't know why I thought I'd come here after being warned. Well, I know why. It's because I'm a psychopath and I'm always looking for an avenue to walk that out on. This, however was not the time or place to be stretching those legs. I thought to take my last sip of whiskey and head back to the flat.I was draining the last of it as I watched the one they called Grime motion for Pilly. Pilly leaned in to hear him whisper something as I headed back toward the bar.

"Oi, be a dove an fetch us another round, yeah Foster?" came the clarifying words from Pilly.

Another round? So that's the game. They meant to shake me down for drinks all night and who knew what else. I was in for it. They wore it on all of their faces as I looked back.

"Not gonna happen, Pilly." I replied, "I've gotta be getting back to the-"

"You what?" he interrupted, stepping in closer.

" I'm done for the night. You guys have yourselves a-"

"Nah, mate. It ain't going down like that." He interrupted again. "Gwan and fetch us another round."

So I cracked him in the face with my short glass, shoved him into his crowd of friends and broke for the door. Hurled pint glasses bounced around me as the rumble of heavy feet on the wood floor spurred me on. I burst past the threshold and ran down the street to the sound of yells as a few more pint glasses shattered on the ground around me. I wasn't pursued but I didn't stop to look back either.

That escalated quickly, I thought to myself as I rounded one corner and another before slowing down to catch my breath and check the time. It was only just a quarter past twelve. I still had a few hours before I'd get in the car and head toward the Essex train station to do the dirty deed.

I headed back to the safe house, nervously watching the shop glass to my right shoulder for any of the lads from Charlie's lurking about. Paranoia. They were well into their next round by now, laughing about the yank they'd wound up. When I got back to the safe house the concierge was wearing a little smirk.

"That didn't take long." He commented. "Found it alright?"

"Pig n' Anvil. Great suggestion." I should have taken it.

I made my way to the elevator, or lift in the local parlance and enjoyed a moment of peace. In that moment I began to finally shut down. The long flight and the night's events had taken their toll in addition to the copious amounts of whiskey. I felt as though I could sleep for a full day. Shit timing.

I exited the lift, walked a few doors down and entered the safe house right for the sofa. There I fell asleep where I'd only intended to collect myself and prepare for my early morning errand.

At 4:16 my ringing Monolith had been going off for a full six minutes before it woke me. I looked to see a private number and took it to be a Prelacy contact of some sort. When I answered there was no one on the line. I pulled myself together in a rush, thankful for the wakeup call. I went to the bathroom, ran warm water and splashed my face. When I returned a text had come in from the Judicious Scrivener.

J.S. – A polite reminder. No response necessary. Enjoy your day.

A shiver coursed through me as I wondered what trouble I'd be in if I'd slept through my task. I gathered my pistol, mask, gloves, map and keys and thanked the Scrivener aloud for that merciful reminder. I went to the dinette and checked the data on the photo and writ one last time to review the details then cursed myself for not destroying the documents as instructed. That would just have to wait until I'd returned. Closing the door behind me I headed for the garage in a nervous rush I could only compare to the first day starting a new job.

Naturally, I opened the wrong door on the gray BMW and cursed myself some more. Once I'd rounded the vehicle and situated myself in the driver's seat I exited the garage nearly turning the wrong way into oncoming traffic. After that I had no problems to speak of navigating the busy London congestion. Eventually I found my way onto the A12 expressway where I finally relaxed and focused on the business at hand. Over the hour long drive I imagined the events to come over and over, the way an Olympic swimmer imagines their seemingly routine strokes in such detail. Truth, I had no idea what to expect, I just needed something to chew on for the drive and my restless mind obliged.

I pulled into Shenfield station parking at 5:37 and located lot 5, space E straight away. Utterly nerve-wracked and unsure of what to do I simply pulled forward a car length and idled for nearly ten minutes, terrified I'd be approached by someone, which never happened.

At 5:45 as outlined in my assignment documents a blue Subaru hatchback pulled into the spot and I watched as a middle-aged Londoner in business casual exited the car. I fought the nearly uncontrollable urge to speed off. Was this fear? If so, it was thrilling and I quite liked it. I watched him so routinely retrieve his briefcase from the back seat. I breathed in deep once followed by numerous fast and shallow breaths as I chambered my weapon and walked over. This was it. Now or never.

I left the car idling and the door open, pulling the balaclava down over my face as I walked toward my mark and leveled the pistol at him. A simple, classic 9mm Parabellum with the wood grain grip and 9 round mag. I was to empty the entire mag into him. As I closed the distance to about 10 feet he looked up at me, right in the eyes and I hesitated. Stopped dead in my tracks, a single second felt like an eternity. In that time I read in him, first surprise, then fear and finally resignation. My heart beat three times in that second. I didn't want to do this. No, not want, couldn't. I couldn't kill this man. I began to lose my nerve and I swear that renewed his fear, even intensified it. All of this in just a single moment. As I found I could no longer hold the weapon sighted for his body I panicked and fired off a single round toward his feet before running back to the car and speeding off. Had I killed him? Had I even hit him? I couldn't know because I had somehow engaged my flight response. OK, now this was definitely fear. I recognized this feeling.

On my self-loathing, baleful drive back to the Fountain of Stars my mind would not rest. I had failed myself, proven myself a fraud and possibly even earned my own dismissal from the Prelacy. I wanted to just keep driving, but where? What if I returned to the safe house and found a Prelacy assassin waiting for me? Would I even make it back home? Might I just die here in London? No doubt the law would be looking for a grey BMW. I was confused and in light of that, I suspect my mind did it's best to remedy confusion with the power of coping. Calm washed over me as I deceived myself I'd sufficiently executed my task and that I had best stick to my orders by returning to the safe house.

After an hour of driving back toward London I arrived in the garage. I parked the caper car where I'd found it and returned to the safe house, all per plan. When I opened the door there at the dinette table sat Monsieur Herman de Boheme, my superior in le Chemin de l'Epee. He had in his hand my undisposed of assignment documents and a poker face that brought chills.

Monsieur Herman stood and approached me, documents in hand and I stiffened a bit when he put his arm around me,

"We're going to need to work on your attention to detail, Monsieur Godefroi." He calmly said, crumpling the documents. "Relax. I botched my first job much worse. You're going to make a fine Main Rouge."

Main Rouge? Was I already meant to be promoted to the rank of Red Hand if I had pulled this off? I went from panic to relief to excitement then disappointment all in one moment.

On the TV, SKY One news was abuzz with the details of my half-assed assassination attempt. "Man in balaclava shoots banker in leg and escapes into morning traffic". Relieved, I just wanted to pass out and wake up to a totally different world; one where I wasn't a psychotic, delusional fuck up. Instead I sat with Monsieur Herman and silently derided myself, imagining Pilly, that chav tough from the bar last night, somewhere having a laugh at my amateurish wet work.

TWENTY-SEVEN

West Seattle, WA - Mon Oct 13th 2014

     With our faceoff at the Maharajah in West Seattle behind us, Arlene and I have begun to find we share little in common besides time to kill. We somewhat resentfully relent to staying close while I await the next writ from the Scrivener. In the back of our minds is a well-placed fear of the Prelacy Guard, our order's police apparatus. We share a confidence that the order is unaware of the Covenant's actions, though we are on edge and prepared for anything. Well, I may have my doubts but Arlene is reassuringly certain that the Prelacy is mostly unaware of Covenant operations and I'm inclined to follow her lead. From what I've seen she and the Covenant are much better informed than I am. This is their affair and despite my key role, I'm woefully under informed on vital details, so I have no choice but to defer.

     It's only been a day and I've yet seen any contact from Sébastien. It is routine for him to check with me after my writs have been prosecuted, often in person. Otherwise things appear to be business as usual. Since the meeting we've taken up lodging in a Covenant safe house on Alki in West Seattle. I find going to ground a bit nerve wracking, as I've taken to vacillating between gusts of delusional confidence and creeping panic. Together Arlene and I do our best to affect routine and get along, despite the numerous threats looming over our tense accord. Tonight we confer over wine and try our hands at small talk which as it turns out, doesn't stay small for very long. I've convinced her to allow a visit to one of the local bars after we've eaten, though we're supposed to be lying low. One of West Seattle's salty maritime dives wouldn't be any place we'd run into the Prelacy Guard, I guess. I don't give it much thought, my mind's made up and she seems okay with it. For dinner, I volunteer to make us my own proud facsimile of Phở and Arlene keeps me company while I dice the vegetables.

"Godefroi, there's something I have to tell you."

"If this is going to be how it is, can you please not call me Godefroi?"

"No. I don't care about that." She halts. "Don't ask me that again."

It stings a little but I get it. We're not long lost pals or anything. It's not like I'm used to hearing my given name very often anyway. Never Foster, always Godefroi. I'll have to mind myself a little better. Cooking a meal for someone, staying under the same roof as them, it begs a level of familiarity. I feel a little shame for seeming so simple and strive not to show it. Probably I'm just wishing to manufacture romantic inroads but I'm too proud to admit to myself something so pedestrian, so patently male and dim.

"That's fair, no of course you're right." I say.

"Listen, you need to hear this."

She's standing there in a form fitting crew neck and denim, all black. Why do we wear all black? I know we must wear the shoulder length hair in defiance of Roman custom and out of respect for the ancient Kings of Europa but with the exceptions of Sébastien in his white and Chilperic in his blue every Prelate I'd ever met wore all black. It's a curiosity that I'd worn long hair and all black for most of my life. Is that a commonality all Prelates share? I wander my mind back to her form fitting all black outfit and care a little less about knowing why Prelates favor black. I'm more focused on her and to a lesser extent, whatever it is that she's about to reveal.

"I know your secret." She says hesitant.

For a man who is full of secrets, there's little more an exciting thing a stunning woman in black can say. If she doesn't bring up the ghost of Al Davis I'm mostly certain this is the beginning of a conversation I might find exciting. I try to play it cool, like I know what that is at all.

"Oh, yeah? What's that?" I ask and dice vegetables.

"I know you've never killed anyone."

Jesus fucking Christ, can't I catch a break? I stop chopping and take a breath. I want to run, to just disappear. Is this fear? Yes. Yes, it is. Perhaps my worst fear. My fear of being found out. Fear of being seen for the phony I am: The professional assassin who has killed no one; the pitiful emulation of an assassin who is not an assassin at all. This was not the "I know your secret" I was hoping for, nor expecting.

"OK," I stammer. I put down the knife so I can steady myself on the stove, "you have to tell me everything. I can't keep doing this."

"You don't think I'd be here with you alone if I thought you were actually dangerous, do you?"

"Can you not?" I flail. "Just tell me what you know."

"I know that you botched your first job and blew off the next one," she explains, "and after not prosecuting that one you realized that someone was taking up the slack for you. I know that in spite of blowing off every job since London you accepted your promotion to Red Hand after your second mortal writ in Donbas turned up successfully prosecuted"

I grab a chair from the dinette in the little kitchenette and sit down.

"And it's been like that every step of the way since." I admit for the first time ever, head in hands.

"You've never asked yourself who it was executing all of those bankers that you wouldn't?"

"Of course I did!"

"And?"

"And what?"

"Well who do you suppose has been doing it, Godefroi?"

"I don't know!"

I sit for a moment with her standing over me. This is a horror I wouldn't wish upon anyone. To be the phony scrambling to acquit himself; a minor hell I imagine most of us go our entire lives without playing out in the real, at least at these stakes.

She takes a seat across the table from me and I feel even more shame in our shaky congress. In my head I think I'd imagined this as an evening of me glibly unfurling my contrary, impossible charm, instead here I am grasping at any sense of humanity, like a drowning animal clawing for purchase, dry ground out of reach. No feeling quite like being caught in a big lie.

"Well your ascension through the lodges is obviously important to someone other than yourself."

"Yeah, well who?" I ask.

"For someone who acts like he has it all figured out you'd think you might know."

"Fuck you."

"I wouldn't worry about it" she toys, taking a sip of Cabernet. "It's probably just Sébastien's doing."

"Fuck off." I pout as if a ridiculed child.

She quietly sits swirling the wine in her glass, challenging my fragile, diminishing peace with her smug look of knowing. Knowing what I was comfortably certain no one knew. No one but me and whoever had been prosecuting my writs for me, anyway. It occurs to me that even she may have been shadowing me, prosecuting my writs, killing those bankers I couldn't bring myself to kill. And so I wonder, just who is this woman I sit across the table from? Once again I feel I'm in over my head with the Prelacy. I sit and wish I were normal. Why couldn't I just be normal? How does someone get this far gone? Over and over, these words in my head.

TWENTY-EIGHT

Los Angeles, CA – Thurs April 3rd, 2014

J.S. – Art thou the Folded Hands?

Me – Nay, 'tis I, the Red Hand.

J.S. – Whither go ye, Red Hand?

Me – Where so ever faith shall guide.

J.S. – Hast thou faith given you a sign?

Me - Indeed.

J.S. – Very well, what is the sign?

Me – It is the Cup.

J.S. – Very well, fill thy cup at the Fountain of Bambi.

Such were my orders from the Scrivener little more than a year past the day of my fiasco in London. I checked my guide which revealed that the Fountain of Bambi was in Hamburg, Germany (not Disneyland, which wouldn't have surprised me if it were.) Routinely I over-packed, only now a bit more experienced. Gone were my black denim and Chuck Taylors, replaced by inconspicuous trainers and a black military style jacket with a banded collar, much like what I'd seen many European men wearing on my trips; all for looking less American in less American places.

As I sat in my apartment laboring to reach my target blood-alcohol level in preparation for the intercontinental flight ahead, Al dropped in to visit. This was not unusual. He seemed to pop up at these moments, though unlike real friends, Al sometimes dropped by just to visit and say hi. I had grown used to it by now, sick as it feels to admit. Besides Al and Sébastien no one really ever looked in on me. I was otherwise long between normal friendships at this place in my life, and by my own careful design.

"Hamburg, huh? You excited, kid?"

"C'mon, Al. It's whatever."

"The Rhineland! Lotsa cool Nazi shit over there, I figured you'd be pumped!"

"There's no good Nazi shit in Germany, Al." I waved him off as I tried to drink. "It's illegal there, besides I don't care about all that. Stop making me feel weird about my collections."

"What's with all the negativity, champ?"

"Have you even been to Hamburg?"

"Of course I have. Have you?"

"No, Al. This will be my first trip to Hamburg."

"Oh, it's great there, you're gonna love it, kid!"

"Let me guess, you had to go back in the '90s for some NFL Europe game or something, right?"

"NFL Europe?" Al laughed, "Hell no. Me and Hef took down some Stasi rogues trying to infiltrate their porn industry back in '72." He seemed to boast, "Why would I watch gridiron in Germany when I can watch it in Oaktown, baby?"

I let it slide. Al is full of bluster like this and I try not to encourage it, but I do enjoy it somehow.

"What's so great about Hamburg?" I asked.

"Beer, for one."

"I don't care for beer, Al. You know that."

"What about German people! You love German shit!"

"Al, if German people excite me at all it's probably because I seldom see any."

"You seldom see anyone, kid."

"Touché."

"By my count, only people you see besides your Prelacy weirdos is me." Al jabbed, "Correct me if I'm wrong but that's almost nobody."

"I'm know plenty of people."

"Like who? Name three"

"Tucan, Guitar Tommy, Chivo."

"From the Copper Pot" Al scoffed.

"Bucket, it's Copper Bucket, Al."

"I thought you were 86ed from that place."

"No thanks to you." I parry, "I'm just saying, that's three people."

"Sounds lonely."

"It is lonely

"Kid, you'd be lonely in a crowd. You'd be lonely at your own birthday party. You're only lonely because you can't stand people."

"Which is why there's nothing exciting for me about going to Germany."

"So you're really not excited about Germany then?"

"Hamburg will probably exhaust me the same way the Slauson Swap Meet exhausts me. They're both really fun at first, I'm sure but it's not long before you're just tired of feeling like an invader and you're ready to go."

"Kid, you need to get over all this anti-social bullshit. Be free, baby."

"Just be an easy going hippy who loves everyone, right Al? That's your generation. I envy it but that's not how the world is now. Everyone hates everyone else, that's just how it is."

"You exhaust me like Hamburg and Slauson never will so, good luck anywhere."

"Yeah, I get a lot of that."

Al set to poring over a curio full of Samurai artifacts I had in a corner of my living room while I continued overthinking my travel preparations and dwelled on how solitary and misanthropic I felt now.

"Kid, tell me something."

"What now?"

"You got all these historical artifacts from everywhere you been in the world, right?"

"Yeah, and?"

"But you spent a year hunkered down in Afghanistan and I don't see anything from over there."

"Everything I brought back from there is in my head."

It just sort of washed over Al like a melodramatic response does anyone, I guess. I could feel him rolling his eyes if I couldn't actually see him doing it. Al just gave it bye and moved on to whatever might next command his attention, in this case one of my katana in its cradle.

"Hatori Hanzo?" he asked taking big sweeps with a very rare katana I wished he wouldn't handle.

""Hatori Hanzo? Really?"

"What? I watch the chop-socky flicks. I know this stuff"

"Chop-socky flicks?" I laugh. "Al, you watched one Tarantino movie and now you think you know a Wakazashi from a Stiletto."

"What's your point?"

"It's a Hatori Masanari, Al. Please put it down."

"Hanzo, Mansari. Two field goals, a touchdown." He grumbled, resetting the blade back in its cradle, facing the wrong way, of course.

"Just win, baby" I replied disinterested as I vainly labored to match identical black socks and situate them next to neatly rolled matching black cotton t-shirts.

"Just win, baby." He cooed as he surveyed the Stephen K. Hayes titles on my bookshelf.

"Don't handle the blades without bowing to them first" I said as I walked over and righted the Masanari blade in its cradle. Al just waved me off.

"Why you always wear all black, kid?"

"Why do you?"

"I don't always wear black, that's just my team." He protested, "My best outfit is this silver sharkskin Italian number. Electric blue shirt, black skinny tie. Style, baby."

He said this with a proud wave of his hand across his whole get up. He really was looking sharp in that thing, no denying. 60s Al was usually how he presented himself to me but not always. 60s Al was best Al, Crypt Keeper Al gave me the screaming heebie-jeebies. Thankfully he seldom appeared to me in that incarnation.

"I wear all black because segregating your laundry is racist and I'm like you, Al. I don't see race. I love everyone."

"You mean you hate everyone." Al said. "Why do you always gotta take the clever way out, kid? Why can't you just be real?"

"I don't know, Al." I relented, flustered. He was getting on my nerves good.

"You depressed?"

"I don't know. Maybe."

"You're probably richer than I am. Why you so depressed?"

"Really? I'm richer than you?" I laughed. "How's that?"

"I doubt it but that's a lot of Merovingian gold you've been sittiing on."

"C'mon, you really think it's worth that much?"

"You never added it all up, never even estimated?"

"Nah, I never thought to."

"Kid, you're lost. I don't mean to judge but you're pretty bad."

"What, you really think all that gold is worth a lot?"

"Are you kidding me? Kid, you're probably a multi-millionaire and you didn't even earn any of it!"

"Whoah! Really? You don't want to judge?" I cringed, pausing to find Al bowing to my Massamune tanto as he correctly set it back in its cradle. Al. God damned Al. I wanted to yell but wound up stifling a laugh.

"C'mon, man. You get paid to kill these squares and you don't even kill them! You just pick up the gold for it, meanwhile, for some creepy reason your marks always wind up dead anyway?" Al pressed, "That doesn't freak you out?"

"I don't want to talk about this shit, Al. You should probably go."

"You wish."

"Al, I need to get my head straight for this mission. Stop fucking with me." And just like that I'd had enough Al again for a long time.

"Mission? What mission? You need to get your head straight to get on a plane wasted and pick up some gold for killing someone you and I both know you're never going to lay a hand on?"

"Fuck you!" I yelled as I launched the TV remote at the place he was just standing.

I'd need to fetch another TV remote and clean that one up. Nothing new there. That was the umteenth one I'd broken on a wall throwing it at Al. At least he was gone for now.

I went and retrieved a new TV remote from my A/V closet where I'd taken to storing a supply of back-ups for just such events. Yes, I had already programmed them all. I have no friends and a meticulous attention to detail as I believe I've made pretty plain. I walked back, sat down and set the new remote on the glass coffee table then returned to calmly matching my socks. I rolled them neatly and arranged them in my suitcase alongside the t-shirts then headed to the kitchen for another whiskey. Al was standing there appraising his nails as if he'd just come from a manicure.

Temper redlining, I grabbed the bottle of Jameson from on top of the fridge and tried to pretend he wasn't there. As I poured, I steeled myself for his first words which never came. I took my drink and headed back for the sofa where of course, there was Al sitting, legs crossed and fidgeting with a tanto.

After a while it was apparent I was supposed to say something so I said nothing and looked for other tasks to focus on. I read about Hamburg on my mobile while Al finally stood again and went to picking over my curio displays of WWII model tanks.

"Panzer division. Lotta people say the tanks-"

"Shut up, Al. Just shut the fuck up." I cut him off hissing through clenched jaw as I clicked through a picture set of the Reeperbahn, Hamburg's red light district.

"What the fuck is eating you, kid?"

I ignored him and continued to pretend giving a shit about pictures of peep shows and triple-x kinos.

"You need to get it off your chest to someone." Al urged. "You're in a snafu and you know it. I might be the only friend you can-"

"You're a fucking ghost! A hallucination or some by-product of my insanity!"

"I'm as real as a bullet in your head, kid." Al interrupted. "Maybe not as real as a bullet in someone else's but I'm right here, right now, you can't get rid of me and if that ain't real then neither is Marcus Allen."

"Marcus Allen is real. You're dead."

"You wanna argue semantics with a guy who isn't real?

"Fuck you."

I looked for something to break by throwing it at Al. Something I could replace. Not another remote.

"Kid, you only ever bring up the crazy when you don't like what I'm saying."

It's true. By now I'd watched a few hundred hours of TV with, smoked a few hundred joints in front of and had a few hundred drinks around this imaginary friend of mine. The only time I tended to get testy was when we were talking about rubber-on-the-road pragmatics. About my completely insane life.

"I have to be on a plane for Hamburg in six hours, Al. I don't want to start rethinking my life right now."

"Who says you have to rethink your life? I just want to talk about what you're doing with it."

"What the fuck? That's not semantics?"

"No! It's logistics!"

Again, I looked for something to break by throwing it at Al. Something I could replace. By my count there were 10 more TV remotes in my A/V closet and the fresh one on the table begged throwing now.

"Throw the ashtray."

"I'm not throwing the ashtray!" I protest, "I got this in Monaco!"

"Fine, throw the whiskey tumbler."

"Fuck you, Al."

I looked at the tumbler then grabbed a half-smoked joint of Hindu Kush from the ashtray and lit it while Al went back to putting his fingers all over my 1/72 scale Hasegawa replica WWII Zeroes. As the designer weed worked its magic I began to relax and anticipate whatever it was Al was so anxious to talk about.

"There ya go, you hippy sucker-head. Smoke up that grass and calm the fuck down, for Christ's sake."

I just ignored my imaginary friend and returned to looking at pictures of Hamburg on my mobile. I tried to collect myself and think of what I'd like to see while I was there. In the awkward silence I planned out a trip to see the statue of Arminius at Teutoburg a few hours south, knowing I'd never go through with it. My Prelacy excursions were usually full of unfulfilled plans like this. I'd get excited, plot something recreational, then just get dejected about it all after fanning on a kill, collect my gold, take it to one of my stashes and come home.

"So that's how it's gonna be, kid?" Al pushed, "You just gonna act like I'm not here?"

"But you're not here."

"For anyone else, as far as you know."

"What do you want, Al?"

"I want you to face yourself, kid." He stood tall. "Something ain't right."

"What's not right?"

"You tell me?" he said walking to face me over the coffee table. "You have caches of hidden gold you didn't earn, people are dropping dead and you think it's just whatever?"

I could neurotically agonize over matching identical black socks when packing for a trip but I didn't always bear out that same meticulous analysis for everything else. Some things were just too big and beyond my control so I buried them. I was all too accustomed to tucking these things far from concern. Things like having an imaginary friend or being a pretend assassin. To have a hallucination or apparition bringing some of it to the surface just felt crazy. I was sorting through feeling crazy and facing the lies I'd been telling myself all at once. Justifying my stupid ways was the sort of shit that made me hate having friends. Especially the kind you couldn't just hit with a toaster or a TV remote or an ashtray and chase off.

"It is all just whatever!" I yelled, hoping the neighbors didn't hear- well fuck the neighbors at this point."This shit is all just whatever!"

"That's you?" Al said looking at me with a sort of disappointment I wasn't used to seeing. Why did I care what this figment of my imagination-this ghost-thought of me? "Just, whatever." He mocked.

"Well what would you do?" I flared.

"This isn't about me, kid."

"Well then why the fuck are you here?"

"I've told you before! It seems like you need a friend and you've got all this cool shit I like to check out."

"Fuck you, Al."

As I did so often I went back to ignoring him and Al went off toward my office room down the hall. I still had a good 4 hours until I had to be at LAX. I occupied myself with details like reserving the black car for my ride to the airport and drinking more. Al occupied himself with trying to play 'Smoke on the Water' on a Les Paul signed by Jeff Hanneman which I kept hung on the wall of my office. He really wasn't going to leave it seemed so I went about the business of killing time while he played some pretty decent power chords. I steeled myself for a good enough talk to get him to leave me alone as I went about my travel details.

The last thing I wanted was Al sitting next to me all the way to Germany, chiding me about how I was letting my life unfold all askew, how I needed to take control. I'm a control freak, but like most control freaks I had no idea how to control my way to success or happiness. Whatever Al wanted to talk about, I'd have to fake it through because I couldn't seem to figure out how to make the ring master of pro football's biggest circus leave me to directing the big top and three rings my own life had become.

TWENTY-NINE

West Seattle, WA - Mon Oct 13th 2014

We're sitting in a local merchant marine dive called the Rusty Anchor. I'm trying to convince myself I could kill her if it was a matter of life and death for me.

"Whoever's finishing these writs you wouldn't, it's not me." Arlene assures. "I know you won't trust that but it's true."

I'm feeling too far removed from control, too undermined and uninformed to trust anything. Trust is my only option at this point but it's far from easy to muster. That's the rub with trust though. It requires an absence of certainty to mean anything. And here I'd been doing so good in the absence of certainty, so long as it was elective anyway. Times like this I swear there has to be a god because there's no way chaos has such a cruel sense of irony. Trust is great and all but I think I'd rather take another stab at feeling in control.

I could end this all by killing her and contacting Sébastien, right? If I were to do that right now, would I be any better off? If I wind this out longer will I be more informed, on more stable ground? I want to know more and it seems the only way to do that is to stay this foggy course. In the back of my mind is something I can't yet consider fully. There is the fearful hint of my having become enchanted. I can't yet bear to consciously toss around the idea that I might be making these high stakes decisions informed by a misguided curiosity, informed by my interest in this woman, Arlene. If I admit to myself I'm bewitched, I'll have to parse that eventually, but not now. For now I suppress an ugly potential I wish I were above.

"Have you ever killed anyone?" I ask.

"That's not important, Godefroi. I'm telling you that I haven't been shadowing you and taking up your slack. That is what's important for you to know."

"Yeah, but as a matter of trust I just want to know if you've ever-"

"No, I'm not a killer." She interrupts then gulps her wine with a look of impatience. "I'm just a good liar."

"Thank you. I believe you."

We share a laugh at that little twist, an uncomfortable laugh that goes miles towards lightening our mutual tension, if not complicating our situation just as much.

"It doesn't mean anything." Arlene says. "Don't think I wouldn't do whatever it takes to advance the Covenant's plans."

"So, you'd kill me if Canan ordered it?"

There's another uncomfortable silence as we both seem to wish I hadn't brooked this line of dialog. We could use a change toward less heavy topics but covering these things is inevitable.

"Are you forgetting that we came to you with intel that could spare your life? Sébastien's been using you and he means to kill you."

"I'm just asking."

"There is no scenario imaginable where the Covenant would benefit from your death right now." She says. "I don't know why I said what I did, I'm sorry. I got a little dark."

"You just like being in control." I try to tease.

She smirks and takes a drink.

"Do you really think there's ever a situation where I'm not in control?" She parries, confident and menacingly feminine.

"So you're a not a control freak, you're a control regular." I volley back, a little too self-satisfied at keeping up with her.

She smirks again.

"Touché, Monsieur Godefroi."

It's evident we're both respectfully laboring through the necessary questions, trying to keep the mood as light as possible. Any reprieve from all the gravity seems welcome between us.

"You know, you accused me of the same thing at the house earlier." I say.

"What? Of being a control freak?" she asks. "When did I say that?"

"Well, you said I think I've got it all figured out."

"That's not the same thing," She chides, "You need to relax and stop over thinking everything."

"That I'll give you but I want you to know, I don't feel like I have anything figured out." It sounds so melodramatic in my ears. I'm immediately ashamed I said anything. "The only thing I'm certain of is everyone has it wrong."

"So everyone else is wrong?" She ribs.

"No, all of us are wrong. Nobody has a damned thing figured out." I say. "But people have always told me I think I have it all figured out."

"You're doing it right now."

""Doing what?"

"You're acting like a know it all" she says with this smug vocal fry that feels so disengaged and belittling. Arlene finishes her wine and fixes on me awaiting my response.

"I just, I enjoy making people question their certainties. I obsess over these hypocrisies and blind spots we all have." It sounds so lame as the words tumble out of my stupid mouth.

"You think way too much." She dismisses, "Shut up and go get us some drinks."

Brusque and belittling, she certainly can be. Her redirect is a welcome break from sitting there being made to feel stupid. Whatever fates have arranged to force this alliance, I'm momentarily disarmed by her confident aptitude. Thankful even? No, that's a hand too far. I am yet to wrap my arms around this notion that Sébastien has been using me with the intent to kill me in the final act of some power play. Not Sébastien. I suppress laboring over the heavier stuff and return my attention to renewing the levity between Arlene and I.

"Gimme your glass." I say as I rise to make for the bar.

"That's more like it." She teases, "Less talk, more action."

I take her empty wine glass and head for refills, playfully giving her the evil eye over my shoulder as I go. She doesn't acknowledge but I tell myself she notices.

I approach the ancient looking rustic bar. It was intentionally made to look rustic 40 years ago when it was thoughtfully crafted. Now it just looks ancient. Decayed fishing nets, haggard bobbers, rotting wooden rudder wheels and sad starfish taxidermy in the dim laboring overheads, the pronounced scent of pine cleaner masking vomit; the depth of my love for these places exceeds the plumb of whatever oceans they seek to invoke. I'm glad we're here and not in that safe house building towards a palpable cabin fever.

Sat at the bar are a solitary white-bearded old salt in a Greek fisherman's cap and a couple of Seattle archetypes, salt-and-pepper flowed 40-somethings in fleece vests, high waist denim, affected geek glasses and for some reason costume shop Indian head dresses. The bartender, a 250 pound tattooed man in a sleeveless Iron Maiden shirt defies common sense, with the current temperature in the low 50s. He watches me the entire walk to the bar, not suspiciously, more like the way a cow watches anything that moves, never scared, never attracted, just watching.

"Hey, man. Can I get a couple more Cab-Savs?"

"Cab-Sav? " He re-animates, warmly. "You got it."

The Jukebox is playing a Heart song I don't recognize. I consider pissing off the head dress-and-fleece couple by asking them what Hole song it is. That would be breaking the rules though. Never break the ice. There are rules to winding up strangers in bars.

"Happy Indigenous Peoples Day!" the woman in REI fleece exclaims, raising her glass toward me.

God, how I love Seattle. For a contrary asshole like me this place is an amusement park. It's as much fun as Orange County with less chance of getting a black eye. Shoulder-chipped normies just overflowing with certainties they suppose are so self-evident, all waiting unawares to have them challenged, the Seattle variety being much less likely to go raped ape over it, unlike their OC counterparts.

Need a black eye? Tell someone in Orange County that the 80s defense industry which paid off the home they inherited was a Reagan administration welfare program for the middle-class. You'd have to work a whole lot harder than that to get a black eye in Seattle. Orange County, California had put me in the hospital more than once for yanking at the carpets they so confidently stood upon. Seattle never could muster that kind of violent indignance. Seattle was mostly just good for dirty looks and muttered insults whenever they had their sacred truths recreationally assaulted.

"Happy what?" I ask, confused.

"Indigenous Peoples Day!"

"I'm sorry, I don't know what that is." I say as I go through my wallet for the cash to pay for our wine.

"Oh! We don't celebrate Columbus Day here, we celebrate Indigenous Peoples day." She explains, so satisfied in her evident righteousness.

Columbus Day. As usual, I'd totally spaced it. I never even notice Columbus Day unless I've pulled at the locked door of a bank. In all my life I've never met anyone who sincerely celebrates this foisted holiday. The only people given to caring about it seem to be the ones who need something to be angry about, but this is low hanging fruit even for them.

"Indigenous People's Day?" I snort, "Then why are you celebrating it? You look alot more like Columbus than Geronimo to me." I say feigning offended, with all the requisite facial pantomime. Wrinkled nose, knit brow.

"It's 'cause it's racist to celebrate Columbus Day." She squirms

Racism again. Everything is racist in Seattle. Broken escalators are racist in Seattle. Late trains are racist in Seattle. And it's always white people in fleece separates leading the charge against these racisms.

"I don't get it. What's that got to do with you getting wasted in mock indian regalia?"

"What's not to get? Columbus was Italian and this is Indian land!"

"So that's what's going on here" I say nodding at their head dresses and their drinks. "You're celebrating the Natives?" I give it a beat and watch the confidence drain from their faces. "You sure you're not just trying to divorce yourselves from the shame of being white or maybe just looking for an excuse to get holiday wasted?"

Crickets.

"OK, well by all means then, let's toast." I say as the wine arrives.

"That's more like it, friend!" the white squaw says raising her glass a foot from her novelty head dress.

"To the sinister undertones of three white invaders celebrating Indigenous Peoples Day. On stolen land. With the whiteman's firewater. In mock native head dresses."

They lower their glasses, irritated and eager to be rid of me. I pay the bartender whose poker face remains unchanged.

"Happy Indigenous Peoples Day." I say to the couple raising my glass again as I turn and head back to sit with Arlene. W.C. Fields once said, "If you can't dazzle them with brilliance, baffle them with bullshit." I try to do a little of both.

"Douchebag." I hear the woman mumble as I make my way. So very Seattle. Orange County would've tried to kill me if I'd insulted any of their hollow customs. Seattle just looks at the ground and mumbles. At least Orange County assholes are overt and self-aware, albeit as violent and depraved as any of the right wing caricatures from the Hunter S. Thompson canon.

I return to find Arlene reading a book. Reading in a bar, something I liked to do when I was still allowed at the Copper Bucket so long ago. I hadn't secluded myself with a book in the corner of a bar for quite a while. I look for the cover but she has it creased at the spine and I can't see.

"What's this? Bridgette Jones? Devil Wears Prada?" I ask sarcastically.

"Harry Potter? Fifty Shades?" She mocks,playing along as she reveals the cover.

"Evola?" I laugh as she shows me a worn paperback copy of Italian traditionalist Julius Evola's Revolt Against the Modern World. "Really?"

"What?" she protests, "What would you suppose I'd be reading?"

"I have no idea." I say. "I guess I'm not surprised."

"You've read him then?"

I shrug and nod a waffling affirmative. She lets it go. I've read him a little but I wasn't bowled over as much as Mussolini must have been. I'm mostly an apolitical egalitarian and a bit of a salad-bar-philosopher, picking and choosing from hither and tither, but ultimately I'm an individualist, a live and let live type, believe it or not. I might go as far as a classical liberal, if only in personal practice but not politically. I try to resist political impulse and stick to observing the Golden Rule. The only time I really break it is when I'm winding up strangers in bars. Suffice it to say, Evola's not exactly my tumbler of Jameson but it says something about Arlene that he appeals to her. There is an awful lot going on in that beautiful head of hers. An awful lot of scary things I wish I were smart enough to let go.

"I see you had your fun at the bar." She remarks.

"Gotta find it where you can." I sigh.

"You're really embarrassing to be seen with, you know that?"

"Which is why I'm always alone." I joke sidling up next to her.

"Awww, sad trombone." she snarks, smirking as I set down her wine. She puts away her book and I oblige her with the sad trombone sound. We laugh.

"So, this captious little pathology of yours; it gets you beat up and thrown out of these places," she starts again with her smirk, "but it's very interdisciplinary, I'll give you that." Compliment? Criticism?

"How so?"

"Well, I've seen you make someone want to fight you over an indefensible opinion about music and now I've seen you turn the only other couple in the bar against you by needlessly insulting their casual politics."

"Oh, so we're a couple now?"

"I knew I'd regret that right when I said it," Arlene volleys, "don't deflect."

"OK, look, it's just a game, really. I think I might be able to devil's advocate anyone's assumptions and that's what I try to do. Sometimes, it's a lot less than that. Sometimes it's just about me being annoying."

"No, I'm afraid it's the other way around. It's always about you being annoying and sometimes it's about you getting to assail someone's assumptions." She says. "You really should have taken the path of the Cloak in the Prelacy. You would have advanced faster and we wouldn't have to be solving this mystery of who's been prosecuting the writs you won't."

I would give just about anything to go a few hours without thinking on the whole ugly truth of my mysteriously prosecuted writs. It's an unwelcome specter that I figure on seeing frequently from here forward. I try to sway the subject.

"How do you know I was offered the path of the Cloak?" I ask.

She dismisses my stupid question with an eyebrow shrug then softens the blow with that taunting smirk I'm starting to see so often.

"Assailing assumptions is a vital part of determining actionable intel." She says. "You would've made a very talented analyst for the Cloaks but I also think you might have a habit of doing the opposite of whatever you think you should, which would explain why you're a Sword with such clean hands."

"Tou-fuckin'-ché" I say as I take a drink. Opening someone wide and probing seems to be her thing the way getting beaten up and thrown out of bars seems to be mine. We play the same game in a different way. She does to me what I so deftly do to strangers. For me, it's pathology, for her it's just tradecraft.

We watch the couple at the bar squawk about how shitty white people and Columbus are, sipping our drinks in silence while the bartender cow-eyes a spot on the wall. Down the bar from our sanctimonious cherohonkees the old salt in the Greek fisherman's cap side-eye's the goings-on in mostly painless suffering. After a sizeable peace Arlene and I take up again.

"So, at the Maharajah last night you told me that you're not a nihilist but I've seen little more than nihilistic, radical critique from you." She prods. "It's a cute game, this hobby of yours but you have to believe in something, no?"

"No, I don't." I challenge. "Not even nihilism."

"Don't get bored and think to wind me up, Godefroi, I'm not impressed with your bullshit." She softly cautions. "You can go back to the bar and take it out on those two pitiful Yanks if you want but I'm not your cat toy, I claw back."

I'm shocked she would even dignify me as an opponent at this point. A lot has happened to indicate she takes me as much less than a match.

"No," I plead, a little too much perhaps, "I'm being sincere."

Arlene gives me a look which I interpret as space to elucidate. Or is that a glare warning me to dial it down? She has what is popularly referred to as resting bitch face and I can't read her with any consistency. Or maybe I'm just too attracted to her to marshal any objectivity. This very realization alerts me once again to my fear that I've let her in my head; that I'm permitting my enchantment to valet for her murky agenda.

"Look, I know this just looks like contrarian fuckery to you but I'm genuinely suspicious of everything and everyone, myself included." I explain. "I can't understand this world, but I can misunderstand it with the best of them."

"Nihilist." Arlene prods lifting her glass to her coy perma-smirk. Keep it up, that smirk will hold no charm over me if you continue to abuse it, you ol' bootleg Mata Hari.

"That's how it looks, sure, but what's going on inside my head is more an urgent search for something to believe in than it is some recreational deconstruction of what everyone else believes in."

"Oh, bullshit. You really need to feel like you're not a nihilist, don't you?"

"I despise nihilism, even if it is my most useful model for maneuvering through a sea of morons who can't see that they don't know shit."

She rolls her eyes and takes a drink of her wine. I ride another uncomfortable quiet.

"You're so on the spectrum." She chides. The spectrum, a reference to autism, something I've imagined I might have a touch of, though I've never verified the suspicion.

"I wouldn't be surprised if I was" I volley.

"I'm joking, Godefroi. I dislike that you've been made to think that something is wrong with you. I shouldn't have said that." She says, inexplicably softening from her new hobby of menacing me. I don't buy it.

"You know what, Arlene? You almost had me but no, you enjoy prodding me. You act like you don't get me but you're doing exactly what I love to do. We're not so different, you and me."

"Maybe so."

"Maybe so?" I laugh, bitter and just below a whispered shout. "That's exactly what you're doing. You think you've got me so pegged but how about you tell me who you think you are? It's one thing to know someone else, but what do you know about yourself?"

"You want to know who I am?" she laughs. "Really now?"

"I can't possibly know who you are but I'd sure be amused to hear you tell it."

"And I'd be amused to see you do the same. This hobby of yours: this over analyzing-this faux objectivity-it won't protect you from a single thing, Godefroi. Being dodgy isn't going to protect you from the perils of the world. Reality is whatever persists in spite of whether you believe it or not. So what's your reality? I dare you to put it into words, if you think you have the moral courage to simply define yourself."

"Maybe I will if you go first."

"I'm not ashamed, I do not avoid characterization, I am not some wishy-washy hipster, some special individual who resents standards and insists on defying definition. What do you want to know about me?"

"I don't know, characterize yourself. Who would you say you are, Arlene?"

"I would tell you that I am a traditionalist, Godefroi." She says, "and a God fearing deist, that I am proudly European to the point of chauvinism, and that I think you and I will probably never see eye to eye on anything that matters to me."

I'm disgusted that instead of defending myself, I'm tempted to admit my fondness for traditionalism, how I admire and even crave the simple, archaic ideals of culture and tradition. How I long for those very things which this post-modern world has little use for. I'd like to tell her but she would just see it as insincere pandering. At this point there's little I could say that wouldn't reaffirm her increasingly apparent prejudices about me. Yet, instead of defending myself, here I go pandering and trying to find common ground. Yeah, I'm losing my objectivity with her and I'm going to have to sort that out sooner than later.

"Look, I'm not a nihilist! I actually respect traditionalism, I'm just no good at using those ancient maps for navigating these contemporary landscapes. Where old mountains are now just islands, peaking above oceans of shitty ideas that have flooded the fertile soils where vital ingenuities once grew." I pause to drink and finish, "What's the point of clinging to culture if the world no longer has any use for it, Arlene?"

That did not sound sane and she's not the customer to be serving word salad like it's the daily special. I can tell she's irritated and I think now might be another welcome moment for one of those prolonged quiets. I should be so lucky.

"Holy shit, you're annoying." She finally relents. "You really are. I thought I could stand you but I don't think I can."

And there's that long quiet I was craving. My mind wanders and I silently beat myself up for being so impossible. As we sit now incommunicado, I imagine that somewhere, there's a raging party where no one has a single thing figured out. Where no one gets beat up or kicked out for not having it all figured out. I imagine that somewhere, in some century in some land, a bunch of 1,000 year old shamans are all high on psychotropics, not having it all figured out together and then there's me, not having it all figured out right along with them and we're all loving every minute of it.

THIRTY

LAX Airport, Thurs April 3rd, 2014

    I was sat in First Class to the right of a glamorous looking, middle-aged L.A. woman. She had her nose buried in Instagram on her iPhone. A miles-long scroll of duckfaced selfies taken beside reluctant Hollywood D-listers. Here's me with a very uncomfortable looking Heidi Montag. She has no idea who I am but I'm straining to make us appear as if old friends. Here I am with my arm around Nick Lachey, pay no attention to his hover-hand, we're super tight. That's me and gal pal Dina Lohan and here's me with my buddy Ian Ziering (he pronounces it EYE-an). Pathetic. And a little creepy, to be honest. A few tiers up the creepy scale from side-eye snooping a stranger's Instagram on a plane anyway.

    Being that the seat next to mine had filled, I was assured I had no worry of Al sitting there instead. Neither he nor his incessant questions would fit. None of his pestering me with "Who's killing all these bankers, kid?" It would all have to wait until we'd landed. Thankfully, the quandary of my mysteriously prosecuted writs would be something that could only be pondered alone for the rest of the flight.

    With that realization, I sunk a little and actually began to long a little for Al's distractions. Fending off his intrusive demands I consider who was killing the bankers I hadn't, that might actually be preferable to laboring over the same question in my own head alone for the next 12 hours or so.

    If I wanted some kind of distraction to get me out of my own head, it was doubtful I could lean on this 40-something career divorcee with a surgical trout-pout sitting next to me. Nope. Just me and my crazy head trapped in the same old monotonous circuit of fear and self-suspicion for the next half-day.

Good times. Why didn't I bring any Xanax?

If I was still allowed at the Copper Bucket I probably could've picked some up from Tucan or Chivo. That would've really helped me get through this long flight. Instead, here I was, barely half-drunk with no diversion from worrying about what I was doing with my life. Fuck my life. Not entirely, just presently.

As the flight attendants were going through the rigors of what to do in the event of a loss of cabin pressure, the Janice Dickinson stunt double to my left was full sail into her routine pond-hopping trance, sleep mask over her eyes and ear buds inserted. I sat there and thought about not thinking. As I labored to think about not thinking my mind wandered to this woman I didn't know who was sat next to me. I seldom got any joy in winding up women and I had a rule about winding up strangers on flights, so that was out. I had no problem with a little bit of silent profiling, however.

It wasn't so much the tan line where a wedding ring had recently been which lead me to suppose her for one of L.A.'s numerous professional wives; women who had skilled themselves in amassing wealth through divorce. It was more the entire gestalt of her composition that effectively announced her résumé to anyone paying attention. I couldn't seem to muster any moral judgment, so I wondered if I wasn't admiring more than I was loathing.

I puzzled over how it was that motivated men of power and wealth ever consented to this inevitability. This getting married, divorced and ultimately parting with much of their wealth. How do you not see it coming from a mile away and organize your contingencies ahead of time? It didn't add up for me. How can men so financially adept, so capable be so easily marked? My mind wandered to questioning my own hormonal health. What made me so cautious where most men weren't? Was something wrong with me? I slammed the hatch on that corridor of introspection and returned my thoughts to wondering what made Hollywood millionaires so reckless in marriage.

It couldn't be a one-way street, right? They had to be cognizant and consenting. Was this a new norm? You're rich so you simply resigned yourself to the first wife shakedown? Expected it? Truly there were mysteries in this world I'd never understand, the same way the Prelacy was something I couldn't possibly explain to the uninitiated without being laughed off and dismissed as crazy.

I trained my meditation again on this woman next to me. What had her youthful aspirations been like? As a teen, I'd foolishly dreamed of finding a woman who understood me and loved me anyway. Had this person in similar fashion dreamed of marrying a wealthy man and dividing him from a large fraction of his riches then moving on to her next mark? And after that, on to range for more kill? This just seemed alien. In that moment I couldn't help but feel so simple and common.

What had my mother and father imagined? I seldom bothered to think about it. They were simpler people than this woman, my mother and father. Mom was first-generation German from Chicago and my father the progeny of generations deep Oklahomans comprised of god-knows-what lineage, though he was born in Bakersfield after the big Dustbowl migration. Neither had the pretentious sophistication or ambition I imagined the woman next to me had. My folks just did what every generation from them on seems to have done. Gave it a go and gave up when it turned out to be something they'd have to work at. I had seen my dad only four times since childhood and then he died in '96, a few months before my 17th birthday. I felt like a bigot for imagining it was any different for ol' trout pout sitting next to me. Like her whole life experience was somehow insincere just because it made no sense to me. The whole life experience I'd completely concocted for her out of boredom. Being a recreational bigot can pass the time like nothing else.

If feeling like a bigot wasn't so familiar I guess I might have felt more guilt than I did. Instead of flogging myself for it, I pulled out the Skymall and set to distracting my busy head with pictures of $500 hummingbird zappers and $900 automated cat petters.

"Hey, you don't have any Xanax, do you?"

I may be flying first class but I'm coach at heart, which is why this question felt sleazy to me. Things are different in First Class, though. You'd feel like a scumbag hitting someone up for Xanax in coach. In First Class, it's just an ice breaker.

"I was thinking about asking you the same thing." I responded.

"Uggghhh." Trout-pout moaned, replacing the sleep mask she'd only slightly lifted to acknowledge me as she asked.

"Well, I can probably part with half of mine for $200" she added before checking out entirely.

Oh, this was a pitch, not a buy. She's a dealer. My lucky day. I didn't even hesitate. I dug out $200 American and handed it to her. She took out a fistful of Xanax and handed them over without even removing her sleep mask.

I took a half a Xanax and immediately stopped worrying about my stupid life, Frankfurt and then Hamburg in the distance. Thanks, lady. Sorry I was hatin'. I still figured I had her pegged, though. $200 drug deal in First Class and we didn't even exchange pleasantries, let alone names. My bigot's guilt was suddenly less cumbersome. Probably just the Xanax kicking in.

Some pill-poppers will tell you they feel the effects the second they have the pills on their tongue. I'm probably exaggerating but simply knowing I had a bunch of bars in my hand relaxed me immediately. This flight wasn't going to be the monster it first threatened to be.

After I choked down a half a Xanax I signaled the flight attendant for drink service. The fit, blonde German in his mid-twenties responded cordially and promptly with my Jameson double, which I faced and handed back signaling for another.

"Was someone running late today?" He amiably ribbed in an ever-so slight continental accent. "A little behind on the pre-flight cocktails, hmmm?"

I suppressed a belch, squinted and gave him the thumbs up. The belching American. So much for bucking stereotype. The young man smiled and soon returned with another Jameson which I nursed.

"Let me know if you need another."

I gave him a downcast nod, pulling the corners of my mouth wide and my lips tight into that smile looking expression you make which is less jocular accord than shameful admission. "Yes, I will definitely need another and I will immediately alert you to this need when it strikes." the little shame-smile says.

At 40,000 feet I finally began to feel relaxed enough to survey the cabin, a routine in-flight distraction from surveying the contents of my own head.

Before me was a neutral colored poly-cotton panorama of serene civility sustained by the comforts of prescription pills, free alcohol, blue in-flight blankets, neck pillows and On-Demand viewing, all of which bathed in the palliative spectra of calming soft overheads. I drifted into visualizing how this entire radius of repose would turn into a wailing, god-bothering cacophony of shouted promises and pleas for mercy were we to lose 10,000 feet in a short stroke.

The fantasy of crashing has always been one of my routine in-flight meditations. It brings me a measure of peace, but also an irresistible mystery to coddle. What becomes of the people inside of a plane that is going down? Who do they reveal? Are they reticent? Rowdy? Do they fight? Fuck? Do they all just bow their heads and mumble their bargains with god? To crash in a plane would be a fascinating way to go and every time I board one, I'm not long from pouring myself into this knickknack of mortality.

The cynic I am says that they can't stay seated, won't accept their fates. That they are all flailing arms and inarticulate but unmistakable blunt expression. The idealist I am gives them the benefit of the doubt, that they are quiet lambs, gripping their chair arms, smiling. Lending a look of strength and understanding to the stranger or loved one beside them, the last face they would ever see.

I peered across the breathing corpse of trout-pout in her headphones and sleep mask to observe a couple of Shiites; a man in business black and no-bullshit red tie, and a woman in a moderate hijab, powder blue and chiffon two-tone paired with complimentary navy blue separates. As cool and conventional as a couple alone on an elevator, these two. These were the people I would want to be surrounded by on a crashing plane. I couldn't imagine them making a fuss. Just calm and resigned, mutters of "Allahu Akbar" as we careened out of control.

A seat ahead of them was a woman who looked as out of place in first class as I felt. A young American stereotype, bleach blonde with a bedazzled pink baseball cap twisted sideways, bopping her head to music I thankfully could not hear. This is the perfect example of a person I would never want to die in a plane crash with. I imagined her in slow motion taking out her earbuds to loudly soothe the ill-fated nearest her with the wisdom of Lil' B or worse, just screaming entitlement. "Why is this happening to me?!" I shuddered thinking that the last words I might hear on this earth could be whatever makes it from her head past the gateway of her mouth. Then there was coach.

Though I more belonged in coach by virtue of the economic status I was raised in and am comfortable around, as much as by virtue of my petty little bigot mind, I knew that the entirety of coach could never go in peace and for that fact I was thankful to be dying in first class should this flight fail. There I might calmly succumb across from that placid muslim couple, trout-pout as my physical shield from the ablutions and litanies of that idiot In the bedazzled pink baseball cap.

There I sat, relieved, so many feet from the great unwashed in coach who would surely ruin a good death by plane crash with their screams of, "My babies!" Obscured from my sight-lines with their blame laying and hateful reckoning. Their frantic breaking of the no-cel phone in-flight rules. Loud, desperate declarations of "I love my family" followed by confessions of infidelity. Cries of injustice bookending pleas to a war demon first worshiped in the Levant 3,000 years ago.

In first Class I could at least feature the image of ill-fateds I might readily tune out. I looked again at trout-pout sleeping in the seat next to me. Less and less a human being each time, more and more a shield I might use against the panicked people who weren't as composed as me and that muslim couple. Just longing to take it easy as my fantasy plane plummeted toward earth.

As my routine meditation on the inside of a crashing plane's cabin unwound, I drifted into a Xanax fortified sleep and all seemed right with the world. No thoughts of unfulfilled writs. No Al. Just me and a really relaxed muslim couple getting comfy as our Airbus of chaos sped towards the white caps folding above the cold, welcoming Atlantic.

Four hours into our flight plan I awoke with a dry mouth that would make a Bedouin sirocco clock out early. I also had to piss badly. At first I couldn't decide whether to signal for water or head for the lavatory but that sorted itself out in a breath or two.

I nudged trout pout apologetically as I maneuvered for the aisle. She tsked and mumbled something plaintive, never really stirring herself awake or removing her sleep mask. A couple of contortionist wriggles and I had achieved egress, making my way toward the loo. Along the way I was ensnared in a narrow-aisle dosey doe with the flight attendant.

"Excuse,me. Sorry" I said in a polite hush before pulling a quick Allemande Left so I might ask him if he minded bringing a bottle of water to my seat.

"Just give me a wave when you get back to your seat." he yell-whispered, disappearing behind the blue curtain into coach.

No dice. It was worth a try. I turned away and in a few paces found myself doing the pee dance in front of an occupied lavatory. My luck.

While I waited I found the time to fret over the Hamburg job ahead. I wondered if one day I might find the courage to prosecute one of these writs. If so, when? This one? Was it even a matter of courage? Principle? Did I have principles? It sure didn't feel like it. Of all the things Sébastien could advise me on, this wasn't one of them. For all he knew I was fulfilling my duties and that could not go any other way. With a conscience like this, who needs Al?

As I was cursing the very thought of Al the lock on the lavatory door popped and I went to making myself small enough for the blonde in the bedazzled pink snap-back to slide past. Hopefully without any chit chat.

A polite nod to her and I was finally latching the lavatory door behind me. As I relieved myself I began to feel a bit of headache from withdrawal and thought to take the rest of that Xanax I'd halved earlier. I was probably going to want more than just a bottle of water, too.

I zipped my trousers and turned to wash my hands in the lavatory sink. Sanitized, relieved and somewhat recomposed, I surveyed my appearance in the mirror. I looked like a million bucks; green and wrinkled. I pulled a towel from the dispenser and to no surprise, there loomed Al over my right shoulder. Old, liver-spotted and veiny Crypt Keeper Al, not sharp-as-a-tack 1964 Man From U.N.C.L.E Al.

"Not gonna happen, Ugly. We'll talk in Hamburg." I told him as I left the lavatory and closed the door on him. A shiver ran through me as I walked back to my seat. Dodged a bullet.

I sat going through my jacket pocket looking for the Xanax. I couldn't be bothered to find the one I'd already halved so I broke another one. No sooner had I choked it down than the flight attendant was hovering over me with a bottle of water.

"Could you bring me another Whiskey? A double?" I asked.

"You got it." He said and walked off quietly down the mostly snoozing aisle.

A couple seats up I spied the blonde in the bedazzled pink snapback watching a movie on her iPad. On screen I could make out the unmistakable image of Jean-Paul Belmondo dragging his thumb across his lips, aping Bogart in the mirror. Goddard's "À bout de soufflé". Was the #YOLO generation big on French New Wave? I think I had pegged her more for the Fast and Furious type. I wondered how often I was dead wrong about people, given my habit of constantly pre-judging, or thumbnail profiling if I'm sparing myself the guilt. I was grinning at the imminently watchable Belmondo's antics on-screen when the flight attendant had returned with my whiskey and water. Twenty minutes later I was once again asleep, this time for the remainder of the flight.

When we de-boarded in Frankfurt some seven hours later I made my routine stumble toward the nearest airport bar. No wind-ups here either. Strictly business until I'd arrived at the Fountain of Bambi in Hamburg. My connection wasn't for another three hours so I expected two solid hours of feigned interest in soccer, or I guess Fußball as it were here. That and a lot more Jameson, gods willing.

The Frankfurt airport didn't disappoint as I was seated at a bar within a hundred yards of my arrival gate and another hundred yards from my departure gate. I took up an empty chair in the mostly empty lounge and ordered my Jameson while Bayer Leverkusen were losing on the road to Hamburg SV up on the flat screen.

To my surprise, Trout-pout had sidled up next to me to text and mumble a number of curses aloud at her mobile. I doubted she even knew we had spent the last 12 hours inches apart so I tried not to notice.

"Those Xanis treat you OK, hon?" she asked, never making eye contact.

"Feeling tan, rested and ready." I responded, eyes on the match, hand on my Jameson.

"That's awesome, baby." She said, never looking up from her mobile.

I didn't bother carrying on the conversation. If she wanted to talk more nothing on earth would stop that. I wasn't interested in more conversation so I sat and hoped she had enough going on with her phone.

"I still gotta go to fucking Hamburg." She said. "This shit is so long."

Hamburg? Maybe it was time to pretend we were friends. I had slept through 12 hours of transatlantic travel with this woman next to me but we might still be in for another six hours of pretending we're friends. It wasn't close to a tragedy having to shift my attention from the most tedious Bundesliga match televised to my new pretend friend, but I could think of better things I'd like to do, bored to death in the Frankfurt airport. Happy slapping strangers, smashing shop windows, pissing all over the luggage coming in on the carousel.

"Yeah, I'm waiting on Hamburg, too." I said.

"You're shittin' me." She said, finally peeling her eyes from her mobile.

I shrugged and smiled.

I could almost follow her feeble profiling as she tried to imagine who I was and why I was going to Hamburg. I expected her to ask if I was in a band. The long hair tends to fetch that assumption. She revealed more about herself than she did about me when she finally voiced her suppositions.

"So what? You're in banking?"

What the fuck? Too close but how? I was a long-hair wearing a military jacket and trainers. Banking? I honestly questioned my recent self-satisfaction over adjusting my wardrobe to blend in across the pond.

"In a manner of speaking." I responded.

"My old man's in banking, too." She said, "So I gotta meet him in Hamburg."

Oh, of course. That's why she asked if I was in banking. Everyone who has to go to Hamburg is in banking to this moron. Then again, she still wasn't far off. Maybe she's a genius.

"You don't look like a banker."

With that, I finished my Jameson and didn't wait for a refill. I pulled my plastic flask and looked at this brilliant piece of god's toil before me. If I could only fathom what was informing these assumptions.

"I don't look anything like a banker but your first guess is that I'm going to Hamburg because I'm a banker?"

"Calm down," she said with disgust. "God, you think too much."

I thought to myself that someday I might meet a woman didn't say that to me. I shrugged and went back to work on my whiskey. As the only match in the Bundesliga played out on the flatscreen, Trout-pout typed furiously on her Blackberry. I was concerned I wasn't pretending to be friends good enough. Bad operational procedure. I silently fretted and tried to think of creative ways to remedy this failing.

"I'm sorry, let me buy you a drink. What're you having?" best I could come up with. Maybe I'm the moron.

"Shot of Patron with a Xanax back" she says with a shrug, eyes on her mobile.

I'm being wound up. This is why I never fuck with people who are used to getting what they want. I suppressed a laugh and straight-faced ordered her shot of Patron. When it arrived, I slid her Xanax alongside the shot. She pretended not to notice and took forever to get to it all.

"Thanks, baby." She genuinely beamed, eyes front and the whole show.

Through the premature surgeries and layers of Clinique I could tell this woman was naturally attractive by classical standards. Still, here she stood, so needlessly augmented and enhanced. Hey, whatever it takes. 2 gauge plugs or 400cc boobs. We all do what makes us feel pretty. Or black denim and long hair, I guess.

"So you're meeting the old man in Hamburg then?" I tried to engage.

She just shrugged and shot her Patron.

"What bank is he with?" I asked.

"Kaufmannsbank."

"Oh, OK." I leave off, hoping she'll volunteer more.

I thought about how weird it would be if the name on my writ was someone from Kaufmannsbank. Longshot or no, it occurred to me that I should assume it was in the interest of operational security. Espionage wasn't my strong suit but it was still something I tried to be mindful of when needed, shitty pretend assassin though I be.

"Yeah, he's here because of some shake up in the bank or something. I don't know."

"Really?"

"Yeah, he called me all worried about a promotion and blah blah, wanted to see me. Whatever, free trip to Europe is all I know."

"Hmm."

"I'm boring you."

"Oh, I'm not bored, I just-"

"Don't worry about it. Look, you're going to be in Hamburg, you're in banking. You should look us up if you like to party. Let me give you my number."

I took out my blackphone and entered her info. It would probably prove to be nothing pertinent to my writ but I figured at the very least it might make for a fun night in Hamburg meeting up with her and her husband.

"Who should I ask for?"

"Oh, don't call just text us." She said.

I just tilted my head low and glared through the top of my brow. She didn't notice.

"I'm Jasmine. Jazzy for short."

Jazzy. I suppressed a sigh of frustration.

"Foster." I reciprocated, right hand hanging in the air unshook as she stared down at her Blackberry. "I'll just text you right now so you'll know it's me when I buzz you guys later."

"Foster? Like the beer?"

And so there I sat for the next two hours watching the glacial-paced action of Bundesliga and pretending to be friends with Jasmine. Jazzy for short.

"...Heidi Montag, Nick Lachey, Ian Ziering, Dina Lohan, Jazzy..." I imagined Dr. Anglethorpe saying into a bouquet of mics from the Supreme Court steps.

THIRTY-ONE

West Seattle, WA - Tues Oct 14ᵗʰ 2014

During my brief and sparse dry spells, I usually start my day with meditation. It's not a spiritual thing in any way, just a practice, a method of exercising my attention muscle. It's not so I can pay attention better, mind you. It's so I can attend to other things than the nominal anguishes I'm prone to dwell on if I don't babysit myself. I only practice meditation so I can better muster a focus on things like breathing, grass growing and paint drying. Things that are better attended to than terrors like what I might do if I lock myself out of my apartment or what domino effects might be set into play if I find I'd left my debit card at a bar an hour away. Meditation, when I can be bothered to do it, keeps me in practice of refocusing away from the myriad hypothetical hells my mind can conjure.

Being that I am not amidst one of those long overdue dry spells, my first intent this waking moment is not meditation, rather a healthy dose of indica to reset me from the anxiety or dread that typically accompanies my initial waking state. Long ago I would have awakened to a simple hangover but in my advanced dependency I usually bolt from somnolence in abject terror of the world's relentless onset. Looming horror and creeping panic have long ago stood in for headaches and nausea. A morning joint of Blue Cheese or Hindu Kush has been my regular treatment for those ails since my late 20s, if not the hair of the dog itself.

As I roll over on my back and the day comes crashing in my first thought is to find the little green bottle in my bag that holds the joints I'd rolled before I left Los Angeles. Next comes crashing in the realization that my bags are still at the Fountain of Emeralds, the Prelacy safe house back in Seattle. Things are off to a crunchy start. It will be a challenge avoiding the Jameson as a means of alleviating my anxieties about the potential offensive of withdrawal related anxieties. Anxiety about anxiety. I can't be the only one who has this hang up, can I?

In my nose is the unmistakable eye-opener of breakfast cooking. I roll over to look at my Monolith and see that it's 11:45 am. I'm surprised to see that Arlene isn't the drill instructor I thought she might be. Though I'd given it no real forethought, I guess I'd just assumed she would be waking me hours before I felt like getting up. Yet here I am at a quarter of noon rising by my own lay-about schedule in the guest room down the hall from where Arlene slept the last two nights. Hungover with no kush, but permitted to sleep 'til around noon. So far this day is a push. Before my feet have hit the floor my ledger is at zero and that is something I could definitely drink to. I'll have to go to the kitchen. Jameson bottle's in the kitchen.

I slither into last night's clothes and shuffle socks down the wood floor corridor toward the Jameson kitchen where just beyond it Arlene is finishing her breakfast and reading from her Monolith at the dinette.

"I made egg white omelets with fresh mushrooms. There's some left if you've gotten your appetite yet." She says without looking up.

I say nothing and head for the Jameson which does manage to elicit the attention of her appraising gaze. I smile as I pour and she returns her attention to her reading.

"Late start?" I ask, cage rattler that I am. "I took you for a crack-of-dawn type." In my stupid head, I think this is me being waggishly gregarious. Once the words have passed the gates of my fool mouth I know that to her it sounds nothing like friendly ribbing but entirely like a degenerate's deflecting, trying to get out in front of judgment.

"I've been up since 8. Ran a few klicks down the shore, stopped off at the grocer on the way back, did some analysis, made breakfast and now I'm catching up on some personal business." She says. "I see you're off to the races, though."

After that remark, my ledger now shows me in arrears so I make quick work of my Jameson and nurse it back to a zero balance.

"Thanks for letting me sleep off last night." I say after a quiet.

"You're not my ward." She says cold, no break in her concentration, eyes fixed on her Monolith.

Instead of pouring another Jameson I quietly go over and walk her empty plate to the kitchen sink before serving myself breakfast and wary my way back to sit across from her. She mercifully masks her annoyance as I try to make myself as small as possible in the room and eat what she's cooked. I dare not compliment her cooking, though it's the sort of cooking I envy. Expert, simple, understated. This is what someone cooks to be better, not feel better. I shudder to think of how my clumsy attempt at Phở last night must have appeared to her. I was trying to show off. I should have just made fuckin' tacos. At least that would have been honest. I kill it at tacos.

I want to say something to reset the morning mood but I think better and hold my tongue until I've finished eating, better yet until she's done with whatever personal business has her preoccupied on her mobile. Once I've finished with breakfast I make my way to the sink, wash the dishes and breakfast skillet then run a glass of water and return to the table. I sure could use that joint of indica right about now. We sit in silence looking at our mobiles across the table from one another.

"It's not safe to return to Seattle for your things so I used one of my burner Visas to order you clean clothes online. They should be here any time now." Arlene finally says.

Shit, I guess that means there won't be any going to the Fountain of Emeralds. Now instead of just worrying about getting my weed I'm worried about wearing clothes I hate. I've pretty much worn the exact same thing every day for more than a decade and I feel naked in anything else.

"Thanks." I lie.

"I hope you don't mind, I looked at your labels and just ordered a few pairs of the exact same thing you were wearing last night." She says. "I know it's thoughtless but I couldn't begin to guess what you like and since it's only for a few days I decided it would be safest erring on the side of proven percentages."

Thoughtless? Be still my heart. This skilled operator was anything but thoughtless. That was expert analysis, but that's what she does. Her tradecraft is an enviable asset even in regard to the smallest details.

"I guess I'll get in the shower then." I say.

Arlene looks up to smile politely but not warmly and I shuffle back toward the hall.

"Good, you smell like hell took a shit in an Irish landfill."

Was that humor? Humor is good. I resist the urge to turn back and look for accord and instead opt for flipping her the bird over my shoulder as I slide down the planks toward the shower. I think that ol' morning ledger might be well into the black by now but who am I kidding? I do my best to ignore ledgers until the bank comes knocking. Suffice it to say, things seemed less and less dire, given that my world had recently shifted on its axis. If I could cloud my head with weed, alcohol and foolish longing for a woman I had nothing in common with, I might actually be able to go through with this massive betrayal I've been set on a course for.

The hot shower water makes quick work of the dark turn in my thinking and I begin to relax. Thoughts of Jameson, fresh black denim and another night of parley with Arlene replace the horror of betraying the Prelacy and Monsieur Sébastien, the man I call mentor. Sébastien is the one person in this world who seems to care about me, barring Al, of course. So, I guess he's the one person who cares about me who isn't imaginary. Details, whatever. It gets exhausting living inside this head. It really does. I don't know how Al handles it.

"Fuckin' Al." I mumble as the warm water cascades over my slight, doughy frame. A jolt of terror wakes me to the disaster that would be Al returning as I'm trying to seem sane around Arlene and her handlers. I shiver at the thought and wrap up my shower in a hurry to get back in the company of Arlene. That is where I'm confident he's less likely to rear his antagonizing countenance. Saying his name is usually tantamount to courting his presence and he is the last thing I want to deal with right now.

"Don't do it, kid. It's a trick. She's gonna get you swept up in all kinds of shenanigans," Al's last words to me as I walked out of the W with Arlene the night before last. The words echo in my mind as I towel myself dry, scared to look at the foggy mirror lest I find him standing there behind me. I really could use that lost reefer right about now.

I slide wet feet down the hall to my guest room and find boxes on the bed, deliveries from Arlene's online order of fresh clothes for me. I find my house keys and open the packaging. In a few minutes I'm draped in an outfit identical to the one I wear every day, just like Fred Flintstone does, or Homer Simpson, or Albert Einstein or any other fictional psychopath does. OK, Homer Simpson and Einstein are only semi-fictional but they wore the same exact thing every day, same as me. OK, maybe Homer isn't even a psychopath. Anyway, I'm trying to say I wear the same clothes every single day and I know how weird that is. The fact that right now I get to wear my comfortable, familiar superhero costume is remarkable, considering the situation. It's like if Amelia Earhart crash-landed on that atoll to find it filled with racks of aviator jackets and chinos. That's the most poetry I can call up. Long and short of it is I really like not having to break routine, especially right now in the face of so much sudden change.

I slide on my black trainers and military style jacket then head toward the living room where Arlene is sitting quietly studying something on her laptop. On the table in front of her I spy a slim, green pharmaceutical bottle and I'm immediately sorting through suspicions of how thorough her profile of me must be. Does this cold-hearted fascist have a soft, stoner side?

"Is that for me?" I ask pointing toward the reefer with my chin, trying not to seem too pleased.

"You require your comforts, I know." She says, "I'll provide as I can."

Without questioning how she got it, or how she knew to, I take up the little canister and see that the label reads "Blue Cheese". I'm too relieved to sweat the fact that her profile is thorough enough to know my strains. She's a Cloak. Intel is her specialty.

"Thanks, Arlene."

"Rolling papers are on the table." She adds, hardly interested. Still, I detect a vague, nonverbal expression of satisfaction. I try not to look directly at her face as I soak in what I take for a restrained delight. Is our Arlene a reluctant nurturer? A closeted provider? I have my suspicions. If I'm right, I imagine it must be rough going through life an emotionless authoritarian when you're hiding the heart of an accommodator, a giver. The layers on this person. I set it all aside for now with a private laugh and set to breaking up weed. Maybe I misunderstand her and her philosophy. Again, I set it all aside and continue breaking up weed. Meditation, refocusing like I was saying earlier.

A nice cone rolled up and poised on my lips now, I look at my Monolith to see that it's 12:40 in the afternoon. I light the larger than usual joint and let the relief of this minor miracle take effect before letting my mind find my mouth.

"So what's the plan today?" I ask Arlene. "We're just waiting here until Sébastien contacts me?"

"Until the Judicious Scrivener contacts you, but if Sébastien were to contact you for a meet that would be of equal importance."

"Well, he usually meets up with me no later than a day past prosecuting a writ." I say, exhaling another fog of indica smoke.

"It's been two days."

"I know."

"So that's not normal?"

"I mean, sometimes, it's within a day of me getting back state side, but yeah, it's abnormal." I say, "I should have heard from him by now."

Arlene closes the lid on her laptop and sits back on the sofa. I offer her the joint in my hand but she just laughs in derision and shakes her head.

"OK, there's nothing to be too alarmed about. We can't assume anything. My orders are to pend everything on contact from the Scrivener but I can't help being mindful of your unusual relationship with his Grey Imminence." She says.

"What does that mean?" I ask, "Grey Imminence. He's used those words before but half the time I just tune out his eccentric nonsense."

"Your rare suspension of cynical analysis speaks volumes about your blind trust of this man. " Arlene says. "It boggles the mind how someone managed to actually break through your routine paranoia so well."

I'm too high right now to give a fuck about her judgmental bullshit. If she wants to make it so plain that she has a stick in her ass about the only decent person in my life she's not exactly winning me over to her cause. As far as I'm concerned, this entire cabal is still a jump ball. Jump cabal. Hah! I feel pretty great right now. Blue Cheese.

"Oh, let it go. I'm asking you, Grey Imminence, what does it mean?"

Arlene lets me off with a masked laugh. Did she just catch herself over-analyzing? Being overly critical? We have so much more in common than she'll admit.

"It's a French thing." She says. "It basically means the power behind the throne. Sébastien holds the rank in the Prelacy directly beneath the King-in-Waiting. He is essentially the King-in-Waiting's counsel. While it is not uncommon for high ranking members of any house or any regime to groom select members of their lower ranks, his affinity for you is deemed highly suspicious among the few who are privy."

"You sound just like one of them right now." I say blowing a cloud as big as I feel like my balls must be at this moment. "You're talking just like some Prelacy devout. This whole thing is just turning out to be so much bullshit, I can't bring myself to care about it all one way or the other."

"I'm not judging you Godefroi, it's just very conspicuous that the 2nd highest ranking member of House Merovingi would hand select someone for recruitment and then sponsor their rapid advancement." She pleads. " And then there's the whole thing so few know of, the fact that you're ascending so swiftly through the Path of the Sword, all the while never having taken a single life."

"Who else knows about that?"

"What, that you haven't prosecuted your own writs?"

"Yeah."

"Monsieur Herman, Canan and presumably Monsieur Sébastien and I suppose whoever is finishing your jobs."

I don't like it. I have the urge to just bolt and be done with it. I could just shake Arlene, round up my gold and vanish and there isn't a thing her, the Covenant or the Prelacy could do about it.

"You know, I could just disappear. You could wake up tomorrow and I'd be gone, Prelacy gold in tow and none of you would ever find me."

"Believe me, Godefroi, the Prelacy would find you."

"Nope. I'm from Boyle Heights. I know too many smart Mexicans to believe any of that's true." I laugh. "I could be in the wind tomorrow and you, Sébastien, Herman, that bald douchebag Canan, none of you could do anything about it. You'd all be stuck in the same whirlwind of phony, esoteric struggles. Meanwhile, I'd be living as some anonymous gringo down South way off the grid."

"And whatever life you might make for yourself would be over in a few months when the entire world is in total collapse. All of that Prelacy gold can't buy you a stable world to hide in. You can't see it with your own eyes, you can't see it by turning on the TV or reading about it on the internet but there is war simmering, and the upshot depends on the Covenant weakening the Prelacy's influence, now more than ever."

"You sound just like one of them. My sole hope was that your Covenant was somehow a little more grounded but you're all just as crazy as them."

"You don't have to believe any of it, all you have to believe is that the Prelacy believes it, the Covenant believes it, the Vatican, the BRICs, the Masons, Gladio and every other shady cabal believes it and each of them is committed to the idea that there is a massive secret war for control of this planet. What you have to believe is that you happen to be caught in the middle of it and you don't have the luxury of seceding into anonymity because these people will happily turn this world into a desert of black glass if we don't stop them."

I give up. I'm still trying to get my day started and already we're on about this Luke Skywalker fable bullshit, full sail, no anchor. I take a big pull from the cone and lean back in my chair. She's going to have to come down a little closer to earth if we're going to be able to close handshaking distance on any of it

Right now, in my head, my bags are packed and these zealots have 'til tomorrow. If things don't start to appeal to my sense of truth I'll be a ghost and this will all just be another odd story in an already odd life. I'll look back someday and wonder where these people are as I sip Mezcal and eat fish tacos. Is Arlene alive and happy somewhere? Is Sébastien the secret king of the world? Is that bald shit Canan murdering the poor for kicks? I'll probably just turn to Al and say, "Fuck those weirdos." And take another siesta.

As a miasma of discord settles on the room in our cold break, Arlene goes about her business between Monolith and laptop. She's attending to whatever Prelacy or Covenant business begs her attention and I'm thinking how I'd like to get a peek at whatever she has on her blackphone and that laptop.

As the silence cools and hardens I get my cone smoked down to around the halfway mark and set it to rest on the table top. I relax and close my eyes to imagine being away from this all, somewhere in Costa Rica or Nicaragua and I'm delighted by the thought of these idiots stuck sorting out their fantastic and petty war pageant, all under the nose of the public at large.

What a childish and infirmed world the powerful and their sycophants have crafted. Comfort and security seems wasted on the worst among us, the earthbound. And then there's me, trying to explore my limits in their highest secret cathedrals. I'm just as sick as they are. Right now I just want to drop out and be some wayward beardo on Playa Del Fuckyou in el Estado Real de Anywhere But Here. I'm tired of civilization, tired of the very irony of the word.

It's my sole certainty that I've decided I'm putting the clock on these fruitcakes. If I don't see something soon, good luck Arlene, good luck Monsieur Herman, good luck to my beloved mentor Monsieur Sébastien and fuck you, I hope you die first to that creepy Covenant baldy-locks Canan. And to Al, well I figure I can't ditch Al but good luck and fuck you, too just to be safe. Who am I kidding? Al, I'll see you on the beach, but still, fuck you.

"Why don't you prosecute your writs?" Arlene says finally breaking our prolonged still.

"How do I even respond to that?"

Arlene shakes her head, eyes ever fixed on her laptop she says, "Has to be a reason."

"Well, I suppose Skinner would say it's because I've developed some sort of reward mechanism for remaining in perpetual crisis while Freud would of course say it's because of unresolved mommy issues of some sort. Sopolsky might say it's because my primate neurocircuitry-"

"Oh, for fuck's sakes." Arlene cuts me off. "There you go already. When you hear hoofbeats the first thing any normal mind thinks is to look for horses, but not you. Off you go looking for Zebras. Forget I even asked. You don't want to figure this out then why should I care?"

I let the silence grow until the mood lightens a little and pay some mind to a more human response. I have trouble putting my thoughts into simple terms usually. Is that what people mean by honesty?

"Look, I haven't prosecuted a writ because I can't. For some reason I've had it in my head for years that I'm cut out to be a soldier and I keep trying to prove it to myself that I am but when the time comes to do the dirty deed, I can never pull the trigger."

She takes a moment to collect her thoughts about what I've just said and softens her tone.

"So you never even took a life when you were in Afghanistan then?"

"You know about Afghanistan, too? Christ, what else do you know about me?"

"It's what I do Godefroi. If it puts your mind at ease, I didn't gather any intel on you. What little I know about you comes directly from the Covenant's file on you."

"Can I see it?"

"I don't have it. Are you going to answer my question?"

"No, I didn't kill anyone in Afganistan. I was a chronic non-firer and it caused me a lot of problems once it got around that I couldn't pull the trigger."

"Why do you continue to put yourself into situations where you'll be expected to kill so frequently, then?"

"It's not like I planned it that way. I wasn't clear this was what the path of the Sword was all about. I mostly just made a bad decision without really thinking and I've been paying the price ever since."

"You, who overthinks everything, I'm expected to believe that?"

"I do overthink everything. I spend almost every waking moment overanalyzing situations and babysitting myself but I'm not infallible. I had no business joining the Army and I had no business taking the Path of the Sword. I'm an idiot for doing it but kicking myself isn't going to fix anything. "

In the brief silence that follows I make sure to kick myself, none the less.

"You know, you're infinitely more likeable when you're vulnerable. Way less of an asshole."

"Suits your purposes, anyway." I snark at her playfully, eager to steer our rapport back toward something more amiable. "Somehow I doubt that vulnerability is a trait you look for in a man romantically, but it's definitely what you want to see in your mark."

"You're not my mark, Godefroi." She says, finally looking up from her laptop.

"Sorry, I didn't mean it as a swipe."

"Don't worry about it." She says. "And you're right. I do find that too much vulnerability in a man is unattractive but a little every now and then looks good on you. You should try it more often."

"If you knew what my inner monolog sounded like, you wouldn't be saying that."

Arlene smiles and returns her focus to whatever cloak work and skullduggery she's been attending to on her laptop. Meanwhile my mind sets to wondering how I might get a look at it all. What sort of files she might have on me, what things I might learn about her. This urge to snoop is informed by equal parts attraction to her and healthy distrust of her.

With nothing but things to avoid thinking about in the current quiet I reach for the universal remote on the coffee table and switch on the giant flatscreen across the room from us. On screen, Dr. Anglethorpe is on the courthouse stairs, looking into a news camera speaking.

"...Miley Cyrus, the cast of the View, V. Stiviano, David Miscavige..."

I laugh and lean back in my seat as the good doctor continues reading off names from that terrific list of people who have inspired his legal battle to lawfully end his own life.

"I love this guy." Arlene says pausing to look at the television.

"He's great, right?"

"So great."

"...Neil de Grasse Tyson, Glen Beck, Russel Brand..."

"Aw, what's he got against Neil de Grasse Tyson?"

"Are you kidding me? Do you know how much mindless zealotry that man inspires? He's as insufferable as your American TV preachers were 20 years ago." Arlene says with a shudder of affected contempt. "Americans refer to science with this dogmatic authority so long as it makes them feel smarter or more dignified but when scientific dispositions transcend their moral sensibilities with things like crime statistics, human bio diversity or the benefits of stem cells or eugenics programs, they scream 'lies, damned lies and statistics.' Science has just been reduced to another religion in the hands of you Yanks."

I tune Arlene out as I would one of Al's insane rants and focus on Dr. Anglethorpe. As I'm looking at him I can't help but scratch at that old itch of wondering why his face is so familiar to me.

"...Nancy Grace..." the doc continues.

"I hate that bitch." Arlene and I say simultaneously, then laugh.

"High five." I say holding my hand up toward Arlene.

"Not gonna happen." She says as I lower my hand in shame.

The doctor continues reading his list and my mind sets to wandering, wondering about Arlene again. The more I learn about her the more she seems to be like a library of unpopular beliefs. I wonder what informs these taboo creeds.

"So, you're not like one of those anti-science people are you?" I ask. "You're not like an anti-vaxer or one of those people who thinks we faked the moon landing are you?"

"Of course not." She says. "Those things are the glorious result of applied sciences. Science is just a method. It is not a religion but Americans like your Bill Nye and Neil DeGrasse Tyson are reducing it to that. Today's Popular Science evangelists are every bit as tedious as yesterday's televangelists. In fact, they are worse. At least your televangelists didn't leave morons feeling like smug intellectuals for parroting things they'd heard them say."

"Well, OK, that may be so, but to be fair I don't think those guys are worse than televangelists." I say. "I've never heard of Bill Nye fleecing lonely old pensioners out of thousands in church donations." I'm surprised to find myself somewhat agreeing with her. What she just said was just delightfully cynical and that's probably why it resonates with me. I'm a simple man, so sue me. I know what I like. Then again, I used to think I liked Seattle.

"So you're more of a faith type of person?" I ask.

"Faith and science needn't cancel one another out. You're buying in to pop sci dogma. Some of the greatest scientific achievements were made by men of faith. Faith is as much about uncertainty as science is. One is a method of consolation and encouragement while the other is a method of understanding and determination. One is disabused of curiosity, the other obsessed with it. Both have their merit and utility."

"OK, but you pray to god and all that, right?"

"I tend to keep those things to myself, Godefroi. They call it a prayer closet for a reason. I don't evangelize."

"But you said the other night that you believe in God, right?"

"I do, but I also kind of believe that what God does is none of my business. I tend to avoid talking or thinking about it all. I just live my life by a set of virtues and hope that if there's a God, he approves."

"What virtues?"

"The virtues of my culture."

"What, French culture?"

"Of course and to a lesser extent Catholic and Muslim culture."

"But you're not a Catholic or a Muslim."

"I am culturally, to a degree. My Father is Persian, from Iran. Both of my parents are apostates, strictly speaking. My Father was raised Muslim and my mother Catholic though neither is practicing."

"That's heavy. I had no idea you were half Persian. How did those two wind up together?"

"I don't know. It's not unusual. France in the 70s, things were different. They were young and more interested in getting loaded at the discoteque than they were in cultivating spirituality."

"And you've obviously rejected that, you old rebel."

"You have no idea how much I've rejected it. I resent their endless party, disco bullshit." Arlene says. "My generation is paying for their generation's frivolous diversions and by the looks of things, so will the next one and the one after that."

"So, you renounced their debauched secularism and embarked on a spiritual path that lead you to the Prelacy then, am I close? "

"Pretty much and that eventually lead me to the Reformed Covenant of Arius." Arlene says.

"Did you ever consider Jihad?" I rib, only half-kidding.

"Je suis Français, Godefroi." Arlene responds. "I have certain appreciations for Islam but not an affinity. My place is where I am now: assisting the Covenant in keeping insane zealots of all Abrahamic faiths from destroying the world, not assisting one of them in actually doing it."

"Hmph. That all surprisingly makes sense."

"It does, does it? Maybe you should try it some time." She says.

What's that?" I ask.

"Making sense." She jabs.

I shoot her a playfully stern look and we share a brief laugh.

"So, tell me, what are your parents like, Monsieur Godefroi?"

"Well, they're both gone now but I suspect they're not much different than yours."

"I'm sorry, I don't think I knew that already. "

"You mean that's not in my file?" I kid.

"No, it's not in your file, smart ass." She volleys. "Were you close?"

"Not really. My mom, sort of."

"And you were raised in Los Angeles, you've always lived there?"

"Yeah, for the most part."

"I can tell you don't like talking about it."

"I don't want to bore you. It's the same old story everyone has."

"Oh, and what story's that??"

"You know the one. 'I came from a broken home in a tough little neighborhood and fought my way out of poverty and adversity and blah blah blah'. I hear that same little badge of honor story from everyone else so much it makes me want to gag if I have to hear it coming out of my own mouth."

"Well it sounds interesting. You should tell me sometime." She says with a soft look.

"Meh. I'd rather listen to you tell me about your life. That's a much better story."

I light up the other half of the cone I'd set on the table earlier and spend the rest of the afternoon in repose as Arlene tells me stories of her youth, how she never felt she fit in among her peers, all easy going kids in love with pop culture icons and American music. How she loves France and ironically couldn't wait to escape it as a young woman. The day joyfully drags on unrushed as we make plans for the evening. A nice dinner followed by the two of us tempting fate among the locals down at the Rusty Anchor just once more. For the first time in a great while I feel at ease and in good company. As the cone I'm smoking gets smaller and smaller I sit and calmly imagine the different methods I might employ to hack her Monolith blackphone.

THIRTY-TWO

Hamburg, Germany – Fri April 4ᵗʰ, 2014

The Fountain of Bambi turned out to be an ivy-covered two story walk up on Paul-Roosen Strasse, a few blocks off of Hamburg's infamous Red Light District, the Reeperbahn. An Austere looking appointment by Prelacy standards, it stood in apparent disrepair amid graffiti covered store fronts, coffee houses and night clubs. In daylight it looked downright Bohemian. In the American sense of the word, not the German.

I shouldered my luggage, found the front door open and made my climb up the stairs to the flat. Inside, the décor startled with its contrast to the run down exterior façade. Polished birch floors and immaculate white plaster with tastefully framed photos of the Beatles were wire-hung from the crown moldings. For Prelacy digs, this place held a certain cool. The anachronism of Beatles pics and blonde wood floors laid out among the immaculate antique traditional style walls and furnishings felt whimsical and brought a smile to my jetlagged face. It was all distracting enough for me to miss the reserved, Italian-suited young man sat before me in the foyer. He rose slowly out of a serious looking high-back chair and approached with his hand out, in them a set of keys for me.

"Monsieur Godefroi, I am Adam, the caretaker here at the Bambi Kinofläche. My number is on the keychain. Please, do not hesitate if there is anything I can do." He said with a slight German accent.

He handed me the set of keys along with a sealed envelope, no doubt from the Judicious Scrivener. I offered Adam an American $20, which he declined politely.

"Sorry, haven't had time to hit a currency exchange." I explained which he waved off with a gesture. "What's with all the Beatles stuff?"

"This was their home in 1960. Hamburg was a launch pad for them you might say." Adam explained with what I took for a delighted confidence in the subject. "On the coffee table you'll find literature detailing the history of the house and the Fab Four's time here. The flat is in fact named after the Bambi Kino, a theatre that used to be downstairs. You'll find it's all outlined in the book."

"I'll check it out." I said, setting down my bags at last. "Thanks, Adam. I'll be in touch if I need anything."

"Of course, Monsieur. Good day." Adam said politely leaving me to unwind.

So this Prelacy hideout was in fact the Beatles' former residence at one time. These weirdoes were full of surprises. The mysteries never ended.

Most of the Prelacy's safe houses, hide-outs and compounds had some sort of staff. Usually just a caretaker. Often, they were the porters, doormen and concierges in the lobby of the buildings where I found them. The Fountain of Bambi was a private residence, and by the looks of it a high-dollar timeshare the Prelacy might even use for generating revenue. The caretaker here, Adam had the same inscrutable, game qualities all of their properties' staff had. As if I could call on him to dispose of a corpse in the middle of the night and he would do it unblinkingly, then decline any tip afterward. Still I never suspected any of these men for members of our order, though whether or not they were was unclear. Out of discretion I always treated them as kindly as if they were and as cautiously as if they were not.

My first impulse upon having the place to myself was showering and repairing to the couch with a drink. Before I could do any of that though, I would have to review my writ. I opened the envelope Adam had handed me and read the coded instructions found within.

M. Godefroi,

The Fountain of Bambi is behind the Knight if you face South upon entering the Foyer.

Destroy after reading.

Cordially,

Your Judicious Scrivener

I smiled at the minor absurdity and located a framed picture of Sir Paul McCartney on the wall south of the entrance to the flat. Behind the picture was a safe which the smallest key on the ring unlocked with a little beep. Inside I found the standard fare. 2 pairs of surgical gloves, a pair of black knit gloves, and this time a loaded .44 revolver along with a folding map, a Prelacy Writ and a photo of my mark, standard coded message printed on the back:

Kaufmannsbank Building

75 Ferdinandstraße, Hamburg

Black 2012 Smart Fortwo

Underground Garage

Level 2, Space EX-3

07 APR 2014 MON 7:45am

Destroy photo and writ after reading.

What were the odds? The same bank as the one Jasmine, Jazzy for short's boyfriend worked at. Reluctantly, I took the writ from beneath the picture of my target and skimmed the encrypted instructions penned beautifully in the Prelacy's usual ornate script. This one was instructing me to take the S-Line from the Reeperbahn to Jungfernsteig Station at 7am then walk to the parking garage beneath Kaufmannsbank where I was to shoot my mark until dead as he emerged from his car, afterwards I was to return as I had come.

I deciphered the instructions as my mind blanched at the thought of this whole giant fraud I'd been perpetrating. Since the Fountain of Stars I had fanned on over a dozen of these assignments, all of them mysteriously carried out none the less by another hand. Lest I deceive myself this was something ultimately manageable, I had only to consider the fact that to date there were dozens of other bankers besides those I'd been assigned, all of whom had been felled, no doubt by other Prelacy Red Hands. A chill went through me as I considered my own imminent day of reckoning. When the Prelacy would inevitably become aware of my deceit and send one of those same loyal swords to settle my account like one of these banksters. What was once exhilarating and novel was more and more a dawning sense of terror and dread. No sane man wakes up each day to this cup of tea. This affinity for challenging the world to undo him. How could it be I had thrown myself in front of so many oncoming trains, only to watch dumbfounded as they jumped the tracks one by one? How long could I go on living this way? Assuming I could escape my fate with the Prelacy, my own psychotic nature seemed to insure I'd eventually find some new path toward self-destruction.

For the first few writs after London, I had still actually gone to carry out my orders. I'd simply lost my nerve each time and turned from my duties. Before long I had all but given up on performing the tasks myself. Seeing as they were being carried out anyway, I'd taken to quietly sitting in bars. There I'd drink alone or wind up the occasional stranger while I waited for local news to report the dirty deed had been done. After that I'd check in with the Scrivener, fly home, collect my gold and wait to hear from Sébastien.

I'd done this so many times now it had become routine but something was different this go-round. Something was bubbling toward the surface that I preferred stay well submerged in my subconscious: curiosity. The thing that I'd avoided thinking about on that long flight was now creeping toward the surface and demanding answers. I wanted to know who had been prosecuting my writs. I also wanted the suddenly burgeoning interest in this line of inquiry to go back to wherever it had come from. While I was busy fending off my need to know more, I was left defenseless against my urge to quiet my head with whiskey. It was Friday afternoon and thankfully I had until Monday morning to talk myself out of the crazy notion that I find out who had been prosecuting my writs.

My customary ransacking of the kitchen cabinets yielded an unopened handle of Jameson, which I uncapped and poured tall in a blink. Tumbler in hand I went back to the sofa where I sat and eyed the finely bound Beatles histoire on the coffee table. It looked like a one of a kind artifact made specifically for the lodging but I couldn't be bothered to investigate it. On my mind was Hamburg in the now, heavy and breathing down my neck.

I sat and thought about a shower but before I had even finished my whiskey, jetlag had caught me unawares. There on the sofa in the Fountain of Bambi I did fall asleep, drink in hand as I dreamt of floating through billowy white clouds in blue skies over Los Angeles. A different Los Angeles than the one I was from. Idyllic, Elysian, a pastoral panorama of overpasses succumb to tendrils of ivy, city streets sprouted with abundant crops and a beautiful teeming human rumpus where monsters once ruled.

It was just past nine o'clock when I was awakened by my blackphone buzzing on the coffee table. There was seldom a call which came through that phone unexpected and unexpected phone calls invariably sent jolts of terror through me. The last thing I wanted was a surprise visit from Monsieur Herman or Sébastien. That hadn't really been anything I'd come to expect from them but I could think of nothing else that might cause my phone to buzz. I reached for my Monolith as if sneaking up on a cobra. Once I had unlocked the screen I found something perhaps worse than a message from the Prelacy.

Jazzy - Hi Foster! Dis iz Jazzy. We r @ Bar Zero on Talstrasse. U shud cum hav drinks w us!

Holy shit. Jasmine, Jazzy for short. I had totally forgotten. I straightened in my seat a little and polished off the drink I'd left unfinished before my snooze. I decided I should shower up and go find this place. I just couldn't overlook the providence of meeting someone from Kaufmannsbank before I was meant to kill one of their top-dogs.

"S'at the broad from the plane ride over, Champ?"

Speaking of shit I'd totally forgotten. There was good ol' Al. Always the expert at picking just the right time to show up and startle me. There he was, sitting across the room from me thumbing through the Beatles histoire in a satin black Raiders jacket with a band-aid on his corpse-white, liver spotted head. My only friend in the world, Al.

"Don't sweat that, Wrinkles."

"Whatever, kid. How 'bout these digs, huh?" Al cooed, taking in the layout. "Pretty cool, right?"

"You a Beatles fan, Al?" I asked, getting up to pour another whiskey.

"Me? Nah. I only go for the good stuff, Ace. Four Seasons, Sinatra, Nat King Cole, stuff like that."

"Right. Got it." I said, refilling my tumbler. "That good stuff."

"You know one of these guys was in your little secret club?" Al said, staring down at the book.

"What, The Prelacy? One of what guys was in the Prelacy, Al?" I nearly spat.

"One of the Beatles, man."

"Which one?"

"One of the dead ones."

I gave that a moment to sink in, taking a nervous sip. If Al stuck around too long I'd start nervously tipping these back faster than usual, which I really didn't want to do.

"Which one?" I demanded, but interrupted myself. "Wait, let me guess. Paul, right? Was it Paul?"

"Nah, man. One of the dead ones I said."

"Paul's been dead since before Abbey Road was released, Al."

"Oh, c'mon. You don't believe in that tin-foil hat nonsense, do you, kid?" Seriously? My entire life was tin-foil hat nonsense.

"I don't know, man! So which one was it? George?"

"No, god damn it, I said one of the dead ones!"

"George has been dead for over a decade, Al."

"Oh. Well not that one."

"Then who?"

"Stuart Sutcliffe!".

"Who? Who the hell is Stuart Sutcliffe?"

"Their first bass player, man! He quit the band in '61 when Lennon got hip to his membership in the Prelacy. A year after that Lennon zapped him with a stolen CIA beam weapon that gave him a stroke."

"Get the fuck out of here!" this was typical Al insanity. Why did my imaginary friend have to be crazier than me? "And I'm the one with the Reynolds Tricorn? C'mon, man."

"I'm layin' it on you straight, baby. Lennon was OTO. He took out your boy Sutcliffe and then your Prelacy buddies took him out in 1980."

"Are you telling me Mark David Chapman is in the Prelacy?"

"What? No! Jody Foster is. She was controlling Chapman with neurolinguistic programming techniques."

"If you're not fucking with me, how do you know all this shit?"

"I told you kid, I was CIA back in the day. It was my job to keep tabs on all you creeps. The Prelacy, KGB, Cosa Nostra, OTO, Mossad. I've had my eye on all you weirdos since before you were even a slick line your dad laid on your mom."

"Al, even by your standards, this is level 10 crazy, but-hey, wait a second. Jody Foster? Jody Foster wasn't Mark David Chapman's thing. That was Hinkley, the guy who shot Reagan."

"Yeah, so?"

"Yeah, so? Yeah, so you're full of shit."

"How am I full of shit? Your girl, Jody was fucking around inside both of those poor kids' heads. Shoot, Sport. She came to your Prelacy club fresh out of the Monarch Program. Look it up sometime."

"Alright, that's enough Al for the day. You gotta go."

"You wish. Do whatever you've gotta do, kid. I'm just gonna hang out and look at this book right here. Read up on the Beatles and that."

"Whatever. Knock yourself out, ugly." I told Al as I finished my drink. "Why are you so ugly?"

"What? You don't like the black satin?"

"I just don't understand why you appear to me as crazy old, wrinkled eccentric Al sometimes and then young, sharp dressed 60s playboy Al at others."

"It's all in your head, kid. I got nothin' to do with it."

I gave that a thought and decided to let it go.

"Whatever, I gotta get in the shower. Try not to burn the place down."

Al just ignored me, his face buried in the Beatles histoire from the coffee table.

I set the empty tumbler on the coffee table, saw my Monolith sitting there and remembered the text from Jazzy. I picked up the phone and sent her a reply.

Me – Hi Jazzy. I'll be there a little after 10. See you soon.

I set my mobile back on the table, took another look at Al still sitting there reading about the Beatles and headed off to find the bathroom.

After my shower I went through my normal routine of agonizing over which black shirt and which black Levis to wear while Al sat in the high-backed chair quietly poring over the Beatles book.

"You know, kid. You've gotta figure out who's taking up your slack on these hits. It's no good you letting that go like you've been."

I came off the tracks a little at that and had to take a deep breath. After a pause I pulled a shirt over my head and answered.

"I know, I know. Look, I'm on top of it. I'm gonna sort that out on this mission. I'm even thinking about prosecuting the writ myself."

"C'mon, kid. That ain't you. Just worry about finding out who's doing the wet work that you won't and leave it at that for now."

"I can't keep doing it like this. I made some mistakes, got a little off course but at some point I have to right the ship." I said, sitting down on the couch, reaching for my trainers.

"It don't work like that. I know you want it to but it don't work like that."

"Work like what?"

Al put down the book and looked me right in the eye. I looked away to tie my shoes. Or more honestly not to look him in the eye, as I could tell I might not like what he was about to say.

"How many people you kill over there in Afghanistan?"

"None."

"That's right. None. And how many hitters did the Prelacy pair you with during your apprenticeship?"

"Like how? What do you mean?"

"They ever have you shadow another assassin on one of his hits? You know, just to sort of show you the ropes?"

"No. Never."

I heard Al lean back in his chair and I could feel his glare, looking right through me. I didn't know what else to say and it felt like an eternity waiting for him to talk.

"Right. They had you picking up big shots from the airport, fetching Zankou Chicken for that old kook Sébastien and occasionally sweeping crime scenes or disposing of evidence for them."

"So?"

"So why no tasks related to developing your skill set? What does picking up food orders and taking out the trash have to do with becoming an assassin?"

"I don't think that's how they do things, Al." I said, feeling like Al was overthinking things a little.

"You think a 15 century old secret society just relies on trial and error? Kid you have to look at this from a more critical perspective."

"Sébastien says they've been training me my whole life."

"Yeah, but for what?"

"What do you mean? Where are you going with all this, Al?"

I had my trainers on and I was ready to head out toward the Reeperbahn but something told me I wouldn't be leaving anytime soon.

"Look, I don't know about all that 'training you your whole life' jive but it wouldn't surprise me if they had that sort of long game. All I know is that since you've joined their little club they've been training you for something but it wasn't to be an assassin."

"Would you get to the point already?"

"Just look at your initiation tasks. There were all these easy little low risk, high reward assignments. These guys weren't cultivating a killer instinct in you, they were making you into a lazy, mistrusting sucker. Patting you on the back like they're old friends, making you think this was all some easy-breezy Country Club shit that it's not."

"Bullshit. They don't operate like that. The only thing wrong with this picture is I haven't been giving the Prelacy my due diligence and I have to get on track, that's all."

"Let me tell you a little something about the human animal. I spent 4 decades in the NFL, I know a little bit about the animal in man."

"Is this gonna take long, because I really had other plans tonight, Al."

"Relax, this is important stuff, kid. Stay with me on this."

I just shrugged, sat back in my seat and figured on meeting up with Jazzy and her guy a little later than planned.

"Just get on with it."

"You ever see wolves fight?"

"Where would I see wolves fight, Al?"

"I don't know, cable? Wild Kingdom? You never seen wolves fight?"

"No, I've never seen wolves fight." I sigh, already tired of this.

"Well, it's an interesting thing. See, wolves are one of nature's killing machines. When a wolf gets into it with another animal, its single intention is to eviscerate that beast."

Al's eyes flicker in the light with life as he relates this all. He is positively lucid and engaged.

"Alright." I follow.

"But when a wolf fights another wolf, as they often do, they only fight until one of them yields. They'll go at it, fur flying, all teeth and growls until eventually one of them will lie on the ground and offer his neck in a gesture of submission. And just like that, it's over."

"That's really cool and everything, Al, it really is but what's this got to do with what we've been talking about?"

"Well, kid, here's the thing. Killing your own species is pretty unnatural, even for one of nature's killing machines. I know you think it's as simple as making up your mind and doing it but it's not. It's not like some light switch you can just flick off and on."

"I'm not a wolf, Al."

"Damn right you're not, kid. Listen, when you were in the Afghanistan, did you have any non-firers in your unit?"

And just like that, a sore subject had been unearthed. I knew where Al was headed a little more now and I would rather not go there. In the military, only about one in five soldiers are actually reliable shooters. I wasn't one of them. While the shooters would take care to actually sight a target and take them out, the rest of us would "posture fire" as it's called. This phenomena has occurred on any side of any battle for as long as guns had fought wars.

"I don't want to talk about this anymore, Al. I'm going down to the Reeperbahn to meet some people for drinks and I'd appreciate it if you weren't here when I get back."

I stood and began to pat myself down for keys, wallet, phone before I made for the door.

"It's OK if you don't want to talk about it but you have to listen to me. You have to just hear me out a little longer and then you can go."

"I don't have to do anything, Al."

"C'mon, kid. Hear me out, just a little longer. I'm sorry to bring up a touchy subject."

"You've got 5 minutes and then I'm out of here."

"It'll only take two."

"Go. I'm listening" I told Al, checking the time on my mobile.

"Here's the deal, kid. And bear with me, this is all from my experience in the league. This is real deal shit and I know what I'm talking about."

I offered no response, looking at him, brow arched with impatience.

"Combat releases testosterone. Victories and accomplishments load your body with it. Testosterone makes you aggressive, invigorates you. The more you fight and the more you win the more drive you have to fight again and win again. And again and again."

I wanted to take a crack at his Raiders, instead I just shrugged and stared as Al continued trying to communicate whatever it was in his crazy head.

"On the other hand, you've got submission. Submission floods your body with cortisol. Cortisol relaxes you, makes you soft. The more you let shit slide, the more passive and complacent you become."

"Wrap it up, Al. You've gotta bring this all home pretty fast, buddy or I'm out the door."

"So why do you think the Prelacy picked you, Foster? Why you? And why did all of their initiations seem geared toward easy reward, rather than challenges you'd have to fight through?"

And bring it all home he did, like a category 4 tornado. I suddenly needed a seat, and found myself back on the couch.

"In you, kid, they weren't looking for an assassin, they were looking for an unquestioning, loyal patsy. Someone who wasn't a killer."

"I think I'm gonna need another drink before I go out drinking."

"Sorry to lay it on you so heavy but something's going on, kid. A whole lot more than meets the eye and you need to realize that before you can get to the bottom of whatever it is."

I passed Al on the way to the kitchen for one more and he returned to his chair to read about the Beatles.

THIRTY-THREE

West Seattle, WA – Tues Oct 14th 2014

Back at the Rusty Anchor for a little more fun, Arlene and I have seated ourselves at the same table where we sat last night. Arlene agreed to join me only on the condition that under no circumstances was I to ply my hobby of winding up strangers. As my new friends from last night, the REI fleeced white natives appear to be absent, it seems I will have no trouble respecting her demand. The bartender and the old salt in the Greek fisherman's hat are right where we left them, but the place is otherwise lifeless and empty.

Arlene, nose already buried in Evola, is quietly sipping Cab Sav at glacial speed while I am doing my best not to pace her with my usual Jameson neat. I'm considering a walk over to the jukebox to look for Slayer as I fidget with my phone when a bolt of lightning hits me. I know how I can get into her blackphone. I see that my mobile's battery is still at a near full charge so what I have in mind will require me to wait. In preparation, I mute the phone and begin running audio, video and other demanding apps, lock the screen and wait for the charge to drain. If my clumsy ploy works, in about 20 minutes I'll have access to Arlene's Monolith and we'll be listening to Slayer on the jukebox. I stop nursing my Jameson, take it down in one swallow and head off to the bar for a refill.

I return unimpeded, empty bar parted wide. I shuffle back to our table, a spring to my step if I'm telling the naked truth. My mood has been on an upswing since last night and I dare say it's trending in spite of all the peril and mystery I'm recently beset with. This very realization invites a momentary darkening of spirit once I've identified the source of my levity: I'm enamored with Arlene. Irresponsible, delusional, whimsical and a thousand other words I use to describe men at their skirt-chasing dumbest. That's me right now.

Jameson be thanked, I can ignore those specters yet and just go right along feeling good. Being happy is for simpletons and I don't rate it high on my list of needs, but apparently right now I have an inexplicable determination to be just that. Something I normally have no clue how to be is now all at once the only way I'll permit myself to be. Go figure. I suspect the down turn following this level of mania is going to be hell to pay so I might as well enjoy it while it lasts.

"Madame Aureline, does your cloak work keep you in the States mostly or are you constantly traveling?" I ask, situating myself again next to Arlene. She looks up from her book and shrugs.

"The Prelacy sends me to all of the same places they send you, I would imagine."

I squash down the well-earned paranoia that she's being literal. I've mostly stopped wondering if she's been prosecuting my writs for me. Her words have an ominous entendre, none the less.

"Do you like it here?"

"In the States or here in Seattle?" she asks.

"Either, both." I respond.

After a pause Arlene says, "I haven't seen much that I like about either, to be honest."

I let her words hang and watch as she sips her wine.

"I prefer the countryside. The Prelacy only ever needs me in the city." She finishes.

"You seem perfectly at home in the city." I say a bit disbelieving.

"Of course I do, I have spent most of my life in cities but I prefer the pastoral. Give me a vineyard over a penthouse any day."

I resist breaking into the Green Acres theme and instead sit trying to adjust my perception of Arlene, reconciling this information with the cosmopolitan archetype I've credulously profiled her as. She's very much the intelligent urban sophisticate in presentation but peel back the layers and she's what? This cold European god botherer who reads fascist philosophy and hates the city, if not the world as a whole. It's a bit dizzying unpacking it all when you're looking on what appears to be a perfectly packaged woman of the world. Her outward display is a bright contrast to the person she masks. As I'm staring like a deer in headlights Arlene finishes her wine and rises from her place at our table.

"I need to use the ladies' room and I need more wine." She says, gulping the last of her wine and patting the top of my hand with a brief smile. "I'll be right back."

Immediately on my mind is trying to get into her Monolith while she's away. I do my best to stay casual as I set my play into motion.

"Hey, don't go yet. I want to show you something." I tell Arlene.

"What is it? I have to go." She says suffering my antics, playful though impatient.

"They have an internet jukebox. Wanna see me hack it?" I say as I pick up my Monolith and unlock it.

"Godefroi, you could probably buy this pig pin with your walking around money, why would you care about hacking their jukebox for some free songs?"

"Because it's fun!"

"I'll be right back, you're being weird.""

"No, don't go yet, my battery's dead." I say showing her the now depleted charge on its meter. "Let me use your Monolith, yeah?"

"Really, a social engineering hack?" Arlene scoffs. "That's the best you could think of?"

"What? I wasn't trying to do anything shady."

"Save it. I've got to use the ladies' room. I'll be right back." She says, dismissing me. "That was weak." She adds, laughing over her shoulder as she walks away shaking her head.

I think I'm more surprised that she'd use the rest room in this dump than I am at her catching me in a hustle. I really thought I was being slick, too. What's even more surprising is that she just up and left her purse behind with her Monolith in it, in spite of what I'd just tried to do.

Naturally, as soon as she's out of sight I'm rifling through her bag for her Monolith when I find it situated right next to another blackphone much like the Prelacy's Monoliths but not identical. Of course, she has one for her Prelacy communications and one for the Covenant. I should have figured on that.

I try accessing both devices with no luck. The phones both contain a biometric security feature unlocked by facial recognition and once that primary security feature is defeated there would be a secondary code authentication, same as my own blackphone. A little frustrated, a little defeated I replace the mobile devices in her purse and head over to the jukebox to pay for some Slayer. If only I'd had the foresight, the operational imagination to load a hacking script onto the blackphone she handed to me in the cab the other night.

By the time I'm done kicking myself, I'm back at our table, the opening riffs to Angel of Death have finished and Tom Arraya's banshee howl is signaling the song's second movement. I reseat myself and sulk over my Jameson as I consider trying a Bluetooth or Near Field Communication exploit later.

"Any luck?" Arlene says, with an antagonizing grin as she returns, pulling out her chair.

"With what?"

"Getting into my blackphones."

"I wasn't trying to hack you, Arlene."

"You're an awful liar."

Her sense of humor about this is disarming but I'm embarrassed just the same.

"I'm not mad." She says. "It's inevitable that you would try to gather intel on me. I'd want to do the same thing if I were in your shoes."

"I wasn't trying to hack you." I say, nervous laugh be damned. I may be an awful liar but I'm sticking to my story. Arlene just shakes her head at me. Is that pity? No, that's amusement.

"I was hoping that we were closer to feeling more like allies than adversaries by now, but I understand." She says.

"I thought we were!" I protest." I mean we are. What, you can't tell I'm starting to feel comfortable around you?"

"Comfortable enough to lie to my face." Again with the teasing smirk.

"Can we change the subject?" I plead as she pauses to gulp down her wine uncharacteristically.

"Did you at least pay for the Slayer?" she asks after a lull.

"Yeah." I say sheepishly. She just laughs and I give in as well, laughing along with her.

"Poor baby. I'll get the next round, maybe you won't feel so bad." She says, grabbing my glass and heading for the bar.

I watch Arlene slink to the bar, all black clad, mysterious and smoldering. My attention is soon broken by the racket of our new best friends, the white natives from last night. The two are piss drunk and the woman is rapping the words to "Baby Got Back" at the top of her lungs as giggly and awful as it's ever been done. As they pass she sees me and wrinkles her nose at me, then stumbles the rest of the way to the bar. Nothing else to do and unfocused, I shift my attention toward my Monolith to browse social media while Arlene is away. I defeat its security features and am promptly reminded that I drained the battery when the screen goes black. Under normal circumstances my first impulse would be to go wind up the Cherohonkees some more but tonight, the only thing I want to do is listen to Arlene talk. The last thing on my mind is winding up those idiots. Is this what contentment feels like?

"Looks like your new besties finally made it in." Arlene kids, setting my Jameson down in front of me before seating herself.

"You think I should go say hi, maybe invite them over for a drink?" I ask; a playful empty threat that elicits a smile from Arlene.

"God, no. I would rather play Russian roulette with 5 bullets in a six shooter than listen to those morons prattle on."

"I'll drink to that." I say.

To my slight surprise Arlene raises her glass.

"To not suffering the company of idiots." She toasts.

Was that a compliment? I waste no time bringing my rocks glass to clank with her stemware and effort to conceal any evidence of feeling flattered.

A comfortable silence settles on our table and I glance over at the couple bellied up to the bar. Arlene has returned to poring over her dog-eared copy of Revolt Against the Modern World. Occasionally she stops to write something in the margins and I admire her a little more if that were possible. I had a pretty nice little library of my own I'd been growing at home and not a single book on the shelves had been dog-eared or written in, let alone read twice, many yet unread, unopened even. My pristine, meticulously lorded over piles-no, shelves, never piles-of tsundoku feel shameful in comparison to Arlene's single haggard paperback edition of a book I can't even imagine taking serious. Though she and I have little in common philosophically, I admire her for having the moral courage to stand behind her taboo beliefs. OK, maybe I won't go that far, maybe I'm just a little too enamored with Arlene to ever imagine challenging her proscribed beliefs. In any case, I'm satisfied I respect her a lot more than the mediocre rabble I'm used to winding up when they trot out their dogma in some dive like this one; people like those two morons at the bar right now.

If nothing else, I'm comfortable saying that I admire the way she apparently owns her books like I don't. I treat my books like treasures but I don't engage them on the level Arlene obviously does hers. I imagine she's one of those people whose books all look lived in. My entire library looks like it's being kept in shape for selling back to the bookstore at the end of the semester. Watching her read is arousing me as much as it's making me feel like a pseudo-intellectual, if not a fraud entirely. I brush it all off and finish my drink before getting up to brave the bar for another. I'm not looking forward to drawing any attention from that couple, though normally I would relish exactly that.

"How's yours, Arlene, you good?" I ask, nodding at her near full glass. She smiles and shakes her head, returns to reading and I make my trudge across the DMZ bracing for an encounter with hostiles.

"Uh-oh, here he comes," the formerly head dressed woman

announces in a well lubed slur, "Hey, buddy. Who'd you vote for in the last election?"

I try to ignore her. Normally, I'd love for this couple to set the table so I could clear it but right now I just want to relax with Arlene.

"I'll bet it wasn't Obama. I'll tell you that." Her old man says.

The one thing in this world I so love to do is fuck with these two and all of their clones throughout creation but right now what I really want to do is get back to talking with Arlene, if not just watching her read. There's a qualia in that. A thing that isn't totally clear to me but a thing I enjoy for better or worse, no matter how uncomfortable. Even when she makes me angry or makes me feel small or stupid I'm sprung on having it out with her.

No sooner do I roll this awful realization around in my head than I hear myself laugh out loud at the fact that there's little if any chance Arlene is having the same experience with me. I'm seeing signals but I can't seem to get past worrying it's all just part of her Mata Hari tradecraft. I'm most likely just a temporary annoyance she has to tolerate in light of bigger goals. I might soon have to deal with the truth of being misled by her because I've become enamored. The bartender just nods and refills my glass. I snort another laugh at how stupid I feel.

"What? Something's funny to you, mister? The President's funny to you?" the Costco jeaned, grey waterfall haired man in fleece demands, as if I've insulted his Queen.

My laugh to myself about Arlene. It wasn't intended for them but they don't know that and now I'm going to have to access parts of my brain I've put on vacay If want to defuse their aggression.

"We're Canadian you Big Mac Guzzling gun nuts, we can't vote in your fixed elections so leave us alone." Arlene casually says swooping in to rescue me.

"We hate guns! We're anti-gun" the woman cries out mortified she might have been confused with one of the bad Yanks. In her head she's the good kind of American.

"We don't eat McDonalds!" the man protests. "We're all about locally sourced organic."

"Liars. Filthy racist, GMO-fueled warmongers is what you are." Arlene slays, "Now stop harassing us, eh." She deflates them in an affected Canadian accent.

I just look at her in amazement. I've never wanted to grab someone by their beautifully pronounced cheeks and squeal so much in my entire life. I tone it down to a look of relief and she flashes back that smirk. After I've paid for my drink we're back at our booth.

"That was-"

She smiles and shushes me with one finger over my lips.

"You toy with these people and their truths when you should just devastate them with a disarming lie and get on with your life, love."

I'll spend the next few hours convincing myself that wasn't the Mancunian pronoun 'love'. She hung it that way on purpose, I know she did. I am really starting to hate her in the most spellbound of ways.

THIRTY-FOUR

Los Angeles, CA – Thurs Oct 28th, 1993

A quarter of three and Mrs. Broughton was wrapping up her lecture to the class on the infamy and terror that white men had brought to the Americas 500 years ago and how they remained here to this day, eager to spoil any chance of a good life for most everyone in the classroom. In 15 minutes she'd be in her Volvo driving back to the safety of lily white Simi Valley while I'd be left to walk home among the chicanos and blacks she'd just obliviously spent the last 45 minutes encouraging to do their worst to me. The only other white face in our class was a girl named Hannah Goertz, an upper-middle class Jew from Hancock Park who lived with her mother 20 minutes West of the 5. The only reason she was even forced to attend this school is she'd been kicked out of everywhere else, private and public, always for drug offenses. We didn't talk.

I might have had an honest expectation of an ass kicking on that walk home but it was more likely some recreational harassment from the closest thing I had to friends at the time. I'd lived in the neighborhood off and on since my mom and I first moved there some nine years ago and by now I knew everyone. I stopped getting shit for being white around third grade, but there were still some guys who were assholes about it. To be honest, by the time I was thirteen I was more worried about running into kids from Highland Park or El Sereno than running into any sort of racial abuse. I'd fallen in with one of the abundant local Surenos gangs in the area and in short order, the beatings for being from the wrong race had given way to beatings for being from the wrong place. Beatings were still a pretty frequent fact of life, none the less. Some days I gave them, some days I got them. And on some rare, blessed days there were none at all.

188

Back then I was more inclined to use my smart mouth for getting me out of a beating, rather than tempting one. Still, I got really good at knowing when I wasn't going to be talking my way out of anything and I might as well just start running or swinging.

When the bell rang and class let out I met Chico at the bike racks toward the front of the campus like I did every day and was excited to see Sailor and Joker and skipped their last class to meet us there. We sat there for a while, had a word or two with other kids we knew and waited to see a couple girls we meant to say hi to before heading home. Eventually the place would empty out and we'd make our way home through a drainage ditch and then North along the Union Pacific railroad tracks. Most of the time Chico would have a joint for us to smoke while we walked and talked about who was a ranker, which hyna was fine, which teacher needed his ass kicked and on and on.

"Hey, Huero I'm not talking shit but the older homies said if you're going to get put on you've got to handle one of these mayates like we talked about." Sailor said to me as he skipped a rock off of the tracks.

Mayate is a Spanish pejorative for blacks and Sailor was talking about finalizing my membership in the neighborhood gang. If it was going to happen, I had to kill a member of a black gang they were pressuring out of the area. I had been up every night trying to think of how I would ever survive in this place if I didn't have strong, tough people like them to run with. I also thought about how there was no way I wanted to do what they were asking of me just to gain membership in the neighborhood. My thirteen year old brain just couldn't see its way out of this damning conundrum. What's worse is I knew if I failed to complete the dirty deed, I'd be in worse standing. I'd never make it out of Boyle Heights alive. With each new day it seemed as though my only option was clear and I'd just have to do it, regardless of how I felt.

I had no problem with the violence of this life I seemed to be headed for; fights, beatings, law breaking and what not-but this was different. What they expected from me was far less chaotic far, less random. They wanted me to commit an up close and personal act of premeditated murder. The very thought made my stomach tingle and my knees weak.

"I know, eh? I've just never see any of those vatos around and whenever I go looking for them there's always a placa or sometimes, like today I can't sneak the strap you gave me past my mom and out of the house or-"

"It's all good, don't trip." Chico told me. "We're going to go handle it with you tonight."

Sailor nodded at Joker who lifted his Charlie Brown Cascade to reveal a revolver tucked in his matching Ben Davis work pants.

"Don't be scared, Huero." Joker reassured me, sincere and understanding. "I was all fucked up when I had to make my huesos but we do what we gotta do, que no?"

Sailor and Joker were all three years older than me and Chico but they were my closest friends, them and Chico. I always thought they felt sorry for me and took me under their wings. I was never as cool as them, never as tough but to them, it never mattered. They looked out for me anyway.

These three and I had spent most of the last year meeting at Joker's house every day after class where we would listen to oldies, crease our clothes and drink wine we'd stolen from a distribution warehouse at the bottom of the hill. We'd spend the nights driving around in a borrowed car one of the older homies would lend us or in a caper car we'd stolen. We'd pick up girls from other neighborhoods, smoke weed, share stories and work on perfecting our cool.

I'd come to lean on and trust these three as much as a thirteen year old can know about those things, skipping right past childhood in a place where no thirteen year old should have to figure out how to become a man. The last thing I wanted to do was disappoint them or lose them as friends. In spite of the chaotic violence and constant lawlessness, life was finally starting to make sense to me. I couldn't see blowing that off for anything, and so I went along with them down the railroad tracks steeling myself for whatever lay ahead.

"Mira, I seen one of them fools coming out of this pad on Isabel a mess of times. We'll kick it up here at the wall and down some pistos." Sailor said. "When it gets dark we'll try to catch him slipping."

After a few more minutes walking along the tracks we came to a cinder block wall that divided the rails from San Fernando, the main road running parallel. Three of us sat along the tracks and smoked another joint while Chico ran to the store for beer.

"Serio, Huero, we'll just snatch the fool up, bring him back here, handle it and dip back to the varrio. It ain't nothing, homie." Sailor comforted.

"We'll get this handled and it'll be on. Next meeting the older homies will let us court you into our clicka."

A round of back clapping and hand-clasping followed with a "Fuck yeah, homes" here and an "Orale" there.

I smiled with a measure of pride at the thought of being put on the neighborhood and for a time I was relieved of worry. Inside though, I carried fear, even shame. It felt fucked up doing this. I didn't even know this kid, had nothing personal against him and the only thing that seemed to be motivating this was some sort of deranged, racial cleansing of the neighborhood. I fought and fought with my own guilt, the shame and nausea over the whole thing until Chico returned with a twelve pack of Budweiser and a bottle of Night Train. I wanted only to drink in enough courage to do this thing which I did not want to do at all.

There, the four of us sat and drank for another hour or so as the twilight went from hazy heather blue to the California sky's signature shade of post-golden hour coral and eventually gave way to the yellow-lit black of old

Los Angeles night. Budweisers depleted and the last of the Night Train passed around, Joker stood, removed the pistol from his waistband and handed it to me.

"Alright, carnal. I'm gonna see if I can hem this puto up. Once we get this handled we'll go kick it in Joker's garage. I got some firme kush from the older homie, Happy so we can celebrate." Sailor told me.

"You ready?" Sailor smiled, hand on my shoulder.

"Don't trip, Huero." Chico reassured. "It'll be over in a minute and we'll go kick it. It's all good."

I think what stands out most in my mind looking back is how supportive they were. I think stereotypically one would imagine brutal ridicule, goading and a lot of blood thirsty excitement. The truth is, none of us wanted to do this but all of us had to make our bones to get in and tonight it was going to be my turn.

We must have waited a full ten minutes before Joker could be seen walking up the tracks towards us, apparently with one of the Crips he said he'd seen around the area. To my astonishment, the guy seemed jovial, boisterous even, telling Joker some story I couldn't hear from where we were standing. Joker had apparently manufactured some sort of consensual rapport, probably with the false promise of women and party favors or a good deal on a stolen item. He would've had to have lied about our affiliation, too and that would have definitely come up. Still, it seemed as if the two were comfortable enough around each other to suggest a mutual familiarity. The thought made my heart fall to my stomach.

The dark skinned young Crip stood about a foot taller than Joker, dressed in standard Hoover blue. As they got close enough for me to see their faces, I was stunned to recognize him. Walking up to us was Rocklynn Coleman. It seemed he had taken the same wrong turn in life we had, finding his way among the gangs. I watched the look on Rocklynn's face go from gregarious to terrified when he saw Sailor handing me the pistol. Rocklynn turned to run but tripped over Joker's extended foot and fell face first into the gravel along the railroad tracks.

"Vaminos, Huero!" I heard Chico shout-whisper as he spurred me forward with a shove.

I bolted forward, pistol angled down at Rocklynn, hammer cocked as I stood over him. The world around me spinning and buzzing, the urging of my friends in my ears.

"Smoke him, Huero!"

"Bust, fool, bust!"

My hands shaking, heart pounding, each draw of breath faster and steeper than the last, eyes tunnel-visioned with panic as I tried to make my finger pull back on the trigger. It wouldn't do, my finger just would not obey the command. Rocklynn was trying to get up and each time he did he was laid back down from kicks to his head and ribs, Chico and Joker pitching in. I realized I had lowered the weapon and as I was raising it again, hands impossible to steady, Sailor grabbed the gun from me and pushed me aside.

A shot rang out then another and two more as I just stared away in shock, eyes fixed on the pinhole blips of air traffic to the North over Burbank. Fear in my heart, I looked down at Rocklynn's body as my friends consoled me with arm-hugs and back pats.

"Don't trip, Huero. It's all good, homes." Sailor said, disappointed but understanding none the less.

"It ain't for everybody, eh. We don't care, you're with us." Joker said.

"We're gonna tell the older homies you handled your business. You're getting put on the varrio, we don't give a fuck." Sailor said.

And that was it. In just the few short hours between the last school bell and those gunshots my life had changed again. I had thrown in with the only friends I had to cruelly betray someone who had once helped us, someone who didn't deserve to die.

"Don't trip, eh. I know it's fucked up. Rocklynn was cool but it was him or us, homes." Joker said.

"Serio, he was Cripping, Huero. He would've eventually taken one of our gente out if we didn't get him first." Chico added.

"C'mon, Huero. Let's go kick it. Try not to think about it. It had to be done." Sailor urged as we headed back down the railroad tracks towards Joker's garage.

I've been surrounded by death and dying my whole life. Surrounded by killers in spite of not being one myself. I couldn't pull the trigger then and I can't do it now. Somehow I'm always supposed to be doing it though. I wonder how many of us in this world are out there leading lives we were never meant for, faking it every single day to get by. Being a fraud gets exhausting after a couple of decades.

THIRTY-FIVE

West Seattle, WA – Tues Oct 14th 2014

Arlene and I have conceded the Rusty Anchor to its locals but we are not yet ready to return to the Covenant safehouse. In discussing our options we've decided to grab a pint of Jameson from the corner store then sit and share it on a bus bench outside the Rusty Anchor. Mostly my idea, as she doesn't really care much to keep drinking. To put it in more honest terms, she's consented to my dragging her to the corner store for a pint of whiskey and then sitting on a bus bench in the intrusive Seattle cold while we talk more, because I'm not ready to head back to the safehouse. In any case, we've both had enough of the Rusty Anchor.

Inside the corner store a group of five black teens in gaudy hood-chic are making a racket while they stuff things in their pockets they have no intention of paying for. Arlene and I trade smirks at their antics. The simple counter-intuitive idea of being the noisiest person in the store you're stealing from is sublime comedy lost on neither of us. I ask the stout, well groomed Sikh behind the counter for a pint of Jameson as he sorts through whether to call the police or confront the kids himself. As I pay for the bottle and we head out the door I hear a cacophony of indignant interrogations shouted at the Sikh. "Y'all ain't got no burners?" and "Where the Gummy Bears at?" and "Why you ain't got no Magnums?" Arlene and I share another stifled laugh as we head back toward the bus bench.

We sit close to one another under the bus stop shelter as I crack the bottle. I take the first sip, trying not to get too carried away by the fact that we're somewhat snuggled together. Just to keep warm, no doubt. Something just shy of actual cuddling but a little more friendly than rival schools surviving a plane crash in the Andes.

"You're an only child, aren't you?" she comments, elbowing my ribs.

"Is that deduction or are you confirming intel?" my playful rejoinder.

"No, seriously, can we not be adversarial? I thought we were pretending we're friends."

"OK, yeah I am an only child, how could you tell?"

"It's in your file." She can't help laughing.

"See how you are?" I laugh back, shaking my head.

"I'm kidding, the Covenant's not omniscient, Godefroi. There's plenty I don't know about you." She assures. "I don't know anything about your childhood."

"Not much to know, really."

"Well, tell me something. I want to know." She presses, seeming genuinely interested.

I'm eager to please Arlene. Enough so that I would tell her most anything about myself but this is well out of my comfort zone. I'm ashamed of my family and background, more so ashamed of the fact that I'm not grown enough to be over it all. Better men just tuck away family resentments and get on with living. I'm that small person who can't get past it, so I bury it. I give it some thought in private but it's never discussed with others, let alone with strangers. Arlene is still a stranger for all intents and purposes though I guess we can pretend we're friends.

"What's there to talk about? Same story as everyone else." I say, "Mom and Dad made a good go of it. Didn't work. Here I am."

"Ooh! Minimalizing! Now I'm intrigued." She says, a little too game.

"Not gonna happen, shorty. Why don't you tell me about your family." I counter.

"I've been talking about myself all day, it's your turn." She shuts down.

"Then let's talk about something else." I say offering her a swig which she declines.

As I take a swig of Jameson Arlene elbows me in the ribs and points her chin toward the kids from the corner market coagulating at the bus bench across the street. They spread out and posture then cluster again intermittently. One is doing pull-ups on the bus bench's shelter while two others are laughing at something they're viewing on a smart phone. Another pair share a blunt and converse while surveying their plunder from the store run.

"God, I was just like them once."

Arlene shoves me away and looks at me with what I can only interpret as disgust.

"How were you ever like those kids, Godefroi?"

"I mean, OK, I probably wasn't as bad ass as they are but I didn't give a fuck, the same way they don't."

Arlene just dismisses the notion with a snort of disbelief and returns to hugging up against me.

"You were never as sad and hopeless as them." She says finally.

"Do those motherfuckers look sad to you?" I ask as the one doing pull-ups starts making overly sexualized moans while his friends laugh at his display.

She takes a moment to respond.

"No, you're right. They look too shallow for the sort of reflection a proper ennui would require."

"Harsh." I say, hoping we don't have to talk much more about the kids across the street.

The overt, racial hate I was raised around in Boyle Heights comes calling back at the sight of Arlene's bigotry. I'm not repulsed by racism as much as people who've seldom seen it in regular practice appear to be. Those people love to make a show of how it offends and injures them so, whether it actually does or not. It doesn't affect me that way and I'm not on the lookout for the hypothetical racism that drives the modern paranoia either. I'm affected by overt, conscious, conscientious racial hate. I have seen plenty of that cruel, casual brutality, lived among the regular and accepted racial chauvinism that occurs far outside the color of law or the security of wealth. Being around it doesn't move me to protest but it affects me in that I'm eye-rollingly exhausted by all of it, from every side.

The hateful tone of Arlene's remarks resurfaces memories I'd rather stay buried, sure but more than made uncomfortable, I'm just annoyed by it. I've yet to meet many people of any race who aren't petty bigots, so I know better than to let it bother me. Regardless, hers is a childish hate practiced by the poor and ignorant of which Arlene is neither. It's likely I've lost at least a little respect for her tonight, this beautiful woman who ought to be intelligent, mature and secure enough to be above this sort of banal loathing. Then again, people who have the stamina for hate seldom permit their intelligence or maturity to disabuse them of it.

"How funny you are, Godefroi."

"What's that supposed to mean?" I ask.

Arlene shoves herself away from me again and takes the Jameson from me this time. She unscrews the lid giving me a judgmental once over, never returning the bottle.

"Do you really identify with those kids?" she asks, "Do you see yourself like them, somehow? Or are you just being contrary right now?"

"What? You don't think those kids are a fucking riot?"

Bad choice of words. She laughs at my unintentional entendre then let's it go.

"So you think they're pretty neat, do you?" she presses. "We just watched them shake down that little corner market."

"And we both laughed about it. I don't get it, what's your deal?"

"Well, I think I was laughing at how, if you're keen to rob an American market you apparently have to be obvious about it instead of sneaky. What were you laughing about?"

"I think I was laughing at that, too, for the most part."

"Maybe you were laughing because you were nervous." She says.

"Oh, c'mon."

"You were. Maybe you wanted to say something but you were scared of seeming racist."

Her emphasis on the word racist similar to the way someone might tease the word boogeyman.

"Racist." I sigh. "I don't give a shit about that vague, emotional, thought terminating cliché everyone loves to lean on. I just can't be bothered to give a shit about a bunch of kids ripping off the corner market when I used to do the same stupid shit."

"And you say you aren't a nihilist. Here I am trying to imagine you as someone who has a morality of some kind."

"I do. Do you really want to unpack this all right now?"

"Kind of."

"It's not pretty." I caution.

"So you thought it was cute, them robbing that place blind while we gave them cover buying your booze?"

"Cute? Yeah, like a shark on the other side of 4 inch plexi-glass is cute."

"So what do you find so endearing, so funny?"

"It is what it is. I see kids like them all the time so why bother giving a shit what they do? Their entire circumstance of hopelessness forces a dependency on plunder and contraband. I can't fix that and I get a kick out of their shamelessness."

"And it doesn't bother you that they're almost surely convinced you came into this world with a debt to them by simple virtue of being born white? That their tragic fable is all your fault because you were born with the original sin of white skin? "

"Being hated for being white lost its sting for me long before high school." I shake my head, tiring of this conversation. "All I'm trying to say is nobody wants to get by like they are."

"Oh, is that it? They have it so bad it's OK if they steal? Your poor are the envy of the rest of the world's poor but to hear your kind tell it they're always entitled to more. At least as much as they can carry while running."

"Wow. You're seriously harboring some resentment in that heart of yours aren't you?"

"Oh, don't feign moral outrage, love. That's how imbeciles make themselves feel dignified and intelligent. You're better than that."

Love? She did it again. I try to act like I don't notice. I know it's just colloquial but it shrinks the distance between us none the less. Puts her right inside my head and makes me nervous.

"Nope, you're deflecting. You just trotted out some prize-winning hate and brushed its silky mane. Now take your Best-In-Show ribbon and deal with it." I tease, trying to lighten the mood a little.

She drives an elbow in my ribs again playfully. I pretend it doesn't hurt and I am too enamored to acknowledge that it annoys the shit out of me. How is it I'm coming to adore this cold-hearted, god bothering fascist? I'd say it's equal parts stunning good looks and her ability to wind me up like no one else can.

"Well what's to be done, then Godefroi? Is it alright for them to behave that way?"

"Oh, yeah. Let's go ahead and figure out black kids. You and me, a couple of smart white pseudo-intellectuals here, we'll just sit on this bus bench and figure out what's best for them, yeah? That what you think?"

"You go from phony moral outrage to genuine moral cowardice." Arlene claws. "Why can't we discuss it?"

"I just don't see why you need for me to care about what they do, one way or the other. It's taboo for me to discuss them and that taboo is quite convenient for me because I don't fucking care what anyone else does."

"Well, it wasn't your corner store being robbed, was it?"

"That's right. God help them if it was."

" Oh , c'est si bon! They better watch out messing with you. You might do absolutely nothing and then they'd mysteriously drop dead while you'd get some more Prelacy gold for your trouble!"

Ouch.

"You're right again, Arlene. You always are." I take the bottle back and drink.

It stings. Arlene has repeatedly proven herself an expert at revealing my own hypocrisy. A beat passes where we say nothing and I watch the kids across the street thinking of how I spent my nights in Boyle Heights as a kid. Chico, Sailor, Joker. They're all dead now but when we were wild and young we lived as if there were no tomorrow every single night, because there really might not be. For them, that proved to be true. And then there's me, my life kept going and it's just gotten weirder and weirder since.

"Seriously, why do you hate those kids, Arlene?"

"I don't hate them, I don't even know them."

"OK, but you don't like them. Why?"

"Are you kidding me, Godefroi, what's to like? They're animals, look at them."

She says a lot of things that make me uncomfortable, but I'm having a hard time disagreeing with her as I gaze across the street to see two of the kids slap boxing with their shirts off in the 42 degree chill while one is pantomiming sex acts to the other two who laugh as they follow along with his story. I can't do it, though. I can't join her in disdain. What she sees repulses her and what I see makes me light hearted and nostalgic. If those are animals then suffice it to say, I too was an animal once and I spent every day among beasts in fear for my life or making others fear for theirs.

"Well, what was it like where you grew up, Arlene?"

"Oh, so you seek to qualify my opinion now?" she teases in that affected neutral accent I've become so fond of.

"Look, I'm just saying, I don't care about them. They're kids being kids. I was the same once."

"How so?" she presses. "Why won't you talk about it?"

I'm not doing this with her right now. We can do a lot of back and forth but I'm not opening up my past to her. I shouldn't have hinted at it. Maybe someday we can talk about it but not now. In fact I'd like to think that's where things could be heading, but just now I think I'm too crushed out and delusional to feel safe going that far into my background with her.

"Arlene, you've got something right here." I say pointing my finger just below the collar of her black button down.

Arlene looks down to see what I'm pointing at and I snap my finger up to flick her nose. She goes stiff, glares at me and stops short of slapping my face. We share a little laugh and she politely pulls away from her current line of questions. She also pulls a little further away from me which I pretend not to notice.

We quietly sit and watch the black kids at the bus stop across the street for a while, passing the bottle of Jameson between ourselves. After a time, Arlene sets the table again. I feel appreciated because of her curiosity. I even begin to wonder if her world is as lonely and secret as my own. Why would it be? She's so attractive, so intelligent and confident. I lose a little confidence admitting to myself that someone like her is already well spoken for, if she even cares to be.

"Monsieur Godefroi, do you believe in good and evil?"

OK, she's perfect and all but just once I'd like to hear something as banal as whether or not I thought Kim Kardashian was talented. I quickly recover from that horrible, shallow pang and thank my circumstances for never having to expect something so low-brow from her. Now that I've reconsidered my position, I warm to her query.

"I went through what I think was a pretty normal phase of disbelief, I guess." I finally respond.

"But now do you believe?"

"Well, no. I think I missed out on getting convinced."

"How so?"

"Aren't ideas of good and evil pretty much culturally transmitted?" I ask. "I'm from a broken family. I think I learned most of my boundaries from state authority."

"You don't leave much to the imagination, do you?" she ribs sarcastically and takes the bottle for another swig.

"Good and evil have little use for me. 'Can I get away with it?' Now that's a practical boundary."

"You long for that, don't you?"

"What?

"Sensible, predictable boundaries. Family, culture, tradition."

I shrug.

"You do." She prods, elbowing me a little.

"Not the kind where I'm from."

"Why?"

"I don't want to get into this. You're making me feel more crazy than Al does."

"Who's Al?"

Why did I just go there? I shouldn't even speak his name, for fear he might appear.

"It doesn't matter."

"Godefroi, I see that you struggle with purpose but I think you are a good man at your core."

"Thank you, Arlene. I want to believe that."

"But your works do not demonstrate this." She accuses with another playful shove.

"Here we go."

"I'm not judging, I believe in you. I just think that your experience may have stunted your potential."

"What's that supposed to mean?"

""I think that had you been raised in a strong family supported by a clearly defined culture you wouldn't struggle with this at all." She sermonizes "You'd have developed a rudimentary certainty of what is right and what isn't."

"You ought to lend some of the same understanding to those kids across the street."

"You should stop comparing yourself to those hopeless morons. You're not as much like them as you think you are. You know wrong from right, you just never learned any certainty in it from your environment."

"I tend to think my environment developed a pretty clear certainty that might and wealth are right and everyone who has neither is wrong."

"No, mon frer, you are fixated on plumbing the depths of right and wrong with no certainty at all, always as this captious bar room contrarian."

Mon frer, the Prelacy's French endearment. That verbiage summons thoughts of Sébastien. How had I come to respect this man so much? He never challenges me like this? All reward and placation if I take account. It makes me think back to Al and I's conversation at the Fountain of Bambi in Hamburg. About how the Prelacy was training me to be a patsy and not an assassin. I find this too troubling and quickly chase away the entire line of thinking.

"So what? You think you have some clear idea of what's good and what's bad?" I ask.

"I do and so do you. You just don't feel the confidence, the agency to plant your flag on the side of good and proclaim, 'this is right, that is wrong and with my life I will defend the line between there and here."

"Yeah, I'm not a crusader."

"Yet here you are, rich beyond belief for your part in a crusade."

I take a deep breath. She can lay bare my conflicts so effortlessly it seems. This rapport Arlene and I have developed is sort of exhausting but when she's winding me up I can't help but be drawn in. I wish she were still sitting close to me.

It begins to drizzle as a quiet beat passes and Arlene finally closes the space between us once more, for warmth I suppose. Ancient adversaries fending off death together in the rain, Arlene and I on a bus bench in Seattle at midnight. As we sit in silence Arlene puts her elbow in my ribs again and points with her chin at the bus stop. I smile to myself at her aggravating but funny way and peer across the street.

Our white native besties from the Rusty Anchor are about 20 feet from the bus stop across the street and closing on it slowly. Arm-in-arm, they babble back and forth, oblivious to the parade of young toughs ahead of them.

"Are you thinking what I'm thinking?" I ask Arlene.

"That we're both horrible racists for thinking there's anything to be thinking?"

"Bingo."

"I wish we had popcorn." Arlene adds. "This is going to be good."

We share a wicked little laugh and snuggle in a bit tighter as the annoying couple approaches the bus stop. With Arlene squeezed against me I begin to think about our playful repartee over my failed attempt to hack her blackphone in the Rusty Anchor earlier. I want to kiss her so much right now but I simply don't dare.

As the white native couple is being beaten senseless by the black teenagers across the street, Arlene turns and kisses me.

"Should we do anything about that?" I ask after a moment of engagement.

"Nah. That couple might call us racists if we try to help them. I just don't think I could bear the pain of such an insult."

I don't even have the chance to laugh at her cold humor before she kisses me again.

And here we sit making out while our besties from the Rusty Anchor are mercilessly beaten across the street. Arlene's soft fingertip traces the lines of my cheek as I hear a fabled war-cry in the background.

"Wooorrrldstaaaarrrrr!"

THIRTY-SIX

Hamburg, Germany – Fri April 4ᵗʰ, 2014

My walk South toward the Reeperbahn was cold enough to call for a parka, which this trip I thankfully had the good sense to bring. The blocks leading there were still, the trees along the way naked and boney against the heathery fell canopy where Hamburg's sky should have been. As I neared the Red Light District, the cars and people congealed, skittering away the privacy of the previous blocks' walk. After a short wade through the hustle and hum of reveling Stadtvolk, I finally arrived at Bar Zero.

It looked to be the sort of hip and loud spot young people might love but I would never think to enter. Nothing whiskey can't fix, I figured. I showed the doorman a phony Canadian passport under my traveling name, Remy Foster. After a glaring once over from the ogre I paid my fare, checked my coat and set to locating Jazzy and her guy. In a short beat I spotted Jazzy at a table near a small back bar where she was waving me in. Next to her was posed a well and deliberately configured clothes-horse of a like mind to Jazzy's own; bleach blonde, efforted complexion, over-priced prêt-à-porter wardrobe, face fixed in a look of permanent dispassion and pointed down at the screen of her iPhone. I waved back and swam past the rabble of locals to meet them, wondering where her man was.

"Foster, Hi." Jazzy said, taking both of my hands and air-kissing each cheek. Très Européen. I just went along with it. "I want you to meet my friend, Hanna. Hanna, this is Foster. We met on the flight."

"Hallo, Foster. Very nice to meet you." She said smiling and attentive as she shook my hand, then immediately returned to her iPhone.

"So glad you made it. I can't wait for you to meet Jürgen. You're going to love him."

"Yeah?" I doubted it.

"Oh, yeah. You guys are going to get along so well." She said, visibly drunk and far more warm and social than the Jazzy from the flight over, understandably. "He just had to go to the little boy's room but he should be back any minute."

"No worries." I said. "I'm just going to order something from the bar and I'll be right back. You guys good?"

Both of them had over-sized stemware filled with some luminous magenta bullshit, garnished with a lemon rind, so I was given leave without a word as Jazzy talked to Hanna and Hanna looked at her phone. While I stood at the bar waiting to order I scanned the place for a bit of the old recreational disgust.

The DJ was situated against a wall toward the front of the house, the club's entrance to his left. He was playing something I couldn't identify, let alone anything I wanted to know. It sounded like flatulent robots over a mid-tempo 808. He was really into it. I watched as his orange shutter shades bobbed up and down with the beat, his spikey frosted tips following close behind. The dance floor, a sea of backs turned toward him, none of them dancing. I imagined him bitching to other DJs about DJ problems. Things like sell outs and posers and getting ripped off by club owners. This leisure pursuit that he was probably fortunate enough to see pay his bills, if I knew anything at all about people I knew he took It for granted. Thought of it like a shitty job. Even hated it along with the people he was paid to entertain. I thought about going over and asking him to play Skrillex because I read online somewhere that it pissed serious DJs off if you did that. Aside from the fact that Dr. Anglethorpe had named him on his list I had no idea who Skrillex was. Maybe after a couple drinks I'd walk over and make that request.

"Ey, vat can I get you?" came the bartender.

"Ein Jameson, doppel. Neat."

"Comin' right up." He said in sharp German Englisch.

"Danke." I thanked him and returned to looking around the place.

The club was crowded as one would expect for a Friday night on the douche side of town. I wondered what the people who didn't suck did for fun around here. Where was the quiet watering hole where stoic old krauts hung out alone together? No matter, for all intents and purposes I was on the clock. Jazzy's old man worked for Kaufmannsbank and come Monday morning, either I or my sinister shadow would be murdering a very important executive of that same bank. This was peripheral to my actual assignment but curiosity had gotten the best of me, so here I stood.

"Twelve Euro" the bartender said, setting down a generous pour in the rocks glass just to my right. I paid the man, gave a nod and was on my way back to the table where Jazzy and Hanna were laughing about something I had missed. I could use a laugh but doubted it was anything I'd find funny. Then again, these two seemed as if they might be as cruel humored as me.

"What'd I miss?"

This question only elicited a bigger laugh so I let it go. Just as I was shifting my attention elsewhere, out from under the table came a short, dishwater blonde man of about 40, hair mussed as if he'd just fallen down or something.

"I think Jürgen's a little drunk." Jazzy laughed as Jürgen straightened his shirt and swept his hair back into place. His disposition seemed a little turned up, agitated but his physical character betrayed what I took for a persistent jovial undertone. He had a life-of-the-party thing going on that came across effortless and immediate.

"Fuckin' stupid floor!" he cursed, which evoked another peel of laughter from Jazzy and Hanna. "It's all fuckin' wet and shit."

I wasn't sure whether to laugh or to offer help. The giant wet spot on the front of his shirt indicated he'd lost his drink when he slipped and fell.

"Let me get you another drink, yeah?" I offered trying not to seem like the smirk on my face was there out of ridicule.

"Bah!" he said, with a dismissing wave accented with a uniquely exaggerated animation all his own. It was evident that Jürgen was quite a character. He dipped into his back pocket with another loud flourish and returned with a flask in hand. After the vaudeville production that was him unscrewing the cap and taking a drink, Jürgen wiped his hand on his slacks and jabbed it toward me.

"I'm sorry, you must be Foster," voice loud and amiable as the rest of his presentation. "Jürgen Austermann."

"Remy Foster," I lied, feeling a little guilty as I shook his hand. I liked Jürgen so far and he inspired in me that cursed simplicity of heart that made lying to him feel shitty.

"Jasmine tells me you're in banking?"

"Uhh, yeah." I suddenly felt my liars guilt dissipate, as I was reminded that my entire life was a lie. I only hoped he wouldn't ask which bank I was with.

"What do you do?" he asked then interrupted, "No, don't tell me. Let me guess."

I sipped my drink and waited for him to continue. Jürgen took a step back and gave me an appraising once over.

"You really don't strike me as a banker, Foster," he said with a squint of suspicion. "but if I had to guess I'd say you're in management. Something on the corporate side, not the branch side. Am I warm?"

"Ahhh, well," I stammered and stalled.

"Murders and executions!" he near shouted, "Am I right?"

A pop culture reference that would annoy me, were it not so ominous due to its on-the-nose entendre. I forced a laugh, self-conscious of looking nervous and raised my glass in an affirmative gesture. Why the fuck did I come here? Besides indulging my curiosity and throwing myself into uncomfortable social situations, what was I even doing here?

"I knew it. You're a shark, you. You have that silent but deadly thing about you."

If he only knew. Silent, yes. Deadly? In a manner of speaking, but not really.

"Well, you boys look like you're getting on well." Jazzy broke in and not a second too soon. "We've got to go to the little girls room, so you two stay out of trouble."

A welcome interruption, as that line of dialog was getting a little uncomfortable. I had to be prepared to steer our conversation away from banking, should Jürgen regain that train of thought. Still, I wanted to get him talking about Kaufmannsbank. I wondered how to do this without so much lying and pretending on my side of things. I wasn't entirely confident I came off as convincing with this spontaneously embellished identity.

"So what do you think of Hanna?" Jürgen asked. "Pretty good, yah?"

Oh, no. Hell no. Things just kept going from bad to worse. How had I missed this? Was I being invited here for match making? I was totally unprepared for all of this. I highly doubted this woman had any interest in me and I had no interest in changing her mind. Charm has been something I've pulled off in the past but it's never been a skill I've focused on honing, let alone one I've relished employing. It was at this moment that I began to consider pulling the rip cord on this little plunge into operational improvisation.

"Um," I paused, nose wrinkled, eyes squinted. "Yeah, I don't know, I guess she's-"

"Nah, you're right." Jürgen interrupted, "She's a dingbat. Fuck her. I told Jazzy you wouldn't like her."

Spared yet again and I couldn't help liking the guy's terminal case of the fuck-its.

"How long you in town for?" Jürgen aksed.

"I fly back to L.A. on Tuesday."

"Smart man. Avoid all those weekenders flying home."

"The worst." People who fly for business will usually take steps to avoid people who fly for recreation. Weekend flights are generally more expensive and on continental flights, more crowded. International flights were crowded, no matter what day you flew. Midweek flights were at least less likely to have too many vacationers. No small concern for people who lived on planes. Flying out on amateur night could make a 12 hour jump feel like a quick dime in Turkish prison.

"Jazzy's going back tomorrow night but I have to stay."

"Business, huh?"

For just a second, Jürgen's light disposition shifted. His face darkened as if that question had somehow distressed him and no sooner had I noticed than he'd caught himself and tucked it in.

"Yeah. Business."

Just then Jürgen hit me in my chest for no reason. Or so I thought at first, but he was just shoving his flask at me.

"Drink, Foster."

I still had a rocks glass full of Jameson but I didn't think details like that were of any concern to Jürgen so I just rolled with it. I got the impression one does a lot of that with Jürgen, just rolling with it.

"So what do you think of Hamburg?" he asked.

"I haven't seen much of it, to be honest. Slept all day and came here."

"Eh, it's just like every other metropolitan. Hipsters and yuppies. Everywhere hipsters and yuppies and the occasional gangster. They're all the same, everywhere you go."

"Are you from Hamburg originally?"

"Me? Hell no. I'm from Vienna." He said with more than a hint of chauvinism.

"Sorry, I'm still a dumb yank when it comes to these Central European accents."

He just grabbed the flask back and drank. I think I laughed to myself a little at his brusque, care-free timbre. I imagined that most who knew him either liked him a great deal or hated him entirely, and that he didn't give a shit either way. A trait I always admired in someone. Or hated.

"Look at these fucking assholes." Jürgen ridiculed, turning to face the crowded club behind us. "The lot of them, fucking chiefs."

I didn't have much to offer but a nod in agreement. To me most of these people were beneath contempt but I could see that Jürgen might be likely to swing at one of them given a cross word or a lingering stare. I'd have to be on my guard for that, steer him towards other courses. Unless it was the DJ he wanted to steal one on. That might be worth a little trouble.

"I hear you. That DJ makes me want to root for Al-Qaeda."

"Fucking douchebag."

"That's probably what he'd say about us."

"I wish he would."

We both had a little laugh as Jürgen raised his flask to toast.

"To fuck this place." Jürgen said

"To fuck this place." I responded, raising my tumbler in accord.

"Careful, kid. Don't get him riled up. I've been watching and I can tell you, he's a handful, this one."

Fucking Al. Barging on me among crowded company like this was unusual, even for him. This was all getting pretty tricky. I turned and found a handsome, youngish 1961 Al in a light grey Italian number with black button down and matching black skinny tie, hair pomade slick and shining. He was dancing alone with some kind of orange and pink umbrella drink poured in tall, fluted glassware. I shot him a knit-browed, tight-lipped look of warning with a slow shake of my head before returning my attention to the crowded club and Jürgen.

"Break it up, love-birds." Jazzy came crashing in with Hanna in tow. Say what you want about Jazzy, her timing was impeccable.

"There she is, the love of my life." Jürgen said planting a kiss on Jazzy with his typically over-the-top flare. Jazzy happily played along and I felt a sincere love was shared between these two middle-aged party-animals. It was kind of sweet, I guess.

"Awww, cocaine love." Al leaned in and whispered sarcastically, shattering the moment with his cold shot of cynicism. "That's cute right, kid?"

I had to do something about this.

"I've gotta use the restroom, I'll be right back" I announced and made off in search of one, but not before pointing a glare at Al and jerking my head toward the bathrooms in a gesture for him to follow me.

I slithered, elbowed and "Entschuldigen Sie'd" my way through Bar Zero and eventually found the Men's room empty, save for a couple of guys doing blow in the wascheschrank or whatever it's called. Al was there leaning against the wall when I arrived.

"You've gotta go, Al. I can't have you looming all night. It'll drive me nuts."

"Drive you nuts? Well there's a short trip." Al teased. "Why waste gas driving."

"Don't get cute. I'm serious. You've got to shake the spot. Now!"

"Relax, kid. I was just checking in on you. I'll be on my way soon enough."

"I'm fine, just go. I'll see you later."

"Just one thing, kid."

"What?"

"Don't wind these people up. Charm them. I know you think being charming is beneath you but I have a wild hunch you need to make a good impression on your new pals. Don't be a dick."

"I'm fine, Al. I'm not going to be a dick."

"Good. Remember. Use your charm. No wind ups. Don't even let them see you doing that stuff."

"I'm not. Now go away!"

As Al danced off the two yuppies in the bathroom emerged with the sniffles. I held up my phone and made like I was hanging up on someone, worried they might wonder who the strange yank was just arguing with. I gave them a quick nod as they passed and they went back to feeling awesome.

Alone, I looked in the mirror over the sink and decided against splashing water on my face, though the urge was there. I wondered what that was all about. Why was Al suddenly so concerned about me turning heel on these people? I admit, I wasn't exactly fond of Jazzy when we hung out in the Frankfurt airport and I knew Jürgen was sort of a douche but they were really growing on me. I figured I deserved Al's suspicion but I don't think I ever intended to wind these folks up. Maybe in the back of my mind it was an option if I got bored of them but it wasn't my conscious intent. Mostly I'd just come here to see what I might hear from Jürgen about Kaufmannsbank. Not sure why, other than curiosity. It was too much of a coincidence and I was usually drawn in by coincidence. That's pretty typical of crazy people.

"Fucking hell, I've really done it, Alter." It was Jürgen and he looked properly tormented.

"What's wrong?"

He wouldn't say. He just leaned over the sink, arms out to bear his weight. As I stood there, he gently banged his head against the mirror one, two, three times.

"Fuck fuck fuck fuck fuck. What am I going to do?"

"What is it? Whatever it is we'll fix it, man. Don't trip."

Jürgen twisted his head in my direction to laugh.

"Not this, Foster. Can't fix this."

What I first thought to be another faux pas, like slipping and spilling a drink or punching out a DJ began to seem something much bigger.

"Well, what's going on? You wouldn't mention it if you didn't want my help."

Jürgen stood up straight and backed himself against the wall behind us, where he fished out his flask and tilted to his head to find it empty.

"Fuck!" he shouted, throwing the flask on the ground.

I closed in to pat him on the shoulder, hoping he wasn't the kind of person to respond to contact with a violent reflex. My little gamble was rewarded with a suddenly more relaxed Jürgen. In a beat he had begun to sob and laid his head on my shoulder. I was both uncomfortable-as I barely knew this person-as much as softened by it. Something was really eating at him and it was disarming, seeing this cocky, self-confident hotshot so suddenly vulnerable.

"I'm seeing the love of my life for the last time and it's driving me mad, Foster. I'm trying to hold it together but it's wearing me out."

"Jazzy? I don't understand. She said you brought her here to celebrate a big promotion."

Jürgen relaxed a little and leaned back against the wall again as he began to tell me what was going on.

"I did. Well originally." Jürgen explained, producing a gigantic diamond ring in its case. "I was actually flying her out to propose to her."

I tried to chase the judgment from my bigoted head, but I couldn't help thinking Jürgen was dodging a bullet if marriage was off the table. I had Jazzy figured for an alimony hound, recalling the tanline I spied around her ring finger on the flight over.

"She'd lost this ring a week ago, before I left." Jürgen explained. "Her mother's ring, she'd given it to her before she died."

Well, that explains the tan line. My bigot's guilt was starting to flare a little.

"Her mother never married. Raised Jazzy on her own. This was just some gold ring she wore. Had this crummy little cheap stone in it but Jazzy loved it, as you can imagine."

I'm such a dick.

"And so you found it?"

"Yeah, she lost it doing dishes and was just broken up about it the whole time before I had to fly out here."

Jazzy doing dishes. Now there's something I couldn't feature. Am I just wrong about everything all the time?

"When I was feeding the dog before I left for LAX, I spotted it on her kitchen floor next to a planter. I just grabbed it without really thinking."

I offered no response, just nodded and followed. I was starting to really feel for Jürgen and hate myself for such baseless negativity towards Jazzy.

"I don't know why I'm telling you all this stuff, Foster. I'm sorry."

"Nonsense, I want to hear this." I protested. "You've got a friend, Jürgen. Please, go on."

"Well, I just, I got to Hamburg and when I got word I was being promoted I finally felt I had earned the right to ask Jazzy to marry me."

"Really? Is she that interested in the size of your salary?"

Jürgen shot me a bit of a warning glare and softened again when I acknowledged.

"She's not like that at all. Jazzy's a self-made millionaire."

"Jazzy?"

"Yeah, she's got a Master's in business and a minor in nutrition. She owns a multi-million dollar vitamin and supplement brand she built on her own. Jazzy pulled herself out of poverty. She's amazing, Foster."

I'm such an asshole.

"I could have asked her to marry me at any point but I needed to feel like I deserved her. I needed this promotion to even find the courage to ask her."

I could feel a dark turn ahead and I didn't like it.

"So when I got the promotion, it was like providence. I had her mom's ring and it hit me like a bolt of lightning."

"What's that?"

"I got her mom's ring replated and had a 2 karat brilliant Princess cut set in it and planned on popping the question with the very ring she loves so much."

"You weren't worried she'd be bothered about you messing with her favorite ring?"

"Not at all. You don't know Jazzy. This was going to blow her mind." Jürgen said breaking down into sobs again. Oh, man. This wasn't good. I'm a fake hitman, not cupid but I'll be damned if I didn't want to help him with whatever it was eating at him.

"So what's the big deal? C'mon, man, it can't be that bad."

"You have no idea."

"Well tell me!"

"I'm ruined. I've lost everything and I'm ruined. I can't ask her to marry me now."

"What do you mean?"

"I mean Kaufmannsbank. A rival within the company stole every single asset I had, engineered my firing and had me blacklisted. I'm ruined!"

"What the fuck? How's that even possible?"

"Oh it's possible. And there isn't anything I can do about it."

"Who did this to you?"

"A man named Jürgen Neuhaus, he's an exec at Kaufmannsbank who never liked me. From the very moment it became clear that I was going to be promoted to COO he undermined me, framed me for things I didn't do and drained my accounts. I'm completely ruined, Foster."

"Wait, this guy's name is Jürgen, too?"

"It's just a coincidence. Jürgen is like George. It's a common name here."

I tried not to get too distracted by the coincidence. I also tried not to wonder too much if this Jürgen Neuhaus was the man I was meant to kill Monday. If it was, I was certain I could do the dirty deed myself. Might I finally be able to right the ship? To get off the shneid and finally lay low one of these bankster scumbags myself?

"Do you mind if I ask how much money he stole from you?"

"Would you believe 2 million Euro?"

"How the fuck is that even possible?"

"If you only knew how common it was."

"So what're you going to do?"

"I'm going to kiss Jazzy one last time tomorrow, lie to her that I'll be back in L.A. to see her in a few days and drown myself in the Elbe."

"None of that, now Jürgen. I can't imagine what you're going through but you can't do that. I can't let you. You have to let me help."

"What can you do, Foster? You can't get my money back. You can't restore my job or my reputation."

"I'm not sure exactly what I can do but I want you to trust me. I want you to hang on for now, don't do anything crazy."

"Foster, I'm trying to hold it together the best I can but this bastard has utterly destroyed me and there's nothing I can do to fix it. I just want to hold Jazzy in my arms one last time and-"

"and you will, but you can't do anything crazy. You have to give me a chance to help you." I interrupted.

"What can you do?"

"Promise me you'll give me until Tuesday. Spend the rest of your weekend with Jazzy, sit tight through Monday and meet up with me Tuesday. Can you do that?"

"I guess."

"Is that a yes?" I wasn't sure what I could do either but I felt like I had a calling here. I only knew I wanted my new friend to hold on to his life and give me a chance to help him. I felt like I was getting through t

"Yes. I will."

"Give me your phone." I said.

Jürgen handed me his mobile and I entered my number into his contacts, then called myself so I would have his.

"If anything new happens, call me right away. Got it?"

"I will. Got it."

"We're gonna fucking fix this guy, Jürgen. You don't deserve this. Now fix up and look sharp. We've gotta go back out there and close this place down with the love of your life and her mercifully mute friend."

"You're a good man, Foster."

THIRTY-SEVEN

West Seattle, WA – Wed Oct 15ᵗʰ 2014

Waking up next to Arlene is probably the best feeling I've had in as long as I care to remember. I haven't felt so content since I'd left the Army nearly a decade ago. In the midst of a life that has become an unmanageable chaos, here I lay feeling completely right, which naturally courts panic.

Last night, after making out on that bus bench to the sounds of screams and beatings, the two of us walked back here to the safe house and continued our pawing and kissing 'til their logical conclusion. We held each other in bed, joking and sharing our thoughts as we seem fit to do, then had sex once more before the alcohol caught up and left us to sleep. I hadn't been with a woman since my last failed relationship nearly five years ago, living here in Seattle. Andrea, a sweet but jealous woman; she made it a full two years with me before it was apparent that I was nuts. My petty, vindictive male hubris considers how great it would feel for her to see me with Arlene. I shake those juvenile thoughts and quietly sneak out of bed to surprise Arlene with coffee and breakfast. I'm too swept up to care that it might violate her sense of copacetic distance. I want to do something nice for her and she'll just have to withhold judgment.

I grab my Monolith so I can browse the news while our coffee steeps. In the kitchen I make with the motions, kettle to the stove, eggs, veggies, knife, cutting board on the counter and so on. After I locate the café press, grinder and beans I return to the dinette to muse over the latest news on the good Doctor Tobias Anglethorpe, the certified sane man in perfect health who is taking his fight for assisted suicide to the Supreme Court.

"...Bono, Honey Boo Boo, Swaggy P, Fred Phelps,Dr. Phil..."

As I'm laughing over his comic antagonizing of our justice system I hear a ringtone coming from Arlene's room.

Immediately, I'm reminded of my once urgent intent to attempt hacking her blackphones, only now I'm suddenly less interested in doing so. My hardwired sense of distrust is flaring up and urging me to do it anyway. As her phone rings a second time I realize I likely have a now or never decision to make and fast. I let my sense of operational diligence overtake my soft-headed crush and begin paging through my apps for the Bluetooth exploit I keep on my Monoltih. I'm too far away for the Near Field Comm exploit so I'll have to take my chances with this one. As I hear her answer her line I activate the app. In seconds I'm alerted to a successful access and downloading a copy of her communication data which should include chat and text logs, private emails as well as an assortment of saved documents. By the time Arlene is entering the kitchen I've already received the data and set down my Monolith. Now I'd just have to convince my fool heart that it's still important intel which needs to be analyzed and that no matter how I feel I have a duty to go over it.

"Making breakfast?" Arlene asks walking in, sleepy eyed and relaxed.

"I wanted to surprise you." I say walking over to grind the coffee beans.

Arlene, somewhat to my surprise closes in to peck my cheek.

"That's sweet." She says.

I was expecting ridicule, not affection. I think I've honestly begun to give up trying to read her.

"Was that one of your Covenant contacts calling?"

"No, I wish." Arlene laughs. "That was my mother calling from Marseille. 6pm there and she sounds like she's been drunk since brunch."

"So you both keep in touch pretty well?"

"No, not at all. A little Marie goes a long way for me. I talk to her as seldom as possible."

"Marie? That's your mom's name?"

"I don't want to talk about my mom anymore. Hurry up with that coffee." Arlene says, playfully pushing me back toward the stove.

"Speaking of phone calls, you still haven't heard from the Scrivener or Sébastien?" she asks.

"No, not a peep."

"Should we be worried?"

"I hadn't thought about it since yesterday but now that you bring it up."

"It's unusual?"

214

"The Scrivener, no, but Sébastien, yeah that's a little bit unlike him. I should've heard from him by now."

Our conversation goes cold with mutual contemplation and I pour hot water over the coffee grounds to steep. As I'm cracking eggs over the hot skillet, Arlene puts her arm around my stomach from behind and kisses me on the neck, raising goose flesh from the bottom of my ears to the tip of my pinky.

"Don't let it worry you. They'll call and when they do, we'll know what our next play is." Arlene reassures. "We'll get through this."

Arlene shuffles over to the dinette while I cook, sits down and begins scrolling through one of her blackphones. A jolt of guilt-informed dread jumps down my spine and I effort to shift my focus toward the eggs in the pan and away from thinking there's evidence of my hack that she's looking at.

"RT is having a field day with the American justice system over your Dr. Anglethorpe trial." Arlene says, eyes fixed on her screen.

"I bet they are" I respond, relieved to see she's just reading the news, "the whole thing is a giant circus."

"If he wins do you think he'll actually go through with his suicide?"

"I don't know but I think it would be hilarious if he won his case and then held a presser to announce he'd changed his mind." I say.

"Or what if he read his list in its entirety and suggested everyone named on it consider exercising the liberty he'd just won them?"

"I don't know if I could possibly love that man more than I already do, but if he did that-" I trail off, pouring our coffee and walking our cups over to set down on the dinette.

I eventually serve breakfast and after we've eaten, the two of us adjourn to the couch in the living room where we snuggle in front of the big screen and binge watch episodes of Lost on Netflix. The rest of the morning is spent quietly relaxing and saying nothing while that band of wacky castaways try to find their way off the island. Around five episodes in the front door opens and the two of us leap from the couch, startled and looking for weapons we've foolishly left out of reach.

"Oh, my, have I come at a bad time?" Canan's hectoring taunt as he closes the door behind him and stands staring at us.

"This isn't what it looks like, Canan." Arlene pleads, visibly defensive and embarrassed.

"I'm sure it's none of my business, Arlene. "He says. "I'm more concerned that neither one of you is on alert for anything and neither of you has a weapon in reach. What if I'd been the Prelacy Guard?"

Well, this was off to an interesting start. No surprise, really. Things had been getting a little too rosy and sedate, all things considered. It was due time the real world came crashing in.

"Don't tell me, tell the assassin, here." Arlene spits.

It's completely apparent she does not want whatever's going on between us to be out in the open and I cannot disagree with that. Here we are supposedly rolled up in some mythic struggle over the fate of mankind and the two of us are just holed up nesting like a couple of careless doves. I'm ashamed for myself plenty but I feel awful for her right now.

Arlene's face reddens as she excuses herself from the room and Canan seats himself on the couch.

"Sit down, Godefroi."

I'm half expecting something akin to meeting a girl's father for the first time. This is already awkward. I take a seat next to Canan doing my best not to seem rattled.

"I know what you're thinking, Canan and-"

"I doubt it but that's not important." He says, cutting me off. "If you're letting her wrap you around your finger, just be aware that espionage is her trade. If you allow yourself to become attached to her, I can assure her that one day duty will call and you will wake up with her gone, never to be seen again. Whatever you're getting into, do yourself a favor and keep it in perspective."

I have disliked Canan from the moment I met him but just now he's talking good sense and I know I need to heed his cautioning. My heart, however is telling me he doesn't know any more than I do about Arlene or the feelings she may have for me, that he's somehow jealous and just trying to drive a wedge between us. Stupid man thoughts I can't seem to extinguish.

"There's nothing going on."

"It's none of my business and I've said all I'm going to say about it. Whatever the case, you need to stay frosty. I meant it when I said I could have been Prelacy Guard. You should have a weapon in reach at all times and always be on alert."

"No, you're right. That was embarrassing."

"If you'll excuse me, it's important I speak with Arlene."

"Of course."

Canan stands and walks down the hall toward Arlene's room and knocks on the door.

"Yeah, just give me a minute Canan and I'll meet you at the table in the kitchen."

He returns and on his way to the kitchen asks "So, no orders yet from your superiors I take it?"

216

"No, they've been completely silent."

The bald man mouth shrugs and walks to the table to wait for Arlene. When she returns, I pretend to watch Lost as I strain to listen in on what they're saying. I can only tell they are speaking in what I'm guessing is Arabic so I can't make out any of it. Add that to the growing list of Arlene's many layers. I can't understand their words but what I can completely understand is the tone of their conversation. It sounds more like a jealous boyfriend bullying his woman into guilt and tears than an intelligence agent being debriefed by her superior.

When the conversation ends, Arlene walks Canan to the door, her nose red, eyes misty, and composure forced. My mind races, heart heavy and extremities numb with a lover's dread. I get the feeling that whatever we had between us has been snuffed out under orders of the Covenant, or worse, her boyfriend. Husband even? I really don't know what to think and though I want to ask, I dare not. Not just now anyway.

Arlene walks past me without a word, heads down the hall and I hear her door close just a little lighter than an angry slam. I reach for the Indica on the coffee table where I left it yesterday, roll myself a cone and try to focus away from what's on my mind. After a few pulls from the joint I can't put off drinking any longer so I shuffle to the kitchen and pour myself a double.

A couple of Jamesons and a couple of episodes of Lost later, Arlene emerges from her room at last, cold and distant. She blows right past me without so much as a glance, then turns to address me, all business.

"Listen for your phone and no more going out, OK? If you get hungry order delivery on the land line and pay in cash."

"OK, will do. I've been paying cash for everything."

"I know, I just have to say it."

"No worries."

"I'll be back in a while." She says and before leaving turns to add "And keep your gun close. No more acting like we're on vacation."

And just like that she's gone and I'm in the dark. Whatever the case, everything changed the second Canan walked in that door and saw us together.

I down my Jameson and pour another, panicked, angry and powerless to do much about it, save what I'm already doing; getting loaded and binge watching Lost. I coax myself off the couch to go get my AF-1 from the dresser in my room and on returning spy my Monolith on the end table next to the couch. The blackphone hack from earlier, I'd totally spaced it. I may have lost interest in it but now I had every impetus to scour it for info on Arlene. The Covenant's play, Arlene's integrity, my role in all of this, all of these things and more might be cleared up by going over the files I'd obtained from that hack earlier. Suddenly I felt a little less lost at sea. I need to stop watching this show.

I unlock my blackphone and access the Micro SD card where the hacked files are all stored and begin to browse the data for anything pertaining to me. What is immediately apparent is the blackphone I was able to access was Arlene's Prelacy Monolith and not her Covenant blackphone. Most of what I'm looking at are files and communications that aren't exactly pertinent to me. No smoking gun about my being marked as some sort of Covenant asset or anything. No real indication of anything going on between her and Canan. No evidence of Canan's existence, actually. His existence would be entirely kept secret from the Prelacy so naturally there is nothing pertaining to him to be found on this device.

As the day winds on I sip Jameson, smoke cannabis and prowl her files for other intel. All though there is nothing definitively pertinent to our relationship or mission, I find numerous interesting insights, not just into Arlene's private life but things about the Prelacy I had no idea about. I found a document illustrating the entire hierarchy of the Prelacy and House Merovingi, specifically the eight lodges of the Prelacy under the Tentacles of Abraxas. I see for the first time everything laid out and acquire an understanding of just how large we are as well as what each of the eight Paths or Tentacles are responsible for in actualizing the Prelacy's goals. Finally, I learn personal details about Arlene.

I verify Arlene's strained relationship with her family reading through emails between herself and her mother. I forge on and gain some insights into her assignments and duties within the Prelacy, notably the fact that a lot of our assignments involved corresponding times, places and entities. I learn that she's likely done a lot of the intelligence field work that preceded most of my own writs. Perhaps the most concerning thing I learn is confirmation that a large part of Arlene's Prelacy espionage is achieved through the application of sexual tactics. Amorous emails from her marks litter her saved correspondence. This gives me cause to doubt her sincere fondness for me. I'm less worried that she might be playing me than I am simply convinced she is. My heart sinks to just above my stomach, my limbs and groin go numb and tingly with a cocktail of regret, betrayal, shame, jealousy. As my breathing becomes shallow I indulge further in intoxicants and renew my thoughts of flight, of leaving it all behind or coming in from the cold and telling Sébastien everything.

About three more episodes into Lost and a quarter of the way from the bottom of that Jameson bottle I hear someone outside and peek through the curtains, AF-1 in hand. Seeing it's only Arlene I return to my sulking on the couch and watch the fat one and the Indian guy skulk around the jungle. Arlene is smiling and buoyant on her return, which for a moment miraculously frees me from my pouting, though it quickly resets. She walks over to kneel, taking my hand in hers and alcohol on her breath, kisses me as if I'd just returned from war.

"I'm sorry for all of this, Godefroi. I'm sorry for all of it; for the Prelacy, for dragging you into it, for going cold on you earlier. I was just caught off guard by Canan showing up and I hadn't planned on anyone knowing about us. I hadn't even really given it much thought and then all of a sudden here I was forced to figure it all out on the fly."

I say nothing, only shrugging as I hold her hand and look off at the fat one climbing through thick brush.

"Are you OK?" she asks.

I nod yes as she kisses me again then lays her head on my chest. A wave of relief washes over my cynicism and renews my distant, poorly considered hope. As I lay there with her, my mind volleys between comfort and distrust, settling into an odd synthesis of fear and resignation. An emotion I've known but never named. Is this called belief?

We lay there, piled together on the sofa barely watching the castaways, quietly closing the brief and reaching rift that had shot between us. After a few more episodes I follow Arlene down the hall to her room where we spend what's left of our energy on what might be best characterized as make up sex, though we hadn't even fought.

Arlene is able to sleep though I am not. My mind races as I toss and turn. More turn than toss, shifting and agonizing over what I couldn't know. I was careening headlong into a loss of agency and sensibility, led by my fool heart toward surrender to an ostensible enemy. As I near a merciful yield to sleep I am cruelly roused by the buzz of a text message coming in on one of Arlene's blackphones. I lean over her sleeping frame and reach for the offending item to see it's her Covenant blackphone.

Canan is my first guess and subsequently I spend the rest of the night in roiling doubt and paranoia, stomach knotting and worry redlining. My fears vacillate between her vanishing from my life as Canan had warned and me being killed in my sleep. Eventually, sleep wins out over dread and my conscious worry dissolves into dreams of home.

THIRTY-EIGHT

File data recovered from the Monolith of *l'Honore Manteau Madame Aureline de le Pyrénées*

Original source unknown.

Les Tentacules de Abraxas
de Maison Merovingi

1. le Trajet du Chamberlain
2. le Chemin de la Nonpareil
3. le Chemin de Exquisite Paragon
4. le Trajet du Thaumaturge
5. le Trajet du Disciple
6. le Chemin de l'Épée
7. le Chemin de la Manteau
8. le Chemen de la Garde

Hiérarchie de La Maison Merovingi

et

la Prélature Familier de Infernal Arbitres

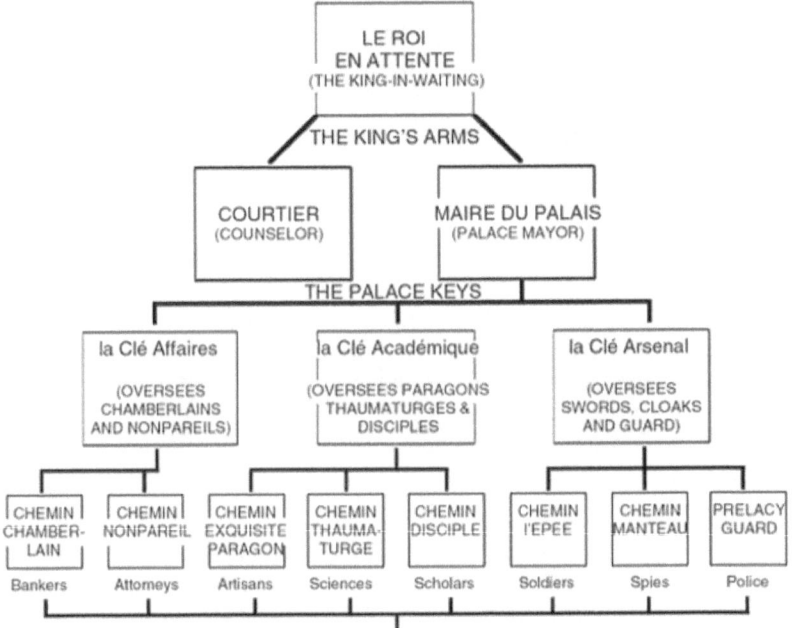

THIRTY-NINE

Hamburg, Germany – Sun April 6th, 2014

There is a popular optimism sustained by the conceit that synchronicities are meaningful; that there are no coincidences, only artifacts of one's harmonizing with the fate he has imagined for himself. I tend to dismiss this sort of thinking as bullshit but as I sat in the Fountain of Bambi, I was marveling at an odd set of coincidences, dizzying synchronicities that made my palms sweat.

Yesterday while recovering from Friday night's excesses, I had done some internet investigating on Jürgen Neuhaus, the scoundrel bankster who had ruined my new friend, Jürgen Austermann. That they were both named named Jürgen was the least remarkable of these coincidences. A much more intriguing fluke would be the one where I found a picture of Jürgen Neuhaus on a Kaufmannsbank website and sat gazing on an image of the same man depicted in the photo accompanying my Prelacy writ. I had to let it all sink in for a moment before I could make sense of what had been revealed. That being: if this man-the target of my writ-hadn't usurped my new friend Jürgen Austermann, logic follows that I would've been here to kill my new friend and not this man who'd ruined his life. This was indeed a set of circumstances rich with intrigue and coincidence. Providence, as the contemporary mysticism would have it, though what it meant in any cosmic sense was beyond my grasp. Not my department.

How I proceeded with this writ was suddenly much more than just a matter of getting to the bottom of who had been prosecuting my writs or finally getting a handle on prosecuting them myself. I not only wanted to take this heel down myself, I wanted to make him restore my buddy Jürgen's life. At the very least, I wanted to squeeze this creep enough that he'd return the money he'd stolen from Jürgen. Then I wanted to finally fulfill my duty as a Prelacy Sword. This guy deserved everything he was going to get.

My plan was so simple it felt flawed. I was just going to get into the guy's car before he could get out, put the gun on him and make him conduct a bank transfer by phone. Once that was done I would finish him and be on my way. I'd been calling Jürgen to let him know my plans every few hours with no luck getting an answer. I had to let him know that I was taking care of everything; he needed to sit tight and trust me. I couldn't get a response from him so there was little I could do besides worry.

"What've you got your nose buried in, kid?"

I wondered to myself how long Al had been over my shoulder snooping as I investigated Jürgen Neuhaus.

"Just getting to know the target of this writ a little better."

"You ever done that before?"

"Nope."

"Is that a good idea?"

"It is for this one."

Al didn't press the issue and I didn't complain. My persistent imperative was to get a hold of my buddy Jürgen so I could tell him to sit tight and not do anything drastic, just like we'd talked about. I dialed his number again but it went to voicemail.

"Jürgen, where are you? Why won't you call back, alter? This is Foster, gimme a shout whenever you get this message. Just want to make sure you remember what we talked about. Don't do anything, just give me 'til Tuesday like we discussed. I think I've got this handled. OK, man? Hope you're alright, just hang in there and I'll talk to you soon."

Al was sitting across the room in that high back chair just looking at me.

"What?" I asked him.

"Nothin', I'm just watching you operate. Seems like you've got everything under control."

"Yeah?"

"You don't need my help."

That wasn't a very Al thing to say and I wasn't sure how to take it. I got up and walked to the kitchen for a whiskey and when I returned, Al had gone.

After another hour of sitting in the Fountain of Bambi I started to worry about Jürgen and became impatient. I decided to text him.

Me – Jürgen just making sure you got my message. Hang in there like we talked about. I've got a plan. Please call or text when you get this message.

Not much more I could do but sit around and pass the time until my assignment. I'd hoped Jürgen might call before then but things are seldom so simple. I sat back on the couch, nursing my last glass of whiskey for the night. Between mental walkthroughs of my encounter with the bad Jürgen, I worried about my Jürgen and what lay ahead for him if I didn't intervene. As the quiet, solemn panic of night-before-jitters frittered by I finally thumbed through that Beatles histoire..

FORTY

West Seattle, WA – Thurs Oct 16th 2014

I stir from dreams of my childhood home in Boyle Heights, a smoldering ruin overlooking a flattened, black glass desert where Los Angeles once stood. As I rub the sleep from my eyes and acquiesce to the waking world, what I find is little more comfort. Next to me are ruffled sheets and the tossed aside comforter, imprint of where Arlene slept but no longer lays.

A minor panic besets me as I imagine her gone without as much as a word. Should I worry? Has she just stepped out for breakfast? Coffee? Had she been called away by her Covenant handlers? Would she return? Was this to her plan? Like a Santa Ana wind, the whole scene hits me sudden and irritating. There is so little I know of what is going on and what lay ahead. I felt such little control over any of it, a cruel truth in light of the fact that I'd foolishly begun to trust this road only a couple of nights before.

I lurch out of bed and shuffle toward the kitchen. My panic says Jameson, my apprehension says coffee. I survey the safe house for evidence to solve the mystery of the vanished Arlene. No note on the kitchen table. No trail of belongings to suggest she'll be back shortly. As an abrupt case of the fuck-its takes hold I recall the text message on her blackphone in the middle of the night and lament that she's gone, called away, mission aborted or simply left for the arms of her true love, whomever that is.

I locate the handle of Jameson in the cabinet and pour myself a wake-up. The night before gives way to a warm morning buzz as I rifle around for coffee with no luck finding where I'd placed it last. Frustrated, I return to the kitchen table where I sit and nurse my whiskey, puzzling over what's at play.

It starts to bother me that Sébastien has yet to call and check up on me as he routinely does following an assignment. If I don't hear from him today, I consider it genuine cause for concern. I wrestle with the unwelcome reality that if Arlene is gone and Sébastien does not call, there might be good cause for me to go ghost. A day I'd long dreaded may have finally arrived.

Not long after the fiasco that was my first writ in London, I had the good sense to organize a bug-out strategy. In the event I ever found myself alone and hunted, I knew I'd need the ability to become a ghost in the wind. I obtained an emergency identity, complete with passports and papers. A clean, untraceable weapon and a host of other mundane items pertinent to becoming someone else and disappearing into the night. This cache I kept hidden in a location only I knew of, close to home.

As I finish my drink I think out my contingency. I would steal a vehicle from long-term parking at the Sea-Tac airport and drive back to L.A. There I would retrieve my bug-out stash and make arrangements for flight to somewhere new.

My list of options in this event was very short. I would need to start over in countries where the Prelacy had little influence, somewhere the U.S. had limited or no extradition treaties. My options are very definite and few. Andorra, Lebanon, Serbia, Croatia and Brazil.

Brazil has the easiest path to citizenship of these destinations. All I would need to do is find a wife. My stash of Prelacy gold could sort that out handily. Because I feared Brazil to be a place the Prelacy still operated in a minor capacity it sat low on my list, tempting though it was. Andorra sat near the top though it didn't belong there by any sane measure. Andorra is a microstate situated smack in the middle of the Prelacy's backyard but it is one of the few places in Europe where the Prelacy has no Fountains or safe houses listed in Le Livre des Fontaines. I have always been most attracted to this choice, in spite of how foolish it would be to hide from the Prelacy in a country tucked between France and Spain, both Prelacy strongholds. A country that is smaller than the San Fernando Valley. More accurately, Andorra is smaller than Simi Valley. When I had the wherewithal to be honest with myself, I knew that Lebanon would be my smartest choice. I simply don't relish the thought of hiding out in the Muslim world. Serbia and Croatia had always remained in the middle on my list though I never once really considered them as genuine options.

As I near the bottom of my glass of whiskey I'm beset with the grim notion of sneaking home and then on to a new life of running from my past in a place I know nothing about. It looms hauntingly in the near-distance. What have I done with my life? I think genuinely, longingly of my mother for the first time in years. Is this fear? Regret? I pour another tumbler of whiskey and retrieve my pistol and Monolith from Arlene's room. I set them on the table and stare at the AF-1 as I nurse my drink. A meditation which continues for what feels like hours, though it is only a few minutes.

As I look at the firearm laid out in front of me I begin to quietly assail myself with shame. I look at the garish brushed steel slide and become disgusted with myself for selecting such a pretentious arm for regular carry. I look with self-loathing at this gaudy pistol which belongs to a so-called assassin who has never even taken a life. It has never even been fired outside of the range. I attack myself over and over for being a fraud, meditating in my hair shirt, drink after drink after drink.

Before long, my ruminating shifts to a more immediate antipathy. My lapse of reason, my brief and costly regression to wide-eyed juvenile infatuation with a beautiful woman I stood no chance with. I should have known better. I did know better, I saw it as it was happening and still I went along. I knew better and still I gave in to this mortifying gullibility, this reckless trust. I start that Arlene played me with expert aplomb, then relent that she hadn't. I had simply made myself into an easy mark. I'd allowed myself to be taken. She didn't hustle me so much as I'd delivered myself to her wrapped and bowed. I made it so easy for her and now I might spend the rest of my days paying for it.

But how? It had yet occurred to me that I was just paranoid. What had she gained in this? I'd made no admissions, gave her no valuable intel. As far as the Prelacy knew everything was business as usual. Had the covenant aborted her mission? As I take the last sip of my drink I consider reaching out to Sébastien. Maybe it would be wiser to come clean. Other than Arlene's dubious word, I had no reason to distrust Sébastien.

I turn in my chair and reach for my blackphone. As I'm about to call Sébastien the front door swings open. I drop my phone and move for my AF-1 on the table behind me.

"Oh, good. You're up! I brought you Vivace." Arlene chirps, "Hope you like Americanos. I didn't peg you for a Carmel Macchiatto type."

I try to collect myself and act normal as I pick my phone up off the floor. Fuck, say something!

"Nailed it. Only thing I like better than an Americano is drip from 7Eleven." I say getting up to take the coffee out of Arlene's full hands. I effort to seem like everything is normal, business as usual, like I hadn't just spent the morning drinking through a paranoid gust and planning my heart-broken flight into a new life on the run.

Arlene pulls the coffee aside and maneuvers herself into my embrace and gives me a probing kiss. One of those studying, reconnaissance kisses only women can do. I'm convinced a woman can pretty much read a man's mind with a kiss, and that's exactly what she does.

Arlene pulls away and locks her gaze on mine appraisingly. I want to disappear. I've spent the morning in an entirely different place than her, psychologically. She can tell something is wrong and I don't want her to know I'd spent the last hour mentally rerouting my entire life.

"You thought I'd left." She smiles. She thinks she's being playful and

I try not to look hurt. What I feel is a destabilizing speedball of relief and embarrassment.

"What?" I feign, clumsy. "Why would I think that?"

She spies the gun and near-empty handle of Jameson on the counter, puts down her coffee and locks her arms around me.

"I'm sorry." She says, softly, reassuringly. "I'm sorry I worried, you Foster. You were asleep and I didn't want to wake you."

Those simple words, a kindness that repairs my psyche. I sit back down and she holds my head to her chest. A breath of relief swells in me as my Monolith buzzes with an alert. Slowly I part from the cradle of Arlene's arms to check the message that's come in.

J.S. – Art thou the Folded Hands?

FORTY-ONE

Hamburg, Germany – Mon April 7th, 2014

My walk to catch the S line out of the Reeperbahn mostly retraced the same steps I'd made toward Bar Zero two nights ago. As I walked to catch the train I lived inside thoughts of right-tracking my haphazard ascension through the Prelacy's ranks. I fanaticized about finally growing into my role as an assassin and putting these embarrassing failings and half-measures behind me once and for all. I thrilled inside at the thought of repairing Jürgen's unfairly razed future and moved on to electrifying my own potential satisfaction from finally prosecuting a writ on my own. A writ targeting a genuine villain who deserved everything he had coming.

I stepped on the train bound for Jungfernsteig Station at 7am and quietly took my seat among the throngs of anonymous commuters. Tucked inside my black field jacket was the Prelacy revolver left for my mission inside the Fountain of Bambi's wall safe. I took to scanning the train for looks of suspicion and relaxed at the realization that I was blending in just fine. No signs of Al all morning, no signs of anxiety, I didn't even hit the Jameson before undertaking my duties. Everything seemed right on track.

I arrived at Jungfernsteig Station at 7:16am and exited the train with a flood of Hamburgers on their way to work. I had a half hour to make the 10 minute walk to 75 Ferdinandstraße where I would hold Jürgen Neuhaus in his car against his will, force him to return the funds he'd stolen from Jürgen Austermann and then end his life of plunder by putting a bullet in his temple.

On my way out of the train station I picked up a Döner from a street vendor and paused a moment to eat, to people watch, and reflect.

For so long my only want was to live up to my duties as a Sword in the Prelacy. Today it seemed I was finally going to do this. Rather than savor it, my restless mind was moving on. I'd been in this rut for so long, it occurred to me I had no direction, no actual goals or desires that I'd bothered to identify or define. For the last couple of years all I had been doing was getting drunk, winding up strangers in bars and pretending to be an assassin. As I chewed on a mouthful of braised lamb I began to ask myself, beyond the Prelacy, who am I? What was I doing and what was it I wanted out of this? Was I just going to let this be my settling? Was this it? Before I could find the courage to answer any of those questions I was chasing them to the depths of my conscience and moving on. On toward the subterranean parking beneath 75 Ferdinandstraße where I would right a wrong and commit a mortal sin, possibly a first time on both counts.

I round the corner into the garage beneath Kaufmannsbank at 7:40am, unseen and in sight of Jürgen Neuhaus' black Smartcar. Heart pounding I quickened my pace and confirmed I wasn't too late. I cut it so close on timing that I worried I had blown it. I tried not to dwell on another near failure. Self-doubt already making itself at home in my head, I moved on to fretting that I may run into my shadow if I couldn't wrap this up quick enough. I was cutting it so close I could very well run smack into whoever had been prosecuting my writs. I hadn't even considered what I might do should that happen. Well what should I be prepared to do? Did I confront them? Interrogate them? Shoot them? What if it was someone I knew from the Prelacy? I quashed these concerns for the time being in the interest of completing the job at hand.

I drew my weapon and crept along the rear quarter-panel of the tiny vehicle, quietly grasped the handle and in a single motion flooded myself into the passenger seat of the vehicle.

"Don't move, Herr Neuhaus. Don't make a sound, do only as you're told and no harm will come to you." I lied.

"Was ist los?" he yelped.

Reflexively I buried the butt of my pistol in his nose and jabbed the muzzle into his ribs as hard as I could.

"Do not speak again unless I ask you a question. Vertanden?"

"Ja, ja." He said hesitantly.

"Sprechen sie Englisch?" I ask.

"Yes, of course I do." He said rubbing his ballooning nose.

"Good, let's make this fast. Does that sound favorable to you, Herr Neuhaus?"

"Yes. Whatever you say, just don't hurt me anymore."

"Get out your mobile device."

Jürgen Neuhaus looked at me blankly and confused. I shoved the pistol hard into his ribs again.

"Do it, now!" I said and he withdrew his smartphone from his coat pocket.

"Now I don't want to repeat myself. I want you to do exactly as I say without questioning and if you don't, now this is very important, if you don't do this without hesitation, if you should stall or question I shall cut my losses. I will kill you where you sit and be well into my contingency plan before your body is even cold. Understood?

"Yes, anything you say!"

"Herr Neuhaus, I want you to access your banking app and wire the full amount of the funds you've stolen back to Jürgen Austermann. Understood?" I said pulling the hammer back on the Prelacy revolver and pointing the weapon at his temple. "I know you are an executive with Kaufmannsbank and there is no excuse you can make. I know you can authorize all of this and so you will. Understood?"

"Yes, right away." He said near tears.

I watched as his shaking hands fumbled with the device and within a minute he was showing me visual confirmation that the transaction had been made. As I fixed my eyes on the figure, 2 million Euro returned to the account of Jürgen Austermann, a shot rang out and Jürgen Neuhaus slumped forward in the seat beside me.

"What the fuck?" I spat, completely panicked.

My shadow! Everything was going so well and just like that it had completely gone haywire. If I had only been a few minutes sooner this might have gone to plan. One might think I would have reflexively returned fire but I didn't. I'm just not a shooter, no matter how much I ought to be. I was actually, in that split second deciding whether to return fire or roll out the passenger side door. As I was fixing my mind to fire my weapon, a head peeked in the driver's side window.

"Foster? Holy shit, alter are you OK?" Jürgen said looking down at the gun I had, still jabbed in the dead man's ribs.

"Jürgen? What the fuck? Why haven't you answered my calls?"

"There's no time, c'mon, we have to get out of here before the polizei respond!"

I rolled out of the tiny Smartcar and followed Jürgen to another Smartcar he had left running a few feet behind the one I was just sitting in.

"You Euros sure do love your Smartcars."

"Fuckin'24 kilometers per gallon, Bruder!" he said, without missing a beat. "Park them anywhere. You Americans with your enormous gas hog SUVs. I'll never understand it."

"Yeah, me either."

"What the hell, man? You scared the shit out of me."

"You scared the shit out of me."

"I could've killed you."

"I could've killed you." I countered.

"Bah." Jürgen dismissed.

Jürgen wheeled into traffic and made his way calmly toward St. Paul Hafestraße as we mixed ourselves in among the glut of Smartcars and scooters in every direction.

"Listen, this is a lot at once. My head is spinning. I have to ask you something." I said.

"What?"

"Have you been shadowing me?"

"Shadowing you? Like how?"

"I mean, do you know what I do?" I ask, "More accurately what I don't do?"

"What are you talking about, Foster? You're talking crazy."

"OK, so you haven't been going around killing a bunch of bankers?"

"What? The BRICS murders? You think that's me?" Jürgen laughed.

"Bricks murders? What are you talking about?"

"All of the banker suicides over the last couple years. What are you talking about?"

"Those aren't suicides, Jürgen, those are all murders."

"You think I don't know that?" he laughed.

"So you know about them?"

"Of course I know about them. I was an executive at Kaufmannsbank." Jürgen scolded me for what he must have took to be a daft query. "I know all about them. I've lived in fear for the last few years."

"So you're not killing bankers? You're not in the Prelacy?"

"Prelacy? Foster, what on earth are you talking about? What is the Prelacy?"

As we continued to talk Jürgen pulled off the road and parked in an urban ghost town of warehouses along the Elbe.

"You're not in the Prelacy?"

"Foster, I'm sorry but I just killed a man, why are you more panicked than I am?"

232

"Because I was supposed to kill him. That's the whole reason I'm even in Hamburg to begin with."

"You? Are you working for the BRICS coalition? No, it can't be that, you're American. Are you mixed up with those Gladio B operations?"

"What the hell is this bricks shit you keep talking about?"

"BRICS, Brazil, Russia, India, China and South Africa. They're a coalition of nations trying to sink the American dollar and replace the Petrodollar. So you're not-"

"No, man! I'm in the Prelacy."

"Prelacy? What is the Prelacy?"

"It's the 1500 year old clandestine martial arm of House Merovingi, the former Kings of-."

"You have to forgive me, Foster", Jürgen interrupted, "but you're talking crazy. I don't understand a thing you're saying."

"Kid, we need to talk." Al chimed in, crammed sideways into the tight cargo area in the back of Jürgen's Smartcar.

"God damn it, Al, not now!" I snapped at the man in the back who wasn't really there.

"What? Who are you talking to?" Jürgen puzzled, "Foster, let's get out and walk. Maybe you need some air."

We exited the car and I followed beside Jürgen as he headed toward the retaining wall at the river's edge.

"I'm sorry, I know this all sounds crazy but I'm in over my head with these Prelacy guys and honestly, I thought you were one of them." I said keeping pace with Jürgen.

"What are you into?"

"Well, I'm meant to be killing all of these bankers for the Prelacy so they can reinstall themselves as the rulers of Europe. Or, I don't know, maybe the world. Hell, all of space-time even. Nothing would surprise me."

"Foster, slow down, OK? No more crazy talk. So, what you are telling me is that you've somehow been involved in the killing of all of these bankers?"

"That's the thing. I take the assignments but I never do the deed, and yet they still wind up dead. Every single time."

"And this is all at the behest of some shadowy group of powerful men?"

"Yeah, man. The Prelacy, that's what I've been-"

"Listen, Foster, I've been in this whole executive banking thing long enough to know that it's all bullshit. There are tons of these cabals, mafias and cults all over Europe and all of them are the same. They're all bad. They've all been fighting to control our economies, some for decades, some for centuries and it never matters which one is in control. None of it matters. Templars, Masons, BRICS, the Vatican, House of Saud, Gladio, the Turks, House Rothschild, the Yanks, the Zionists. None of it matters. The only thing that matters are the people you love. I found that out too late."

"Foster. I need to talk to you, now." Al fumed.

"Jürgen, lay low for a minute. I've gotta find a bathroom."

"We're in the clear, Foster. Take your time."

"I highly doubt that." Al said as I skittered off after him.

I followed Al to a public restroom a few yards off the water's edge and lost sight of Jürgen.

"Look, kid. You did good. You got the guy his money back and the writ was prosecuted but you have gotta shake the spot kid. The Polizei are going to be all over this guy like flies on shit any minute."

"Nah, we're in the clear, Al. Relax."

"You're not in the clear for nothin'. He's calm because he doesn't give a shit. He's suicidal."

"Oh, shit. That's right, he's not well. Al, I haven't even mentioned to him that I got his money back for him. I have to hurry and tell him before he does anything!"

"OK, kid but step to. We gotta make tracks."

"Alright Al, I'm going to let him know and then we'll be out."

I returned to the water's edge to find a pile of Jürgen's clothes where I'd left him standing. I bolted to the retaining wall and peered over but saw no sign of my friend. Had I only remembered to tell him his money had been returned, he'd still be here. Instead, it seems he had gone through with his tragic plan to drown himself in the Elbe. I blamed Al, I blamed myself but mostly Al. Then again, Al was a figment of my imagination, so when it came down to it, I blamed myself.

As the sound of sirens swelled in the distance I made myself scarce and eventually wound up on the couch back at the Fountain of Bambi, watching the news report how my overnight friend Jürgen had murdered the top exec at Kaufmannsbank and was missing and presumed dead, having drowned in the Elbe River. The report went on to detail the contents of a suicide note they'd found in his Smartcar, which was parked nearby and how his clothes and pistol were found at the edge of the seawall.

Everything was going so well, and just like that, here I was back in the same mess I was in before Hamburg. The Prelacy would surely have something to say about this publicly botched job. I wouldn't be advancing to the rank of Sword Hand or the Tentacles of Abraxas any time soon. It was the London job all over again only much worse. I drank myself to sleep with thoughts of withdrawing to the solitude of my home in Los Angeles until my broken spirit healed. Al would be persona non grata for a long time to come.

FORTY-TWO

West Seattle, WA – Thurs Oct 16th 2014

There have always been people like me and there will never be a shortage. People who convince themselves they are clever enough to have found an unseen angle. A shortcut everyone else has somehow overlooked. Some as yet identified crux or fissure, obscured from plain sight, circumventing the rainbow and leading directly to the pot of gold. People who over estimate their ingenuity; self-published novelists, coke dealers, gamblers; people who think hobbies should put food on the table. But there's nothing new under the sun, no new font of easy money waiting to be exploited and by the time that truth comes crashing in, people like me are already all in on a zero sum game that will never pay out, halfway to our graves. For some reason there's never a shortage of people like me, though. The world just keeps churning us out. A man named Barnum said there's one of us born every minute. Soon enough though, the margin call comes for every sucker. I have a feeling mine has arrived in the form of a text message from the Judicious Scrivener.

"Sébastien?" Arlene asks.

"No." I respond gravely.

"What is it?"

I take a beat to breathe and calm myself, a bit of anxiety to stave off.

"The Scrivener."

"You've got your orders?"

"Yes."

"Where are they sending you?"

"The Fountain of Renewal"

"Do you have your copy of Le Livre des Fontaines"

"Don't need it, I already know where this one is."

"Where is it?"

"The penthouse of the Citron Lofts in Pershing Square.

"In L.A.?"

"Yes. Looks like we've got a little travel ahead of us."

"Well, it's too risky to fly or even rent a car. Your Greyhound doesn't record IDs so we should leave straight away, pay in cash for the tickets."

"Good thinking." I agree.

We set to sorting out the details of our little road trip but are interrupted by my phone buzzing again. I pick it up to see Sébastien calling. When it rains it pours. The grave look on my face tells Arlene who is calling before she can ask.

"If that's Sébastien you'd better think of something to stall him until we can get back to L.A."

I have to remind myself that she's being bossy because I've entered into her cabal as a subordinate, not because I slept with her. What an unusual insight. Normally, I rely on Al for pointing out things like this. Am I finally growing up in my mid-30s?

"Monsieur Sébastien, so good to finally hear from you, mon ami." I start in answering the call. "I was beginning to wonder."

"Monsieur Godefroi, there you are. Wonderful to hear your voice." He responds warmly. So far so good. "I understand you've done well for us on your business at the Fountain of Emeralds."

"Piece of cake, Sébastien."

"Excellent." Sébastien says as the line goes cold for a long beat. I nervously jog my brain for some detail to fill up the dead air but to no avail. It's getting uncomfortable.

"Monsieur Godefroi, we need to talk before you embark on your next assignment. Has the Judicious Scrivener contacted you yet?" Sébastien says at last, breaking that long, cumbersome still.

Here is where it could get sticky. I need to provide routine responses here and I have none.

"Yes. Just minutes before you rang me."

"Then we must meet soon. Find me at Macarthur Park, our normal place. Tonight at 7."

Here we go.

"No can do, Sébastien. I'm in Joshua Tree and I just ate a bunch of mushrooms."

"Oh? Off on a little vision quest, Monsieur Godefroi?" Sébastien says with a chuckle. I think I'm in the clear. Sébastien is fond of my eccentricities so I figure if I can amuse him he'll be well disarmed to my less than stellar ability to lie.

"Yeah, I needed to hit the reset button on my ego." Don't push it.

"My dear Godefroi, you are a strange bird, indeed." Sébastien relents. "Fair enough. Meet me tomorrow at Macarthur, noon and not a second past."

"Will do, mon ami."

"Very well then, safe travels in the spirit world, Monsieur Godefroi"

"Thanks, Sébastien, I'll tell God you said 'Hi'. See you tomorrow."

Arlene's smirk says all I need to hear. We've dodged a bullet and now all we need to do is get on the road.

"C'mon, we need to pack. I called a cab to take us to the Greyhound station."

"There's no time. I have to meet Sébastien tomorrow at noon."

"We can't fly, Foster. We have to stay off the radar or the Prelacy Guard could be alerted to what we're doing."

"I know. We'll have to steal a car from long term parking at Sea-Tac. We can get there in time if I drive through the night."

"Works for me. Why the airport?"

"If we take one with a window tag dated yesterday it won't likely be reported stolen while we're using it."

"Look at you, 007. Where'd you pick up that sneaky bit of trade craft? The Prelacy? Uncle Sam?"

"Boyle Heights. C'mon, let's get moving." I say stealing a kiss as we begin inventorying the safe house for our things.

"Was that your plan if I didn't comeback today?" Arlene asks sheepishly after a moment of collecting her things.

Not much gets by her. Though I'm moved by what comes across to me as genuine empathy and concern, I feel a little ashamed that she's in my head so easily and try to change the subject.

"No. If you didn't come back I was gonna go track down that Thrift Store song guy and torture him."

"Well, if I'd have known that I might not have come back."

We share another laugh as we continue gathering our things before the cab arrives.

"Fuck!"

"What's the matter?" Arlene asks.

"I just remembered that I never got my suitcase back from the Fountain of Emeralds."

"Well we couldn't. What was in it?"

"Four identical pairs of black Levis, four identical black t shirts, four pairs of plaid boxers and four pairs of black socks and some good weed." I recount to Arlene who is smirking at my idiosyncratic obsessiveness.

"No IDs or weapons, no electronic devices or anything like that?"

"No, nothing like that. Before I went out drinking I grabbed my pistol, keys and phone and returned the items from the Prelacy's cache to their safe, so that's all square but my clothes and suitcase are still in there."

It's neurotic, I know but secretly I fret over the loss of a suitcase, four pairs of levis, four t shirts, and four pairs of socks and boxers. I can easily replace them but it eats at me nonetheless.

"My god! How will you go on living after suffering so much loss?"

"I'll have to pick up the pieces somehow, start over new."

"I'll pray for you."

The playful banter could be to blame for why we wind up in each other's arms waiting for the cab to arrive.

FORTY-THREE

West Seattle, WA – Thurs Oct 16ᵗʰ 2014

Circumstances aside, it would be nice to hit the road for a change. I've traveled by air enough to merit a handful of miles accounts but, truth be told, I never cared for flying. The road on the other hand always held a sentimental draw over me.

Growing up, my mother had dragged me back and forth between Los Angeles and Chicago on a near yearly pace. I was in sixth grade before she finally relented to raising me on her own in Boyle Heights. Until then it was back and forth between her dreams of independence in L.A. and the safety net of her working class family in Chicago. Once, sometimes twice a year we did this boomeranging, always in a U-haul, always without warning. To this day, I'm fairly certain a great deal of U-Haul's revenue is owed to the caprices of single mothers. Between the age of four, when she left my father and on through to the age of 12 when she finally took root in L.A. for good, my summers held the dubious promise of these road trips and I coped by reveling in them. Relocating, changing schools, leaving behind the friends I'd struggled to make, alone and afraid trying to make new ones, these were the banal nightmares of my youth but they were always punctuated by those lingering tours through the dog days across I-80 and I-40. In those summer junkets I can't overstate my excitement for the outdoor pools of roadside motels in places like Flagstaff, Tucumcari and Tulsa. To know me, is to know that my foolish American dream was cultivated on the bleach-scented pillows of those roadside fugues. My American dream: the freedom of reinvention. My hometown: a full tank.

I was looking forward to a nice, quiet drive over the pass, down through the Sequoias and over the Grapevine as Arlene and I got to know each other more. First there was the matter of acquiring our car. Our plan, to steal one from the sprawling multi-level garage at Sea -Tac airport. This is easier said than done, considering I haven't done anything like it in 15 years.

After we've stolen a vehicle, there's still the issue of getting it out of the parking garage. We'll have to pay an attendant in cash or pay a machine with a card. I would prefer paying a machine to paying a person if I'm sitting in a stolen car. For this reason I had our cab driver pull over at a convenience store on our way to the airport. There, I paid cash for a couple of pre-paid debit cards, which couldn't be traced back to us. They would come in handy for quick fill-ups on the road as well. Any digital trail might tip the Prelacy Guard to our unusual movements, which could have dire consequences. I also picked up a pair of burner phones we could use for safely keeping in touch. Everything we did had to be in shadow.

We arrive at Sea-Tac on the heels of dusk, the October sky changing shades of salmon and grey. I wait beside the cab as Arlene pays the driver in cash. We take the elevator up to the arrivals level and cross the skybridge into the parking lot to begin our search for a car.

I'm not a professional in the habit of carrying thieves tools so our vehicle options are restricted to domestics made prior to 1984. Not exactly a cornucopia. After about 10 minutes of trying to look like a pair of weary travellers who can't remember where they parked, we happen upon an '82 Firebird that is perfect. Its ticket indicates it's only been here 20 minutes which makes it a risk. Another five minutes of searching and we're beginning to lose hope in finding an old enough car that has been parked for long term. Just as I'm about to break down and take our chances with the Firebird we'd fanned on I spy a '78 Regal that was parked last night. Not as pretty as the Firebird but we're in business nonetheless.

The easiest thing here would be to punch open the tiny back seat window, reach in and unlock the door but I don't want to drive through the Oregon pass this time of year in a car that is missing a window. Mindful of the CCTV cameras I peel back the passenger side window and direct Arlene to snake her thin arm inside the car to access the lock. With just over a minute of grunting and fiddling around we're inside the old Buick and I'm cursing as I try to remember which wires will turn over the ignition. Another minute of fiddling around behind the steering column and we're on our way. We pull up to the auto-pay machine, present one of the pre-paid cards we purchased earlier and just like that we're on the road to L.A. free and clear with a car that might even make it the whole trip, knock on wood.

"Bravo, Monsieur Godefroi! Bravo." Arlene ribs. "A genuine renaissance man, you are."

"Whatever. You know that was sexy."

"Oh, it was. I, why I think I'm just a little bit faint." She says feigning the overwhelmed damsel.

I only smile back at her smart-ass remark, keeping my eyes on the rear view and the road behind me with the rational paranoia of someone who's just stolen a car.

18 hours stuck in a car together lay ahead of us. This should tell us something about each other, though I'm not sure what.

"Should we see what's on the radio?" I ask.

Arlene just shrugs and I'm fine with that. I'm not much for musical accompaniment but I'll require background noise at some point if it gets so quiet I start thinking. Arlene reaches over and puts her hand on top of mine and the gesture is a welcome reassurance. I don't know what to make of what's developing between us but it comes at a time when I'm feeling pretty outnumbered and alone, so I'm keen to just go with it and try not worry or expect too much.

After about 10 minutes of backtracking on the 405 we're shot out onto Interstate 5, southbound and beginning our journey, proper. I estimate if we make no stops other than to use the restrooms and refuel a couple of times we should reach Los Angeles by about 10am tomorrow.

"Just let me know when you want a break and I'll take over."

I check to see that the car has about a half a tank of gas so I've got a few hours before I'll have to refuel.

"I'll probably try to push it to Sacramento. If I start getting tired by then it might be time for you to take over."

"How far is Sacramento?"

"We should be there a couple hours before dawn."

"OK, your call. I might fall asleep so wake me up if you need anything."

"No worries. I've made this drive dozens of times. Piece of cake."

We slide quietly through the brume of I-5's slavering plane, glancing Fort Lewis and bending south past Olympia. As the evening hours peel off, we whisper down through Centralia between a sea of evergreen and press forward toward Portland. Remembering that in Oregon it's against the law to pump your own gas, I decide to refuel in Vancouver before crossing their state line, the Columbia River.

Back on the highway, Arlene stirs from her nap and I feel her smiling just outside my line of sight. I point out the coffee I got for her sitting in the console and she takes it, thanking me with a touch.

"We'll be entering Portland in a few minutes."

"You're making good time."

"So far so good."

"Don't worry. We'll make it."

I want to ask what if we don't. What if this all goes sideways? Then what? I know what I'll do anyway. I'll go dig up my bug-out bag, try to monetize as much of my gold as possible and disappear into my new life, but what of Arlene? Would she join me? Try to stop me? Try to kill me, even? Better to stay focused. I might not want to know the answers to these questions just now.

"You said you'd made this trip dozens of times?"

"Yeah, I lived up here for a while. Used to drive back down to Boyle Heights to visit my mom from time to time. We also used to come this way sometimes on our trips back from Chicago, my mom and I."

"For vacations?"

I laugh at the idea of vacations. I was never from the kind of family who took vacations.

"No, we moved around a lot when I was a kid."

"Back and forth between Chicago and L.A.?"

"Yeah, basically."

"That sounds awful."

"The road trips were fun but yeah, moving sucked."

"Tell me about your family."

We'd graciously spared ourselves this course of discovery so far but we'd also grown closer in that time. I feel genuine interest from Arlene compelling me to trust and to share, though not without some apprehension.

"What do you want to know?"

"What's your mom like?"

"Look, I gotta be honest. I want to share with you but I'm not too good at talking about my folks."

"That's OK, if you don't want to talk about family stuff, we don't have to."

"Maybe some other time." This already feels rotten. "I mean, I want to share, I'm really interested in hearing about yours, too. I just think you're going to tell me all these great things about your family and then I'm going to feel all weird talking about how mine were just crazy."

"You want to know about my family?"

"Of course, I want to know about your family. I want to know more about you. I want to know who made you."

"I don't mind telling you but if you're expecting a flowery tale about growing up on some pastoral vineyard in the South of France, you're going to be disappointed."

"I hope so. I really do want to be disappointed here, because I'm totally expecting the vineyard and the perfect parents and all that."

"Perfect parents? I never even had parents. I had Abbas and Marie, hip, hash smoking, rock and roll loving pals who fucked and made me but never wanted to be a drag like their folks. And naturally when marriage got to be a drag for them, they didn't want to do it anymore so they didn't."

"Harsh, how old were you when they split up?"

"10. I lived. I resented them for it, they're so spoiled but depriving me of a family is hardly the worst they did."

"It gets worse?"

"Oh, much worse. Divorce is the least of what I hold against them. I despise them and their entire party first, work never generation, Godefroi."

"Aha! And now I know why she reads Evola."

"You asked and I'm going to give it to you. Let me tell you about my grandparents."

"Please do."

"Jean-Yves and Marine, Marie's parents, they married young and never parted ways. They sweated their entire lives, tending their little vineyard in the South of France. That vineyard had been in our family for three generations before them. They worked it sun up to sundown every day until they died and today they lay buried side by side in the church grounds at Ste Adèle, down the road from that Vineyard."

"God damn it, you promised, no vineyard."

"I lied, there's a vineyard." Arlene shushes. "My mother inherited that vineyard and rather than work it, rather than keep it in the family she and her husband, my father, decided they'd sell it."

"Why?"

"Because they had no interest in such things. They wanted the lives of urban socialites, not humble farmers. They sold the vineyard so they could move to the city and squander three generations of blood and sweat in just a few years, living as frivolous hipsters in Paris. They wasted their twenties getting high in discos like the rest of their generation, then entered their thirties in divorce and hit burn-out in their forties as they settled for unrewarding state jobs that barely provide for their retirement."

"So you would prefer the family was still in the wine business."

"As opposed to being wrecked in a single generation? What do you think?" Arlene says, a pain in her laughter.

"So where are your folks now?"

"I haven't seen my father since I graduated from University. He's probably in Paris, womanizing and doing coke like he's still 25 and it's still the 1970s. I keep in contact with my mother but I haven't seen her since around the time I joined the Prelacy. She's in a shitty little rental outside Marseille squandering her retirement on champagne brunches, pretending to be rich in hopes of attracting a pensioner with more money than she left herself with.

"Do you ever help them out?"

"Abbas, no, never. Marie, I am always bailing out of financial problems but I try not to spoil her."

"You've got your Prelacy wealth, why not just forgive them for being idiots and take care of them?"

"I'm nowhere near as well cared for by the Prelacy as you've been, Monsieur Godefroi. I will be fine and yes, I can afford to help them but they can't know enough to ask questions about where the money comes from and honestly, they don't deserve my help. I know that sounds cruel but there's a lot I'm not telling you. Maybe someday I'll tell you more."

"It's not that cruel, I mean, I get it. Really it just sounds like normal, healthy rebellion against the folks. They were slackers, so you rejected that and became an uptight reactionary. Who wouldn't?"

Arlene laughs in agreement with my overly frank, overly simple observation.

"Maybe, but trust me, it's a little deeper than simply wanting to spite two people who took four generations worth of our family's proud endeavor, four generations of civility and heritage and squandered it all to get high every night and feel sophisticated and cosmopolitan. Like I said, there's more than what I'm telling you. They did some pretty unforgivable things."

"Well, like what?"

"Maybe someday."

"So, did your folks even make it through college like you or did they just blow it all off to party?"

"Abbas finished but Marie dropped out after three semesters to be a performance artist or dancer or whatever she thought she was doing. I'm sure Jean-Yves and Marine were just thrilled about throwing all that tuition away."

"I feel like I shouldn't be bringing this all back. I'm sorry, Arlene, let's talk about something else."

"No, it's OK, It's not just my parents I'm angry with, Godefroi. It's their stupid Bohemian generation who took a majestic, centuries old dominion of freedom, culture and tradition and turned it into a decaying slum in just a couple of decades. My parents didn't invent the degeneracy that seduced them. I'm less rebelling against them than I am the counter culture they bought into."

"I know how glib this is going to sound but don't you think you could be happier if you could just let it all go, just forgive it all and get on with it."

"I know you're being sincere but the need to constantly feel happy has degraded France. I want to feel accomplished, not happy."

"You know, I had you pegged for Swedish when I first saw you." I quip, hoping to steer the conversation towards lighter fare.

"Have you ever noticed how wrong you are about everything?" Arlene laughs and leans in to kiss my cheek.

"It's starting to become pretty apparent."

"Like, always. About everything, all the time." Arlene ribs.

I let it go with a grin rather than verbalize any response, but there's a lot of truth in her joking. More and more I've found myself asking how often my ridiculous prejudices and judgments are miles off the mark.

"So feel free to tell me about your family, Foster." She says. "Can't be any meaner than what I've got to say about mine."

I give it a moment of thought. I feel a little less self-conscious about discussing my background after such bold and trusting admissions but something else is begging my attention. It's her. This insight into her family doesn't explain her so much as it sparks more curiosity, more questions. She's mean and tough and a little unhinged. And while it's sexy as hell, that isn't what deepens my curiosity. She said there were things she wasn't telling me and I suspect it's a lot. An awful lot.

"I don't mind talking about my family as much after that but I've gotta tell you something."

"What?"

"This is gonna sound judgmental but don't take it wrong, because I really like this about you, Arlene."

"What, Godefroi? Say it." Arlene says leering from across the car a little.

You're kinda scary. You should've elected the path of the Sword when you joined the Prelacy."

"It wasn't offered or maybe I would have." She relaxes and smirks.

"So when you were tapped, you saw the Prelacy as a way to restore France to better times, by returning House Merovingi to power?"

"Honestly, I don't know what I saw it as. I only knew I was angry at my family, angry at my country, angry at religion and angry at the world. Since then I've changed. Since being approached by the Covenant I've found faith and I've found a little peace and now maybe I've even found a man worth the risk of caring about."

The boldness of her heart stuns me, assuming she's talking about me. I fight off doubt and jealousy before it takes rise. I know for someone as hardened as her, this sort of confessional honesty isn't natural. She's either winding me up or taking a big risk. I delude myself it's the latter, fearful it's not. Moved by her words, I reach across the car and caress her hand. Far clouds seem to marshal against us, my only hope is to find calm seas once we've weathered the coming storm. I dare to hope and I think I should know better, but I hope nonetheless.

"Why are you in the Prelacy? Why aren't you someone's husband or father, Foster?"

It worries me that she seems to see me as a kind man hiding behind a coarse façade. Not because I'm a wretch in truth, but because I can't face the world as a kind man. I see myself as an unpredictable psychopath but I'm usually wrong about everything, where she seems to see things for what they are. I don't want to be a kind man. This world makes quick work of kind men. Unpredictable psychopaths have hidden stashes of gold and bug-out bags buried with new identities. Kind men have cancer and alimony, kind men are estranged from their children who hate them and answer to bosses who fire them the day before their 401k vests. I can't greet this world a kind man; I don't have that sort of courage.

"A father or a husband? Is that how you see me?"

"Well you're not much of an assassin, no offense." She says gently, looking me square on to convey accord, not judgment.

"I have never wanted be a father or a husband, Arlene."

"I don't believe that. Not for one second."

"OK, maybe I wanted those things when I was a kid but those things are illusions, Arlene. Those things don't exist anymore. Sure, I could have been someone's ex-husband or someone's real dad but there are no husbands and fathers where I'm from anymore. Just exes and real dads. I was lucky enough to realize there's nothing in it for me, so I did other things. Fought some wars, developed a drinking habit, joined a cult. You know, fun shit. Dude shit."

"I wish I would have met you a hundred years ago."

"In France?"

"South France, in a vineyard."

"I could clear the land and work the land, you could bear us some ungrateful kids and we'd leave them the yield of our lifelong toil to squander on dope and Warhol prints."

Arlene bolts across the car, throwing her arms around me laughing. She kisses me recklessly and I can't see the road and that's just fine. Nothing could be better.

FORTY-FOUR

Hamburg, Germany – Tues April 8th, 2014

The Monolith is a secure mobile communications device that relies on GSM encryption to obscure all peer to peer transmissions between it and other devices. A blackphone. The Prelacy uses these blackphones for everything and all members are issued their own Monolith after initiation. We are instructed to use them strictly for Prelacy business and to use no other device for Prelacy business, though my hack of Arlene's Monolith had revealed she uses hers for nominal personal contacts as much as I use mine for the same. The day after the Hamburg job my Monolith was blowing up with calls and texts from Monsieurs Sébastien and Herman both. Hungover and defeated by the previous day's fiasco I missed my flight and ignored all attempts to contact me. I just kept sleeping, snored through a light coma on the leather couch in the Fountain of Bambi's living room all morning and only awoke in the afternoon when Sébastien and Herman had come to physically raise me. That they had to confront me in the flesh was not a good thing, to be certain but it was not at all unexpected.

"I take it you haven't seen the news on television, Monsieur Godefroi." Herman started, his patience stretched as I slowly stirred from the couch and sat upright.

"I'm sure I already know what it says." I yawned, getting my bearings.

"Monsieur Godefroi, you're in no position to be flippant." Herman responded sharply. "Your folly has set us back, this is very serious."

I stiffened a little at Herman's tone. My few contacts with him had been very pleasant and I sunk inside a little having obviously disappointed him. I wanted to disappear.

"Nonsense, Monsieur Herman." Sébastien interjected, massaging the mood in the room. "This is indeed a complication but nothing so severe as to divide us from our calm or esprit de corps. We shall assess contingency and we shall see to its satisfactory redress."

"Of course, Monsieur Sébastien. Please, excuse my impatience." Herman deferred, reclaiming his standard poise. "Monsieur Godefroi, I bear no malice."

"It's all good, Herman. I guess I've earned a few lumps," I said, "and if I have, I intend to take them."

"We're not here to mete penalty, Monsieur Godefroi." Sébastien assured me. "We are simply here to execute remedial action."

"How did you guys even get here so fast? What time is it?" I said, still trying to shake off yesterday and find my feet.

"Monsieur Godefroi, we are la Prélature Familier des Arbitres Infernales. If I tell you we have business on the dark side of the moon, do not worry about whether or not we can get there, only make sure that you yourself can get there and that you arrive with a nice Vinho Verde to pair with all of that wonderful green cheese." Sébastien quipped.

Sébastien was rarely anything but straight forward, but this was one of those times when I couldn't tell if he was boasting in sincerity or just yanking my chain. I tried not to imagine Sébastien walking around the Sea of Tranquility with Jesus Christ negotiating a wine shipment for his Chalet.

"Fair enough." I laughed then pinched it off when I recognized that Sébastien and Herman were not laughing.

"OK, so how bad is it?" I ask after an awkward beat. "How bad did I screw up? What've I got to do?"

"There's nothing to be done, really." Sébastien said. "We must simply restart the ritual."

Every operation in the Prelacy was ostensibly seen as some sort of Ritual or Pageant by its devouts. Taking your oath of induction into the Prelacy? You're conducting the Ritual of the Blind Apprentice. Killing the King-in-Waiting? You're conducting the Pageant of Clovis. Wiping your ass? You're Composing an Epistle to the Pope. And on and on.

"What we must do is debrief you." Herman said.

"That's it?" I asked.

"For now, yes."

"And there is the matter of your promotion to Sword Hand in the Tentacles of Abraxas." Sébastien cut in. "As I'm sure you'll understand, this must be deferred, pending proper satisfaction among the elders that you are indeed deserving of promotion."

What a ludicrous, misguided entitlement, this dejection I felt being passed over for promotion. Though I hadn't even nearly earned it, I was unfittingly eager to reach the next lodge, the Tentacles of Abraxas. This was all but a done deal, had I simply prosecuted my writ here in Hamburg. Had I finally gotten things on track, I would for the first time know the feeling of a promotion earned within my order. No more being a phony, no more shorting the race. Had I never crossed paths with Jürgen Austermann, had I but properly dispatched Jürgen Neuhaus, I would be righting the ship as it were and I would have been promoted to Main l'Epée or Sword Hand.

Coulda woulda shoulda.

"Of course. I understand." I sheepishly said back.

"Very good, Monsieur Godefroi. What say you prepare yourself a coffee and collect your thoughts, then we will begin your debriefing."

"Coffee, yeah, that sounds like a great idea." I respond. "How many cups should I make?"

As I shuffled toward the kitchen I turned to receive a response of cold silence from both men standing in the foyer. Monsieur Herman checked his watch, lips tightening across that otherwise idling countenance chiseled from the same dauntless druid slabs which comprised Stonehenge. I wanted to never again test this man's patience. He could evoke dread with little more than a cocked eyebrow. How does someone so ascetic in demeanor manage to command the same regard as a bare-fanged wolf?

As I rifled through the cabinets I found only single cup filters and an ancient looking tea kettle to heat the water in. For all of its modern and luxurious appointments, the Fountain of Bambi lacked one simple thing I suspected any German home might have: a Braun electric coffee maker, better still a Keurig. Growing more self-conscious and agitated by the minute I filled the old Melitta and placed her over a medium flame to wait. What I really wanted to do was throw the teapot at the wall and pour a whiskey.

"It'll be a few minutes before the coffee's ready. Should we just get on with it?" I asked, studying Sébastien for even the slightest demonstration of mercy.

"Non, Monsieur, we will wait. I want no distractions."

My propensity for manipulation in social settings was not going to abide a prolonged silence gracefully. I fought the urge to make small talk and gritted my teeth at the disquieting silence. I felt as if a cruel child's caught stray, cornered and prodded.

As I waited expectantly for the watched pot to boil I longed for a whiskey and channeled my impatience into a petulant loathing of my own illicit appetites, which in turn gave way to a study of the human appetite in general. Craving and its demands, valet for immediacy and convenience, lazy usurpers to our proverbial Mother of Invention's throne. What Pageant of Clovis had dethroned you, Necessity? Who were the assassins responsible for this matricide, who were these installers of convenience and craving as your successors, oh, necessity, you once great Mother of Invention?

Was it Henry Ford and his assembly line, which made a glorious liberator like the automobile affordable to the common man but in more perverse and clever hands made a thing like chocolate bars a cheap new food group? Epiphany: diabetes was a tangential by-product of the automobile.

Was it Ted Hoff, whose microprocessor helped bring power computing into every home, but would eventually give way to putting fast-food workers and barbers and baristas and delivery drivers out of business, consigning their sacred charges to unambiguous machinery? Epiphany: Ted Hoff is why unskilled labor will arrive by google cab in the streets every day to riot over a living wage, spurred forth by fast, cheap coffee, with full stomachs and great hair. Where necessity once drove invention, appetites and convenience now did and it was ruining us in a sense.

We are all on our mules, winding toward the basin of a valley between technology's freeing us from toil and figuring out what to do about the emerging horror of too much free time. Meanwhile, I was in my own valley between boiling water over an open flame for five minutes to make coffee and simply pressing a button on a Keurig to have it in seconds. Somewhere in the very near future was a confused former barista rioting in the streets for a return to the good old days of bitching about tips. Epiphany: tomorrow's reactionaries will bomb fully automated Starbucks and demand a return to traditional values like "an honest day's work" because free time and abundance make for a terrifying boredom. Utopia will never happen because we simply don't want it. Worshipping at the feet of God, basking in his love and glory, free from sin and suffering? That just sounds like a drag and we know it. When we've finally defeated the devil, we will simply re-invent him.

The whistling kettle spared me from further meditation and prompted me to place grounds in the little paper filter over my cup. I engaged the banal toil with a delusional sense of sanctity after my dizzying flight of fancy. Once the task had been attended to, off I went-coffee in hand-to join Sébastien and Herman who had both relocated to the couch.

"So what's the score, fellas? What're we doing?" I said taking my seat in the high-backed chair across from them.

"Monsieur Godefroi, we have some questions about yesterday's events." Sébastien said.

"Shoot." I said and sipped my coffee.

"The media is reporting that the target of your writ was killed not by your hand but that of a man named Jürgen Austermann, who later drowned himself in the Elbe River." Herman tagged in. "Did you now this man, this

Jürgen Austermann?"

I didn't know whether to answer honestly or lie. The sociopath's familiar quandary. I would have to provide a seemingly assured answer and maneuver around the upshot. I elected to lie.

"I don't know anyone in Hamburg."

"That was not my question, Godefroi." Herman pressed. "I asked you if you knew this Jürgen Austermann."

I responded with a frown and shook my head then sipped my coffee again. Herman looked gravely at Sébastien who urged the proceedings with a shrug.

"Monsieur Godefroi, would you please provide for us a full account of yesterday's events?"

"The whole day?"

"From the moment you awoke to whenever you passed out here on this couch." Herman replied. "Spare no detail."

I most assuredly did not do this. Instead, I provided a sterilized account of my performance, leaving out any detail that involved Jürgen Austermann, or Al for that matter. I explained that when I arrived at the Kaufmannsbank parking garage my target was in his car already dead. I returned to the Fountain of Bambi in shock and drank myself to sleep as I awaited contact from the Judicious Scrivener, which never materialized.

Satisfied with my debriefing, Sébastien and Herman assured me there would be no consequence for my failing and reminded me that my promotion to Sword Hand and the Tentacles of Abraxas would have to be deferred, pending my satisfying the Elders that I indeed deserved the new title and station. They explained that it was in fact a minor setback but nothing unusual, something that was bound to occur from time to time. As our impromptu court wound down the pair stood to depart with a less stern demeanor than the ones they'd arrived with.

"Monsieur Godefroi, are you familiar with the Pageant of Childeric II?" Sébastien turned to ask, stopping short of the door on their way out.

"From the Codex Merovingi?" I asked. "I've read it but it's not one of the gospels I'm very familiar with."

"You should take the time to study it when we meet again. I'll contact you when you've returned home so that you may."

"Thanks, Sébastien ." I say. "I'd like that."

"I'm sure you'll find it insightful if you consider it's pertinence to this particular writ as much as your duties as a Red Hand."

I watched my Elders out the door, closed it behind them, poured my coffee in the sink and refilled my cup with Jameson. The rest of the day was spent in the Fountain of Bambi drinking myself dull as I booked a new flight home and frittered away the down time scanning German television and browsing the internet for information about the death of my fast friend Jürgen who had found his unnecessary compromise at the bottom of the Elbe.

FORTY-FIVE

Los Angeles, CA – Fri Oct 17ᵗʰ, 2014

Magic Mountain means you've made it back. It passes on your right and you look at it, sight for sore eyes every time. Any Angeleno who flees north only to find that they miss Los Angeles knows the feeling of relief that is passing Colossus on the right. Pity those of us who miss Los Angeles. We're out there and we're real like so much of this place isn't. Mugu Rock along PCH offers a similar hail embrace for the returning Angeleno, home at long last.

If these bluffs and basins bring to mind lying on your back in the hills, stoned and studying air traffic, or turning right onto Chavez toward the beach as the sky turns pink, Vin Scully on the radio calling the final innings of the Dodgers game you've just left, if they bring you thoughts of frustrating, dry Santa Anas bounding off of terracotta walls on an April afternoon, or a black eye from a rough Dawn Patrol at El Porto, if they conjure longings for Loncheras and elotes, a smile for the mob of Mexican bootboys and chelseas riding their Vespas through Highland Park, if they remind you of whoppers about undiscovered stashes of Mickey Cohen treasure or what all of those spooky silhouettes painted in the alleys really meant, if those are the sort of rushes and flourishes the sight of Colossus brings to mind, then you know. If for you, this place is just the Hollywood sign, fake tits and real assholes then you probably don't know. Lucky you.

I watch as Colossus gets smaller and smaller in the mirror then lean over to rouse Arlene. I'm tired from pushing through the entire drive but I'm not in danger of nodding out at the wheel, thanks to truck stop coffee and talk radio. Her conversation would be a welcome change from Bill Handel rambling about the parking situation on Larchmont, warm greeting though that is, too.

"Are we there yet?"

"Home. I didn't realize how much I'd missed it."

"You're cute when you're homesick." Arlene teases, already playfully feisty before she'd even rubbed the sleep from her eyes. "How long's it been?"

"I don't know, six days I guess?"

"Oh, poor baby. Did you ever think you'd see it again?" she quips, her affected neutral accent fading into the territory of extraneous deceits no longer viable or necessary; her natural French accent peeking through adorably.

"Well, to be honest, I had some concerns."

"Yes, I suppose you did." Arlene soberly agrees.

Our conversation slows like our forward progress as the morning rush coagulates in the veins of the bloated 5 freeway. The rising quiet isn't sleepy, just a fitting tension. Strange times lay ahead. If this were a new found love we were sharing it would be tested and soon, this we know though neither of us speak of it. In the back of my mind lingers that perfectly rational distrust I still dread entertaining. That Arlene is a run of the mill Mata Hari, just doing her job.

"Is there a Covenant safe house you can hide out in while I meet with Sébastien" I ask breaking the tension.

"Yes, there are several. I should stay in the one closest to you."

"I'm in Glassell Park. Do you know if there's one near Dodger Stadium or in Hollywood?"

Arlene took out her blackphone and started to enter those details before I stopped her.

"Is that safe?" I asked.

"Cloak work means I travel more than most other Prelates but maybe you're right."

"I should just take you to one you've stayed at. We need to leave as small a digital foot print as possible, no?"

"No, you're right. I know of one in Hollywood, for sure. It's in a Scientology building."

"You've got to be shitting me." We share a laugh.

"I told you, the Covenant has infiltrated everywhere."

"Do you have the address stored on your phone?"

"No but I remember the cross streets are Fountain and Normandie."

"That's perfect. I can take the 170 in a few miles here. We should get there in a little less than an hour, traffic permitting."

"Is that going to make you late for Sébastien?"

"It's 10:15 right now, Have to meet him at noon, so I should make it to Macarthur Park with time to spare."

Arlene smiles and gives my hand a squeeze.

"See? We've got this. Don't worry."

Plenty of time just means plenty of time for things to go wrong. I don't want to think like that though. I smile back in accord.

"I should check in with Monsieur Herman and bring him up to speed, arrange to stay at the Covenant safe house and all that."

"Oh, yeah." I'd sort of forgotten about Monsieur Herman being a member of Arlene's Covenant of Arius. Suddenly I feel a little less worried, knowing that we were in this together with the Master of Swords and my immediate superior in the Prelacy. Things were about to get far more serious than I was likely cut out for dealing with but I take comfort in knowing his capable, deadly hands were on our side. We can do this. I can do this. It has to be that way.

I drive on as Arlene pulls the Covenant blackphone from her purse to text Monsieur Herman. Sneaking around apparently means lots of different phones in this modern world. As we navigate the late morning rush and wheel onto the Hollywood Freeway I consider the odd item of my next promotion within the Prelacy. The Covenant's contingency is pendant on Monsieur Sébastien's proposition of regicide which they expect to occur shortly after my advancement to the Tentacles of Abraxas. Once I've prosecuted my next writ, my advancement rite will be scheduled and it will be nothing less than nerve wracking to go through. Carrying off the ceremony straight faced, knowing I'm about to betray our order is no small task and it will likely pale in comparison to the more serious skulduggery which lay ahead. There are indeed a lot of moving parts in this operation. I'd spent the last couple of years free of having to do anything so precise, so detail oriented. I would need to get my head in the game.

"You know, there'll be a ceremony for my promotion to Sword Hand and the new lodge." I say to Arlene. "I'd sort of forgotten all about it."

"I know. Don't worry, you'll do fine."

"I'm worried I'm going to act weird now, knowing I'm a turncoat."

"You're not a turncoat, you're the next head of House Merovingi, le Roi en Attente, en attente" she says comically. The King-in-Waiting, in waiting. I'm too anxious about it all to laugh at her wordplay.

"I feel like a turncoat."

"If anything, they're the ones who've betrayed you. They've been using you all along, don't you see that?"

I offer no response and drive on. Arlene texts with Monsieur Herman as we proceed south toward Hollywood.

"OK, I'm all squared away with lodging. Herman says there will be an attendant there when I arrive and he also says I have to meet with him tonight."

"With Herman? Should I be there?"

"No, he said the next time he sees you will be at your promotion ceremony. He also told me to let you know that you're doing good and that you shouldn't worry because everything is going to plan."

A relief to hear, no way I can overstate it. The closer I get to my meeting with Sébastien, the more anxious and unsettled I become.

"Did Herman say where he was meeting with you?"

"He said the Ukrainian Culture Center on Melrose."

"Do you know where that is?"

"No, do you?"

"I don't."

"He said it's walking distance from the Covenant safe house, so I should be fine."

"OK, well, call me if you need anything, OK?"

"I will, don't worry."

We press on down the Hollywood Freeway and eventually take the Western/Santa Monica Blvd off ramp to exit. In a few minutes we are pulling over in front of a nondescript four story apartment building on Fountain that looks to have been built nearly a century ago.

"This is a Scientology building? Wasn't what I was expecting."

"Yeah, they own all of these old apartment buildings around Hollywood where they house their acolytes."

"Why is that creepy to me?" I wonder aloud.

"Yeah, no creepier than us hiding a Covenant safe house inside one, I suppose."

"Yet another weird little Matryoshka doll of conspiracies and cabals."

"The rabbit hole goes deep." Arlene says.

"In deed."

With that, Arlene plants a little kiss on my cheek, gives me a reassuring look and brushes my hand as she exits our purloined Buick.

"I'll be in touch."

"OK." I say.

I wave her off and watch as she ascends the stoop into the old concrete flat house. A man dressed like what I would describe as a Mormon crossing guard opens the door to let her in and then she's gone. A little emotional, I wheel the Buick onto Kingsley and nearly wreck into another driver, distracted by a gigantic mural of a man who looks like a cross between the warden from Cool Hand Luke and a Mexican Einstein. The Armenian man in the black Acura I nearly crashed into yells something then flips me the bird for driving shitty and speeds off toward Normandie. I'm home.

FORTY-SIX

From the Codex Merovingi

Excerpt from

l'Évangile de Leodegar le traître

(aka The Pageant of Childeric II; The Ritual of the Insulted Noble)

Translated from the **Le Volume du Maire du Palais**
from memory by Foster Revell,

formally l'Honoré Godefroi de Les Anges de le Prélature Familier des Arbitres
Infernales

Chapter III, vs. 1-32

1. Among the wardens of Neustria and auld Aquitaine, callous and dull sat the last long-haired king.2. Installed by his sire, his sole virtue: his name. 3. Impotent and spoon-fed, wed his cousin in shame. 4. Childeric II born to Clovis II and St. Balthild of House Merovingi. 5. From the salt and to the salt, those long-haired kings of the Frisian Sea.

6. Insolent and arrogant, he insults the Burgundy Nobles 7. Doling out titles to Alsace warlords as payment for their loyal swords. 8. Imprisoning your humble narrator and so many more 9. When he ordered the noble Bodilo bound and then flogged. 9. A step too far that cost him all.

10. His cousin-wife Bilichild slain in his sight at the hand of Bodilo who'd caught them on their hunt. 11. Driven into the sea, he swore to return. 12. An empty threat his last recalled words: 13. "House Merovingi will forever live on!"

14. They buried his empty robes beside his consort and laughed at the thought

he'd survive to restore House Merovingi to the throne of the Franks. 15. No corpse just his robes found along the banks. 16. Death to House Merovingi, Long live House Merovingi. 17. No corpse , just his robes found on the shore.

18. By the hand of Bodilo, the long-haired kings were no more. 19. They buried his empty robes beside his consort and watched evermore in dread both beachhead and port. 20.Death to House Merovingi, Long live House Merovingi.

21. The ritual replays and replays again. 22. The insulted noble returns to kill the king. 23. To go forth and forge the land's new accord. 24. That a new house may rise by might of the sword. 25. But for Red Hand and Cloak's intervention 26. Assuring the next long-haired king's ascension. 27. Death to House Merovingi, Long live House Merovingi.

28. All Kings and Dynasties will fall in due time. 29. If by the hand of the insulted noble, a new House may rise. 30. If by Red Hand, long live House Merovingi, death to the Insulted Noble. 31. Death to the King, long Live House Merovingi. 32. From the sea, and to the sea and from the sea once again, long live House Merovingi.

FORTY-SEVEN

Los Angeles, CA – Fri Oct 17th, 2014

After a 20 minute roll down Virgil and on to 5th I'm looking for a parking spot near Macarthur Park. After a few more minutes hawking for a place to dock my hot Buick, I find myself sitting on the usual bench in view of the Fountains, waiting somewhat nervously for Sébastien to show. I worry about how disheveled and tired I look after some 20 hours on the road. I then remember lying to Sébastien that I was out at Joshua Tree doing hallucinogens, so I can relax in the knowledge that I should look a mess. Nobody who spent the night in the desert talking to god is going to look hygienic and unblemished, all ready for court. Neurotically I begin to wonder if I shouldn't look a little more of a mess.

I watch as a couple of ancient and mustachioed Diamond Streeters nod off on the grass nearby, high to the gills on Eme dope, their black-inked prison sleeves pocked with scabs and abscesses. Across the lawn a pair of young Dieciochos shake down a churro cart guy and I casually brush my hand over my pants to trace the outline of the AF-1 pistol held there for reassurance. There's a joke about overcompensating masculinity in there, I'm sure. This nervous habit of inventory is something I do every time I leave the house, more likely anytime I panic that I might be incomplete or unprepared. There's zero chance this pair of young mafiosos extorting the old guy at the churro cart have any interest in me, but if you stay ready you never have to get ready, something I picked up in Afghanistan. I return my attention to the fountains out on Macarthur Park Lake and gratefully greet the unfolding calm the scenery elicits.

In these rare moments of quiet I usually expect Al to show up. It occurs to me that I've seen neither hair nor hide of him since the night I met Arlene at the W in Seattle. That's actually an unusual stretch for Al. In this tranquil, day-lit park setting, the clarity from going a full night without a drink threatens to set in and beg deeper analysis of things like Al and my current state of affairs. I usually do a pretty good job of just accepting the insanity of having a phantom friend, rather than digging into myself in effort to better understand why he is. At some point I fear I might lose that high ground and succumb to a painful introspection that has me seeking help where I know there is none: in therapy and elaborate pharmaceutical regimens. The way I see it, I have a better shot at sustaining a functional insanity by just accepting Al as a quirk and frequently self-medicating my myriad conditions with marijuana and alcohol. And of course cutting loose every few days by irritating the shit out of some strangers in a bar. Always that. Never shrinks and Thorazine, though. Those things might render you more agreeable to others but I've never seen them help anyone become the person they wanted to be. I hadn't yet given up being that person someday, or at least figuring out who that person was, anyway.

"You appear as a Panda among the Bamboo, mon ami. A Koala, peacefully chewing his Eucalyptus leaves." Comes the voice from behind me- Sébastien.

I turn to greet him but he is already taking his seat next to me, bedecked in his ostentatious white and gold as always, impeccable vision of the sophisticated eccentric. A modern wizard.

"I take it you enjoyed your little vision quest?" Sébastien muses.

"As much as someone can enjoy getting lost in the desert without water, I suppose." The first of many lies I would today tell the man I call my mentor.

"Well, you seem no worse for the wear. A little bedraggled, perhaps but whole and attendant, nonetheless."

"Yeah, I'm fine. No worries."

"Good, good to hear."

A somewhat typical silence unwinds as can happen whenever sitting with Sébastien in his economical and deliberate manner of speech. I wait for him to ask about my writ and he just stares out at the Fountains.

"Monsieur Godefroi, tell me how things went at the Fountain of Emeralds." Sebastien asks finally breaking the silence. "Were you without hindrance?"

"Couldn't have been more routine. A nice trip to be honest."

"You have a curious rapport with that city, mon ami."

"That's one way to put it, yeah."

"I imagine you were at your leisure briefly 'winding up strangers in bars' as you like to call it?"

"Old habits die hard. Yeah, after my writ I spent the rest of the evening being a nuisance to the locals."

"Of course you did."

In light of recent circumstances, these routine questions all feel dubious and probing. I effort relaxed composure under the haunting fact of my own treachery. His questions about my activities in Seattle whisper a subtext in my ear; that his inquiry into how things went is unnecessary, as he knows so much more than he lets on. "Of course you did" comes across to me as patronizing and sarcastic, the implication that nothing I say is true. These are the same interactions we would have in any case, but under the duress of my own well-earned paranoia and guilt they sound like card calls in a high-stakes hand.

"Why the trip to the desert afterward? Was this something you had already planned?"

"I sort of decided on the drive up to Seattle." I say, thinking on my feet. "Not to get all spiritual and weird on you but I guess I felt like it was time I did a little soul searching."

"Anticipating your promotion to the Tentacles of Abraxas?"

"Yeah, I think that has a lot to do with it."

Sébastien let those words hang in the air for a while as he stared out at the lake.

"So, you drove to Seattle?" Sébastien asks. "Why not fly?"

"Some more alone time to reflect, I guess. I like the drive North. Always have."

"Hmmm. Rental car I presume?"

"Yeah. Used my rewards points to pay for it." This conversation is getting a little itchy.

"And how did you get back?" In my guilt informed paranoia, this really is starting to seem like a little more than our standard light debriefing. I wouldn't even characterize our routine meetings after a writ as debriefing. I have always taken them as little more than checking in and catching up. I'm getting into big lie territory now and I worry I'll have to recount all of this bullshitting someday in flawless detail.

"I don't think I was prepared to tell you all of this stuff, Sébastien."

"What is wrong, Monsieur Godefroi?" Sébastien asked. "You needn't worry. When have I ever judged you? What is it you're apprehensive about?"

"I don't know, I guess I know you're not judging me. I don't know why I'm feeling so self-conscious."

"Is there something you want to get off of your chest?"

"No, nothing like that."

"OK, well if you change your mind you know you can come to me with anything, mon ami." Sébastien advises with grave import, "I am your sponsor in our order and I would give my own life to protect you."

I offer no response at first. This is getting heavy. I need to steer the conversation toward more banal tones.

"Thank you, Sébastien." I say. "You are the best friend I have."

"The only friend you have, it seems at times. I admit, that is perhaps the only thing about you that worries me."

If you only knew, old friend, I now have some new friends who expect that very soon I must kill you. This is an itchy exchange indeed. I take a deep breath.

"I know. I need to stop isolating from the world. I have no life outside the Prelacy."

"Well, you have a life." Sébastien says. "A life that seems to consist of getting drunk alone and thrown out of bars. That and collecting nazi artifacts."

"They're not all nazi artifacts! I have katanas, too."

"Fair enough, Monsieur Godefroi," Sébastien chuckles, "I do not judge. So tell me how you got home."

"Well, I hitch hiked."

"Hitch hiked? This does not sound like you, but then again, it is you entirely. Socially adventurous: not you. Capricious and risky: entirely Monsieur Godefroi de les Anges."

"I know. It's weird and I don't even know why I did it, really. It was exactly that, a caprice."

"You are a strange bird, indeed, Monsieur Godefroi."

"I figure between driving to Seattle by myself instead of flying, the hitch hiking home only to spend a night in the desert alone, high on mushrooms, you must figure me for a little unstable right now."

"You are dependably unpredictable, mon ami. Aside from your predilection for Jameson and black denim suits, there is little I can be sure of with you. Well, besides prosecuting your writs, of course. In that regard you have been quite dependable, save for a couple of snares along the way."

As this all drags on I want more and more to simply disappear into a glass of Jameson or 10. I vacillate between thinking he's winding me up good and thinking the old guy truly is a loving mentor who knows nothing of the skullduggery afoot. Back and forth between feeling like shit for lying to him about every writ I've ever been credited with prosecuting and the dread horror of thinking he knows I've never successfully prosecuted a single one. This is way too Texas Hold 'Em and I fucking hate Texas Hold 'Em. I don't even like Go Fish.

"Yeah, London and Hamburg, I still get a little embarrassed when they're brought up."

"You shouldn't. Few Swords even live as long as you have, let alone prosecute as many writs as you have as fast as you have."

Well that isn't a shit-your-pants scary thing to think about now, is it?

"OK, now you're just winding me up."

"Non, mon ami. The Sword is a dangerous path in our order. Surely you know this by now."

"Yeah, I mean, I guess so. I just never heard it put in such concrete terms."

"Did you not study the Pageant of Childeric II like I suggested so many months ago in Hamburg?"

"I did, you were there when I read it."

"Indeed I was, Monsieur but what did you take from it? Did I not advise you of its pertinence to your writ in Hamburg?"

"I guess you did, but I feel like there's something I'm missing."

"Well, perhaps you should continue to meditate on it. Read it again and think on it more. Hamburg was not the giant fiasco you seem to grief yourself for. You have acquitted yourself adroitly in your work since then and following the completion of your next writ, as you know, we will be eager to welcome you as a Sword Hand into the Tentacles of Abraxas"

"The writ that's waiting for me at the Fountain of Renewal?"

"The same, Monsieur. This is a writ of crucial importance so regard it with severity. "

"I will, Sébastien."

"Very well, then. Once you've prosecuted this writ, take your leave and expect the Scrivener to contact you with the details of your advancement ritual and initiation into the Tentacles of Abraxas. The next time I see you, we will be welcoming you into House Merovingi as a titled courtier."

"It's a lot to take in. What's the ceremony like?"

"It will be a closed ceremony in Frankia with myself, The-King-in-Waiting and Monsieur Herman attending. Much more ritual than your Black Hand and Red Hand advancement ceremonies. Similar to your initiation as a

Blind Apprentice. After your initiation, I should like to meet with you privately to read a particular chapter from the Codex Merovingi."

"Of course, Monsieur. Which one?"

"It is a passage from l'Evangile de Saint Dagobert. It's not important for you to know more than that now but you'll understand when the time comes."

And there it is. His mention of l'Evangile de Saint Dagobert, the book of the Codex Merovingi which contains the Pageant of Clovis. This is his segue into soliciting my hand in the commission of regicide, just as the Covenant said it would play out. I try not to get distracted and keep the conversation on track.

"I'm looking forward to it, Sébastien. I'm also looking forward to being known to you as Monsieur Chevalier Godefroi de les Anges, Épée Main de les Tentacules d'Abraxas; titled knight in House Merovingi. I can't believe I've made it."

"A rare achievement, mon ami. Something to be very proud of. Who knows, perhaps you will even be the King-in-Waiting someday."

There go those alarm bells again. I just want to wrap this up and get the fuck out of here. I don't know who's conning who at this point.

"Now go home and clean yourself up, get some rest. Big things lie ahead in the days to come."

"Will, do Sébastien, good to see you again."

"Always good to see you, Monsieur Godefroi."

Sébastien turns to leave and I look out on the lake as the odd little white wizard saunters off, cane in hand, past the fountains and churro carts, winding up the trail and off toward the buildings in the distance.

FORTY-EIGHT

Los Angeles, CA – Fri Oct 17th, 2014

Coming home is a banal ritual anyone can relate to, no less potent for all its ubiquity. Most people arrive home to the delighted squeals of their children, a kiss from their spouse or a tail-wagging pet, re-initiating them into the realm of the safe, the sane and the familiar. And then some are like me, turning the knob on the asylum of their muted solitude and closing the door behind them on more than just what is outside.

When you spend a lot of time alone you come to appreciate the world outside your door as a phenomenon for exploration second to your own inner-space. Places and people become more like gadgets for poking around and tinkering with. "What does this button do?" You press it, it blows up everything you've built and you perhaps grow more cautious about exploring your world-gadget's other functions. People who've dared to take on dependents, they don't tinker at all. They only push the buttons they know to reward. People like me on the other hand; we're constantly blowing up everything we've built just to see what a new button will do. And so we come home to the relief of empty houses, rather than the joyous heralding and fanfare of those who've missed us. And we plop down on the couch to rest before we go exploring our inner space again, knowing that on a long enough timeline, we'll be headed out that door to push more strange buttons and hope for the best.

My spotless apartment-sight for sore eyes-hasn't been on my mind much but already I feel more made whole just seeing it again. I congratulate myself for cleaning it before I'd left. One of my travel rituals has always been cleaning before leaving. Returning to a spotless house is the closest I get to a welcome wagon, a little homecoming gift from my past self. My welcome home isn't a happy dog or family, it's a sterile environment where everything is in its place dusted, polished and uncluttered.

I pile up on the sleek leather sofa in the living room and with no effort I drift off into slumber. Wistful visions of Arlene soon give way to absurd dreams of a Sisyphean epic, in which I'm tasked with retrieving the luggage I left in Seattle. Even in sleep I'm running myself ragged with needless burden and wagging neuroses.

Sometime after sunset I awaken to find Al poking around my curios, one of my pieces of Bauscher Weiden Reichsmarine porcelain dinnerware in his crusty old mitt. I want to protest but I let it go like so many pairs of black denim in Seattle.

"Feeling restored yet, kid?" Al asks.

"Yeah, I guess I am." I respond with a stretch actually surprised to see the old spectre.

"Attaboy."

I look out the 2nd story window and seeing it's dark outside, quickly check the time on my Monolith for how long I've been asleep. 5:14pm. I'd slept only four hours but I feel adequately restored.

"Holy shit, I've gotta get going. I have a writ waiting for me at the Fountain of Renewal in Pershing Square."

I shuffle to the kitchen and pour my morning repast, evening though it is. Moving back to the couch, with Al in my shadow, I sip my whiskey and roll myself a joint. Though no one would know it to look at me, I felt hurried and I am rushing as best I know how.

"Where's your new friend?" Al asks. I have to think about that for a moment before I realize he's talking about Arlene.

"I had to drop her off in Hollywood."

Al looks on as I roll, saying nothing at first. As I light up and begin to relax he continues.

"You think you can trust her?"

"Do you think I can trust her?"

"Probably not. What matters is if you think you can." Al says. "So do you think you can?"

"Probably not."

"But you're falling for her."

As always, Al sees all and pulls no punches.

"Cautiously." I say taking a pull of Hindu Kush from the manicured joint I've just crafted.

"What if she's playing you?"

"What if she is?"

"Could you bring yourself to hurt her if it came down to life or death?"

"I don't know. If you'd asked me a week ago I'd have been delusional enough to tell you I could."

"And now?"

"Now I don't think it matters. I'm running out of 'give a shit.' I'm tired of all this."

"So you don't care if you die?"

"Not really."

"But you'd prefer not having to kill anyone?"

"Pretty much."

"I think you're gonna be alright, kid." Al says smiling as he replaces my Nazi China on its shelf. "I'm not worried about you."

"You worry about me, Al?"

"Less and less all the time, kid."

I don't know this Al. This is some other Al. Agreeable, supportive. Where's the confrontational wise-ass who's all up in my business? I take another drag from my joint, finish my whiskey and head toward my bedroom to lay out some clean clothes before I shower. While I agonize over which black denim pants to wear with which black cotton t-shirt, Al comments over my shoulder.

"You still have that bug-out bag buried somewhere?"

"Pacific View Memorial, locked in a fire safe, slathered in cosmoline and wrapped in moisture barrier bags. Same as ever."

"Good man. You know where you're headed if this all goes sideways?"

"I don't know. Brazil or Andorra, I guess. Flip a coin."

"Andorra? No way, kid. Prelacy's backyard. You're safer in a BRICs nation. The Prelacy won't fuck around there. Brazil's your pick."

"Yeah, but most of my gold is stashed in Europe."

"Kid, if this all goes bad, you better just kiss that all goodbye and make do with the gold you've stashed here in town."

"You're joking, right?" I pause, looking at Al for evidence of bullshit.

"Not at all. You try to get slick and move around through Europe they'll make quick work of you. And smuggling a bunch of gold out of

Europe? How do you see that all playing out?"

"I figured I'd convert it. Sell it at an exchange in Liechtenstein or something. Maybe on the silent market."

"Silent market? What, with all of your 'Ndragheta and Vorodskoy Mir connections?", Al laughs. "You don't know anyone like that. And if you use the exchanges you'll alert the Prelacy. Europe's out, kid."

I let it sink in that he's absolutely right. I'm not connected like that. If I have to disappear into the wind, I can write off all of the gold I've stashed in Europe. For now anyway. I'd have to make do with the amount I had here in L.A.

"OK, you've got a point. So I guess I just bug out to Brazil with what I have here."

"Seems to be your best play, right now. How much do you think you have stashed here."

"In dollar value?"

"Yeah."

"No clue."

"Ball park figure."

I shake my head feeling a little defeated when I calculate a rough estimate.

"A million, maybe."

"Well, kid. You won't be retiring in style. Enough to get yourself set up nice, but you'll probably have to find a job."

"I need to get to Europe."

"You need to put that out of your mind."

He's right. If I were a fugitive from the Prelacy, showing my face in Europe would be suicide. I take a deep breath and try to acquiesce.

"Do you have a way you can quickly move the gold you have over here?"

"I have a couple of ideas but nothing certain. If I do, it's going to cost a shit load."

"Probably half if you're using shady channels."

"Can we not talk about this?"

Al was bringing to light some painful truths. I'd begun considering my bug-out contingencies when I thought Arlene had abandoned me up in Seattle. I knew it was less than ideal but talking to Al right now was making it apparent, I was far from set for life if I had to disappear.

"I think we'd better." Al protests.

"We don't even know how this is all going to play out. For all I know I'll be the King-in-Waiting in a couple weeks, with the entire Prelacy under my command."

Al laughs at this. He thinks that's funny.

"Is that really how you see this all playing out, kid? Is that where this is all headed?"

"I don't know, Al. I don't know what's going on."

"If you're honest with yourself, you'll see you've already left in your own mind. You know you're not being groomed to be the King-in-Waiting. Your bags are packed, you're just waiting around to see if you'll get the girl."

Is that what I'm doing? I don't like the sound of this. I look at the clothes I've laid out on the bed and brush past Al toward the shower.

"Al, I've gotta get ready. You can stick around if you want but I've gotta get my shit together and head to Pershing Square." I say closing the bathroom door.

"I'll just be out here in your living room playing with your Chop-socky swords and Hitler stuff."

I ignore him and let the shower steam hit my skin and nostrils in anticipation of renewal. I disrobe about 1200 miles of road and leave it all in a pile on the herringbone tile, then slip under the flood of warm water.

A week's worth of confusion, bewilderment and bewitching begin to fall away and circle the drain as I consider Al's insights. I'd given some thought to shaking the spot but I've perhaps been proceeding under a self-deceit, entirely unawares. Whether I consciously knew it or not, I may have already decided to weigh anchor, swing helms alee and tack for calmer waters. My coping mechanisms are nothing if not robust and potent. I'd no doubt spend the rest of the night chewing on this somewhere in my mind.

I step out of the water, quickly dry off and once dressed head back toward the living room to find young 1960s Al practicing basic sword strikes with one of my katana;

"Shomenuchi, Kesagiri, Yokomenuchi, Zenpozuki. Slash, step, slash, step, slash, step, slash, step." Al says in rhythm with each motion.

Dressed in his grey sharkskin number with the black turtleneck, Al glides gracefully across the floor with each strike and hardly notices me looking on in amusement.

"Picked up Kenjutsu recently. Been practicing." Al says, slightly winded.

"Terrifying."

"The sword that saves man, kills man. Old Samurai axiom."

"I'll have to remember that one."

Al bows to the sword and replaces it in its cradle respectfully. It wasn't long ago he couldn't even set the thing back right, now he's some sort of expert. Al is full of surprises.

"So you're off to the Fountain of Renewal then, huh kid?"

"Yeah, just gotta call for a black car."

"You gotta stop throwing money around on stuff like that, you're not rich anymore."

"You've got a point, I guess. I could take the car I stole in Seattle then wipe it down and ditch it in a long term parking garage in DTLA."

"Two birds, one stone. Now you're thinkin' with your head."

"Thanks, Al."

"Here to help, kid." Al snarks. "I'm serious though, if you're going to go on the run, you need to stop acting like you can still throw money around. That's over. You gotta tighten the belt."

"I'm not even sure if I'm going on the run, Al."

"C'mon, kid. Cut the crap."

"Whatever."

"Listen, how come you don't own a car, ace?"

"I don't know. I could never drive it if I did." I respond. "I drink too much."

"You might want to change that soon."

"What? The drinking or the no car?"

"Either. Both."

"Why didn't I ever think of that?" I jab. "Good thing I've got you to figure these things out for me."

"Yeah, about that, kid." Al says. "You won't be seeing me around so much anymore."

"What're you talking about?"

"I'm telling you you're on your own from here."

"Get outta here."

"I'm serious, kid." Al persists. "You've got this, you don't need me anymore."

"What am I, Christopher Robin? Little Jackie Draper?"

"You could be Wendy Darling for all I care, kid. I'm telling you, my work is done here. You're starting to get a handle on things so you're on your own from here out."

I finish my drink and stare over at Al. Am I so awful that even my imaginary friend is abandoning me? Al has always been an annoyance but I never imagined this. I always wanted him to go away but I've never wanted him to go away for good. I really don't know what to make of it, a figment of my imagination telling me I won't be imagining him anymore. I don't trust that to be likely.

"Whatever you say, Al. I'll believe it when I see it."

"Believe it, kid. I'm gone. 5,000. Decamped. AWOL. Dust in the wind. Downsized. Made redundant. Off like a prom dress, Out like shout-"

"OK, stop, I get it." I interrupt." Like I said, I'll believe it when I see it."

Al shrugs and picks up my First Edition of El Ingenioso Hidalgo Don Quijote de la Mancha off the coffee table. I cringe as I watch him thumb through the rare collectible and hold my tongue, tempted to tell him to be careful with it.

"Alright, Al. I'd better get going."

He doesn't even look up to acknowledge, nose already buried in the book.

"I didn't know you read Spanish."

"Go on, kid. Get out of here. Go have your fun." He says without breaking his concentration, nose buried in the book he's holding upside down.

"OK, I guess you'll let yourself out then?"

"Don't worry about me."

I shrug and head for the door.

"See ya later, Al."

"Good bye. Kid."

I exit, lock the door behind me and head downstairs. After a few blocks' walk I'm back behind the wheel of the stolen Buick and about 15 minutes from the Fountain of Renewal. As I head South on San Fernando toward DTLA, I think about my strange exchange with Al and wonder what he meant by it all.

FORTY-NINE

Los Angeles, CA – Fri Oct 17th, 2014

    I find a long term parking lot to dump the Buick in a few blocks west from the Fountain of Renewal. I quickly wipe it down again and make my way on foot toward my destination. When I arrive, the concierge at the desk recognizes me and gives me a nod. I collect an envelope and the keys to the Fountain of Renewal, then head toward the elevator.

    The Fountain of Renewal is a lavishly appointed penthouse apartment and as I've been here numerous times, I don't bother to open the envelope. I instinctively head toward a bookcase along the South wall and pullout a copy of Camus' L'Etranger, disabling the latch on the hidden door. The bookcase pulls aside revealing a large walk in safe with numerous lockboxes. I take the key ring and insert the smallest key into the box typically used for writs. The lockbox beeps and opens revealing the usual balaclava, pair of latex gloves, pair of cotton gloves and a .44 revolver placed neatly atop my writ along with the photo of my target.

I look at the coded message printed on the back of the writ straight away

Jensens Melrose Theater

4315 Melrose Ave

Inside Theatre

17 OCT 2014 SAT 7:00pm

Destroy photo and writ after reading.

    The hit was scheduled for this evening. Good thing I got here when I did. I had about a half-hour to get there and by my estimate it was a 10 minute drive. Good thing I brought that Buick. I examined the writ next. The coded wording consisted of boilerplate Prelacy instructions. I was to simply walk into a darkened theater and stop the heart of the person in the picture. I had a good feeling about tonight. I had every intention of walking into this and waiting to see who else might show up to prosecute the writ when I didn't. I'd gotten a more precise view of what lay ahead from my meeting with Sébastien today. Tonight I would learn still more and tomorrow I would meet with Arlene to see what she had discussed with Monsieur Herman. From there we would finally have a clear picture of what our next move was.

I flip the photo over to look at my target and what I find makes my heart fall past my knees. I suspected from my earlier conversation with Sébastien that this writ would be different than the others. I thought it might have something to do with beginning the Pageant of Clovis; even worried a little that I'd turn over this picture and find none other than the Pope himself, or maybe a Kennedy or a Rothschild. Instead what I found was something that hit much closer to home. Pictured there on the page in front of me is Arlene.

The papers fall from my shaking hand as I begin to hyperventilate. I look at the time on my blackphone and see that it's 6:18 pm. I throw it down and go through my jacket for the burner phone I'd bought specifically for contacting Arlene. I call her immediately and it rings.

It rings and rings. And I let it ring, over and over and over until it goes to voicemail, then I call again. And again and again. I waste time obsessively recalling her number over and over with no luck connecting before I snap out of it and decide that I have to go to her. I call back one last time to leave a frantic message.

"Arlene, this is Foster. I don't know why you're not picking up but I hope you're OK. Listen to me, and listen carefully. Something is wrong. I just got my writ and the target is you. I don't know what's going on but the Prelacy knows about you and they want me to kill you. Please, call me back as soon as you get this."

I Google the address on my phone and go pale. Looking at an image of the building I can see that Jensen's Melrose Theater is inscribed in the masonry on the building's crown but the more recent marquee over the door reads "Ukrainian Culture Center." This was where Arlene had earlier agreed to meet Monsieur Herman tonight.

I have precious little time to make sense of it all. Had Sébastien figured out there was a plot against him? Did he know I was in on it? Was this a test of loyalty? Was Monsieur Herman a double agent for the Covenant or the Prelacy? Where did his loyalties lie and could he be the assassin who had been prosecuting my writs all this time? My head is spinning. Regardless of what is unfolding, I only know that I have to get ahold of Arlene and tell her about this writ. I shiver and my stomach knots into a diamond as I burst out the door in an urgent rush

I exit the building and head back toward the parking lot where I ditched the Buick. As I'm fast-walking toward the parking lot I try Arlene again, no answer so I leave another message. I decide I'll haul ass to the Ukrainian Culture Center and hope to intercept Arlene.

"Arlene, listen, I think Monsieur Herman de Boheme might be playing us all. I don't know for sure, I don't know anything but don't go to that meet with him tonight, I'm worried it's not safe. I'm on my way to the Ukrainian Culture Center right now. Do not go in to meet him, it's where my writ has been staged. Please call me if you get these messages, I lo-" I cut myself off from saying that word and start again. "I'm worried about you and I don't want anything to happen to you."

I hang up and after a few blocks of frantic fast-walking and occasional running; I'm back behind the wheel of my stolen Buick. I turn to set the writ and the revolver down when I see sitting there in the passenger seat is Arlene's burner phone. She must have forgotten it this morning when I left her in Hollywood. I curse and pound on the steering wheel near tears of frustration. I try to compose myself as I fiddle with the wires beneath the steering column. After a moment or two the old bucket roars to life and I hit the gas. I brake briefly to pay the automated attendant with the reloadable debit card I'd last night, then turn into the street and stand on the gas.

As I speed to meet Arlene I think about the mad world we'd become a part of. Where we'd so willingly, joyfully made ourselves pawns in some ridiculous game of elites, of grey eminences and the thrones they maneuvered behind. Drawn in by intrigue, secret power and undue access to wealth and resources, we'd rendered ourselves unambiguous pieces on a chessboard. And there wasn't a righteous side to play for, save survival. The Prelacy, the Covenant of Arius, the BRICS nations, the Zionists, the Black Nobility, the Masons, Radical Islam, Google, Ethno-Nationalists, Collectivists, Globalists, the Vatican; our nations or someone else's, they were all just tyrannical royal houses in deed. There was no race, religion, philosophy, secret society or sovereign nation that was going to usher in any new age of peace and prosperity. Nothing was under control; everything was out of control and in perpetual conflict. There was no new world being born, just the same old one soon to be rebranded under new management. None of these factions stood to deliver us a better life or better world. The only ones who could do that were us. The only happiness comes from within. The only enemies to defeat were within. The only freedoms are the ones you'd dare avail yourself of, whatever the price. The only things worth fighting for are the people you love, in arm's length of you. From the third world to the first world, regardless of wealth or station, the happiest people I'd seen were the ones obliviously living their lives focused on what was in arm's length of them. There were no riches to be had. No destination called success. The only currency a man has, that can't be debased or devalued is his own toil and his own free time spent in anonymity. Everything else is just debt. There were no benevolent kings, no angry gods. No battle raging between good and evil. Only the tyranny of men and the liberation of the soul that comes from doing what you love with those you love, in the obscurity of anonymity. There is only that and a peace which comes from doing no harm. Everything else is a cruel manipulation, a sacrifice of freedom for the illusion of righteousness. Everything else is bullshit.

All this time we spend trying to be things we're not. Some of it is vanity but how much of it is just a paranoid survival strategy? All of us; forever trying to find a safe place, passing ourselves off as members of a group of people who are doing the same thing as we are. Tribes, gangs, churches, temples, ethnicities, even nations: these facilitators of culture that provide the comforts of affinity, identity and familiarity, they give us some predictability in our lives but none of them seem to provide the aegis or justice they all promise. More likely they imperil us. They crush our individuality and sap our wonder at this world we're fortunate to explore for a short time. I'd spent my life being everything I wasn't before I realized all I had to do was dare to be me, because that might actually be worth the cost. If I could just start over, I'd keep my head down and blend in somewhere and just be. No legacy, no fables. No horse, no wife, no mustache, a Freemason of the soul with no lodge. For the first time in my life I know who I am and I know what I want. I am a quiet, peaceful nobody who is done with it all, who wants to disappear into obscurity with this woman whom I may love. And I want to live. I just want to live. Both of us.

After stitching and weaving my way north through surface traffic on Temple for 10 minutes I wheel onto Beverly and right up Vermont 'til I get to Melrose. As soon as I hit Melrose, I maneuver into the first parking space I find and begin walking west toward the address on my writ. In a short walk I'm standing across the street from the Ukrainian Culture Center, a two story tall stone masonry theater. I check my blackphone to see that the time is 6:46 pm. I try to remember if Arlene said what time she was supposed to meet Monsieur Herman here but I don't recall. I fade into the doorway shadows of the darkened storefront I'm standing in, trying to decide if I should cross the street and enter the theater or wait and watch the door.

I start to wonder if this writ were part of the Pageant of Clovis. What if Monsieur Herman had no idea that I hadn't prosecuted any of my writs? What if as far as he knew I was an uncomplicated killer who simply fulfilled the orders on any writ handed me? If he knew of this writ, wouldn't he simply be expecting me to take Arlene's life, business as usual? Or had I jumped to conclusions about him altogether? What if he really meant to do no more than meet with Arlene tonight and had no idea about this writ in my hand? If that were true it would be a mistake to break in on them guns-a-blazing. All I know is that I must go inside that building at some point and get to the bottom of what's happening. I'm confused, frustrated, scared and my only certainty is that what happens over the next hour will shape the fates of Arlene and me.

I check my blackphone again and see that it's 6:53 pm, just minutes from the time indicated on my writ. I've seen no sign of Arlene or Monsieur Herman and I'm sweating this whole nerve wracking puzzle to the point of getting the shakes. I steel myself for the inevitable trip inside that building across the street and conduct my nervous ritual pat down for essentials. AF-1 in my waist, the Prelacy revolver in my coat pocket, gloves, blackphone, balaclava. I'm whole and accounted for as I cross the street, palms sweating, pulse racing.

I draw the AF-1 from my waist band and cross the street toward the theater. I reach to pull open the door to the Ukrainian Culture Center then pull the balaclava down over my face, quietly slipping in unseen. I creep in the shadows toward the theater hall, just beyond the dim, empty lobby looking around but unable to see anything at first. As my eyes adjust to the darkness I can begin to make out that the lifeless theater is cluttered with numerous empty cocktail tables and chairs leading to a stage at the back. I'm on stilts about walking around this place in the total shadow, unsure of what I'm doing or what to expect. Worries for Arlene are repeatedly chased from my mind to make room for details about my surroundings and pertinent alerts. One step, two steps, three and I stop, stock still when I feel the muzzle of a pistol poke my ribs commanding and hard.

"Drop your weapon and put those on." says the familiar voice behind me. On the ground next to me lands a pair of handcuffs.

I drop my AF-1 without any delusions of turning and firing. I just reach for the handcuffs and put them on. In a few seconds I'm being led toward stage right. The man then takes another pair of cuffs out, attaches them to the ones binding me and uses them to fasten me to a water pipe on the wall along the floor of the theatre. As I'm sitting, my captor strikes me hard with the butt of his gun and I feel dizzy enough to go out but I hang on. Everything goes fuzzy and he yanks off my balaclava as I struggle to stay awake and alert. My captor then flips on the lights and my eyes strain to focus. As things normalize I'm able to make out Monsieur Herman de Boheme standing over me.

"Monsieur Godefroi, I hadn't expected to see you until we began the Pageant of Clovis after your promotion next week."

"Where's Arlene? What did you do with her?" I ask.

"I thought you would be her."

"You weren't expecting me? So you had nothing to do with the writ?"

"Are you here on a writ, Monsieur Godefroi?"

I say nothing, concerned I've said too much. Monsieur Herman leans down, looming in my face to look in my eyes.

"I asked you a question Monsieur." He menaces.

I try to turn my head as he rams the butt of his automag into my face again hard enough to make my ears ring.

"So Monsieur Sébastien must be conscious of a plot against the King-in-Waiting and himself." Herman thinks aloud. "The Pageant of Clovis has begun a little early it would seem."

I offer no response and Herman kicks me in the gut, knocking the wind out of me as a sharp pain shoots through my kidneys.

"What did you tell Monsieur Sébastien?"

"Nothing."

"You didn't tell him about me or Madame Aureline?"

"No! I've been on board the whole time. At least until you chained me to a water pipe and hit me in the face."

"You really are a sucker, aren't you?" Monsieur Herman mocks. "I'll bet you've even fallen for that low rent Mata Hari, Madame Aureline."

I look away, embarrassed.

"You did, didn't you?" Herman laughs as he paces. "You poor sucker. You're worse than Canan."

"I'm not a sucker! Wait, what? Who?"

"Oh, you don't know about Canan and Arlene? Of course you don't, because she loves him and not you, idiot. She's just manipulating you so you would unquestioningly play your role in the Covenant's gambit to install me as the King-in-Waiting. Once the Pageant of Clovis had concluded, you would have joined her and Monsieur's Chipleric XI and Sébastien in the grave and I would have sat at the top of House Merogvingi, with fealty only to Lord Canan of the Covenant. Alas, Monsieur Sébastien has caught on and there's been an apparent change in plans, but no matter. Your story comes to an end here tonight and I will have to sort out Arlene, Sébastien and Chilperic through more direct means."

I look up at Monsieur Herman, trying not to think about Arlene, instead more set on the remote hope that I can convince Herman I am still useful to him. I doubt I can impress upon him that he shouldn't kill me. As I study his face for any indication of sympathy or yield, I look at his knit brow and steely eyes and hear a crack. I watch his gaze go soft as a trickle of blood streams down his left cheek. Monsieur Herman collapses at my feet and behind him stands Madame Aurilene holding a 9mm. She walks toward me and standing over Herman, puts two more bullets into his back.

"Glad to see me?" Arlene says.

I'm thinking yes and no. She looks at my situation and begins digging through Herman's clothing for a key to the cuffs. After a moment she's locates it and frees me. I pick myself up off the floor, slow and unsteady then walk to one of the tables to sit and get my bearings.

"I think he was bringing you here to kill you. The Prelacy sent me here to do the same so I was calling you like crazy to warn you. I saw you'd left your burner phone in the Buick. How did you know what was going on?" I ask scrambling to retrieve my AF-1 and patting myself for the Prelacy revolver still in my pocket.

"I just didn't want to carry a bunch of phones around so I took the sim card. I called the voicemail a little while ago and got your messages."

"What? Well, how long were you going to wait? What if he'd just put one in my head straight away?"

"I've been here with my gun on him since before you walked in. I put him down the second I could see he'd decided to kill you. He was reaching so I put him down, but I needed to hear as much as I could of what he had to say."

I let that sink in. If not for Arlene I'd be dead right now. In fact, I wouldn't have even seen it coming. I was focused on Herman's face, preoccupied with convincing him to spare me. I didn't even see him go inside his jacket for a weapon.

"So what do we do?" I ask.

"I don't know about you but I'm a little bit upset with the Covenant just now."

I say nothing. She was being used and manipulated by Canan as much as she'd been using and manipulating me. I know exactly how she feels, yet no less resentful of her.

"Everything's gone off the rails. The Prelacy and the Covenant are both going to be coming after us. We need to disappear." I say finally.

"Easy for you to say. I'm half-a-world away from my bug-out cache. I've got nothing here."

"So we'll make do without all that." I say.

"Look, you should just worry about yourself. I'm sorry I got you into all of this. I understand if you-"

"Nonsense. I'm not leaving you." I interrupt. "You may not feel the same way about me as I feel about you but you saved my life and at the very least I owe you for that. We're going to go dig up my bug-out stash, then we're going to find a way to get you papers and we're going to disappear some place safe, far from anywhere the Prelacy operates. What happens after that is up to you."

"You've got your bug-out cache nearby?"

"Buried about an hour from here."

"Passports, birth certificates, emergency cash and all that?"

"I'm sorted. I've got clean papers, about a million in gold kilo bars and $20 thousand in cash hidden, we just have to go dig it up."

"It's a start. Do you have an off-the-grid safe house we can access?"

"One thing at a time. Let's just dig up my cache and then we'll worry about getting you papers and planning our next move.

Arlene looks at me blankly. That may be gratitude, then again that may be pity, I can't tell but the absence of warmth between us is palpable. I can't help but feel like I'm still being played for a fool. I feel like I've run out of trust for all of humanity at this point but some misguided sense of loyalty seems to urge me forward. She just saved my life. I'm not letting that go. I'm going to do everything I can to return the favor.

FIFTY

Corona del Mar, CA – Fri Oct 17th, 2014

We used to bury our dead to give them a head start toward paradise in the underworld. That and because they stink after a while. We'd leave them with their treasures, wish them well and miss them for a time then ultimately not think about them much at all. But not Jeff Hanneman. I thought about him pretty much every time I went to the Copper Bucket to get drunk. I'd been listening to his music since the stoner neighbor next door introduced me to Slayer in 6th grade. Before that I thought music was pretty neat, I guess. I was 12 and I really liked the Bangles, thought the Point Break soundtrack had some pretty good jams on it, figured Mötley Crüe was the ultimate in rebel shit you had to sneak around to listen to so mom wouldn't freak out. Beyond that I didn't give it much thought. Then one day Cuate showed me Slayer. Cuate means twin in Spanish and I have no idea how he got that nickname. Cuate was already a mountain of a man barely in his late teens. Long black haired and rotary gun tattooed, he'd spend every afternoon taking bong rips in his car port, usually among his friends, an assortment of cholos and chicano stoners who comprised the neighborhood regulars on our block. I was walking home from school as I remember it and Cuate was there in his driveway as usual, sitting on a milk crate waiting for his friends to trickle in.

"Hey!" He called from across his yard. "You smoke weed, little dude?"

I never had but I was curious.

"Yeah."

Cuate laughed and held up his bong in invitation so I sheepishly walked up to where he sat. He packed weed into the bowl of the PVC bong in his hand, made a grand production of taking a big hit and holding it in, then handed the bong off to me. I put my mouth over the opening at the top and fumbled to light the bowl, inhaling for all my worth.

"Nah, you gotta put your thumb over the carb or it's not gonna work, eh." He said leaning over to show me the little hole at the back of what I took to be the most ridiculous science equipment a man could use to take drugs. I covered the carb, lit the weed and inhaled as smoke filled the chamber.

"Now take your thumb off the carb."

I did as he said and immediately my face was full of smoke which I choked out into a giant cloud. Cuate grabbed the bong from me and scolded.

"Man, you didn't even inhale. You're just wasting my weed."

I felt embarrassed, found out for a phony. In spite of doing it wrong I still got high to the bejeezus. Suddenly everything was hilarious and I felt great, just great.

"What kinda music you listen to, homes?" Cuate asked suspiciously and I knew how I answered was every bit as important as knowing how to smoke pot right.

"Like, heavy metal and stuff like that." I answered as Cuate used his science pipe to do more pot.

"Like what, man?" He exhaled.

"I don't know, like Mötley Crüe, Van Halen."

"Pussy shit. Check this out."

Cuate leaned over to press play on his enormous swap meet boom box and what came through those speakers changed everything. As the chilling sounds that preceded the opening bars of Slayer's Hell Awaits wafted out of those speakers like so much weed smoke I heard music do things I had no idea it could. Suddenly, music wasn't some carefree backdrop to showering for school or cleaning your bedroom. It was this bold defiance of doing any of those things at all. It was lumbering build-ups to soaring guitars and angry peels of vocal contempt I couldn't decipher verbally and didn't have to. A new world opened up to me that afternoon and it changed my outlook on everything. In the days that followed, my taste in comics shifted from the X-Men to Judge Dredd. My toys all seemed stupid, but drawing pictures of skulls was time well spent. I stopped cutting my hair and I traded in colorful Ocean Pacific board shorts and t-shirts for black denim and band tees. In one afternoon at 12 years of age, my neighbor Cuate had introduced me to two things that to this day still bring me great relief. Weed and Slayer, and I've yet to outgrow them like I have everything else since then.

"This is it. You still got that spade?"

Arlene hands me the tiny camping spade we stopped to pick up at a Target along the way to our present location, Pacific View Memorial Park

Cemetery in Corona Del Mar. A mild California Autumn chill rolling through the rows of marble and stone, I begin to dig with just the moonlight to illuminate my shady business. I dig and dig and I imagine that what I am doing might actually be seen as a flattering intrigue by the man who was laid to rest here just last year.

"Godefroi, who's Jeff Hanneman?"

It irks me to hear that name. Not Jeff Hanneman, I love Jeff Hanneman, rest his soul. It irks me to hear my Nom de Prelature. It irks me to hear Arlene keep her distance from me by using that name but what hurts most is the name itself. As of this night, I'm done with the Prelacy and I never want to hear that name again.

"Arlene, you don't have to call me by my real name if that's too endearing for you but do not call me by that name again. I am not that person and I'm not sure that I ever was."

"I'm sorry, Foster. I understand."

"Are you ever going to tell me your real name or have we not gone through enough together for me to know it?"

"Arlene is my name, Foster. I styled myself Madame Aureline de le Pyrénées as a member of the Prelacy because I fear I lack your creative flare. Well, I considered Madame Dorothée de le Vent du Sud but I thought better of it and went with Madame Aureline."

"Dorothy?"

"Long story."

"So, you got to pick your Nom de Prelature?"

"Of course, didn't you?"

"More and more it looks like everything I did or didn't do in the Prelacy was someone else's idea." I pause to say, deflated. "Sébastien picked that name for me. He's never called me anything else." A moment of rest and I resume digging, the briny sea air gently breathing through the cemetery tree tops as I work.

"Do you think Sébastien chose you for sponsoring into the order because you weren't a killer?"

I stop digging again to face Arlene.

"Yeah, I'm starting to come around on that. With a total body count of one, you've officially killed more people than the assassin who stands before you."

"Yeah, I might have been telling a little lie when I told you I hadn't killed anyone before."

"What?" I'm only half-surprised. "So Cloak duties involve wet work in addition to the espionage?"

"Not necessarily but I had a life before the Prelacy, you know and I also had my duties with the Covenant so we'll just leave it at that."

"Holy shit, there are just layers and layers to you."

"Don't judge me, I just saved your life by killing someone."

"I wasn't judging, Arlene." I plead. "But instead of talking about it I should just be thanking you."

"You're not a killer, Foster. Why is that such a bad thing to you?"

"I've spent years trying to figure it out."

"You realize that's normal, right? Not being a killer."

"A mile in my moccasins and you might not be so sure."

"You've seen a lot of it, haven't you?"

"I don't know what a lot is but I'd guess I've known more killers than most. Seems like I can't get away from them. They're always around me, like I attract them or I seek them out."

"Whatever your experience, being a killer is not normal."

"In a world full of lying, manipulative assholes? I'm not so sure that's a good normal."

"Is that what drew you to the Path of the Sword? You thought you would be doing some good in the world, thinning some of its surplus assholes?"

"I don't know what I thought." I say and return to digging. "Whatever the case they saw this sucker coming from a mile away."

"Well, that makes two of us."

I pause again.

"It's pretty easy to see why Monsieurs Herman and Sébastien would have chosen me for the Pageant of Clovis, but why do you think he chose you to flip me?"

"Did you or didn't you fall for me?"

"I guess you're right." I say, acknowledging the hard truth of my being a sucker every step of the way. "So it was all just tradecraft? You really haven't developed any feelings for me?"

"I haven't decided how I feel about you, Foster, but I like you. I do. I wasn't going to let you die, was I?"

Best I can hope for, still feels like a letdown. I wipe my brow and return to digging.

"What do you think Monsieur Herman planned to do at his meeting with you at that theater?" I ask.

"I think he intended to kill me and take the writ I'm holding with Monsieur Sébastien's name on it. I think he would have killed Monsieur Sébastien at your initiation rite."

"And then the King-in-Waiting after that."

"And he'd lay the blame on you. He would have taken the writ before the Tentacles of Abraxas and the Palace Keys to indict you as an inspired usurper who killed Sébastien and Chilperic. He would have fulfilled the ritual Pageant of Clovis and ascended himself to the highest position in House Merovingi."

"I don't understand why the writ would be so damning though if it was issued by the Order's Judicious Scrivener."

Arlene takes the writ from her coat and hands it to me.

"Notice anything?" she asks.

I scan the writ and on close inspection see that it's not a Prelacy writ, though it looks mostly indistinguishable from one at a glance.

"This writ says it was issued by the Ordo Fraternum Umbrae, not the Prelacy. It looks almost exactly like a Prelacy writ. What is this?"

"It is a writ issued by a secret society of Prelacy Cloaks within the Vatican. Ordo Fraternum Umbrae, the Fraternal Order of Shadows."

"What does it mean?" I ask, handing it back to Arlene and returning to my task of digging.

"I'm not entirely sure.I'm a Cloak and I'd never even heard of the Order of Shadows before joining the Covenant. Canan gave me the writ and only told me I was to use it for leveraging your support in our operation. "

"Well it worked."

"Do you see why they used me to bring you in for this role in the Pageant of Clovis?"

"Of course. They never intended for me to become the King-in-Waiting, they were grooming Monsieur Herman for that role."

I'm getting a little tired of feeling like such a sucker. This whole escapade just keeps going from bad to worse at every turn. I keep digging and try not to dwell on it.

"You would have made the perfect patsy and this document would have served as evidence to have you executed as a regicidal agent acting in concert with rogue elements within the Prelacy and the Vatican." Arlene says as I continue to dig.

"So I guess that's it then?"

"It's what I've pieced together anyway, but I could be way off."

"Well it makes sense to me. I'm just glad I won't have to go through that whole Pageant of Clovis bullshit now."

"Who knows, maybe Canan and Monsieur Herman were wrong about you. Maybe you would've had some wild streak in you to slay your mentor and the King-in-Waiting and bring Monsieur Herman before the Tentacles and the Keys to be held in account."

"Yeah, I could've been King."

We both laugh, knowing full well I would have fucked that all up.

"What do you think would've happened if you hadn't come to my rescue in that theater?" I ask

"Can't be sure." She shrugs. "I figure Herman would have killed me next and embarked on some impossible mission to assassinate Sébastien and Chilperic outside of ceremony. My guess is Monsieur Herman was a dead man from the minute he learned of your writ to kill me. He knew it, I think but he was so stuck on the idea of completing the Pageant of Clovis that he thought he could salvage some kind of contingency outside of ceremony."

"So do you think Sébastien was grooming me for the same fate as Herman and Canan, independent of their scheme?" I ask.

"Maybe not. Maybe he's innocent in all of this but we still have to assume the Prelacy and the Covenant are both gunning for us. Sébastien sent you to kill me. Even if he's not coming after you, he's obviously not going to be giving me a pass."

"Yeah, you're right. And Canan, what do you think becomes of him now?"

"Who can say? I hope the Prelacy finds him and sends him to hell before the Covenant can find us."

"I'd drink to that."

"You know, you're not right about much but I guess you were finally right about one thing."

"Oh, yeah? What's that?"

"These people are all fucking crazy."

"You had to know that, though, no?" I probe.

"Honestly, Foster, I thought I'd found my home in the Covenant of Arius. They were like a family that made sense to me. Canan and Monsieur Herman's betrayal has shattered my entire world."

"You loved him, didn't you?"

Arlene doesn't respond and our conversation reaches a lull as I finally begin to unearth the corner of my buried cache. I dig a little more frantically, partly because the finish line is in sight, partly to distract from imagining her with Canan.

A little more excavating and most of my cache is exposed. I dig my fingers under a corner and manage to dislodge it after some wiggling. Proud of myself I grin and show the moisture-barrier wrapped fire safe to Arlene like some sort of grave-robber's trophy.

"Eureka! We're done here. C'mon, there's a row of motor lodges up the 405. We'll hunker down for the night and figure out what our next play is." I say.

"Fine. Are you ever going to tell me who Jeff Hanneman is?"

"Just some Saint."

FIFTY-ONE

Costa Mesa, CA – Fri Oct 17th, 2014

The Roadside Motor Lodge is as American as having your corpse cremated because it's cheaper than a funeral. Free HBO, free Wi-Fi, free pool. All that freedom. The S.S. Anywhere But Here, all sail, no anchor. I had seriously considered living in roadside motels when I first joined the Prelacy. It's a quirk but I happen to love them, probably because of how often I was in them as a kid. In motor lodges every neighbor's a stranger, just like in regular modern life, but you get new ones every couple days at the motor lodge. Nobody sticks around long enough to become your nemesis. There's usually an adjacent bar where I can wind people up and if I ever cause too much trouble, it's nothing to just pick up and disappear down the road. I tried it out for a while, moving from motel to motel up and down the 5 every few days, the 405, the 1, the 101. It felt right at first, but honestly, it got a little old after a month. I just wound up retreating back to L.A. and renting my apartment in Glassell Park. I still love the roadside dumps none the less and being in one right now I have a certain giddiness that defies the grim import of our current circumstance.

The appointments in our room are late-20th Century Carpetbagger and a chewy layer of aerosol disinfectant masks the previous tenants' challenge of the statewide smoking ban. The bedspreads make no attempt to pass themselves off as comforters and the television has a picture tube. There is a microwave to melt the phone in should that sort of drunken notion present itself as it has in the past, but I doubt it will this time, considerate of present company and mood.

I start my motel check-in ritual of going through the drawers and under the mattresses to see what's been left behind by the previous tenants.

Sometimes there's $100, sometimes there's a bag of weed. A dirty syringe is usually good for a discount if you complain at the desk, not that we need it. I just like getting freebies. After a moment of rummaging on my hands and knees to Arlene's bewilderment I declare my scan for treasure fruitless and set to checking the towels. As I head toward the bathroom I'm distracted by Arlene who looks as if she's about to lie down.

"Don't lay on those! They're nasty!" I shout, stopping her before she throws herself down on top of the notoriously unclean bed covers.

"They never wash those things." I explain as I gingerly remove the offensive article and guide Arlene back to be seated. "If you ran that thing under a UV light it would probably look like a Jackson Pollack painting.

"It already does." Arlene jokes, referring to the ugly print pattern on the bedspread. "Oh, you mean...ugh, that's disgusting."

"Yeah."

"This place is horrible, why are we here?" Arlene asks.

"If the Prelacy and the Covenant are looking for us, it won't be here."

"Good point. You paid in cash?"

"I did, signed in under my new alias and everything." I say handing her the passport we just dug out of the ground in Orange County.

"Martin Van Horn? I don't like it. You don't look like a Martin." Arlene says handing my passport back.

"Whatever, Dorothy," I tease, "It's what the cobbler had. It was either this or Manpreet Jindahl."

Arlene smirks and though I know her spirit is heavy I appreciate her trying to accommodate the juvenile way I cope with trouble. I want to make jokes, and in fact I'm dying to go to the bar at the end of the parking lot to rub some people the wrong way. Though our lives could easily be just days from ending and the overall mood is grave, old habits die hard, old rituals persist. For me, that means a full-blown case of the fuck-its. For a rational adult like Arlene, it means solemnity.

"So, I don't mean to prod but it bears discussion, you do have someone who can set me up with new papers?"

"Well, I did but here's the thing, we're not exactly on speaking terms."

"Monsieur Godef-" impatient, she stops and takes a calming breath, "Foster."

"Or Martin."

"Manpreet, or whoever you are," she smiles and relaxes. "if you know of someone, please, swallow your pride and reach out to them. We are in an all-or-nothing, no, I am in an all-or-nothing situation and-"

290

"I know you're not feeling very trusting right now but you're going to have to trust me. Nothing has changed for me. We were in this together a week ago and as far as I'm concerned we're in it together now."

"Thank you, Foster but can you just make the arrangements, please."

"I'll call."

My only chance of making this work is Tucan. One of his people is the cobbler who set me up with the set of papers I'm using now and my hope is that he can set up Arlene and maybe liquidate some of these gold kilo bars. The thing is, I haven't seen him in more than a year and the last time I did see him I was getting my ass kicked by Chivo and his friend out in front of the Copper Bucket. Regardless, the only shot you have is the shot you'd better take.

I go to the other side of the room for a little privacy. I begin scrolling the contacts in my blackphone for Tucan's number when I get a deathly chill and react off instinct.

"Give me your blackphones" I tell Arlene walking toward her all robotic determination.

I begin tossing her purse without thought when she produces it from her person without any trepidation.

"Oh, my god. What have we done?" she says, full aware.

"We're fucked. We're so fucked." I say taking our phones and tossing them in the microwave. Phones, microwaves. Not at all the antics I'd had in mind earlier.

I cook them 'til I see sparks then hot-hand them onto the floor and stomp them to shards. After that I take what's left outside and hurl them into the free pool.

Arlene, already hip to the game is shuttling our belongings back to our stolen Buick and in minutes we're back on the 405, northbound now asking ourselves how we'd entirely overlooked smashing the shit out of our Prelacy leashes. With those phones on us they would have been able to locate us by GPS and kill us in our sleep.

"You know, it would have been a better tactic to throw the phones into the back of a moving truck or gone to that bar and stowed them in a stranger's purse." Arlene says as we drive.

"I didn't think, I just reacted."

"No, you did good, it just might have sent anyone tracking us on a wild goose chase, bought us a little more time."

"That's why you're the spy and I'm the, shit I don't know what I am. You're the spy and I'm the idiot." I say.

"If they come for us there they'll know your new identity from the desk records at the motel."

"Yeah, I thought about that, too. Looks like we both need new papers now. Meh, I'm not a Martin anyway." I say and we laugh a little, shitting bricks a little. "So what now?"

"Don't worry. This is right in my wheelhouse." Arlene reassures me.

"I hope so, because all of my contacts were in that phone. I don't know how we're going to get papers without them."

"We'll figure this out; you just have to trust me."

Trust is not something I have in abundance right now but what option do I have?

FIFTY-TWO

Palm Springs, CA – Fri Oct 17th, 2014

Somewhere around midnight Arlene and I are breaking into Elvis Presley's house in Palm Springs. Her logic was if the Prelacy tracked us to that roach motel off the 405 south of L.A., they'd figure on us continuing south toward the border. So we went East. Being that we still hoped to arrange an encounter with Tucan, it was a good idea to stay L.A. adjacent. Arlene posited that staying in hotels was out of the question so we picked up a Real Estate guide where she looked into model homes that were going to auction soon. Her logic was that they would likely be empty and comfortably staged. So here we are, breaking into Elvis Presley's house in the desert. Arlene's shrewd thinking gives me a gust of confidence. Like maybe we could really find our way out of this mess.

"I guess there's no sense trying to call the Copper Bucket for Tucan."

"Nah, it's a dive bar. They don't answer the phone." I say. "Fuck! Why didn't I at least get Tucan's number before I destroyed the phones?"

"You were panicked and that's understandable." Arlene soothed. "For all you know, if we'd delayed to get that number it might've cost us our lives."

I take her point as a kind placation but can't stop beating myself up over destroying those phones before we got any useful data off of them.

"So what's our move? Do you think it's safe to try walking into the Copper Bucket?" I ask Arlene.

"I don't know, you have to make that decision but it presents a risk." She says.

"Sébastien knows I was a regular there," I advise, "but as far as he knows I'm 86ed so it seems unlikely they'd look for us there."

"Like I said, it's not without risk but it's our only life line right now."

She's right. I don't like the idea of walking into the Copper Bucket. Prelacy drama aside, I don't like the idea of showing my face there. Last time I was there I got beat up and went to jail. Add to that the fact that there are people who want us dead and they might be looking for us there. I really don't want to walk into the Copper Bucket.

As we consider our plans, I start looting through the kitchen cabinets for liquor with no luck. Arlene used some of her magical Cloak tradecraft to disable the alarms but we've agreed to leave the lights off as much as possible, so I'm fumbling around in the dark for Whiskey in a bar I've located. The place appears to be bone dry and only staged for auction, no liquor.

"You're probably not going to like this but I need a drink. Can we brainstorm this at a bar over a couple of whiskeys?"

"I don't mind. Do you know your way around here?"

"A little bit. I figure we'd just drive up Palm Canyon and find someplace that looks alright."

"Lead the way."

We skulk back to that trusty little Buick that has served us so well and make our way down Vista Chino toward Palm Canyon.

"I think we should find a new car tomorrow. We've had this one for too long. I'm worried it may have been reported stolen by now. Last thing we need is the mundane world coming after us, too."

"Better safe than sorry." Arlene agrees.

"If you stay ready you don't have to get ready." I volley playfully.

"The early bird catches the worm."

"It's always calmest before the storm."

"It always rains after you wash your car."

"Nothing good ever happens after 2am."

"All's well that ends well."

We laugh a little at the non sequitur exchange of clichés and I realize that I have that approval seeker's urge to keep her laughing. In my mind, if I can keep her laughing, this will all work out somehow. We crawl down Palm Canyon in good spirits and I spot parking near a row of desert nightlife possibilities.

"So what do you say? We'll drive out to the Palm Springs airport tomorrow before we head to the Copper Bucket, ditch this hot rod and find something a little less hot to get around in?"

"Sounds fine to me."

We park and head inside of a place called the Desert Rose which is crowded with a diverse group of wasteland trailer trash, high class pensioners and fugitive film vets who somehow escaped from Hollywood, assuming they weren't exiled. Arlene finds us a place to sit and I head to the bar for our drinks. A middle-aged bottle blonde with great big fake boobs shimmers over in her sequined cocktail dress and takes my order. While I wait for our drinks I inventory and profile to pass the time.

There's a perma-tan 40 something dude in white slacks and a parrot print Hawaiian shirt who is a little too young to be living a Jimmy Buffett song so sincerely. He can't unsmile and he looks like he'd be fun to drink with, awful to call boss. His golf partner is sitting closer to him than their wives are and I can't imagine what sort of thing makes these guys stop laughing. I doubt cancer can slow these guys down. Bailing their good for nothing kids out of jail, cutting $60k checks to Passages in Malibu? No problem. Bumped tee time or runny eggs? Fuck you, God. Why me?

Next to me at the bar is their spectral opposite. Red-head biker type, early 40s. The weekend warrior, rides a kitted out bagger kind of biker, not the three patches on the back, rides a raced out drug-mule kind. Sun-dried a painful shade of clay-red from firing a nail gun outside every day, missing a tooth, age a little accelerated by drinking at dawn and all through the workday. Potbellied but sinewy strong working man arms covered in faded ink that has spread to near indistinct over time. He uses them to slap his old lady's backside playfully when she's around. Right now though, she's making nice with an old bluehair who probably leases a new model white Continental every spring.

A little further down the bar is what appears to be one of L.A.'s numerous professional wives. A glamorous looking middle aged career divorcee with her nose buried in Instagram. Probably a bunch of duckfaced selfies taken with reluctant Hollywood D-listers. I recognize this woman from somewhere.

The bartender returns with my order and I try to place the face of the career divorcee down the bar. As she looks up and makes eye contact it clicks and I gather our drinks to retreat in momentary terror. I try to shuffle away nonchalant but it's no use, Jazzy has spotted me and she is following me back to our seats shaking her head, smiling flourescent white.

"Get ready for shit to get weird." I warn Arlene.

"When is it ever not weird with you?"

"Touché." I say straightening in my seat and looking Jazzy in as she approaches all smiles. Why on earth would she be glad to see me? I want to run, I am not prepared for this and I'm too preoccupied with escaping my own despair to be confronted with hers.

"Remy Foster," the traveling alias I used on Prelacy missions, "you stand up and give me a hug, right now!" I'm at a loss so I do as I'm told, trying not count the number of names I've known in this lifetime. I think I'm at five now and still shopping for one more.

"Jazzy, I'm shocked-"

"You? Foster, we have been talking about you and thanking you every day for the last year. We owe you everything for what you did."

"I'm sorry?" I'm baffled.

"I guess you wouldn't have any idea. Sit down, I have so much to tell you."

I take my seat again, Jazzy joining us. All I can do is cast a glancing smirk at Arlene who is just winding it all out in good humor.

"Jazzy, this is Arlene. Arlene, Jazzy."

"You've got yourself a good man here, Arlene." She says reaching over to take Arlene's hand. "A saint. Don't you ever let him get away. "

Thanks to the dim bar lighting no one sees me blush.

"Let me call Jürgen, he'll want to see you. Then I'll tell you everything."

"Jürgen?" I nearly shout, incredulous.

"He's going to die when I tell him I'm sitting here with you. He will absolutely cardiac."

As the kids say, my mind is full of fuck.

FIFTY-THREE

Palm Springs, CA – Fri Oct 17th, 2014

Orwell warned us against surrendering our avail of precise verbal expression with his haunting vision of Newspeak. Good, plusgood, doubleplusgood. In his 1984, these were the only acceptable expressions of an agreeable experience. We'd failed to heed these warnings somewhere in the last 15 years. It seemed we had become incapable of articulating a precise positive feeling without the words amazing, awesome or best ever. These hyperbolic clearing houses for all exclaim of agreeable circumstance were the entire palette of expression for most. Today, the same word that you would use to describe seeing the Grand Canyon for the first time was perfectly apt for describing your ten-thousandth Big Mac. Suffice it to say that what Jazzy had just told me in the Desert Rose a few minutes ago was quintupleplusgood. It was fucking amazing. Awesome, even. Running into her turned out to be the best thing ever.

Right after Jazzy called Jürgen, she proceeded to tell me a story that simply changed everything and gave both Arlene and I a renewed confidence and hope. Jazzy explained to us that after throwing himself into the Elbe, Jürgen was unable to drown himself. The idea of Jürgen drowning himself had always sat strange in the back of my mind but I simply believed the news reports rather than my own common sense. Suicide by drowning is nigh impossible. Humans have an irresistible instinct to return to the surface. Unless they've bound themselves with weights they seldom succeed in drowning themselves. It just doesn't happen.

Jazzy spun for us the story of Jürgen's failed suicide and his watching the news of his own death on television hours later with morbid fascination. How he drifted around Hamburg like a ghost, homeless and detached for a week, and then two weeks, three weeks, a month. Finally he found the courage, or perhaps hopelessness to call Jazzy. He called her and when she answered it was like the skies themselves had opened up and dropped him a vine back to life in the real world, back to sanity.

His returned millions had found their way to Jazzy via a living will he held with Jazzy as executrix. Being that he was officially a missing person and not a suicide, Jazzy was able to assume what would have been his estate, via power of attorney. Jazzy had been going through her own hell, thinking the man she loved had drowned himself in the Elbe. She was beside herself with grief when she finally got the call from Jürgen.

In short order, Jazzy had used some of her more seedy Hollywood contacts to arrange papers for the love of her life and she brought him back to California to start anew. Together, this make-shift Jean Valjean and herself had started over in Palm Springs and prospered.

Suffice it to say, this is an amazing turn for Arlene and I. Awesome. Best thing ever. I'm thrilled to see things have worked out for this pair and to say I'm excited to see Jürgen again would be an understatement. The thing that my mind won't leave alone though, is that Jazzy was able to get Jürgen new papers. This is nothing short of providence and if that's hyperbole then pardon my Newspeak.

"Jürgen should be here by now, I'm mad at him!" Jazzy pouts playfully.

"I'm sure he's just shouting down a shitty cab driver or punching out some asshole who thinks the bike lane is four wide."

"You two. I can't wait to see you back together." Jazzy coos.

"This is all so mind blowing."

"He told me everything, Foster. I don't know what you did to make that asshole return his money but we owe you big time. You saved Jürgen's life, you kept us together."

"I don't know about all that. All I did was tell that scumbag to return Jürgen's money and he did it. The rest was all you guys."

"You saved us and you can never disappear on us again. Everything happens for a reason. Running into you here is no coincidence"

We'll see if she feels the same way once I tell her we're on the run from a pair or murderous cabals. That we need new papers and we have a half-million in gold to liquidate. She's a godsend and yet I'm reluctant to broach the subject of Arlene and I's situation too soon.

Arlene looks on feigning demure but I know that mind of hers is watching everything with meticulous analysis. I'm going to require more whiskey for managing the pressure of walking this fine line between being a competent operator and maintaining a cordial rapport with Jazzy who is for all intents and purposes, an old friend with only the most facile kindness in her heart. I'm keen to put off the heavy topic of our situation for as long as possible. For another couple drinks at least.

"There he is!" Jürgen joyously exclaims leaning into view over Jazzy's shoulder.

I bolt up to greet him knocking the table forward. No one notices and the vibe is warm all around, save for Arlene who efforts a commensurate glow to match ours but is mostly weathering an understandable confusion.

"I know you." Jürgen says to Arlene from across the table, his smile going from effortless to stilted.

Our table-wide levity is briefly given pause as Arlene awkwardly responds to Jürgen.

"No, I don't think we've met."

Jürgen seems puzzled and apprehensive for a blink before brushing it all aside.

"My mistake, I'm sorry, are you a friend of Foster's?"

Arlene doesn't hesitate; she reaches across the table to take Jürgen's hand and lies.

"I'm Foster's girlfriend, Arlene."

"Well done, friend." Jürgen remarks to me as I'm suspiciously unpacking what's just occurred, all the while doing my best to remain casual seeming.

I cast a sideways glance at Arlene but I can't linger. She knows him from Cloak work. There's no question. I don't know who I want to interrogate more, her or Jürgen. I try to remove my teeth from this catch and stay focused on what's pertinent; broaching the subject of clean papers and moving this gold.

"I'm guessing you're as surprised as I am." Jürgen tells.

"You have no idea." I say side-eying Arlene as sly as I can manage.

"I don't know why you did it but you did. You said you would fix it and you did. I only wish you'd said something before I threw myself into the river like an idiot."

"I meant to say something when I got back from the bathroom but you were already gone."

"Why didn't you say something straight away, you fool?" Jürgen teased.

"Well, I was probably still processing that whole part where you gunned down a man in the middle of Hamburg." I joked.

"Shhh! Foster! What're you thinking." Jürgen laughs.

"Jürgen, please. This is Palm Springs. Everyone here has killed someone." I say, eliciting a hearty laugh from Jürgen, a nervous laugh from Jazzy and a smirk from Arlene.

"It's Linus now. Linus Hummel. I had to leave Jürgen in Hamburg, as I'm sure Jazzy told you." He explains, his Austrian accent, ever present in spite of everything.

"Linus?" I say teasingly incredulous.

"It was either that or Harish Singh." Linus laughs.

"So, it's an interesting coincidence that we're joking about you getting clean papers." I say.

"Oh? Did you make someone angry in your little Prelacy?"

"So you remember that part?"

"No one forgets anything from a day like that."

"I suppose not."

"You know, I've spent a lot of time trying to find out whatever I could about your Prelacy."

"Lotsa luck."

"Aside from a few mentions here and there in the most tinfoil-hat websites, the entire thing is an enigma."

"Yeah, it's a mystery to me and I was in it."

"So you've really gone rogue then?"

"Not to put too fine a point on it but the lady and I are running for our lives. We need a full sheep dip; clean papers, passports, background and history, everything and I have about two dozen gold kilo bars I need to liquidate, too."

Jürgen looks gravely at Jazzy and she echoes his sober resolve.

"Say no more." Jürgen says.

"Foster. Anything we can do to help you, we will do. We are here for you." Jazzy reassures.

"Come, mein alter, join me on the patio while I have a smoke." Jürgen urges me.

I follow Jürgen through the low lit hum and bustle of the Desert Rose and on out into the brisk badlands starlight of Autumn in Palm Springs. We take a pair of seats remote from the weekend revelers and I sit watching as my stylish friend lights up a Nat Sherman that looks like a crayon. After a moment of quiet bearing he speaks.

"Someday, I hope to host your regaling us with tales of your adventures in this Prelacy." He says exhaling his smoke to the side.

I weather a brief pang of concern over what sort of webs Arlene is spinning to Jazzy and then shove it down.

"I hope to live so long."

"Things are this serious?"

I give Jürgen a look that sufficiently communicates the severity of our circumstances and he interrupts before I can attempt to put thoughts into words.

"No matter. If they come looking for you here, they'll find nothing but trouble." Jürgen says patting a pistol bulge under the left armpit of his light sport coat. I like that he's taken his new life as worth protecting. The man I met in Hamburg was a little more flippant and unsteady than the one before me today.

"They won't find us." I assure him. I'd rather not spook him with details of our panicked flight from the coast. "As soon as we've secured new papers and gotten liquid we'll be in the clear."

"That should be no problem. I will see to it that Jazzy makes the call first thing tomorrow." Jürgen tells me. "By this time tomorrow night you should be a different man, well on his way to a new life."

"Thank you, Jürgen. I don't know how I'll ever repay you."

"It is I who am repaying you, bruder." He says and takes a sip from his glass, then and sets it back down. "I only hope that when the dust has settled you will stay in contact with us. I don't think you know it but you have friends for life in Jazzy and I."

Feeling a gust of relief, I raise my rocks glass and Jürgen clinks his in warm accord. A silence swells and the mood briefly grays.

"Are you being totally honest, Foster?" Jürgen asks. "It's awfully odd running into you here and all. You really didn't know I was alive?"

"This is dumb luck. We fled here in a panic and broke into Elvis Presley's house to hide out."

Jürgen just smirks and shakes his head.

"Long story. We were just trying to lay low, stay off the grid. Arlene and I came to the bar here to take the edge off of a very stressful situation and that's when we ran into Jazzy."

"Yeah, Melinda, the bartender is her BFF so we wind up spending a lot of time here. I probably would've gotten around to coming in even if Jazzy hadn't called."

I fight off another pang of worried suspicion about the coincidence, about Arlene. Leaving our motel in a rush was my idea but coming east was her idea. No, I'm just paranoid and that's fine but I picked this bar out of a half-dozen on this block. What're the odds? I fortify my resolve to remain trusting by finishing my drink. It's worth a try anyway.

"Look, since we're checking the lines and all, I gotta ask you," I say leaning in, "back there you said you thought you recognized Arlene?"

"It's nothing, alter. I thought I knew her from Kaufmannsbank but it's nothing."

"Knew her how?"

"It was just a mistake, Foster. It's nothing." Jürgen implores.

"You looked like you'd seen a ghost for a second there."

"In deed, I thought I had. I was relieved to see it wasn't." He pauses to drink. "No, your Arlene looks very different."

"Who did you think she was?"

"Foster, it's embarrassing, just leave it."

This sets off alarms that I'm getting worse at suppressing. I'm going to need another drink for any hope in so doing. Our convivial exchange cools over the silence, which Jürgen finally chases off.

"After all you've done for me, you could introduce me to the devil himself and if you told me he was with you, I'd treat him the same as family."

"Fair enough." I tell him. "Whaddya say we head back in for some drinks?"

"Lead the way." Jürgen says extinguishing his butt and rising from his seat.

We slip back into the warm shadows of the Desert Rose snaking past PGA wash-outs, boob jobs older than either of us and dirty denimed desert meth moguls.

"Go on ahead, I'll get this round." Jürgen commands and I shrug my compliance.

"Jameson neat, right?" I say.

I take my seat beside Arlene to find she and Jazzy are getting along fine, which I suspect is just Arlene's tradecraft at work. There is little about Jazzy I can imagine Arlene finding sufferable for long. Then I remember that I'm usually wrong about everything. My analysis, strategy and tactics are for shit but at least they seldom get in the way of my amazing luck. So I've got that going for me.

"Foster, honey, all your problems are solved. I called my guy and he's going to make the arrangements tomorrow."

"You already called? Isn't it a little late?"

"He doesn't mind, we're good like that, baby. " Jazzy coos. "We just have to meet him at his office tomorrow morning, 11 o'clock."

Jürgen arrives with an armload of drinks and a smile so genuine and disarming it spreads to the rest of the table. Even Arlene isn't immune.

"You doing OK?" I half-whisper.

"I am. I think I'm actually starting to relax a little." She leans in to tell me.

And I'm actually starting to relax enough to put aside bending her ear about how she knows Jürgen, and what other things she isn't telling me. Every time I feel like I can trust her, a suspicion flares up and begs putting out. The warmth of amity and whiskey will hold that off for now, but I have questions. Fears that what I don't know might be my undoing, that I'm still being led down the garden path like I've been for too long now.

"When we finish these drinks, let's continue this little reunion at our place down the road." Jazzy announces. "You two OK with that?"

I look at Arlene who shrugs in abstinence.

"I don't know if that's a good idea. We should probably just stay where we've set up camp."

"Elvis's rumpus room?" Jürgen snorts. "Nonsense, you stay in our guest house. You'll be safer there anyhow."

I glance over to check it with Arlene again and she defers. If she had any objection she'd signal. I can't think of a reason why we shouldn't.

"OK, we'll have to go back for our things at the other place but-." I start.

"We don't have luggage, babe. Everything's still in the Buick." Arlene interrupts.

Babe. It's just for show but melts me nonetheless, triggering suspicion and distrust. This wild ride should feel like it's near over but doesn't. I won't to be able to relax until we're on a jet to Brazil.

"Well, I guess we'll finish our drinks and follow you to your place then."

FIFTY-FOUR

Palm Springs, CA – Sat Oct 18ᵗʰ, 2014

Tucked at the back of Jürgen and Jazzy's sprawling desert ranch style property sits a cozy little Mother-in-Law house where Arlene and I slept after extending our night cap with Jürgen and Jazzy well past 3am. I want a shower really bad and I would have taken one last night had we not gotten so sidetracked with listening to Jürgen's stories about being a ghost in Hamburg and Jazzy making us smile with tales of her road to being a health supplement mogul. As due fair, this morning, my head is giving me the rare sign of hangover. I stopped getting hangovers a decade into my problem drinking, but this morning I am feeling the previous night's indulgences come calling back for the vig on a loaned moment of levity. I roll out of bed with every intention of washing the residual crapulence away in the shower but Arlene stops me saying there's no time.

"It's already 10. Jazzy's waiting for us inside."

I grumble and pull myself together, pat myself down for essentials. Apartment keys I'll never use again: check, Prelacy revolver I feel weird about having still: check, AF-1: check. Wallet: check. Blackphone: nope, that's in pieces three hours west. I also feel weird without my Monolith. Off balance without it in my jacket pocket, incomplete. The psychology of my pockets is all fucked up right now. I pull it together and follow Arlene out of the guest house and up the path toward the front of the property where Jazzy is waiting inside her black on black Escalade. We climb in the back to find the passenger seat empty.

"Arlene, honey, you've gotta ride up front with me, I'm no chauffeur." Jazzy pokes.

"Where's Jürgen?"

"Still asleep. After last night I'll be surprised if he's even awake by the time we get back."

At this moment I envy Jürgen, still sleeping while my head pounds, an hour on the freeway ahead of me. Arlene, already in the front seat can't resist noticing.

"You jealous?" she kids.

"So jealous." I groan.

The pair of new friends in front laugh at my wadded-up and grumpy disposition as we pull away from the property and head toward the 10.

"So where are we headed? Who is this guy?" I pry. Unsurprisingly, we spent most of last night talking about everything but the business at hand and I was suddenly feeling a touch of nerves over the whole thing.

"We're going to meet my old friend, Bam Bam Sandoval out in Mo Valley. He has a little postage and shipping place there where he does everything."

"And he was able to set Jürgen up with passport, birth certificate, all that stuff?"

"Oh, yeah he did. Social security, even school records. Bam Bam's legit."

I was expecting a Russian or Armenian name. "Sandoval? Sounds Mexican. Sureno? Mafia guy?"

"Bam Bam? No" Jazzy laughs, "He's a wood from OC, ex-con."

"Can't be too reformed if he's a paper cobbler."

"Yeah, well, you know how it is. He's a good guy, you'll like him."

"He's the only ball game in town. I don't have to like him, I'm just trying to get an idea of what to expect is all."

"Sweety, I've known Bam Bam for 20 years. I wouldn't set it this up if I didn't trust you, let alone him, so relax."

Outside our noise proof canopy the desert air whispers by at a comfortable 70 degrees, warm for autumn even in the California desert. We ride in climate controlled leather comfort down the diamond lane west on the 10 toward the 60 which runs through Moreno Valley, the inland suburb where Bam Bam's store is located. Jazzy flips through her iPhone and puts Social Distortion's eponymous third album on the stereo. Arlene appears to be quietly making good sport of finding something to like about the music while I suffer in silence with the back seat to myself. Jazzy sings along with every song, words by heart and when Drug Train, the last song on the album is finally beginning we're circling the block for a place to park down the street from our destination. As Jazzy expertly maneuvers us into dock I consider the synchronicity of listening to Social D on the way to meet some convict from the OC, and give it no more thought as we exit the vehicle.

We walk toward the strip mall store front of Bam Bam's packing and shipping place. The signage and décor is modern hipster nautical. Anchors, compass points, banners all Sailor Jerry traditional. The name of the place is Ship Mates. I pat myself down, then blush when Arlene catches me in my nervous ritual. She smiles a little and my pensive tension magically washes away. Ahead of us Jazzy is talking and walking like Aaron Sorkin has penned whatever words are flowing from her after-market mouth.

"Catch up, lovebirds. We're late and Bam Bam can be kind of a stickler."

Arlene sobers and I straighten up in follow-that-car reflex. She smiles again at my mannerisms and I wonder if we aren't having a moment. I push it down and refocus.

We follow Jazzy in through the front door which rings a polite alert to new business but the young California archetype behind the counter is already looking us in with a smile. Blonde pomaded side part, tan, 6 feet high, partially paid off Western Dental whites gleaming, beach kiosk neck tattoo of a rose and some shit in cholo script that probably says something heavy like "feelings" or "live life." On the hi-fi is, wait for it, Social Distortion.

"Alright y'all! What's crackin?" the clerk bubbles.

This is a place to mail packages and that's how they greet you coming in the door. Scurvy Joe knock off tattooed demi-Val saying, "What's crackin'?" I was raised in Southern California so I don't belabor myself with trying to understand why we demand a phony cultural experience for something as banal as shipping a package, I just know that we do, and this place gets that. Every new era 1%er in a fitted 5950 who has some weed in a vaseline slathered vacuum bag to FedEx and on down to every Rockabilly Chicana with Disney ink and an Etsy order to fill probably can't wait to come here and send their product off to people in those luckless fly-over states where the post office only has sad depression era murals and brass finish PO boxes. In 50 more years maybe some genius will build out a packing a shipping place in brown brutalist décor with knock offs of those depression era murals overlooking mosaic tile floors because that will be some sort of lost artifact of cool. Or maybe we'll all just be extinct by then.

"Hi, honey, where's Bam Bam? Can you tell him Jazzy is out front with his 11am people?"

"No worries." Young cool says as he presses a button on the desk phone. "Ryan, someone's here to see you. Jazzy?"

"Right on, send 'em back." The voice on the intercom says.
"He's just right through that door." The clerk says pointing us through a door to his right.

We follow Jazzy into a sort of multipurpose shop area that has a printing set up, a wall of PO Boxes, copy machines and packaging stations where plastic wrap sits on rolls at least twice the size of a grown man's arm. Sitting at a shop desk studying his computer screen is a tawny muscular, sable headed man in a teal Izod and blue 501s. This presentation coupled with his black frame glasses and side part deftly toe the line between weed connoisseur hipster and dependable square who pays his taxes. The SS Bolts peeking out from under his left sleeve hint at another set of inclinations entirely.

"Jazzy! So good to see you, homegirl!" He exclaims, bounding out of his chair and yard-walking over, tall-chinned and rigid postured.

"Bambi! How's my favorite Pexican?" Jazzy coos as they embrace.

"Can't complain. You said you had some friends you wanted me to meet?" Bam Bam says with a smile that somehow dovetails genuinely with his curt segue into business.

"I did, Bam, this is my friend Foster and his girl, Arlene. They're in some shit but they've got money and they're good people."

Bam Bam gives Arlene a respectful nod and keeps his distance then closes on me, stretching his right hand forward. As I take his hand to shake it I see a set of dots in three-score on his hand over a cross, on the ditch of his arm is a cholo script tattoo that says "Death Squad". His hands are soft like mine, like he's never done a hard day's work in his life, but his knuckles tell a different story. His are misshapen boulders from excessive fighting where mine are wholly unremarkable. His handshake is firm, a shade beyond polite but miles from menacing.

"Foster is it?" Bam asks.

"Yeah."

"Cool, cool. So, you're from out here?"

"Nah, Boyle Heights." I respond.

"Boyle Heights? Damn, fool. You're kinda gava for Boyle Heights."

"Yeah, well you're kinda tan for Aryan Brotherhood." I volley, with a playful smile nodding toward a Black Sun tattoo peeking out between his tan muscle belly and armpit.

To my own relief and by extension the entire room's, Bam Bam responds with a good humored laugh and claps me on the back.

"You already know what it is." He says, laughing. "You're alright Foster, my kind of people."

This is the sort of winding people up in a positive way I would like to make a better habit of. In the past, being charming has caused me far more problems than being an asshole; problems that take longer to develop and yield greater consequence than just making a bad first impression on purpose. I'd have to grow up and learn to wield these anti-social skills better at some point.

"So what is it, you need passports, birth certs, the whole shot?"

"Full sheep dip. Passports, birth certificates for sure, Social Security, light history and background if you can do it."

"And what else?"

"Gold. We have about a million in gold to liquidate."

"OK, this jives with everything Jazzy told me, I just want to make sure we're all on the same page."

"I get it."

"You know the gold is going to take a hard hit getting liquid, right?"

"I'm prepared for that."

"As long as you know." Bam Bam says. "OK, check it out, I'm going to put some stuff together, make my calls and in a little while I'll come get you guys to pick out which names work for you, then we'll take your photos and all that good stuff. Sound cool?"

"Works for me."

"Few hours from now you guys will be leaving here with your assets in a stack of reloadable debit cards and completely new identities."

"Sounds fucking awesome." I say, looking over at a very content Jazzy and an uncharacteristically sheepish Arlene. Doubleplusgood. Best ever. Literally.

"You're welcome to hang out in here, or out in the shop if you want or I can just call Jazzy if you guys wanna go walk around."

"Thanks Bam Bam." I say. "Ladies, you wanna go out front and pop a couple hundred dollars' worth of bubble wrap while we listen to Mike Ness sing about cool jail stuff?"

FIFTY-FIVE

Palm Springs, CA – Sat Oct 18ᵗʰ, 2014

There's only so much fun to be had burning the clock at a packing and shipping store, so Jazzy, Arlene and I make our peace with the pop-punk soundtrack, the miles of bubble wrap and hipster décor of Ship Mates and head down the block in search of better distraction. A few doors down and across the street we find a clean little restaurant and cantina decked out in terra cotta, teal and peach, the walls painted with pictures of old Mexico; cacti, dunes and missions, images of men and women in traditional garb. The restaurant is empty and I lead us to seats at the bar in front of the flat screen. Jazzy orders herself and Arlene some sort of blended drinks and I my usual Jameson neat.

On the screen I can see the press is crowded around Dr. Anglethorpe at the steps of our nation's highest judicial authority. Dr. Anglethorpe's face look's positively ebullient, his demeanor marking a note of satisfaction.

"Excuse me, would you mind turning it up just a little?" I ask our bartender as he brings us our drinks. The young Mexican man fishes a TV remote out from behind the bar and adjusts the volume.

"Oh, I love this guy!" Jazzy exclaims looking up at Dr. Anglethorpe on the screen.

"Shhh" I reflex at Jazzy, eager to hear what he's saying. Jazzy just giggles and apologizes where I was anticipating sass back.

I sit, riveted watching the mad doctor with the familiar face I can never place, wondering what has him so delighted. He usually affects such a deadpan attitude, which honestly lends itself to any comic value I glean from him and his absurd legal battle. Today though, he is bright and smiling.

"For over a year now I have been fighting for the right to legally put a cosmic, even spiritual distance between myself and the inescapable human debris that litters every glowing screen, every billboard and conversation." The doctor says. "I've simply asked that the state mercifully grant me the legal right to escape these specters of mediocrity and standard bearers of decline who cloud the horizon in every direction; who occupy every waking moment with their bellicose vanity. Thankfully, after my long plight the state has heard my case and seen fit to permit me agency in determining my own course.

For over a year now I have recited for you the names of trespassers on your consciousness. I have listed for you a seemingly endless census of personalities whom you would surely know, because if I were to list the names of the true people I sincerely wish to escape, you would look to me not with rapt attention but as deer in headlights. If I tell you I wish to leave this world because I shall not share it with the likes of Perez Hilton then it registers with you. This appeals to you because this is important to you. If I tell you that I should like to leave this world because I shall not share it with the likes of the Familiar Prelacy of Infernal Arbitrators or the Reformed Covenant of Arius, then I've lost you. You have no idea who that is. You are all standing in the courtyard of hell, eyeing the jester when you should be eyeing the Kings of Hell themselves, like an angry mob might eye a cornered scofflaw.

These names I've listed over the course of this trial served only to concentrate your attention on this day which I've prayed would eventually come; the day I would impel you all to forget every name on that list I've recited, for they are insignificant, wholly irrelevant. Instead, I tell you, learn the names of the Kings of Hell and make a choice; dethrone them with regicide or follow my lead. Forget the identities of your beloved and reviled court jesters and instead learn the identities of the Kings of Hell and refuse to share this earth with them. Instead dedicate yourselves to the perpetual commission of regicide upon these tyrants until you've made for them a new tradition of death so unfailing that no man shall ever again so much as set his eyes toward the dais let alone the throne atop it. Either do this or follow my lead. From the sea, and to the sea and from the sea again, death to House Merovingi, long live House Merovingi."

No sooner does Dr. Agnlethorpe finish his spiel than does he produce from his jacket a shiny chrome revolver, placing it in his mouth and painting the crowd around him with his own blood. As Dr. Anglethorpe delivers his final words, I have at last put a name to his face, solving the riddle of why he has been so familiar to me. The man whom I had spent the last year laughing at with his list of the shamed, he was none other than Monsieur Chilperic XI, le Roi in Attente, the King-in-Waiting of House Merovingi. He was the blue cloaked man who'd overseen my initiation rite in Belgium, whom I'd just once had such brief congress with under Prelacy ceremony. My jaw is down by my knees and I'm trying to process what I've just seen. What effect does this have on the Pageant of Clovis? It's a lot to parse but as best I can tell, I'm guessing Monsieur Sébastien is now in line for promotion and much worse. Arlene and

I share a look of puzzled amazement at what we've just witnessed and relief that soon this would all be part of our past.

"Well, that got pretty intense, didn't it?" Jazzy says, sipping her margarita as the scene on screen descends into a chaos of screaming and ruckus. "Bartender, can you be a dear and change the channel?"

"What would you rather watch?" The bartender asks, picking up the remote.

"Anything." The three of us reply in chorus.

FIFTY-SIX

Palm Springs, CA – Sat Oct 18th, 2014

A couple hours of drinking at the Cantina down the street and Bam Bam has changed my gold kilo bars and taken his fee from the cash I'd dug up. In its stead is a stack of reloadable debit cards. In all, Arlene and I have just under $400k in debit and just under $10k in cash. It isn't retiring rich but it's more than enough to start a new life where ever we go, a better start than most people have when they turn it all around anyway. We'll manage.

Shortly after Bam Bam has taken our headshots for passports and IDs, we're being presented with choices for our new names. Arlene, having gone through a very short list of offered names selects the stunning and beautiful name Anabasis Colonomos which, as far as I'm concerned, she will wear well. It looks to fit her.

I pour over the list of names Bam Bam has and after some agonizing settle on one.

"So whaddya think? What's it going to be, Foster?" Bam Bam asks.

"I'm still thinking."

"You know it doesn't matter, right?" Bam Bam advises and he's not wrong.

"I know, I'm a little superstitious, I guess."

Bam Bam just sighs and goes back to studying his computer screen.

After a few more minutes of deliberation I settle on one.

"I think I like this one." I say pointing at the name on the page for Bam Bam to see. He laughs.

"Leroy Delmer?" Bam Bam laughs, "Are you sure? You don't look like an Leroy"

"It's either that or Rajesh Prasad." I joke, referring to another name on the list.

"Hey, I get what my guy gives me. You want Leroy Delmer? You got Leroy Delmer."

"That's all me. I'm Leroy Delmer from here on out."

And that was that. At 2:45pm Arlene and I were about to walk out of a place called
Ship Mates in Moreno Valley completely new people and on our way to a new, anonymous existence anywhere but here. It's exhilarating. Before we leave I go to shake Bam Bam's hand and he pulls me in for a hug and tells me to contact him if I need anything else. It's just business for him but I feel encouraged and well peopled, nonetheless.

In an hour, Arlene, Jazzy and I are pulling back into the driveway at Jazzy and Jürgen's desert ranch style.

"Listen, I know you guys are in a hurry to go but take some time to unwind. You're safe here, so relax, book your flights and then shower up and let me and Jürgen find some clean clothes for you."

"If you have anything I can wear that would be so sweet of you, Jazzy." Arlene perks up.

"Oh, honey, don't you worry, I'm not letting you leave before you've had a chance to reset. I'm gonna hook you up, you just get all clean and comfy"

"Thank you." Arlene says.

"Why do I love you two so much?" Jazzy pouts, opening the door of her Escalade. "I'm going to miss you both, this isn't fair!"

"I wish we could stay, I do, so much" Arlene says.

I follow the fast and unlikely new BFFS into the beautiful single story ranch style where we find Jürgen sorting out a huge pile of grilled meat he's excited about presenting.

"Perfect timing, love." He says greeting his Jazzy with a kiss on the cheek.

"I hope you like horse. We eat a lot of horse around here." Jürgen says

I say nothing and he lets us off the hook with a laugh.

"Relax, it's not horse, alter. I'm Austrian, not French."

My look of relief says everything and Jürgen laughs. Arlene's lips flattens in contempt for the swipe at her heritage, though she efforts a phony nasal laugh.

"It's kangaroo." Jürgen says, the smiling fiend, turning his steaks.

"Kangaroo? I snort. "G'day, mate, you stereotypical fuckin' Austrian." I say in my best Aussie accent, "You old bogan."

Even Arlene laughs at this.

"Hey, what's wrong with horse?" she asks, warming to the humor now.

"Très français" I poke as Arlene smiles and recoils with a restrained squeal like some happy child evading a tickle threat.

"OK, listen, you kids go freshen up and we'll get you something to change in to for your flight." Jazzy says settling the room.

"Our flight!" Arlene exclaims.

She's right, we haven't even booked one yet.

I'm on it. I take Arlene's ID packet and sit at their dining table to browse our options on my shitty burner mobile. In ten minutes I've booked passage to Sao Paulo for both of us and I can't remember ever feeling better. OK, maybe I can remember feeling better, but never more relieved. First class seats for Anabasis Colonomos and Leroy Delmer, Americans. To think that this time yesterday we weren't sure we'd live through any of this. Now, we're these entirely different people with really weird names. It's every bit as surreal as anything we've been through so far but entirely new and different. Rebirths are no joke and everyone should have at least two per lifetime.

"We fly out 9:55pm." I try not to shout.

"Alright, kids, you've got your flights. Go get yourselves cleaned up and we'll look after getting dinner ready. I'll be outback in a few with some clean clothes for you both" Jazzy says, shuttling us off with blended drinks in big glasses.

"I love you, Jazzy." Arlene disarms, planting a kiss on her cheek as we're shoed out the back door, Jürgen in the background grinning as he loads service platters with kangaroo, or horse or something. It's meat, I know that.

I walk, unhurried, blissfully arm in arm with Arlene down the little cobblestone path to the back of the property toward the Mother-in-Law we're housed in. The dusk so slow, I want daylight to topple like our obstacles have. I won't feel like we've crossed the finish line until we're in the air on that flight but I sure do feel like I can see it from here. It's hard to resist celebrating right now but we're not out of the woods yet and there are still things to discuss.

"So are we going to talk about what we saw at the bar earlier?" I ask.

"Dr. Anglethorpe's suicide?"

"You mean the King-in-Waiting's suicide?"

"It really was him, wasn't it?"

"All this time and I could never pin it. I only saw the King-in-Waiting briefly at my initiation rite so it never really clicked but Dr. Anglethorpe always looked so familiar to me. It used to eat at me trying to figure out who he was, where I'd seen him."

"It never even occurred to me but when he delivered the final line of his speech something went off inside my head."

"From the sea, and to the sea and from the sea again, death to Rome, long live House Merovingi.' It's a verse from the Codex Merovingi, the Prophecies, l'Évangile de St. Éloi."

"He said that and it just hit me like a bolt of lightning, then when he turned to draw his pistol I saw his ponytail and it all came together for me."

"So what does it mean?" I ask, pausing to face Arlene halfway to the door of our accommodations.

"I have no idea but I know this much: Chilperic XI ascended from my lodge, le Chemin de la Manteau."

"He was a Cloak?"

"He was, and if you know anything about tradecraft you know that creating spectacles is all part of the job."

"So you think this was some kind of propaganda?"

"I don't know, I can't even tell what's real and what's not at this point."

"Me either and you know what? I don't even care. We're so fucking out of here." I say hooking my arm through Arlene's again as we resume unburdened our calm, rustic stroll toward the Mother-in-Law at the back of the property.

"So, what do we do when we get to Brazil?" I ask Arlene as she opens the door to the guest house.

"We'll have to talk about that but we should enjoy ourselves right now."

She's the tactical smarts of our operation so I won't argue but I hate being redirected and my mind is racing. I try to take her deflection gracefully.

"I don't mean over all, I mean, like when we get off the plane." I press. "We won't know anyone in Sao Paulo and we don't even know what we're doing, really."

"We'll just check into a hotel and unwind for a couple days, then we'll conduct some analysis." Arlene says. "Foster, we're fine. We're all but there so let's not pursue this pathology of panic. Let's not allow crisis to become our new normal. It's not healthy to celebrate winning a marathon with more running."

Somehow, I think the two of us have been operating in a normal state of crisis since long before we ever met. This is the woman I have come to love and I have somehow entangled myself with her enough to hope someday she might feel the same about me. She winds me up like I do everyone else and I can't get enough of it. Even if she never comes to love me, I intend to savor whatever time I have with her.

"I can't argue with that." I say.

"Do you mind if I take the first shower?" she asks.

"Go for it, I'm just going to sit here and read up on Brazil."

"Fala Português?"

"No. I guess I should work on that."

"That makes two of us." Arlene confides.

"I guess we'll have to speak cash for a little while."

"Money talks ."

"We'll figure it out."

"Yes, we will."

We share a moment of quiet accord before Arlene breaks eye contact and disappears behind the bathroom door.

After Arlene has been in the shower for ten minutes or so, Jazzy comes in with an assortment of attractive clothes that are surprisingly conservative, given her own ostentatious style. On the bed she lays a simple black three button suit with white button down, white boxers and socks for me and a very attractive choice of three dresses for Arlene in Navy blue, midnight blue and Black.

"Give us a shout if you need anything else, sweety." Jazzy says blowing me a kiss as she vanishes through the front door of the guest house.

Immediately I set to convincing myself that I can wear the white button down and white under garments for a day. I've worn all black every day for nearly a decade and I don't like big shake-ups to my routine. Sitting here looking at the offering on the bed I consider it likely I'll opt for wearing the same black denim suit I have on, only changing out the undergarments.

To assuage my anxiety over the disruption of routine I sit and scan the internet on my burner for information about Brazil. Part of me feels as though the more I read, the less I like it. Another part of me looks on it with excitement and wonder. This place, so patently South American yet with its flourishes of Europe that the U.S. itself couldn't boast. Somehow, the newborn Leroy and Anabasis would leave this place and create their next world there. An entirely different world and entirely different lives. I let that sink in. I'd never been to South America and the more I sat with the idea, the more I swelled to yet another rebirth. As best I could tell, for Arlene, this would be her second or third, for me, my fourth at least. Rebirth is for the living. Death is for the dying. We had chosen to live.

As I sit studying rural areas adjacent to Sao Paulo and looking into realtors Arlene is drying off and urging me to get showered. I put my burner mobile down and adjoin with her rational urgency. I disrobe black denim and head toward the steam coming from the shower room she's just vacated.

I go through the motions, the warm water on my head and hair as I imagine the two of us safely in flight away from this all. My mind wanders carelessly to vanities of making right with Arlene, of growing old together, anonymous and simple, happy. I shiver with something that is part disgust, part embarrassment, a teetering coins edge. I should just be thankful that I'm alive and be satisfied with that. Tilting my head back past comfort and letting the warm water pound the center of my forehead, I try to stay in the world of the real. Like everything else in this desert, nothing seems real, no matter how hard you try to make it.

After it feels like I've been showering for a normal amount of time I decide it's okay to stop. I exit and find a towel hanging on the rack. A few diligent swipes across the ol' corpus and a rustle of the hair on my head and I'm feeling like I've sufficiently completed the ritual. I force myself into the white undergarments left by Jazzy and reload myself into the same old black denim, leaving Jürgen's nice suit on the bed where it was left for me.

"You're not going to wear the suit Jazzy laid out for you?"

"It doesn't matter, Arlene, th-"

"Put on the fucking suit, Foster." Arlene orders, smiling and incredulous.

I can't win this one. I retreat to the bedroom and put on the rest of the clothes Jazzy left for me. In my head is a running tally of black denim I've lost since I've met Arlene. Part of me wants to punch the air, part of me wants to cry. A tiny part of me laughs at the absurdity of it all and that's the part I lend voice to with a rattle of laughter.

"What's so funny, Foster?" Arlene asks as she walks in to see me laughing in the mirror. "You look good."

I want to kiss her but I know better. I miss how things were just a few days ago in Seattle.

"You know what time it is?" I ask.

"We should go. I don't want to assume Jazzy or Jürgen will drive us and we still have the issue of that stolen Buick."

"Fuck that thing. Let's take a Black Car to the airport. We're clear, Arlene."

"You know what?"

"What?"

"That's such sloppy tradecraft and I don't even care."

"We're short-timin'"

"Damn right, we are."

"Take this job and shove it!"

"Ugh!" she grunts in carefree agreement.

We gather ourselves, our drinks, lock arms and head out the door of the guest house toward Jazzy and Jürgen's looking sharp. As we walk, I resist the nervous urge to pat myself down, knowing full well Arlene is on my arm and I simply will not break the mood with my compulsion.

A few dozen paces and we are at the back door that opens onto Jürgen and Jazzy's spacious and effulgent Spanish Colonial kitchen. The homey beige and terracotta tones host the aroma of grilled meats which waft out when Arlene opens the door. I playfully cut past her and make for the pitcher of Sangria Jazzy left sitting on the counter as Arlene heads toward the living room.

"Who needs a refill?" I chirp heading toward the living room a few paces behind Arlene, pitcher in hand.

Sat there on the couch are Jazzy and Jürgen on either side of Canan, Arlene's superior in the Cult of Arius and at one point her lover. When we'd last seen him nearly a week ago at the Covenant safe house in West Seattle, he appeared as the owl in our sunlight. Now, here he is once again to ruin everything.

Standing across from me is Arlene, shaking, her glass on the ground and drink spilled across the carpet. I look back at the couch and drop the pitcher I'm holding along with my own drink when I focus on Jazzy and Jürgen who have both been shot through the head.

"How did you find us?" I ask the bald headed Canan who is holding an automatic pistol.

"Come, sit down." He orders, waving the gun toward a chair to my right.

"How did you find us?" I ask again.

"Arius always chips his pets, Monsieur Godefroi." He answers with a grin and I lose it.

I can't take it anymore, I'm so sick of these people and this dilemma and I've never liked this asshole in the first place. In the blink of an eye I've gone full red-out, closed the short distance between myself and the couch and I'm too busy ramming my forearm into his throat to care about the gunshot he's fired. Let alone notice anything else going on. My focus is soon broken when I hear a voice from behind me.

"Foster, can you move to the side just a bit, love?"

I look over my shoulder to see Arlene leveling a pistol at us. Never one to resist the request of someone holding a pistol I oblige the beautiful Franco-Persian woman and slide to Canan's left.

"You don't want to do this, Arlene." Canan chokes and huffs , a bit worn from what were some pretty decent throat shots, if I do say so myself. "You know the bigger picture is what matters here."

"The Covenant was going to kill me. You meant to kill both of us so you could install Monsieur Herman as the King-in-Waiting."

"It wasn't personal."

"I know how irrational this sounds to a big picture guy like yourself but killing me is just something I tend to take personal."

"I would never hurt you if I could help it. You have to see beyond the subjective."

"You're bargaining with house money." Arlene laughs.

"How am I holding house money? You're the one with the gun."

"You're bargaining with house money because it would be so much more satisfying for you to talk your way out of this than it could possibly ever be for me to shoot you dead. I would give just about anything not to have to do this."

"Arlene, please."

And those would be the bald man's last words. "Arlene, please." In my book, a man could do a lot worse. Arlene calmly fires two rounds into Canan's chest and one in his head; the Mozambique Drill. I'm thinking how she was definitely stretching the truth when she told me she'd never killed anyone. Before I can elucidate any further on what's just happened I pull back to catch my breath and everything gets fuzzy. The room starts to spin, I fall into the chair next to me and Arlene rushes over. I haven't a care in the world once I feel her holding my head.

"You've been shot."

"How?"

"Canan fired when you attacked him. You didn't feel it?"

"Not until just now, no."

"Just sit still, let me look at you." Arlene soothes.

"Where'd you get that gun?" I slur trying to make sense of what's just happened.

"You made him drop it." Arlene says. "So I picked it up and used it."

"But I wanted to kill him. I never get to kill anyone."

Arlene laughs a little and looks at the wound in my shoulder.

"He got you pretty good, Foster."

"Ruined Jürgen's suit."

"You little brat, you just wanted an excuse to put your dirty old Canadian Tux back on, didn't you?"

I laugh at Arlene and look at my shoulder. It's throbbing and swollen and if I weren't a couple drinks into the afternoon I might not be able to ignore it.

"Is this bad? What should we do?"

"You'll live, but obviously we have another problem to sort out and the clock is ticking on our flight."

"Yeah. Arlene I want to kill that fucking guy so bad right now." I say, feeling a little woozy.

"Yeah, well he's already dead."

I look over at Canan piled on the couch between two of the only people I liked in this world and cry out in anger at him for taking them from me.

"You motherfucker! Why them? Why them and not me?"

Arlene gathers me into a tight, consoling embrace and I break down in embarrassing drunkards sobs. I catch myself and recoil in shame.

"Foster, sweety, we've gotta get going. You've got a bullet that needs to come out of you and we've still got a plane to catch."

"I don't care about that right now." I sob.

She pulls me in again and this time I relent. My mind racing, I eventually push her away once more, this time worried I'll get blood on her clean dress.

"You think Bam Bam knows someone who can take a look at that?" Arlene asks.

"It's worth finding out. I don't know where else to go."

"Call him."

I pull out my burner and dial up the man who just a few hours ago set us up with our new lives and hold out hope that he answers.

"Bam Bam? Hey, man this is Foster, Jazzy's friend. Is it cool to talk?" I ask and Bam Bam confirms that he's clear to discuss illicit transactions. As I'm about to unload on him, a bolt of lightning hits.

"Hey, man. I'm sorry, this is really important and I need to talk to you but can I call you right back? OK, cool, five minutes. Bye."

I look at Arlene who is staring at me puzzled and I straighten in my chair.

"You've got a chip in you. That's how your Covenant buddy found us."

"Arius always chips his pets." She remembers.

"That's what he said, right?"

"Fuck, you have got to be kidding me."

"You didn't even know?"

"No, but I'm not surprised."

"You think the Prelacy put one in me?" I ask.

"Fuck, did they put one in me? Do I have two of those things in me?"

"Yeah, we're going to need a doctor for more than just this gunshot."

I look down at my burner phone and start to get dizzy again. I wouldn't say I'm hemorrhaging but losing even a little blood can make someone lightheaded. I've definitely lost more than a little.

"Arlene, you're going to have to call Bam Bam back. I'm a little dizzy." I say, putting the burner in her hands. "Find Jazzy's keys and let's get over to Ship Mates."

Arlene takes my phone and I fall back in the chair, grey fog of sleep closing around me.

FIFTY-SEVEN

Palm Springs, CA – Sat Oct 18th, 2014

I reawaken with a dry, furry mouth and a pounding in my head that is giving the pounding in my left shoulder a run for its money. I try to sit up but Arlene is there to put an arm across my chest and tell me to relax. I'm lying on a standard examination table in a small private practice, shirtless, a little cold with an IV in my arm. As my eyes focus I see Bam Bam standing in the background looking grave and distressed. Next to him stands a salt and pepper haired little man with a PGA tan under a salmon colored Izod.

"How are you feeling, Mr. Foster?" the salt and pepper stranger asks.

"You gave him my old name?" I ask, looking at Bam Bam, who smiles back and shakes his head.

"You already know, slick." Bam Bam reassures. "Don't worry about nothing. The Doc here is on the level."

"You lost a lot of blood but I was able to get a handle on that and remove the bullet." The Doctor says, picking the crumpled little slug up from a stainless-steel tray on the table next to me. "I was also able to locate and remove this."

The Doctor holds between his fore-finger and thumb a dime sized chip that has been broken in two.

"He also took a pair of those things out of me." Arlene said, nodding at a couple more broken chips on the table. I notice her bandaged arm and look at my own to find it dressed the same way.

"You're some heavy hitters, eh." Bam Bam said, "I've seen some shit but I've never run across anything like you two."

I look over at Arlene who is either putting on a brave face or is simply made of pure unflappable callous at this point. She gives me a taut, half-smile of resignation that reassures me we're still in this together and that we'll get through it.

"Bam Bam, thank you for everything." I hate to be rude and bring up money but I'm also worried about time. I look around the room for a clock and find one on the wall that reads 5:10pm. By my estimate we can still make our flight if we wrap things up here soon. I'm honestly mortified by the thought of tabling something so banal as business talk, having just seen his old friend Jazzy and her husband lying dead, murdered by the man who had come to kill Arlene and I. I want to disappear. I just want to be on that plane to Brazil so bad and yet it seems like some unreal fantasy that can never come true the closer we get to it.

"You're alright with me, slick." Bam Bam says. "Your old lady filled me in on Jazzy and Jürgen and took care of me and the Doc's expenses. We're all square."

It's like he's reading my mind, more likely my face. I'm not that mysterious when it comes right down to it, this I learn more and more with each new day.

"I've got a bag with antibiotics and painkillers set up for you." The Doctor says. "And I made a little printout with instructions for caring for your wound. You're gonna want to put clean bandages on it before you go to sleep tonight."

I'm listening to him but my eyes have discovered the X-rays he took up on the light board. I wasn't awake for any of that so I'm a little intrigued.

"You want to take those with you?" He asks. "Had to take those to find your tracking chips."

"Yeah, let me have them." I say and the doctor takes them down and puts them inside of a manila flat then hands them to me. I take them back out and look at them again. "Weird, man."

"That's some creepy shit, brother." Bam Bam says looking over my shoulder at the x-rays of our chips.

"You have no idea." I say.

"I don't know what you're into but that guy who killed Jazzy? I'd like to get my hands on every person he loves." Bam Bam says.

"You and me both, Bam." I say.

A respectful quiet falls on the room as we think on Jazzy and Jürgen. Bam Bam mercifully breaks the silence before there's too much time to unpack it all, before it gets uncomfortable, before the temptation rises to start pushing blame around where it belongs.

"You two better get goin'." Bam says.

I nod a silent acknowledgement and look to Arlene who puts out her hand and forces a smile. I take her grip and stand up, a little wobbly. The Doctor comes to my aid and I steady myself with my free hand on his shoulder as he takes out my IV.

"Here, put this on." Bam Bam says, throwing a t-shirt at me. "It probably ain't your style but it's better than trying to get on the plane with your titties out."

I put it on without question and catch a glimpse in the mirror of the graphic on the front. A Sailor Jerry style banner and anchor with the words Ship Mates in the banner and the words Inland Empire, CA in small print across the bottom.

I nod a thank you at Bam Bam who claps me on the back, my good shoulder's side. Bam and the Doc walk us out and wave us off as we pull Jazzy's Escalade out of the parking lot and begin our drive toward LAX.

We proceed West on the 60 without a word. Arlene holds my hand in a tight grip though we don't talk the whole way to the airport. After 2 hours in the diamond lane we circle LAX long term parking until we find a spot out of camera view. I wipe down Jazzy's Escalade and the two of us make our way toward the terminal with no luggage other than a carry-on containing our burner debit cards, some X-rays and medicine, our IDs and after another visit with Bam Bam a little less than $5k in cash.

With enough time to spare we breeze through check-in but don't have to hurry. Once we are in sight of our terminal we detour into a place called the Pie Hole for flight lube. Arlene orders a red wine and I order a double Jameson neat. We sit quietly and I wonder if she's looking for something to say like I am.

"We don't have enough money to last us." Arlene breaks the silence languorously

"What'll we do?" I ask.

"I suppose I could teach Arabic, French and English."

"Maybe we can start a vineyard." I say, revisiting a past humor, only now half serious.

"Get old and die, leave it to some kids who'll sell it and squander the money?" Arlene plays along.

"Nah, no kids. We'll just burn it to the ground when we get old and tired of it."

Arlene smiles and takes my hand.

We finish our drinks in silence and make our way to the boarding call coming over the PA. As our place in line slowly moves toward the gate my heart races a little. We finally get to the front, show our tickets and begin to board. As the line shuffles along I look and see a pair of specters standing cool along the other side of the terminal. Monsieur Sébastien, smiling peacefully, his signature white suit now replaced with the King-in-Waiting's color, Grand Maître Chilperic XI's signature blue. Sébastien silently nods and waves me off with the two-finger salute while behind him to his left stands sharp-as-a-tack 1961 Al Davis making rabbit ears behind the old wizard's head, grinning devilishly. My heart leaps into my throat and I don't say a word, I just wave quietly behind Arlene where she can't see.

We board and I shadow my companion to our seats. I take the aisle as she's selected the window. In a short time we are wheels up, banking over the Santa Monica Bay, the jet adjusting its heading South East toward Brazil.

"Do you think there'll even be a world for us to hide out in a year from now?" Arlene asks, unguarded and fallible as I've never seen her.

I think back to the blue-clad Sébastien waving us off in the airport, Al jestering behind him.

"I think it was all just bullshit."

Arlene takes my hand in hers and looking out at the sea ever so quietly exhales, "Thalatta, thalatta."

www.ingramcontent.com/pod-product-compliance
Lightning Source LLC
Chambersburg PA
CBHW031156020726
47499CB00002B/386